The Calendar of Trinity the Divine
Anniversaries for Holy Month

	1999	December
1	*Wednesday*	Friedrich Engels d. 1895
2	*Thursday*	BIRTH OF ||| MOTHER THE DIVINE 1958
		ST LUCIUS OF BRITAIN
3	*Friday*	CHANUCAH BEGINS. Joseph Conrad b. 1857
4	*Saturday*	Mary Baker Eddy d. 1910
5	*Sunday*	**Advent Sunday.** W. A. Mozart d. 1791
6	*Monday*	BIRTH OF ||| SON THE DIVINE. 1970
7	*Tuesday*	G. L. Bernini b. 1598
8	*Wednesday*	Paul Gauguin b. 1848
9	*Thursday*	Karl Barth d. 1968
10	*Friday*	Alfred Nobel d. 1896
11	*Saturday*	Hector Berlioz b. 1803
12	*Sunday*	**2nd S. in Advent.** Gustave Flaubert b. 1821
13	*Monday*	Laurens van der Post b. 1906. Paul Gauguin d. 1903
14	*Tuesday*	BIRTH OF ||| TRINITY THE DIVINE 1945
		George Washington d. 1799
15	*Wednesday*	Izaak Walton d. 1683
16	*Thursday*	Jane Austen b. 1775
17	*Friday*	**St Begga.** L. van Beethoven b. 1770
		Vincent van Gogh b. 1853
18	*Saturday*	Carl Maria von Weber b. 1786
19	*Sunday*	**3rd S. in Advent.** Emily Bronte d. 1848
20	*Monday*	Sir Robert Menzies b. 1894
21	*Tuesday*	Lockerbie Air Disaster, 1988. Joseph Stalin b. 1870
22	*Wednesday*	**Winter Solstice**
23	*Thursday*	Thomas Malthus d. 1834
24	*Friday*	**Christmas Eve.** King John b. 1167.
		Ivan Turgenev b. 1818
25	*Saturday*	**Christmas Day. The Birth of Christ**
26	*Sunday*	**1st after Christmas. St Stephen**
27	*Monday*	**St John the Evangelist.** Johann Kepler b. 1571
28	*Tuesday*	**Holy Innocents.** Theodore Dreiser d. 1945
29	*Wednesday*	Christina Rossetti d. 1894
30	*Thursday*	Michael Bakunin d. 1876
31	*Friday*	Henri Matisse b. 1896. Leon Trotsky b. 1877
Leap Year		MILLENNIUM
	2000	January
1	*Saturday*	THE RESURRE

Reg Gadney was born in Cross Hills, Yorkshire. He was educated at Cambridge and Massachussetts Institute of Technology. He lives in North London. He is the author of nine previous novels, including *Just When We Are Safest* and *The Achilles Heel*.

MOTHER, SON AND HOLY GHOST

Reg Gadney

faber and faber

First published in 1986
by Faber and Faber Limited
3 Queen Square London WC1N 3AU
This paperback edition first published in 1999

Photoset by Parker Typesetting Service Ltd, Leicester
Printed in England by
Mackays of Chatham PLC, Chatham, Kent

A CIP record for this book is
available from the British Library

ISBN 0–571–19722–1

2 4 6 8 10 9 7 5 3 1

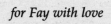

for Fay with love

Somewhere in England, there is said to be a grave which is distinguished not by a splendid monument, nor by its melancholy surroundings, but by a brief inscription, The Unhappiest Man. Someone must have opened the grave, but had found no trace of a body. Which is the most astonishing, that no body was found, or that the grave was opened?

   – KIERKEGAARD

In my life I have frequently been asked what relation the beliefs of my followers have to the theological systems of Christianity, Islam, Buddhism, Judaism and the other religions of the world. Are we to say that mine is the One True Way and deny the infidels?

I say three times Yes and Yes and Yes again.

Do I say to you that I seek some form of world domination?

My beloved friends, ask not that we dominate this world. Rather, ask how the world will allow itself to be dominated by us.

For in my Resurrection – in the first minute of the first hour of the first day of the Millennium in the sacred Square – will the truth you seek be shown to you. Only Love. Only Connect. Only Believe. For in the Sacred Three – in Mother, Son and Holy Ghost – are we united. And the flame of our shining faith will burn in purity to light the path of all generations to come.

   – TRINITY THE DIVINE | | |

New Moon

1

As we approach the millennium, apocalyptic expectations are rising throughout the world. Beyond the symbolic aura of the millennium, this excitation is fed by currents of unsettling social and cultural change. The 'millennial myth' ingrained in culture is continually generating new movements, which draw upon the myth and also reshape and reconstruct it. Many of these movements are volatile and potentially explosive.

– MILLENNIUM, MESSIAHS AND MAYHEM, THOMAS ROBBINS AND SUSAN PALMER, EDS, 1997

It was the method of the executions in Trafalgar Square that was shocking. The killing of the pair of thugs: youths who had robbed some apparently harmless members of the Trinity Chapter, the millennial religious cult. There had been no street violence of this kind in living memory.

Take the robbery that sparked things off. The snatch of paltry offerings outside St Martin-in-the-Fields. The small amount of cash in the canvas bag belonging to the Trinity Chapter.

The public view of the Trinity Chapter was one of vague tolerance. Its followers presented a familiar sight on the streets of London and Europe's other capital cities. Most people considered these street people with shaven heads, dressed distinctively in white, to be happy, harmless souls. To rational minds, the belief that their dead leader, Trinity, would fulfil His avowed prophecy of Resurrection in the first minute of the first hour of the first day of the Millennium was, to say the least, a belief to be dismissed. Nonetheless, it was true that society figures in London, throughout Europe and in the United States had applauded Trinity's mission to offer succour to the deprived and dispossessed. It was fashionable to agree that Trinity had, after all, a point. Commentators in the serious press approved His view that 'the measure of a society is the way in which it treats the weak and vulnerable.' A growing number of the wise, the good and the very rich considered Him to be the Coming Man. And many of them parted with substantial sums of money that swelled His funds, held in offshore accounts the better to avoid paying regular tax. Like donors to the established churches or great international charitable causes, few of them paused to ask quite how the gifts were actually spent. Presumably they just wrote the cheques and felt all the better for that. Trinity was the embodiment of Good, the Future and the New Generations. Whether some sense of guilt persuaded them to part with their money, only they can tell us. Most likely they sought reflected glory and the approbation of their honoured peers who made public donations to opera houses, museums or political parties. Anyway, the kids loved Trinity too and all His ways. The rich, old and young, clapped hands together and felt somehow they had something in common. And the few critics of Trinity the Divine went unheeded.

Thus, during what remained of what was frequently described as this 'momentous' twentieth century, the authorities saw no good reason to pay attention to the Trinity Chapter and its leader's extraordinary promise.

Rather law and order were being concentrated on the wave of national millennial celebration. The great New Year's parties to end all parties. The orgy of nostalgia. The promises of a better future. The small and single harmless click of the second hand that would somehow change the world. Or not.

Rather like those who remembered where they were when they learned of the death of Diana, Princess of Wales, people would recall where they were at the dawning of the year 2000. The last chime of midnight would herald the dawn of the Millennium and everyone would remember the moment.

No one was certain of it, but there was the growing and reasonable suspicion that the cult's capacity for extreme and public vengeance against those who offended it had a very nasty side indeed. And it was the murder of the two youths in Trafalgar Square that suggested to the authorities that they might do well to take notice of what now seemed to be the darker side of the Trinity Chapter.

In Trafalgar Square the midnight hour had passed

uneventfully. Freezing wind and driving sleet and the just-below-zero temperature meant that the night-time crowds in London had dispersed. Raw wind tossed around the lights in the Trafalgar Square Christmas tree. The fountains in the two vast clover-leaf pools had been switched off. Although floodlit, Nelson standing 170 feet above on his column was barely visible. And from the bus shelter on the northern side of Trafalgar Square, in front of the Portland stone base of the National Gallery's portico, it was difficult to see Big Ben, whose midnight chimes were muted. The few pedestrians hurrying home for warmth paid scant attention to the group of three chanters huddled together outside St Martin-in-the-Fields. Saddos chanting:

> *Trin-it-eee*
> *Trin-it-eee*
> *Three in one*
> *One in three*

Of the duty police officers, usually in Trafalgar Square even at this time of night, there was no sign.

The only people on the north side of the square were two men and a woman standing beneath the transparent canopy of the bus shelter, close to the two notices headed NIGHT BUSES FROM TRAFAL-GAR SQUARE and the black tubular City of Westminster waste-bin.

Of those two men and one woman, the eldest was

a formidable figure wearing a heavy winter coat and a Germanic leather cap. He had a powerful dog. Muzzled and on a chain leash, the dog was an unusual cross breed: a Rasselaer with strains of the Pit Bull Terrier and Rottweiler in the blood. Carrying a hold-all, the owner of the dog had just reported something to cause his two companions to look with alarm into his blunt features. Restraining his anger, and as if to emphasize the danger of what he'd said, the big man repeated the news: 'The CIA and MI5 are getting close. On top of that, there's the additional threat of the Moorfield woman's sister, Caroline. She's hired a private investigator to look into her sister's death.'

His female companion, her features mostly hidden by a royal-blue silk scarf, turned her head away from the biting wind. 'Who is the investigator?' she asked. The cold wind brought tears to her eyes.

'A man called Alan Rosslyn,' the big man said.

'How far has he got?' she asked.

'I don't know,' said the big man.

'The Master can't be stopped,' said the second, younger man.

Wiping her eyes, the woman asked: 'But if it gets nasty?'

'Then we'll get nastier,' the big man told her.

'How do you know all this?' asked the younger man, tightening the collar of his coat.

Stretching the muscles in his thick neck, the big man twisted his head slowly. Pent up like a prize fighter, he avoided giving the direct answer: 'We have to believe it, boyo. There's the possibility they have us under surveillance. It's best we don't meet together again. Stay out of touch for the time being. And let the inquest take its course.'

The woman frowned. 'How much do the security service people know?'

'Nothing that will stop us.' There was something in the big man's tone of voice that suggested he lacked conviction.

'There's no going back,' the woman said.

With the tone of the evangelist, the big man said: 'Be warned. Be warned about the man Rosslyn and his client. Call me if anyone asks questions. If you need my help, call me.'

'What if they give us real trouble?' the woman asked. 'What will you do?'

'The usual,' the big man said. Again, he stared out across Trafalgar Square to where his leader prophesied His Resurrection: in the first minute of the first hour of the first day of the year 2000. Here in the midst of the millennial celebrations in Trafalgar Square. The square that Trinity the Divine, the Master, deemed sacred. The place of His Second Coming.

Trafalgar Square, geographically crucial to the Trinity Chapter, was once the main crossroads in London's street pattern: where the east-west axis through St Paul's Cathedral meets the north-south axis through the transepts of Westminster Abbey.

The square is that point to which the Master, Trinity the Divine, and his followers attached the greatest significance. As important to them as Bethlehem and the notion of Golgotha to Christians or Mecca to the Muslims. For the followers of Trinity, it was the place that concentrated thought. The Holy Place.

Something of this holy sense was conveyed by the tone of the big man's reply. Without apparently giving it further thought, he answered the woman's repeated question about facing trouble by muttering: 'Misadventure.'

The woman drew a sign in the freezing moisture on the glass of the notice NIGHT BUSES FROM TRAFALGAR SQUARE. Three vertical strokes: | | |.

'Leave it,' the big man added, 'to Her Majesty's Coroner's Court. The usual.'

It was then that the trouble started on the pavement outside St Martin-in-the-Fields.

Half a dozen youths began to taunt the three followers of Trinity, who suddenly stopped their chanting. The weapons the youths were carrying, baseball bats, were unmistakable even in the sleet. During the struggle, two of the youths succeeded in snatching the small canvas bag containing offerings. Once they'd got the bag, the gang split.

One pair of them ran off in the direction of Charing Cross. Two others sprinted across the road to disappear somewhere near South Africa House. The remaining pair – one of whom was carrying the canvas bag, the other clutching his baseball bat inside his anorak – ran towards the National Gallery and the bus shelter.

Here the younger of the two men who'd just been in conversation in the shelter stepped out to block the youths' path. So did the woman. 'That's not yours!' she shouted. The younger man grabbed at the canvas bag but failed to get a grip on it. As he did so he was punched so viciously in the mouth that he collapsed against the bus shelter's narrow red bench. The other youth pushed the woman back against the black tubular waste-bin. Stooping over her, his hand at her throat, he grabbed her shoulder bag. In his other hand he held a scalpel.

Now the big man made his move. Hidden further up the pavement beyond the bus shelter, as if leaving the scene, he had already unfastened his hold-all. He unmuzzled the Rasselaer. He unwound the chain leash from his gloved wrist. Turning, he walked slowly towards the two youths. Because they had their backs to him they didn't see what was in his hand. Nor did they pay attention to what seemed to be the restrained dog. And they probably never saw what it was the big man had taken from the hold-all or what his fingers were doing with the instrument in his hands: the general-purpose miniature butane gas blowlamp. The precision flame control for paint-stripping. The flame was short, white and blue. The big man swept it in an arc into the youth's eyes and mouth. Scorching flesh.

Simultaneously, the big man jerked his knee in turns up into the youths' crotches. Each sagged to the pavement. And the big man continued to direct the flame into the youths' burning faces. Up and down. Searing the skin. The needle flame hissing. He directed its heat against the flesh with vertical strokes: | | |.

Stepping back, he extinguished the flame. Deftly, he unwound still more of the chain leash. The sign to the dog to jump. Jaws wide, the dog did as it had been trained. It clamped its pointed teeth straight over the bridge of the first youth's nose. Closed its jaws. Cracked the nose bone into splinters. Then bit out both eyes. Panting, it spat blood like thick juice. Putting a paw on the neck of the second victim, it carried out the same procedure. Bit deep. Chewed hard. Crunched bone. Spat. Stuck out its long and quivering tongue. Gouts of blood dripped from its mouth.

The big man patted the animal's head. The 'well done' gesture. Then he nodded at his two companions. The young man's baby face was ashen. The woman swept aside the split fringe of dark hair and tightened the knot of the head scarf beneath her chin.

He told them calmly to collect themselves. To go their 'separate ways, into the night.' To 'say nothing.' Adding lastly, with the calm of a priest delivering a Blessing, that they should await 'the Second Coming that Will Change the World'.

It was only later, after the dawn of the Millennium, that the police reached the obvious conclusion: the two sadistic killings bore the hallmarks of the Trinity Chapter. It was, of course, among the considerable number of the Chapter's members that they eventually identified the perpetrators of the crime. And their enquiries eventually prompted the asking of many awkward questions. Not the least of these was about the recent death of the young American woman in London. Jane Moorfield, a native of Vernon Hills in Massachusetts.

)

First Quarter

2

Cape Cod. Today is the Sunday before Christmas 1999.

Jane Moorfield's younger sister, Caroline, heads home for Moorfield House in Vernon Hills, Massachusetts.

The evening sun has turned the Cape landscape into the colours of some old embroidery. Mostly white, shot through with silk threads of dark blue, violet, grey and pink. 'Like a Currier and Ives Christmas card,' her father used to say, 'come to life from long ago.' The winter horizon seems low, and beyond Wellfleet, on Route 6, the powdered snow curls across the road in wisps. Either side, where the snowploughs have dumped it, it leans against the banks like giant buttresses. The voice on the car radio warns that tomorrow more snow will fall across Cape Cod.

Caroline Moorfield is driving home after an out-of-season stay at Haystack Mountain School of Crafts on Deer Isle, Maine. She's had an intense and happy few weeks of work making chowder mugs and lobster platters. Stacked on the back seat, wrapped in layers of tissue and bubble-wrap inside cardboard boxes, are the mugs and platters, the products of her happy Haystack Mountain stay. Her pots bear her trademark hand-painted designs. The chosen colours are those of the Cape Cod woods and wild flowers. Deserted beaches and mythic sea creatures rising out of the Atlantic Ocean. The creatures always in pairs or threesomes, with facial resemblances to her men, and the woman is recognizably Caroline. The images are barbed and twisted. Her peers consider these disturbing images to be the product of a haunted and somewhat secretive mind, and the couplings suggestive of some fantasy of promiscuity.

Next to the cardboard boxes is her L. L. Bean canvas duffel bag. She prides herself on always travelling light. 'Always ready,' as her mother used to say, 'to accept the summons of good news. Be prepared to leave at a moment's notice for somewhere and something better in God's wide world.' Her duffel bag lies next to two large brown paper bags she's filled with groceries in Bangor and the insulated and leak-proof container of tomalley or lobster's liver. What she calls the *Green Stuff*.

She sees the dark barn rise as if flattened between the snowy ridge and iron sky. The wooden barn that looks as dark as a ghost house is actually the colour of rust. It reminds her of the barn at the back of home. Like it's the twin of the barn she calls *The Wrist*, the barn her mother had converted for her to use as a pottery studio. *The Wrist*, partly because of Caroline's belief that the art of pottery is finally a matter of how you use your wrist, partly out of her mother's respect for Thoreau's description of Cape Cod: 'The bared and bended arm of Massachusetts: The shoulder is at Buzzard's Bay; the elbow, or crazy bone, at Cape Mallebarre; the wrist at Truro; and the sandy fist at Provincetown.' Somewhere beyond the snow banks stretch the desolate sand dunes and the seashore.

Beyond Truro she swerves left onto the road to Sandy Point, narrowed by snow drifts. Now she's almost home. To the familiar woody smells of Moorfield House. The family shelter against the blizzard that's gathering in the north-western night-fall sky above Massachusetts Bay. The house of troubled family memories. The Bay State sanctuary she and her sister Jane have solemnly promised to preserve for future generations.

The approach to Moorfield House is along a gravel driveway. The long curve through the pine trees bearing heavy loads of snow. Caroline at once notices the recent tyre tracks in the snow. *Odd. Who are the visitors?* She feels a kind of proprietorial resentment. *People shouldn't just invite themselves without warning.*

The final bend in the drive is slightly uphill. The trees thin here and the wooden frontage of Moorfield House comes into view. The sight of the lights in the windows serves to puncture her elation. *Whoever's*

inside the house hasn't bothered to close the curtains.
There's some kind of trouble here. Now, the only person
who has keys is Tammy. Tammy Duilac who reminds
her, at every opportunity: 'Twice a week, I clean
Moorfield House out of God's goodness in my heart
in memory of your mother.' Tammy's presence is one
thing. But the headlights of Caroline's VW pick out
two cars parked in the driveway. They're something
else.

The Cherokee's the one her mother bought for the
family priest, Father Scott. The other car belongs to
Tammy Duilac's husband, Police Officer Joe Duilac.
Only this is not the Duilac's family car. It's big Joe's
patrol car she parks next to – big Joe's official Chevy.
Her first worrying thought is that Joe's conducting
one of his rare investigations into wrongdoing in
Vernon Hills. *Jesus, Moorfield House has been burglar-*
ized.

Her rubber Sporto boots make tracks in the
powdered snow across the small courtyard in front
of Moorfield House. Up to the wide wooden steps
beneath its entrance porch. Out of habit, she rings
the doorbell and opens the door to the accompaniment of its muffled chimes.

She sees Tammy and Joe Duilac standing nervously in the hall with Father Scott.

The hall is filled with the welcome smells of the
pine and apple logs burning in the hearth. She
thinks: *Something's wrong. Otherwise, why's Joe twist-*

ing his police cap and snapping his chewing gum with
greater force than usual? Even for Joe.

Father Scott's soft hands are toying awkwardly
with the zipper of his pink parka. 'How are you,
Caroline?' he says. 'How was it in Maine?'

'Great,' says Caroline. 'A lotta snow. You can
imagine.'

Joe stretches his broad neck. 'We've been trying to
reach you,' he says.

'You were? Well, now what are you guys doing out
here? I mean, I wasn't expecting a greeting committee.' Caroline smiles at Tammy. 'I have a lot in the car,
Tammy. It needs to come in. Can you unload it for
me? There's going to be a snowstorm.'

'Sure,' says Tammy, apparently relieved to be
given something to do, even if it means going
outside in the cold.

'And you guys can tell me what you want to talk
to me about,' says Caroline.

'Yeah,' says Joe. 'Sure.' The two men follow her
into the kitchen.

'Caroline –' says Joe. 'We're here to talk about
Jane.'

She sits down at the kitchen table of scrubbed
pine. 'Is she coming home early?'

'Well,' says Joe, 'matter of fact, that's it, Caroline.'
His voice begins to shake. He seems to chew on his
gum too hard; he must have bitten his tongue.

'What's the matter, Joe?' asks Caroline. 'Has
something happened?'

'I am afraid –' says Joe. He hesitates. 'It's my formal duty, Caroline, to tell you that your sister Jane is dead.'

Caroline sits with her elbows on the kitchen table. She scratches at her skin, toughened by hours on the potter's wheel at Haystack Mountain.

Her mouth is dry and filled with a bitter taste. Her mind seems stuck at the end of some waking dream and a voice is urging her to wake up.

Return to reality.

She can hear the sounds of Tammy busy in the entrance hall bringing in the grocery bags. The duffel bag. The cardboard boxes containing the new pots. The pattern of the shock, a kind of terror, is like some *déjà vu*. She's experienced sudden death like this not just once, but twice before –

When her father died in the Vermont road accident in 1990, Patrolman Joe Duilac had brought the news.

Her mother, once a woman of striking beauty, never managed to come to terms with her husband's death. Despair and grief got the better of her. Alcoholism took its toll. It seemed to Caroline that her mother had somehow deliberately sought the fatal heart attack.

Caroline had gained some degree of relief, if relief it was, from having seen her parents soon after death. At least she'd got the proof. She'd been certain of their deaths and able to say her goodbyes.

[20]

A prescient thought told her that she was now about to be denied the same certainty. The same opportunity to see Jane.

She thought to herself: *I wish I'd spoken to you during the last few weeks. I want to see you. Now. Walking into the kitchen here. Telling me, like you did when we were kids: 'Caro, wake up. You're dreaming. The Old Moorfield Bogey Man in the Chimney without a Face will never get you.' Instead, it's you he's got, Jane. He's got you, Jane. And I'm not dreaming any more.*

Floorboards creak above the kitchen ceiling. Sounds of Tammy making Caroline's room ready for the night.

'When did it happen?' she asks big Joe Duilac.

'Like three weeks ago or thereabouts.'

'Where – in London?'

Father Scott reaches across the table for her hand. 'Yes. In London. God rest her soul.'

'Why haven't I been told this before now?' she asks him.

'Like Joe says,' he says. He's holding her hand tightly. His soft skin feels cold. 'We couldn't reach you, Caroline. But you told Tammy when you were coming back. And, well, you Moorfields are never late.'

On the kitchen shelf, Caroline sees the photo of Jane standing outside a Church Family Dwelling in Hancock Shaker Village in high summer. She thinks: *You look so happy, Jane. Serene almost. Now this. I don't believe it.* 'So exactly what happened?' she asks.

'They said that she died from a narcotics overdose,' says Joe.

'Narcotics overdose? You aren't serious, Joe. She never does drugs. Never. You know that.'

'Sure,' Joe says, 'I know.'

'That's what the doctors said in London,' says Father Scott.

'There's to be an inquest,' says Joe. 'An inquiry. A coroner's court in London. The police there contacted us. And we've had other visits.'

'From the FBI,' adds Father Scott.

'Even two people who said they were from the CIA,' says Joe Duilac. 'They want to know about all of this.'

'Why?' asks Caroline. 'What in God's name do the CIA and FBI want to know?'

'Just general background –'

'I've had our embassy in London calling,' says Father Scott.

'I don't understand this,' says Caroline.

'They think,' says Joe, 'that Jane killed herself.'

'Did she? Did she do that?'

'Seems so,' says Joe. 'Seems that, like, she had to have known what she was doing.'

'With narcotics – you say she knew what she was doing – with drugs?'

'Yeah,' says Joe. 'That's what they say in London.'

'What drugs?'

'Heroin,' says Joe. 'Heroin.'

'Joe, you know she wouldn't know heroin if she saw it. Neither would I.'

'Neither would we,' says Father Scott. 'Oh Caroline. In God's name, I am so sorry.'

'Yes,' says Caroline. 'Why? I mean, *why*, *why*? It isn't true, is it?'

'It is true, Caroline,' Joe says. 'The officers of the London coroner's court in some place called St Pancras also called me. They're postponing the inquest so you can be present.'

Caroline begins to shiver. 'I want to see her.'

'If I may say so, Caroline,' Father Scott says, 'I think it would be advisable, I think indeed that it would be God's wish, that you be spared the pain of seeing her.'

'What do you mean, "the pain"? Like whose pain are we talking about here, Father?'

Turning to Father Scott, Joe says, 'What the Father is saying, Caroline, if I hear you right, Father, is that the British were required to perform a *post mortem*. And that the fact is, you know, Jane has been dead some time. And, well, we reckoned on your reaction. And after a lotta thought we decided that it'd be best if Jane, rest her soul, be buried. That's what we believe to be the right thing to do.'

'Excuse me? Look, maybe it's just a terrible mistake.'

'No, Caroline,' says Joe. 'It seems not.'

'No?' says Caroline. 'What else did those people from the CIA say?'

'Nothing. They said nothing. They said they'd no need to come back. We haven't heard from them any more. But I said I thought if you could help them, you would.'

'I would? You're not serious,' says Caroline. 'Help them with what? I can't help them with something I don't know about.'

'That's what I sorta told them,' says Father Scott. 'They said if you wished, you could of course attend the inquest in London and that the American Citizens Services Branch at the embassy could maybe help you. There's a woman there called Susan Isiskind who'll see you.'

'Right,' says Joe. He tears a page from his notebook and sets it carefully on the table. 'This is the coroner's court number. The court will issue what they call an E certificate. They'll take Jane's body to a funeral parlour in north London. They'll fix the funeral for something over a thousand pounds sterling. The court officers said to call them any time they could be of help.' He stares at his broad callused hands. 'I think it best you stay with Caroline a while,' he tells Father Scott. 'If I can help, why, be sure to call me. Maybe Tammy can stay till late.'

'OK,' says Father Scott. 'I'll stay here with Caroline.' He holds her hand again like she's Little Girl Lost. 'You can call the London embassy.'

As if unable to take his eyes off her, Joe, a broad man with a puffy face scarred by acne, walks to the kitchen door. When he reaches it he breaks down.

'I can't believe this,' he whispers in his whisky voice.

'Yeah, well,' says Caroline. 'Neither can I.' She turns to Tammy and Father Scott. 'I'll see Joe out. Then I wanna check the mail. And then we can talk it over some more. First, I need time alone to get my head together.'

There's a bundle of mail on the table in the passage and Caroline takes it into the family library, to which, apart from Jane, she possesses the only keys.

She whispers to herself: *Jane, you have to have written something to me. Come on. Speak to me. Please.*

Once inside the library, she locks the door. A family rule. To the rest of the world the library's off limits.

Caroline sees that the bundle of letters is mostly bills and junk mail. Finding none from Jane, she stares at the many photographs of her parents lined up on the shelves next to the Mark Twain window.

She asks out loud: 'Mom and Dad . . . what would you do?' There is, of course, no answer.

She goes to the mahogany desk in the centre of the library, where there's the sole concession to modernity: the Panasonic combined telephone answering and fax machine, which has spewed out many sheets. She sees some are headed with the address of the Malvern Hotel in London, others with the name and address of an Asian newsagent in London's Gray's Inn Road. *Oh my God, these are the last letters she ever wrote.*

Written in Jane's bold calligraphic hand, the texts are interspersed with drawings of her favourite flora and fauna:

The holly leaf. The prickly pear cactus like the ones we found in Nantucket. The feather from one of your favourite birds. A cardinal – Only, the drawing of the cardinal on the fax is in matt black and its leaden blackness seems to be an omen. She turns to the most recent of Jane's faxes. Her last.

Destroy these letters now. I need you to
know I'm facing real trouble. I know this
will come to the fax machine in the library
like all my letters. No one except you must
see any of them. This is important. No one
knows what I've written to you about.
Destroy my letters. Promise me, Caro. I'll
explain later. I'll call. All my love.
Jane.

Searching for some kind of immediate explanation of the truth, she skims through the letters. Both wanting and not wanting to find out what's happened. Glancing at the headings that always began her letters.

<u>The Funding of Millennial New Religious</u>
<u>Movements with Special Reference to the</u>
<u>Trinity Chapter.</u> Sorry I haven't been in
touch for so long. No news is good news.
The Good News is that above is the title of
my thesis. At long last, I've got academic
approval for it. And it's going great,
maybe so great that I'm in danger of
becoming a victim of my own success! My
Cambridge tutor, Dr Julia Llewellyn, is
really pleased. She's taken off on the idea
of the economic angle. And now that
special reference, the Trinity Chapter –
it's the cult or sect or what we call a New
Religious Movement that's preoccupying me
day and night. I'll write more when I've
time. I'm so happy in England. I feel
totally fulfilled in the work. But no
cardinals that I know of! Love Jane.

<u>I'm counting the days till Christmas.</u> Oh
my, are these people influential? Only I
sense the whole organization is falling
apart – like they are getting at each
other's throats. It seems like they've
exercised a psychopathic need to exploit
the lonely and the vulnerable. To distort
sad people's emotions. It's kind of, well,
what I imagine would be psychotherapy in
reverse. Based on strange revelations and

[27]

visions and theories, their systems trap you. I'm trying to think myself into their very souls and work out where their beliefs originate. What has to be an objective study of the Trinity Chapter is already getting like an exposé of the cult. There's talk of money, a lot of money, having gone missing. I've been told that there's a real chance some people will feel cornered by me and might even resort to personal violence. But I've been down that road before. In the end it's lawyers they hit you with, not clubs. Sticks and stones . . . and all that stuff . . .

Anyone who questions it is not so much a threat, or to be derided, rather an object of pity in need of intensive counselling and care. That means us. They don't use brain-washing or coercion. Only vulnerability and loneliness. The Trinity Chapter gives them the love the world denies them. Believe in Yourself. Believe in Me. Believe in Trinity. For He is Always with You. <u>And He will Resurrect. How? You tell me.</u> What makes some of those who do of real interest to me is their money and influence. They are seriously rich. Plain and simple, these people are waiting and preparing in secret for Trinity's <u>Resurrection.</u>

I like to think of you playing Cassandra
Wilson on your hi-fi in The Wrist. Of your
jean shirt stained with sweat. Your
beautiful fine hands wet and sticky with
the clay. And you inventing some stunning
new arrangement of colors. Remember how
Dad always said color was your strength?
Strange how well he understood us. He had
so much right. Is there a man in your life
again? One or, as usual, two? I'll be home
in time for Christmas and you can tell me.
And if that's impossible, never mind, we
can always dance in the fountains in
Trafalgar Square on New Year's Eve. Love
Jane.

Her rapid reading is interrupted by a knocking at
the door.

'Caroline?' It's Father Scott. 'Are you OK in there?'

'Yeah,' she calls,'I'm coming, Father.'

Back in the kitchen Tammy says: 'Are you sure
you're feeling OK, Caroline?'

'I'll be all right.'

'You know,' says Tammy, 'that if there's anything
in the world Joe, me and Father Scott can do to help,
well, we'll do it.'

'That's right,' agrees Father Scott.

'I know, Tammy,' says Caroline. 'And thanks. But
nothing's going to bring her back, is it?'

Tammy avoids the question. Instead, she asks: 'Why did Jane *have* to go to London? Why couldn't she have found a college nearer home?'

'Because that was what she wanted to do,' says Caroline. 'Study in England.'

'And what was it she was studying?'

'Theology,' says Caroline. 'She was doing what she was passionate about. Same as me with the pots.'

'I somehow feel responsible,' says Father Scott. 'I mean, I encouraged her in her studies. I believed it'd be a good thing if she went to England. If she did what she wanted. She was so dedicated. Yeah, I really do feel responsible. Once or twice she phoned me. Even late at night sometimes. Just to ask how the house was. Little things about home.'

'But you said the FBI and CIA people were asking about her,' says Caroline. 'What is it *they* were asking?'

'They wouldn't say,' says Father Scott. 'I guess they were making checks. From Boston. Up from Washington even. Something to do with the State Department. I don't know about those people. Maybe it had to do with how she died. Or what it was she'd learned about those cults.'

'I've read about those people in the *National Enquirer*,' says Tammy. 'You know about Waco? Devil's works. She shouldn't have gotten so close to evil. Maybe the FBI is interested after Waco.'

'Well, let's not forget we're all God's children,' says Father Scott.

Caroline thinks: *Didn't do her any good, did it?*

'Perhaps,' says Father Scott, 'we can say it was God's will she pursued her interest in evil cults to the very end.'

'What else did she tell you?' Caroline asks him. 'About the cults.'

'Nothing,' he says. 'Nothing.'

'Not about the end of the world,' Tammy asks, 'like Salem and stuff?'

'Nothing,' says Father Scott.

Caroline pockets the notebook page with the number of the London coroner's court Joe has left her. Says she wants to get some sleep. That she'll decide what to do in the morning.

Leaving Tammy opening cupboards and the freezer to find food for breakfast in the morning, she goes to her room upstairs. Where, seated on her bed, wrapped in her Shaker quilt, she reads:

Rich, young and vulnerable. Until recently, one or other of Trinity's secluded centers was home to his chosen members or followers. One was in East Grinstead in Sussex. Another in Wallingford in Oxfordshire. He amassed a fortune. Bought property and Trinity Hostels, like the YMCAs. The secluded centers offered 'advanced treatment and rehabilitation for substance abuse'. Trinity established them as 'charitable foundations'. Effectively, they served as recruitment centers. Most of the 'patients' were vulnerable, loveless, impressionable and young. Many of them were beneficiaries of considerable family fortunes. They'd already been treated in genuine private and exclusive substance abuse clinics, in which Trinity 'monitored their suitability for service' to the chapter. In these places the followers vowed to reject 'The Previous Life' or 'The Meaninglessness of Life'. After that, a selected number – The Select – were encouraged to follow the teachings of Trinity with him in London in strict secrecy at a west London apartment block.

Like the Aum, Waco or Heaven's Gate people, the more they feel threatened by the outside world, the more they realize the rest of the world will deny Trinity's prophecies and the preparation for his Resurrection at the dawning of the Millennium. So their common bond of victimization and persecution grows stronger.

I'm beginning to think the Trinity Chapter has members in a whole network of organizations here and in the US. Like the Masons, Scientologists and what's left of the Moonies. They have their tentacles everywhere. Even in politics. Some are extremist Anglo-American and European political figures. In Washington. The State Department's been mentioned even. New York. Houston. Los Angeles. Hollywood. Others are men and women from the worlds of national and international politics, public service, the arts, sciences and academic life.

It really looks like the Trinity Chapter has been using the most lenient tax regimes in the world to shelter massive donations e.g. Seychelles, British Virgin Islands, Mauritius, the Dutch Antilles, Labuan, Bahamas, Malta and Monaco. The Trinity Chapter had assets in all those places. The works. Only the Swiss have denied them bank facilities. What they don't want is any repetition of Jouret and his Solar Church. The next question is – who provided these apparently unlimited funds?

The Day of Resurrection must be accompanied by Sacrifice. 'For You So Loved Me That You Gave of Your Blood to keep Me in Eternal Life.'

His Resurrection during London's millennial celebrations will be witnessed by millions on TV. Just imagine

the publicity. Think of the opportunity
that the Chapter can seize for the
recruitment of millions, each paying say a
hundred bucks. The increase in their funds
and the increase of their world-wide
influence.

The mystery of it scares me sometimes. I
mean just how powerfully they believe in
all of it. I'll write you in a week.
Meanwhile, I know you never write letters,
but call me if you have time. All my love
Jane. PS I'll call you.

There had been no call.

*I have no other choice. Go to London. Somebody has to
give you a proper funeral. That's what Mom and Dad
would've wanted. And I'm the only person who can fix it
for you. I'll stay just as long as it takes to bring your
ashes home. Mostly, I need to know what's happened to
you.*

After she cries herself to sleep, the blizzard breaks
across the Cape in the darkness of the early hours.

Next morning, when Tammy shows up with Father
Scott, Caroline tells them she's going to London.

'Will you be OK over there in London all alone?'
Tammy asks.

'I'll be fine. It won't take me long to do what's
needed. As long as it takes.'

'As long as what takes?' asks Father Scott.

'As long as it takes to discover the truth,' says Caroline. 'You have to know what I think. I think the British have it wrong. Like she would OD? Oh, please. No way. Suppose she died of a heroin overdose. If that's right, then it wasn't voluntary, was it?'

Father Scott stares at her. 'You're not suggesting that someone else took her life?'

'If you think it was murder,' says Tammy, 'why don't you talk it over with Joe?'

'Caroline,' asks Father Scott, 'are you suggesting that – I mean, that it was murder?'

'I'm not suggesting anything right now,' says Caroline. 'All I'm saying is this. If it's the last thing I ever do, I'll find out the truth, right? If what the British say is true, then it looks like I never knew Jane at all. And you both know that's wrong.'

'What possible interest would the British have in lying?' asks Father Scott.

'Why would the FBI and CIA be crawling around here asking questions?' says Caroline.

'They just wanted to know if we could throw any light on what happened,' says Father Scott.

'And you couldn't, could you?' says Caroline. 'I know what you're thinking. Like don't meddle in things I can't handle. But don't even try to make me change my mind, Father. I'll bring her ashes home here. And also I'll bring back the facts. You know why? Because, aside from anything else, that's what Dad and Mom would have wanted. And no burial.

Sorry, Father . . . they wouldn't have wanted that. And most important of all, that's what Jane would've wanted. And if you ask me how I know, I can tell you that I knew her better than anyone else on earth. And you both know just as well as I do that she *never*, *ever* told a lie. And I am not letting any lies surround her leaving.'

'Well, if you need any assistance, there's the woman at the embassy with the American Citizens Services Branch who may be prepared to help. Is there anything else that I can do, Caroline?' asks Father Scott finally.

'Yeah, one more thing,' she says. 'Wait here until I know I've got the room I want. You know what, it's the same hotel Jane used to use in London. The Malvern Hotel. And you know what, I'm going to ask them if I can use the room that was her favourite. You remember, Father, it was the room you used to phone?'

'Sure,' says Father Scott. 'Number 65.'

'Yeah. And there's something else I need you to do. You can take me to Logan this evening for the flight to Heathrow. Meanwhile, I have to take a look at the hills. I need some peace of mind.'

From the porch of Moorfield House the hills roll away to the horizon covered by the ruffled carpet of white snow. The morning wind lifts streaks of powder snow. The air is dry and cold. Sun edges the dazzling white of the sharper drifts with pale

[36]

blues and pinks. Caroline breathes the dry air and feels the coldness deep in her lungs. The sky is uniform deep blue. Her father used to say, when the snow was fresh in winter time: 'There's no place on earth like this. It's colored like some bleached old flag of Betsy Ross.' Now the snowfields seem possessed of an awful solitude. She runs her fingers along the rim of the railing by the entrance. Powdered snow sparkles in her hand. As she looks out at the magnificence, she shudders.

A rabbit, alerted by her presence, is scampering for shelter. It's the only movement in the landscape. It makes her catch her breath. *I'm positive I see Jane out there. Sure, I see her face.*

Suddenly she lets out a howl of grief.

She stumbles back inside the house.

'Caroline?' says Father Scott. 'Caroline?' He's reaching out to embrace her.

'I'm OK. Really.' She's gasping for breath. 'Listen, once I've made the hotel reservation, you just drive me to the airport.'

Caroline watches the snow across Logan Airport. The rush of the Boeing 747's take-off whips it over the glowing lines of runway lights.

She has boarded the jumbo with her L. L. Bean canvas bag as hand luggage. She's the only passenger who's checked no baggage into the hold for the flight to Heathrow.

She is wearing no make-up, and her long fair hair is French braided. Her rugged outdoor clothing is totally different from that of the fashion-conscious career women among her fellow travellers, who are intent on looking busy with their papers, slim briefcases and personal organizers.

Leaning against the headrest, her eyes on the lights of Boston until they disappear below, she clutches her journal on her lap. Leafed inside it are Jane's faxed letters. She holds the journal tightly like a talisman. Once the plane levels out above the clouds, she scans these pages and she's written even more about Jane than she has about herself.

She finds not a single clue as to why Jane might have ended her life a junkie in London.

3

Jane Moorfield, late of Moorfield House, Vernon Hills, Mass.
USA. Please will anyone who knew Jane Moorfield either
personally, professionally, or in connection with her
researches into the Trinity Chapter in London or Cambridge,
UK, contact her sister, Caroline Moorfield, urgently at the
Malvern Hotel, 2 Coptic Street, London WC1. Telephone:
0171-935-0100.
  – INTERNATIONAL HERALD TRIBUNE, DECEMBER 1999

The immigration officer at Heathrow asks her about
the purpose of her visit to the United Kingdom.
'Business or a vacation?'

'Neither.'

A woman in a blue blazer standing next to the
official butts in: 'Why exactly are you visiting
London?'

'It's kind of a family matter,' Caroline tells her.

While the immigration officer taps Caroline's
name into his computer the woman leafs through
the pages of Caroline's passport. 'Do you have any
friends or relatives in London?' she asks.

'No, I don't,' says Caroline.

'Would you mind telling me about this family
matter that brings you here?'

'Sure, OK,' says Caroline. 'If you want to know,

I'm visiting London because my sister died here a short while back. I've come to arrange her funeral.'

'I'm sorry,' the woman says, with a look of regret. 'What was your sister's name?'

'Jane Moorfield.'

The woman hands back the passport. 'Thank you, Ms Moorfield.'

'Is there something wrong?' asks Caroline.

'No,' the woman says. 'Enjoy your visit.'

'By the way,' the woman asks, 'where are you staying in London?'

'At the Malvern Hotel,' says Caroline. 'Coptic Street.'

Caroline lies exhausted on the bed in Room 65 of the Malvern Hotel. The room is smaller than she'd expected. The double bed takes up most of it, and the bedspread matches the floral pattern of the curtains. In the corner, next to the only window, is the TV. In front of the TV is the small writing desk stacked with tourist brochures and a complimentary copy of the *International Herald Tribune*.

The view from the window is not quite what she'd expected either. The garden Jane had once described to her looks bleak and drab in the snow. Not at all the 'tiny green patch of summer' she had mentioned. Some pigeons are cooing on the sill. At first the pigeons had woken Jane early in the mornings; but finally she'd grown accustomed to them. Like familiar friends, she only noticed their absence and wondered where they went. So she said.

Her face buried in the pillows, Caroline thinks she catches the smell of Jane's scent, Lauren.

Perhaps I want to smell it. To find something of her. Anything.

Now, drifting into sleep, she thinks she imagines the knocking on the door. She gets up from the bed and goes to the door. Unfastening the security chain, she sees a short and rather plump man standing in the corridor. He's wearing a dark double-breasted suit and holding some plastic carrier bags.

'Miss Moorfield?' he asks with a bland smile. 'I'm the assistant manager. I hope this is a convenient time. I was so sad to hear of your sister's passing.'

Caroline shows him into the room.

'Shall I leave these things on the bed? They're your sister's. Clothes, toiletries and so on, I think. We'd quite forgotten we had them.'

Caroline briefly looks inside the bags. *Jane's clothes*. She asks him: 'Did you, by any chance, find any of her papers and work notes?'

'No, nothing else, I'm afraid.' He is looking at the photograph of Jane on the bedside table. 'You've now got all there is in these bags.'

'Well, thanks anyway,' she says.

'Is there anything else I can do to help?' he asks.

'I don't suppose anyone's discussed my sister with you, have they?'

He seems reluctant to venture an opinion. When

he does speak, he says: 'There was some talk of the possibility of drug use. But I wouldn't want to swear to it. Unfortunately, you hear all sorts of stories in my line of work. You learn that whatever your opinions they're best kept to yourself.'

'Did Jane have any regular visitors?' she asks him.

'I'm afraid we don't keep a check on visitors. By and large we like our guests to feel free to come and go as they please. What I would like to say is that if there's anything we can do to make your stay more comfortable, please just get in touch with me.'

From the window of Room 65 she looks at the grey sky blotched with London's yellow light. Once the man has left, she lies down on the bed again and finds herself weeping for Jane. *I want to go home soon. Home to Vernon Hills. Once I've let them cremate you and I've got your ashes.*

Unable to sleep she confides in her journal. She writes:

I cannot believe you died by your own hand or that you ever took heroin. You of all people, Jane. Never. I know it can't be true. I swear to you, as if you were here with me now, that I will find out the truth. Whatever it costs.

The wind is whistling. A long continuous whine. If I listen very hard, I can hear it singing your name. Somewhere in the distance I can make out the sound of church bells ringing.

I find it hard to believe that this is really happening to us.

It's like some nightmare. What I feel is that somehow, even in the middle of all this trouble, you're here with me.

That someone has to have murdered you. But I can't imagine who could be possessed of so much murderous hate that they would destroy the sweetest soul that ever lived.

I love you Jane. Just because you are dead, that has not murdered my living love for you. You are in my body, in my blood, in my juices, in my ears and in my eyes and in my heart. Otherwise, why am I talking to you right now? Tell me . . . But the crying has to stop sometime. What those unseen hands did is beyond belief. I feel almost guilty that it's not me who's dead here because I cannot stop thinking that if only I'd been with you none of this would've happened.

LONDON — I already seem to hate it. But I'll stay with it. Because somewhere here, I'm sure, here in London is the reason for your death.

Her first telephone call is to the United States Embassy and Ms Susan Isiskind of the American Citizens Services Branch.

Ms Isiskind says she'll be happy to see Caroline at her office the following afternoon. Happy to advise on the arrangements for the return home of Jane's ashes.

'Your family priest, Father Scott, says you have a problem with the circumstances of your sister's death.'

'Yeah, I do. I'd like to talk to you about it.'

'Why not wait and see the outcome of the

inquest? In fact, I made a call to the coroner's office. It's tomorrow morning at ten thirty. In St Pancras.' Isiskind describes the whereabouts of the coroner's court and gives detailed directions. 'If you have serious legal problems with the circumstances of your sister's death –'

'I do,' Caroline interrupts.

'OK. Then I suggest you call ASG. That's Alexander Swincarron Gertler. They're a private investigation firm. We can recommend them.' She gives Caroline the ASG Strand Chambers address and telephone number. 'Matter of fact, I spoke to them this morning and they suggest you contact one of their people. A Mr Alan Rosslyn.'

'I'll do that. I really appreciate your help.'

'You're welcome. I'll see you here tomorrow. Say at noon.'

She telephones Rosslyn at ASG. An assistant says Mr Rosslyn's been expecting her to call. He'll see her this afternoon. 'In an hour's time, say?'

Her next telephone call is to the London office of the *International Herald Tribune* in Long Acre. She has the folded copy of the paper open at page six.

'How much is it to place a personal ad?' she asks.

'The line rate?'

'Whatever.'

'It's £11.85 per line per day.'

'How soon can you place one for me?'

'You're too late now to catch tomorrow's edition. I

can get it in the day after for you. How long do you want to run it for?'

'Two weeks.'

'How many lines?'

'As many as it takes,' says Caroline. 'I'll pay by Visa?'

'No problem. If you'd give me your message.'

'OK,' says Caroline. 'The message reads:

JANE MOORFIELD, late of Moorfield House, Vernon Hills, Mass. USA. Please will anyone who knew Jane Moorfield either personally, professionally, or in connection with her researches into the Trinity Chapter in London or Cambridge, UK, contact her sister, Caroline Moorfield, urgently at the Malvern Hotel, 2 Coptic Street, London WC1. Telephone: 0171-935-0100.'

The woman at the *International Herald Tribune* office reads it over. 'If you give me your credit card details I'll see it appears in all our editions.'

The short walk from the Malvern Hotel to the computer shops in Tottenham Court Road. In the first one Caroline comes to, she talks the assistant into demonstrating the Internet: 'Can you show me how to put a message on it?'

The man agrees. As an example of what the equipment on sale can do, he puts up the same message Caroline has given to the *International Herald Tribune*. At Caroline's request, he posts it on to the newsgroup dealing with new religious movements and cults in general: http://www:ex-cult.org/.

Then she heads south, in the direction of Trafalgar Square, to Strand Chambers, on the corner of Whitehall and the Strand.

4

Alexander Swincarron Gertler Limited was established in 1995 by Dr Maxine Gertler and Peter Alexander, formerly of Baumann, the New York based investigations firm. ASG is a business intelligence consultancy which assists decision-makers at critical junctures by providing them with accurate and substantive information on individuals and companies.

Typically, our clients include banks (commercial, investment and private), corporations (manufacturing, trading, financial services and insurance), law firms, creditor committees, auditors, venture capitalists, charities, foundations, religious organizations and individuals. We assist organizations who may harbour reservations about a potential client. Retained by corporations to screen overseas joint venture partners and agents, we can discreetly vet senior hires and develop competitor intelligence.

ASG understands the possible commercial, political, legal and government secret intelligence implications of the information and intelligence which we gather. We have a well developed expertise in tracing concealed assets in multiple jurisdictions.

Our service is acknowledged to be the most effective on any continent. I am confident that, with the approach of the Millennium, ASG will preserve its standards. *Ruth Swincarron*

ALEXANDER SWINCARRON GERTLER LTD,

INTELLIGENCE CONSULTANTS,

LONDON.

MILLENNIAL BROCHURE,

LONDON, 1999

At the entrance, the brass plaque says ALEXANDER SWINCARRON GERTLER LIMITED.

Caroline leans over a frozen pile of Pret a Manger bags, lager cans, scratch cards and discarded copies of *The Big Issue*, to speak into the entry phone.

'I have an appointment with Mr Alan Rosslyn,' she says.

The warmth of the atrium is a relief from the cold. Gleaming metal tubes and brightly painted service ducts hang beneath the steel and glass web of the enormous roof space. Water from a leaking roof fills a plastic bucket on a great square of plastic sheeting beside a defunct fountain. Giant indoor plants obscure most of a temporary notice which says DANGER – OUT OF ORDER.

Behind the reception desk, on which there's a row of CCTV monitors, the security guard asks her for ID. She offers him her passport. He taps the keyboard of his computer. 'Mr Rosslyn is in a meeting,' he says. 'He'll see you in ten minutes.'

Handing her an ASG ID tag, he invites her to take a seat on one of the leather sofas across the marble hall. 'While you're waiting,' he suggests, 'you may care to read our brochure.'

Caroline turns to the biography of Alan Rosslyn in the brochure. She reads:

Junior Associates

Mr Alan Rosslyn was educated at the University of London. In 1983 he was a University Graduate Direct

Entry appointee to Higher Executive Officer Level. Until 1998, he served HM Customs and Excise Investigation Division variously in the Drugs Financial Investigation Branch, Team A Division Arms and Explosives, and Team E Division Indecent and Obscene Material. He was a trained firearms officer. His specialized experience was in Surveillance and Undercover Operations in liaison with Police, Armed Services and the Security Services (MI5 and MI6) and he served in many geographical areas including the United Kingdom, United States, the Caribbean, Middle East, West Africa, South-East Asia and the Indian subcontinent. In January 1999 he joined Alexander Swincarron Gertler Limited as an Associate.

And when the security guard tells her to take the lift to the top floor she gives him an approving smile.

Alan Rosslyn introduces himself to Caroline in the corridor. She notices the strong handshake. Long fingers. Cold to the touch. The short dark hair shows traces of premature grey. He's tall, with the build of a distance runner, and when he smiles he bows his head slightly. The slow smile is attractive. Thoughtful. 'Sorry to have kept you waiting,' he tells her. He seems relaxed. Not the sort of Englishman she'd expected. Harder. Straight. 'This way,' he tells her. 'We can talk in my office.'

Plush crimson carpet muffles their footsteps on the top-floor corridor of Strand Chambers. Caroline notices the framed colour photographs lining the wood-panelled walls. Mostly of desert scenes, they are prominently labelled DUBAI, SAUDI, BAHRAIN. Above them, at intervals, she sees the discreetly-positioned CCTV cameras. The office doors, each with an elaborate locking system, are marked variously PRINCIPALS DINING ROOM, INTERVIEW ROOM, RUTH SWINCARRON, PETER ALEXANDER, DR MAXINE GERTLER. Outside the door to Rosslyn's office is the photograph of Alexander Swincarron Gertler Limited's three principals. The founders of Europe's leading firm of private and commercial investigators.

He shows her into his office, with its view of Trafalgar Square and Nelson's Column against the leaden sky.

She turns to look around the triangular room. At the low table in the centre of the room. The neat piles of the *Financial Times*, *Asia Today*, *Time*, *Newsweek* and the *New York Herald Tribune*. The Apple Mac on the glass-topped desk beneath a reproduction of John Constable's *The Cornfield*.

'Have a seat,' Rosslyn says. 'Would you like coffee or tea?'

'No thanks.'

'Feeling the cold?' he asks.

'Its no different than home.'

'I could do without it,' Rosslyn says.

She is looking hard at his jacket, the pale blue shirt and nondescript tie. Neat, a bit dull, they contrast with the smile in his unblinking greyish eyes.

Rosslyn asks her: 'Did Ms Isiskind at your embassy tell you what we do here?'

'Yes. And I read about some of it in the brochure. It's impressive.'

'We like to think so,' Rosslyn tells her. 'Ms Isiskind told me about your sister Jane. I'm sorry. What can I say? It must be terrible for you.'

'It is.'

'You have my sympathy,' he says. 'OK now. Let's see what I can do to help you with your problem.' He takes a felt-tip pen from inside his jacket.

She tells him about Jane. The postgraduate work in Cambridge and London. Of what little Jane has told her about the Trinity Chapter. How she can't believe her sister could possibly have died from the drugs overdose.

'If you don't mind me asking,' Rosslyn says, 'did your sister ever, just once, do drugs?'

'She didn't, I swear to God.'

'Never?'

'Never.'

'Even soft drugs?'

'No.'

'And have you?'

'Never.'

'Have you any idea, any suspicion, however slight, that Caroline might have been involved with people she shouldn't have been?'

'No. She hadn't done anything wrong. I'd have known about it. We had no secrets from each other.'

Rosslyn watches the look of exasperation pass across her face. He notices her wring her hands. The knuckles are almost white. The furrowed forehead. She gives a short and sudden breath. As if in pain.

'I believe the inquest is tomorrow,' he says.

'Right.'

'Why don't we attend it and maybe go together to see Ms Isiskind at the embassy? You say Jane had been researching this Trinity Chapter. And that was both here in London and in Cambridge?'

'Yeah,' says Caroline. 'Her tutor's based at Cambridge University.'

'Do you know her?'

'No. Only her name. Dr Julia Llewellyn. She sounds to have liked Jane. And Jane her. More than that I don't know.'

'Have you any idea who else she may have been in contact with?'

'No,' says Caroline.

'When she was in London where did she live?'

'At the Malvern Hotel in Coptic Street. Where I'm staying right now. I guess it was convenient for her work or something.'

'And she wasn't short of money?'

'We have enough money.'

'What I mean is,' says Rosslyn, 'and this may be painful to you, she had enough money to fund a serious drug habit.'

'I'm telling you she never had a drug habit.'

'We don't know that for sure,' says Rosslyn.

'You may not,' says Caroline. 'But I do –'

'I'll take your word for it,' says Rosslyn.

'You have to.'

'OK.' He goes to the computer on the table beneath the Constable reproduction. 'Now if you can, please, Caroline, I want you to tell me, in one or two sentences, exactly what it is you want ASG to do for you.'

'This is what I'm asking,' says Caroline. 'I want to know –'

'Not too fast,' Rosslyn tells her. He begins to type.

'I want to know,' she says slowly, 'yes or no. Could Jane have been doing drugs? Like I say, I believe the answer is no. If I am proven right – and I mean proven – then I want to know who murdered her. I want the proof. The absolute proof. I want her killer or killers arrested. Indicted. And prosecuted.'

He turns round to face her in a crouch like a prize fighter between rounds. 'I doubt we'll find out much about the drugs. But we might find out if someone other than herself took her life. We have to discover the motive and the opportunity. We already know the means. Arrest, charging and prosecution come later. That's all for the police. In the meantime, you do know my services will be expensive.'

'I guess so.'

'All depending on how long we work for you,' says Rosslyn, 'you could be looking at in excess of four figures.'

'I told you, we have no problem with money,' says Caroline. 'You can do a credit check.'

'I just felt I should point it out,' says Rosslyn. 'So there'll be no awkwardness down the line.'

'Mr Rosslyn, I really need to know if you can help me.'

He watches her staring out across Trafalgar Square. At the snow. At the tall Christmas tree with its sparkling lights, the gift of a grateful Norway for British help in World War Two.

'Yes,' he says, 'I think I can. First of all I have to check my case load with my superiors. I don't foresee a problem there.'

'See,' she says, 'I need your help. You know the feeling. When your whole world's fallen apart. Oh well, I guess you don't.' She walks to the desk where she's left the ASG brochure and looks down at the photograph beneath the glass top. She sees the face of a pretty uniformed woman police officer. 'Have you ever lost anyone close to you?' she asks. 'Do you know what it feels like, really feels like?'

He looks her straight in the eyes. 'Yes, as a matter of fact I do. If you want to know – I lost my girlfriend in a terrorist shooting some years back. Right in front of my eyes. I do know what it feels like to lose someone.'

'Who was she?'

'The photo. That's her. You're looking at her right now.'

'A cop?' she asks.

'Yes. A cop.'

'What was her name?' Caroline asks.

'Mary.'

He takes his long dark coat from a peg behind the door. *So all I could tell you, Caroline, is that you're going to take a long time to get over your grief. You have to learn to live with it. But you seem to be discovering that for yourself already.*

Caroline says: 'I'm really sorry.'

'It's OK,' he says. 'Why don't we meet tomorrow morning at the St Pancras Coroner's Court? Take it from there. I'll show you to the lift.'

'I can find it on my own.'

'No,' he says. 'Company rules. You have to be escorted. You're my visitor.'

5

There are thousands of [new religious] groups of which there is no doubt that they are of satanic origin. But praise be to God, there are also thousands of new church movements in which, in spite of syncretism, the Spirit of God is at work. Where one ends and the other begins will require discernment that only God can give.

– REACHING MYSTICS AND CULTISTS, COMMITTEE FOR WORLD EVANGELIZATION, LAUSANNE

Her Majesty's St Pancras Coroner's Court is a single-storey, late nineteenth-century building of London brick.

The interior is lit by clusters of lights in glass shades suspended from the ceiling by brass chains. Raised on a dais, the coroner's desk and his chair, upholstered in cracked red leather, dominate the room. On the wall behind the desk is a painted royal coat of arms. A grey noticeboard on an easel gives the room the atmosphere of an old-fashioned church school.

To the left of the coroner's desk there are three wooden benches provided for the jury if the coroner is hearing evidence about someone who died in prison. Or in police custody. Or if death resulted from an incident at work. On a railway line. A further six benches are provided for witnesses. Members of the public. And those known as Properly Interested Persons. The latter may attend the court for a variety of reasons. For example, if they are relatives of the deceased, or if they may stand to benefit from a life insurance policy. It is the coroner's prerogative to decide who may or may not be a Properly Interested Person.

Pinned to the wall on the left of the coroner's desk is a calendar showing the day of the month in bold black and red numbers. At the back of the court-room, to the immediate right of the entrance, is a white electric clock with hands and numbers in black. The clock shows ten thirty precisely as the coroner's court officer enters the courtroom and calls: 'All rise for Her Majesty's coroner.'

All rise.

Of the three witnesses who will give evidence in court this morning, two are women. One is a young uniformed police officer who is busily reading her notebook. The second is a woman approaching middle age, a forensic pathologist. The third witness is a man in his twenties. With an open face, curly fair hair and blue eyes, he wears a neat black suit and a white shirt buttoned at its high collar. Beside him, on the bench, is his folded Burberry mackintosh.

Caroline is present as a Properly Interested Person. She sees Rosslyn at the courtroom door.

The court officer is asking him what interest he has in this morning's proceedings.

'I represent the sister of the deceased,' Rosslyn says and shows the court officer his business card.

The court officer says: 'If you'd sit over there, Mr Rosslyn.'

He sits on the benches reserved for the public, next to Caroline. 'How are you?' he asks her.

'Dreading it,' she says.

'It won't take long,' says Rosslyn gently. 'You'll do fine.'

At the door to the courtroom, at the start of this morning's proceedings, the court officer asks another apparent member of the public to identify herself. A slim blonde, she wears a dark green waxed jacket, blue jeans and strong black shoes. She also presents a business card to the court officer:

> ▆▆▆ ▆ ▆ ▓
>
>   Wendy Lever
>   Home Office
>   Intelligence and Resources Operations
>   Thames House
>   Millbank
>   London SW1P 1AE

The court officer, a former Metropolitan Police officer, recognizes the Millbank address: Thames House, headquarters of MI5 – known to insiders as Box, the domestic security service.

He returns her wide smile and quietly shows her to a seat.

The coroner enters from a door to the left of his desk.

Bowing slightly, he says: 'Please be seated.' He spreads out various papers on his desk. His duty is to establish medical cause of death in all its forms. If the cause of a death reported to him turns out to be unknown, he will have to enquire into it. Say, for example, death is unnatural or the result of violence; or if no doctor treated the deceased during a final illness. He is not about to apportion blame for a death, as a trial would. Rather, he will preside over a limited inquiry to find out precisely who has died and how, when and where, together with any other information required by the Registrar of Deaths.

Mostly his task is easy enough, though the evidence he hears is always unpleasant. If a person has been charged with causing someone's death, say by murder or manslaughter, the coroner will adjourn the inquest until the accused has been tried. Before doing so, he has to satisfy himself as to the identity of the deceased. And as to how he or she died. Having sent the appropriate form to the Registrar of Deaths, once the trial is over he will resume the inquest.

The court officer approaches the coroner's desk. 'This, sir,' he says, 'is the case of Jane Moorfield. The preliminary hearing was adjourned for the *post mortem* and, as you will recall, to allow for the police to contact Caroline Moorfield, the sister of the deceased. You will also recall, sir, that the deceased was an American citizen and her sister resides in the United States, in Vernon Hills, Massachusetts.'

'Is Caroline Moorfield in court?' the coroner asks.

'She is, sir, yes.'

The coroner smiles sympathetically at Caroline. 'I'm grateful to you for your attendance here this morning, Ms Moorfield.'

'Thank you, sir,' she says, almost in a whisper.

'Very well,' says the coroner. 'This is an inquiry into the death of Jane Moorfield, an American woman aged twenty-six. Born in 1973 at Vernon Hills in Massachusetts, USA.'

The court officer walks to the witness stand to the right of the coroner's desk and beckons to the first witness to enter the witness box. The pale, boyish figure has the look of an anxious chorister.

'What religion are you?' asks the court officer.

'Church of England,' says the witness, his blue eyes glancing nervously around the court.

The court officer hands him a printed card and a bible. 'Place your right hand on the bible. And read from the card, please.'

'I swear by Almighty God to tell the truth, the whole truth and nothing but the truth.'

The coroner gives the witness an encouraging smile. 'You are Marcus Luke?'

'I am, yes, sir.'

'And you were Jane Moorfield's friend?' asks the coroner.

Marcus Luke leans forward. His blue eyes hold Caroline's and he gives her a slow smile. 'I was,' he says.

She shivers: *I can see what Jane might have found attractive in you.*

'May I remind you,' says the coroner, 'that you have given evidence that Jane Moorfield, a postgraduate student of theology, lived at a temporary address – the Malvern Hotel, Coptic Street, London WC1?'

The witness breathes deeply. 'She lived there, yes.'

'And you said that you had known her for some five months, Mr Luke. Is that correct?'

'It is, sir.'

The coroner leads him gently. 'And am I right in thinking that a card or scrap of paper with your name and work address on it was found on the deceased when she was admitted to University College Hospital?'

'Yes, sir, I believe it was.'

'And the address was that of the Provident Care and Nursing Agency in Warren Street?'

'That's right, sir, yes.'

'And that you are a qualified psychiatric nurse, Mr Luke?'

'Yes, I am, sir.'

The coroner turns the page. 'And in the presence of a police officer you identified the deceased as Jane Moorfield. A single American woman who was a resident of the United States?'

'I did, sir.' He's looking at Caroline. 'Yes.'

'Is it reasonable then for me to assume,' asks the coroner, 'in so far as you were her friend, that you were close to her?'

'Yes,' the witness says, 'I was.'

'And she was close to you?'

The witness hesitates.

'I want you to take your time,' the coroner says. 'I appreciate this must be difficult for you. I am trying to establish whether she, in turn, felt close to you.'

'Yes, sir,' he says, his eyes once more holding Caroline's. 'I believe she did.'

'And may I take it that, in so far as you are aware, apart from her drug abuse, she struck you as being a generally healthy young woman?'

Once again, the witness seems to hesitate.

'I need to ask you about her general state of health,' says the coroner, 'because she was not, as you probably know, a registered patient of any general medical practice. That means the court has no established or written record of her general medical history or state of mind.'

'She struck me as being –'

'"Generally healthy",' prompts the coroner. 'That was the observation you made?'

'Yes,' agrees the witness. 'Though she hadn't actually commenced regular treatment at the clinic where I used to work –'

'May I interrupt you there, Mr Luke? This clinic, what was it called?'

'The Van Rijn Clinic.'

'In Harley Street?'

'Yes.'

'And when Miss Moorfield attended the Van Rijn Clinic, did she not furnish you with a few details of her medical state?'

'Not in any detail that I can recall.'

'I see,' says the coroner. 'I see that you no longer work at the Van Rijn Clinic.'

'That's correct, sir, I don't.'

'And why is that?'

'Because the clinic has closed.'

'Why is that?'

'Because Dr Van Rijn has retired. He has moved abroad to Belgium.'

The coroner smiles at those present in the court. 'My daughter has just married a Belgian.' The court officer beams with approval, for the coroner likes to add the personal touch to proceedings. 'Whereabouts in Belgium?'

'I don't know. Somewhere in Belgium.'

'Ah well,' says the coroner. 'My daughter is in Brussels. There we are. Now can you tell the court what sort of treatment Miss Moorfield was seeking at the clinic?'

'Just treatment of a natural kind.'

'Based on what I believe is called complementary or alternative medicine?'

'Yes,' says the witness. 'She particularly used acupuncture.'

'Why was that?'

'It was intended to improve her immune system and inner state of harmony.'

'It was. I see. And for some time previous to her death you were aware that she was using drugs?'

'I'm afraid that I was aware of that, yes, sir.'

'Your statement says it was mainly heroin?'

'It was, yes, sir.'

'Miss Moorfield wasn't as far as you could tell, though, prone to extreme depression, or for example to any state of acute distress that might have led her to seek treatment at the Van Rijn Clinic?'

'Not as far as I am aware, sir.'

'Am I right in thinking that she did not seek treatment, shall we say, of a specifically psychiatric nature?'

'No, she did not.'

'But am I right in thinking that, on several occasions, you tried your level best to get her to seek treatment to overcome her drug habit?'

'I did indeed, sir. Yes.'

'But you were unsuccessful?'

'Unfortunately, I wasn't successful. No.'

'I take it that, as far as you were aware, she had never indicated that she might take her own life?'

'That's correct. She never said anything like that to me at any time.'

The coroner writes something on a printed form. 'I am satisfied that the deceased is Jane Moorfield.' He smiles at the witness. 'Thank you for your help,

Mr Luke. You may return to your seat.'

Caroline watches him sit down. He's frowning. Whether the look is one of pain or doubt, Caroline is unsure. When his face relaxes he looks innocent and sweet in a way she finds slightly dangerous.

It's Caroline's turn to enter the witness box. She lifts the bible. Takes the oath and gives her name.

'You are Caroline Moorfield,' says the coroner, 'the sister of the deceased?'

'I am, yes.'

'And you have heard the evidence given by the previous witness as to the identity of your late sister?'

'I have.'

'Would you say, Miss Moorfield, that you are in broad agreement with what you've heard?'

'No, I am not.'

The coroner stares at her with a quizzical look. 'Why is that?'

'Because I cannot accept that my sister did drugs.'

'Well, unfortunately, Miss Moorfield, however regrettable it is, I'm sorry to have to tell that you will shortly hear more evidence given by the forensic pathologist who performed the *post mortem*. The pathologist's findings substantiate your sister's use of drugs.'

'It doesn't add up, sir.'

'That, I am afraid, is as may be.'

'Sir, I can't accept it. She had no psychiatric

illness, nor any problem with drugs. She was the sanest and healthiest woman I ever knew. And she was my sister.'

'As I am aware.'

'So I should know.'

'Oh, naturally.'

'She had no problems. She had her whole life to live for. There was nothing wrong with her. I do *not* believe what I am hearing, sir.'

The coroner hesitates. He seems temporarily taken aback by this outburst of transparent honesty. Perhaps he is moved by the intense and wide-eyed look of vulnerability. 'I very much regret to say, Miss Moorfield,' he says kindly, 'that the evidence already submitted by the doctor who admitted her to casualty endorses the contrary view. I think you should hear it and we can return to you a little later. But first we must take other matters in their proper order.'

Caroline shakes her head in disbelief. The court officer ushers her back to her seat.

Now it's the turn of the woman police officer to give evidence.

The coroner rests his hands on his desk. 'Officer, you attended the place where the deceased was found. The area of wasteland immediately to the north of King's Cross and St Pancras. That was on the second of December, wasn't it?'

'It was, sir, yes.'

'What time was that?'

'At approximately eleven thirty at night.'

'And you personally found the deceased?'

'I did, sir.'

'She was, as far as you could tell at the time, not then dead?'

'No, sir,' the WPC says. 'She was not at that time dead, sir.'

'But obviously seriously ill?'

'That was my opinion. Very sick indeed.'

'And what else did you observe?'

'That there was a great deal of foam around her mouth and a quantity of vomit. It seemed to me she had swallowed her own vomit.'

'And then you called for medical assistance?'

'I did, sir. Yes.'

'And what time did the ambulance arrive?'

The WPC turns to her notebook and flips through it. She appears to find the page she is looking for. 'At approximately eleven forty-five, sir.'

'And next to the deceased, you also found a syringe, three needles, a tourniquet and a small quantity of powder in a folded sheet of paper?'

The woman police officer once more consults her notebook. There is a silence. She's considering her answer cautiously. Thinking carefully. 'I did, sir, find the items you mentioned. Yes.'

'What did you do then, officer?' asks the coroner.

'I heard the deceased say "No. No. No."'

'And what did you infer from that?'

'That she was anxious not to be taken to hospital.'

'Why not?'

'I didn't understand at first. But although she was obviously very ill, she managed to tell me that she was American. I didn't realize then that, in the United States, a drug abuser is arrested once admitted for abuse. I tried to calm her and said she must try not to worry. I told her that all we wanted to do was to save her life.'

'And when you travelled with her in the ambulance to University College Hospital,' says the coroner, 'what did she say to you?'

'Just "For God's sake, leave me alone."'

'And were you with her when she was admitted to Casualty at University College Hospital?'

'Yes, sir, I was with her.'

'Very well, officer. Thank you very much.'

The coroner turns to a letter in the open folder on his desk.

'This letter,' the coroner says, 'is from the doctor who examined Jane Moorfield, Dr Ryan Lancaster. Dr Lancaster is presently abroad on vacation in New South Wales, Australia. I intend to accept his letter as evidence. Item C1: Statement of Dr Ryan Lancaster in respect of the deceased.'

Aware that Dr Lancaster's letter contains medical technicalities, the coroner reads it out slowly:

I am the Senior Registrar in anaesthetics at
University College Hospital and I was called to

Casualty at about ten minutes past midnight on the morning of 3 December 1999 to assess an emergency. A young woman had been admitted by ambulance.

The ambulance staff informed the casualty officer that they had attended the King's Cross area following an emergency call from Woman Police Officer Colette Marshall.

Alongside the woman were a 5cc syringe, two 25g and one 23g needles and a folded piece of paper to which traces of a powder were adherent. They brought these with the patient.

The patient was a young, thin, fair-haired Caucasian woman. I estimated her age as between twenty-five and thirty.

She was by now unconscious. Her pupils were small. They were constricted and did not respond to light. Nor did she respond to painful stimuli. I estimated that she was in stage three to four of the Glasgow coma scale. Her blood pressure was low. Her respiratory rate was five a minute. She was mildly cyanosed. There were a few crackles at the lung bases on auscultation suggestive of pneumonia. Minor contusions to both wrists.

No other abnormalities were detected. No signs of trauma or head injury.

The casualty officer had inserted an intravenous line in the dorsum of the right hand and there were several recent venepuncture sites on the anteriors of the wrists. I remember thinking these were rather awkward sites for self-administered intravenous injections. These were not the venepuncture sites one normally sees in comatose intravenous drug abusers brought to our casualty.

However, given the physical findings and the presence of the syringe, needles and folded sheet of paper with powder traces, I thought the most likely cause of coma was an intravenous drug overdose, almost certainly an opiate, and I therefore administered a dose of the narcotic antagonist naloxone through the existing IV line.

As there was no immediate response to the naloxone, I intubated her and ventilated her by hand and accompanied her to the Intensive Care Unit.

Once there, I arranged for blood to go off for routine screening and a full drug assay.

I also arranged for an urgent CAT scan of her brain, which was done approximately thirty minutes later and was normal.

I stayed with the patient in the Intensive Care Unit as, despite fluid replacement and positive intotropes, she remained hypotensive.

She arrested at approximately 2.26 a.m. and was successfully defibrillated. However, shortly thereafter she became asystolic – a form of cardiac arrest – and failed to respond to resuscitation.

Efforts to resuscitate her continued for forty minutes. But she was pronounced dead at 3.23 a.m.

The laboratory returned samples of diamorphine in the peripheral blood and urine –

The coroner pushes the letter to one side. 'That concludes Dr Lancaster's letter.'

The court officer accompanies the final witness, the forensic pathologist, to the stand and hands her the card for her to swear the oath.

Wearing a dark blue cotton jacket and black linen skirt, she is a slim woman with neat dark hair that falls in a split fringe across her forehead.

Formality requires the coroner to ask the question to which he knows the answer: 'You are Dr Elizabeth Maryon, a forensic pathologist at Guy's Hospital?'

'I am, sir, yes.'

'You carried out the *post mortem* on the deceased?'

'I did, sir.'

'In your report you say that there was evidence of recent puncture or needle marks on the deceased's wrists?'

'Yes. Marks consistent with injection.'

'Evidence of drug abuse?'

'The marks would suggest that, sir, yes.'

'And some evidence of bruising,' asks the coroner, 'consistent with the use of a tourniquet having been tightened?'

'Yes.'

'But no other marks or bruising that might constitute evidence of violence?'

'None, sir.'

'And you found evidence consistent with signs of inhalation pneumonia?'

'Yes, I did, sir. She had signs of recent inhalation pneumonia.'

'You found the presence of diamorphine or heroin in the blood?'

'I did. Yes.'

'And your report concludes that death was the result of an overdose of diamorphine or heroin?'

'That is correct, sir.'

'Thank you, Dr Maryon,' says the coroner. 'Please return to your seat.'

Once Dr Maryon is seated, the coroner turns to Caroline.'I will be happy for you to ask any further questions you may wish in respect of the medical evidence, Miss Moorfield.'

'I have said everything I have to say. I do not believe this.'

'I regret that,' says the coroner.

'I want someone to do something about it.'

'Yes, well, the court officer can suggest what avenues may be open to you.'

'Like what?'

'OK, Caroline,' Rosslyn whispers to her. 'We'll talk about it after.'

She sits on her hands and sniffs.

'Very well,' says the coroner. 'It is now my duty to address the main questions concerning the death of Jane Moorfield.

'First, as to identification. I am satisfied the deceased was Jane Moorfield, a twenty-six-year-old single woman of Vernon Hills, Massachusetts, USA.

'Second, I am further satisfied Jane Moorfield died at University College Hospital; and third, she was pronounced dead by the duty doctor there on 3 December 1999 at three twenty-three in the morning of that day.'

His concentration is momentarily diverted by a chant from the cemetery outside:

> *Trin-it-eee*
> *Trin-it-eee*
> *Three in one*
> *One in three*

The coroner waits a moment.

The chanting outside is almost like the drone of bagpipes. The funeral lament.

'Fourth,' he continues, 'I must be satisfied as to the cause of the death of this twenty-six-year-old healthy female. There is no evidence that any natural diseases contributed to her death. Nor is there any evidence of the administration of violence. The toxicological analysis, however, shows that a lethal quantity of heroin or diamorphine had been taken. I am satisfied, therefore, that the cause of death was an overdose of heroin that led to changes in the brain, cerebral anoxia and cardiac arrest –'

The droning continues: *Trin-it-eee–*

'So, to conclude this inquiry into what is a tragic event. This is the sad history of a young and healthy adult female who decided to take heroin and consequently suffered from the fatal effects brought about by a shortage of oxygen, which led to premature death. This was an unlooked-for and fatal action and was the result of the voluntary action of the deceased. Without further ado, I record a verdict of Death by Misadventure. It only remains for me to draw attention publicly to the danger of heroin and drug abuse . . .' He catches Caroline's eye. There's a second's silence, broken by Caroline, who sobs. '. . . and finally, I wish to convey the sympathy of the court to the family of the deceased.' He is already rising to his feet, gathering up his files. 'Thank you very much.'

The court officer intones: 'The court will rise.'

All rise.

The courtroom empties. Rosslyn stays next to Caroline, who has buried her face in her hands. He takes her left hand. 'It's all right, Caroline.'

'Excuse me? It's not all right. I don't believe it. Please –'

Putting an arm round her shoulder, trying to comfort her, Rosslyn notices the blonde, who's near the exit pulling on her dark green waxed jacket.

'She never did drugs.' Caroline squirms and leans away from him. 'Never. Please –'

'It'll be all right,' he says.

He sees the blonde is about to engage the court officer in an unwanted conversation. He can't place her. But he feels sure he's seen her somewhere before. He wonders what interest she has in being here this morning. He'd like to know. And on Caroline's behalf he'd also like a word with the witness, Marcus Luke. Angel Face. Too late: Angel Face has already left and it'll have to wait.

'Acupuncture,' Caroline is whispering. 'Never . . . Jane had a phobia about needles . . . Jesus Christ –'

'OK,' says Rosslyn, 'wait here a second.' He goes to the centre of the courtroom. To the square wooden table marked with ink stains and he fills the tumbler with water from the jug.

He hands it to Caroline. 'Here. Would you rather postpone the appointment at the US Embassy? They asked me to confirm it with them. Are you sure you're up to it?'

'Yeah. They said they'd help. I'll be OK, Alan. Let's do it. Just *let's do it*.'

'OK,' he says, 'I'll be back.'

At the window of the court office counter he asks if he can use the telephone. He notices the blonde in the dark green jacket is watching him.

Preoccupied with preparations for the next hearing, the court officer moves the telephone along the counter towards him without a word. 'Excuse me,' says Rosslyn, 'you wouldn't happen to know the number of the United States Embassy, would you?'

'It's 0171-499-9000,' volunteers the blonde. She

has a wide face. Pale blue eyes. 'I'm very sorry about your friend's sister.'

'You knew her?' says Rosslyn.

'No,' she says, 'I'm afraid I didn't.'

'So how come you're here?'

'Routine. I'm with the Home Office.'

Dialling the embassy, Rosslyn watches the blonde from the Home Office walk away. He asks to be put through to the American Citizens Services Branch. To Ms Susan Isiskind. Confirming the appointment, he looks outside, where he sees the blonde from the Home Office heading in the direction of St Pancras Road. Making a call on her cellular telephone, she's almost at the far boundary of the Old Church cemetery. The place is favoured in less cruel weather by London vagrants. Winos, lunatics, prostitutes and drug addicts. He watches her hesitate by the Old Church. Builders' tarpaulins and scaffolding obscure the church's light grey brickwork. The strange morning darkness, as ugly as the openings in the vandalized cemetery tombs, seems to engulf her. Then she disappears from Rosslyn's sight.

He peers over the counter at the business card and reads it upside down:

```
■ ■■ ▩
```

Wendy Lever
Home Office
Intelligence and Resources Operations
Thames House
Millbank
London SW1P 1AE

Thames House – MI5? Why's Intelligence Resources and Operations nosing into Jane Moorfield's tragedy? Ms Wendy Lever, you with the pale blue eyes, who are you?

6

There is a great danger that many people in the UK associate cult violence with American culture and liberal gun laws. People do so at their peril. I hope we don't have to wait for a British Waco before something more is done.

— IAN HOWARTH, DIRECTOR, CULT INFORMATION CENTRE, UK

Rosslyn and Caroline cross the city in a cab for the appointment at the United States Embassy in Grosvenor Square.

For most of the journey she stares ahead in silence. At the Christmas decorations in Marylebone. She looks back once at the most garish of the lights. 'Nothing,' she says, 'nothing in the evidence I heard has convinced me that the verdict is a true one.'

Rosslyn's following her gaze to the flickering sign: MERRY CHRISTMAS AND A HAPPY NEW CENTURY.

True. I don't want to be the one to have to tell you that's how it most certainly seems to be.

'True,' he says. Which sounds as if he's agreeing with her. Or it could mean the verdict's true. That's what he thinks it is. His emotions are mixed. He can't quite reconcile the reality of the verdict with Caroline's passionate doubt. He wants to spare her further pain. To avoid raising her hopes or encouraging her to believe some falsehood. To do so might alleviate her distress. Objectively, she's his client. She's paying him to find the truth of the matter. What, as she's asked him so often, what really *happened* to Jane. Subjectively, he feels sorry for her. The stranger in the strange city where her sister died in such unpleasant circumstances. He shares something of her mistrust of what she calls 'this very British system. You people do all the right things for the wrong reasons.'

What can I say to you?

The drug habit usually starts around the age of thirteen and continues until death, which occurs most often some ten years later. On the other hand, victims who have overdosed in the earlier stages of their addiction are a frequent and depressing feature of millennial London. And the police, the doctors and the forensic pathologists – they're all too familiar with the myriad causes of addiction. When it comes to dealing with a drug-related death, they're sensitively attuned to even the slightest suspicion of foul play. The police are supposed to be well aware of even the slightest irregularity.

I can say to you: 'Let's face it, the police don't care about druggies as human beings any more. They don't want to know.' You'll ask me: 'Never?'

I'll admit there may, of course, be an exception to the general rule. But it'll be rare. Very rare.

He stretches out his long legs until the soles of his plain black shoes press against the jump seat. Folds his dark winter coat across his knees. It hangs loosely on him. Like the loose knot of his dark blue tie, tied without great care, so that it doesn't quite cover the collar button of his shirt. The cab driver seems to be watching Rosslyn's reflection in the rear-view mirror. Cursing the weather, the season and the Millennium in half-shout, half-speak, he tries to share his resentment with his passengers. Perhaps it's the intensity of Rosslyn's eyes that persuades him to cease the ranting. The restless flicker of dark eyes set deep above bruises that suggest sleeplessness. The slightly battered features hinting they've witnessed violence, experienced it perhaps in one or other of the services, even dealt it out. The Royal Marine or Royal Navy man perhaps. The look reflected in the rear-view mirror seems to say 'You do your job and I'll do mine.'

Paying the cab driver at the junction of Upper Brook Street and Grosvenor Square, Rosslyn glances at his client standing in the snow. She presents a forlorn figure. She's gazing at the kids begging spare change from an elderly pedestrian near the statue of General Eisenhower. She seems almost as helpless as the young beggars to whom the government has falsely promised a better future.

He wishes that, without hurting Caroline, he could help her find a way to accept the painful truth about her sister. The verdict on Jane Moorfield: Death By Misadventure. Perhaps the US Embassy's American Citizens Services Branch people will dispel her misgivings. Help her to face the facts.

The offices of the American Citizens Services Branch are on the United States Embassy's ground floor.

Here Ms Isiskind introduces herself with a smile and offers them a seat. She's a neat woman. Slim. Greying hair. Maternal. Her voice is soft. Traces of a Southern drawl. The photographs on her desk suggest she's a happily married family woman. Rosslyn notices a rosary lying in a small cut-glass dish. On the wall above a xerox machine is a photograph of a younger Ms Isiskind shaking hands with the President in the rose garden at the White House. And there's a row of Christmas and New Year cards on the mantelpiece. The New Year cards are emblazoned 'Millennium 2000.' 21st: the People's Century. Most of the cards show the count-down numbers. Printed large. Some are scratch cards so you can coin away the number of days left till 2000. Isiskind's cards say there are 11 DAYS TO GO. On a low table in front of her desk are copies of *Sports Weekly*, *Time*, *Newsweek*. And the European edition of the *International Herald Tribune*.

'My client would appreciate it if there's anything at all you can do to help,' says Rosslyn.

'We'll do what we can,' says Isiskind. 'If you have no objection, a colleague of mine's going to join us. One of our legal attachés here, Donna Queron.' She smiles sympathetically at Caroline, who seems edgy. 'Why don't you tell me what it is you think we can do for you?'

'See,' says Caroline, 'it's just that anyone who

knew Jane simply wouldn't believe she died in the way that's been said. I swear she never did drugs. Believe me. You know, that's why I asked ASG – Mr Rosslyn here – to help me.'

'OK,' says Isiskind. 'Tell me, Caroline, about just what happened at the inquest.'

'I don't want to go over it again,' says Caroline.

So Rosslyn summarizes the coroner's findings for her. When he's finished, Isiskind says to Caroline: 'What you're saying is that you want your sister's death investigating, right?'

'Yes,' says Caroline. 'I can't go on not knowing what really happened to her.'

'I appreciate that,' says Isiskind. 'I know that if something like that happened to a relative of mine, I'd feel the same way exactly.' She brings her hands together in a gesture of prayer. 'I guess Mr Rosslyn here has maybe told you already, Caroline, that the evidence will have been considered with great care by the British authorities, police –' Here she's cut short by the arrival of her colleague the legal attaché, who introduces herself.

'Donna Queron.'

She's a tall, thin woman with short hair. Muscular, handsome like a tennis player. Rosslyn puts her at about thirty-five years old. Her face is strong. Rosslyn and Caroline introduce themselves.

'I'm really sorry to hear about your problem, Caroline,' says Queron.

'I appreciate that,' says Caroline.

'It's good of you people to let us take up your time,' says Rosslyn.

'That's what we're here for,' Queron says. She has a slow smile. Turning to Isiskind, she says: 'We can talk in here, if that's OK.' The tone of her voice suggests she wants to be left alone with the visitors.

Isiskind takes the hint. 'Make yourselves at home,' she says, adding for Caroline's benefit, 'I really hope things work out for you.'

'Thanks,' Caroline says, watching Isiskind leave.

Sitting at the desk, Queron says to Caroline: 'Why don't we start at the beginning? Tell me about Jane.'

Rosslyn feels he might just as well be a piece of US government furniture.

So Caroline talks about her dead sister. 'Theology was her passion. She was what she called "a sociologist of religion". So I guess you could say that's what drove her. That's why she came here to the UK to London and Cambridge to complete her postgraduate thesis.'

'How long had she been over here?' Queron asks.

'Since early last summer.'

'And did she tell you what her work entailed?'

'Yes and no,' says Caroline. 'She'd always been reluctant to talk in great detail about the work. I guess she felt that if anyone were to know too much about it, it would've undermined her reputation as a sociologist.'

'Why was that?' asks Queron.

'Because she kind of didn't want cult victims or

anyone who'd fallen foul of them to feel threatened by her. And she didn't want to antagonize practising cult members.'

'Did she antagonize people?'

'No more than anyone else.'

'Did the work ever trouble her?'

'Not seriously as far as I know. She was always aware that some of the people she was looking at were malevolent. Some were even dangerous and violent. She asked questions about cults that some people don't dare to ask. About their history, practices and doctrines and their financial scams. The really secretive ones interested her. Jane was always obsessed with the idea of secrets and secrecy. I guess it's a family trait. I'm the same, really.'

Queron smiles at Caroline's tone of innocence.

'And she was kind of mistrustful of mainstream churches and official bodies,' adds Caroline.

'She liked to go her own way?' says Queron.

'Yeah.'

'And you?'

'Yeah. Me too.'

'Do you think she may have made some enemies here in the UK?' Queron asks.

'I can't think so,' says Caroline. 'She was so lovable. Warm and so generous. And brave too. Yeah, I'd say courage was the word that sums her up. No, I don't think she ever made an enemy of anyone in her life.' She smiles.

Queron smiles back. 'You reckon she was aware

that the public needs warning about cults?'

'Oh, sure,' says Caroline.

'And what about the cult-watching groups?' asks Queron. 'You know . . . people who think *all* cults are totally evil. That you can't be objective about them.'

Caroline leans forward. She seems to have taken Queron's observations as a criticism. 'That wasn't Jane's belief,' she says. 'By the same token she didn't hold with people who said that any religion should be welcomed.'

'Or in total freedom to pursue lunatic ideas,' says Queron. 'To control people who join voluntarily? That's the real world. People have rights to believe in what they will.'

'She never sat in an ivory tower, if that's what you're saying, Ms Queron.'

'Call me Donna,' says Queron.

'She liked to talk to people,' says Caroline. She adds 'Donna,' rather pointedly. 'Hers was the real world. Don't misunderstand her. Jane's world wasn't that of the People's Temple or the Manson Family. She liked to get out into the field. But she didn't hold with making ethical or moral judgements. And if she did encounter a thoroughly malevolent individual or group, well, she didn't tell me about them. She was aware such people existed. You only have to look at the shared experiences of ex-cult members on the Internet. She once told me I could search them out for myself.'

'Like where?' asks Queron.

Caroline leafs through her journal. 'Here,' she says. 'A good starting place there is http:// www:ex-cult.org/. I'm looking. And I'm saying she had no enemies.'

'Most people have one enemy in life,' says Queron. 'Even I do. And Mr Rosslyn here, I dare say.'

Rosslyn shrugs.

'I don't believe in the verdict of that inquest,' says Caroline. 'No way. *I just can't.*'

'This Trinity Chapter,' asks Queron. 'How much do you know about it?'

'Only what I've seen of its followers here in London,' says Caroline. 'Wherever you go they seem to be there, don't they? Other than that, I only know what Jane wrote me about them when she was in London. As I told you, she didn't go into too much detail. She faxed me at home. Only at the time I was away in Maine. And there was no one at home who could mail her faxes on to me. So I never got them until it was too late. In them she told me some of the stuff about the cult.'

'And did she ever mention, maybe, that she just might have gotten on the wrong side of it?' Queron asks.

'OK,' says Caroline. 'Sure, she hinted at that.'

'Would you mind if I look at her faxes, then?' asks Queron. 'Maybe they'll help me advise you what we can do for you.'

Caroline glances at Rosslyn.

'If you'll respect their confidentiality,' he tells Queron.

'Sure, we don't have a problem with that.'

Caroline hands copies of Jane's faxes across the table. Reading through them thoroughly, Queron's face is expressionless. Trained, Rosslyn recognizes, to give nothing away.

Donna Queron obviously has the gift of reading fast. Whatever reactions she has to the faxes, she's still keeping them to herself. Finally, with her broad tennis-player's hands, she tidies the faxes into a neat pile face up on the desk. 'Other than what's in these faxes,' she says, 'did Jane ever communicate anything else about this Trinity Chapter cult to you?'

'Only what's in her faxes,' says Caroline.

Queron licks a finger and searches among the faxes like a cashier sorting dollar bills. 'She didn't want anyone else to see these, right?'

'That's what she said, yes.'

'Has anyone contacted you about this since you arrived in London?' Queron asks.

'No one.'

'OK,' says Queron, 'I want you to look at some ID photos. So why don't you wait here while I get hold of them?'

With Queron out of the office, Rosslyn says: 'We still have to get that guy Marcus Luke to speak to us about why she went to the clinic.'

'Listen,' says Caroline. 'You have to understand this. Jane wasn't ill, was she? You have to believe it. You couldn't even imagine anyone saner than she was. Centred.'

'I believe you,' says Rosslyn.

'She was truly at ease with herself and the world.'

'But things went very wrong, didn't they?' says Rosslyn.

'You Brits, your idea of justice.'

'I want to be fair.'

'Jee-sus.'

Before Caroline can continue with her protest, Queron returns with a file and the photographs. 'I'd like you to look at these carefully,' she says. She puts them on the desk. The photographs are ten inches by eight. Glossy and in colour. She turns them towards Caroline.'Tell me if you recognize anyone in these.'

Caroline points to the first one. It carries the official date stamp. 'This one here – I guess that's the guy who claimed to be her friend, Marcus Luke. The man who gave evidence at the inquest. The one who identified Jane's body. How come you have a photo of him?'

'Because we have a responsibility to be interested in extremists,' says Queron with a tone of reluctance and a look of self-justification. 'He helped out at one of the treatment centres,' she continues. 'But then so have a lot of well-intentioned people.'

'I find it so hard to believe what he claims,' says Caroline. 'That he was ever a friend of Jane's. Or her nurse, or whatever. Don't you really think she would've mentioned him to me, I mean, if she was having treatment? Don't you think she'd have put me in the picture?'

'She was having treatment, though,' says Queron.

'Oh come on, of course she wasn't. She didn't need any treatment. So I just don't know why this man, this Marcus Luke, was trying to help her. I mean, I'm telling you, she didn't need help, did she?'

'Why do you think Luke could've been trying to help her, Ms Queron?' says Rosslyn.

'Because,' says Queron, 'the followers of Trinity think of themselves as friends of all mankind.'

'Are you saying Marcus Luke is a member of the Trinity Chapter?' says Rosslyn.

'Do you know if he is?' says Queron.

'Well, you've just asked us to identify him.'

'We just want to know we have him right.'

'What's that mean?' says Caroline. 'These people are friends of all mankind?'

'It's a figure of speech,' Queron says. 'They're the chosen ones.'

'Yeah, well, it doesn't mean anything,' says Caroline, the anger rising in her voice.

'You've read her faxes, Ms Queron,' says Rosslyn, trying to lower the temperature. 'She made no specific mention of him, did she?'

'Right. OK,' says Queron, who points to the next photograph. It shows a bearded man in his forties.

Maybe early fifties. Dressed in a white and hooded robe. Like a priest. Around his neck is a sort of necklace with a medallion clearly etched with the sign: | | |.

'You know who he is?' asks Queron.

'I don't,' says Caroline.

Queron looks at Rosslyn. 'Do you?'

'No,' says Rosslyn. 'Who is he?'

'The leader of the Trinity Chapter,' says Queron. 'OK, it's a kind of out-of-date ID. But we'd be interested to know if and when you ever encountered him.'

'Never did,' says Caroline. 'No. Why should I?' She follows Rosslyn's gaze. He's looking round to the door, which is open. A small man with a wrestler's build is standing in the doorway.

'Donna?' he says. 'Excuse me interrupting. We have your Langley conference call –'

Queron says: 'You two don't mind waiting here a few minutes longer?'

Once she's gone, Caroline says to Rosslyn: 'What's she asking us about these photos for?' Rosslyn raises a finger to his mouth. *Say nothing*.

He's turning quickly through the file Queron's left on Isiskind's desk. It's marked SECRET TRINITY CHAPTER HUMINT PHOTOGRAPHIC.

There are more photographs in the file. He reads the labels on the backs:

- **EDWARD AHEARNE** (*see* **VIRGINIA AHEARNE, MI5** Legal Adviser, London)
- **WISLAWA MARIA ODONE** United States Secretary of State
- **ASSOCIATES: FELDEN SCHULMANN, MONNY LEHTA, DEBORAH MORTON ZATZ, ADRIANNA CORNEL PERCY**

There are annotations in the margins next to Percy's name: (*formerly a counsel to the Senate Judiciary Committee, now Odone's chief of staff at the State Department*).

- **EVAN MATTHEWS**
- **IRENA MAUSCH**, Odone's mother

Has Queron deliberately left the file open and unguarded for me to see? Is she trying to tell me something, like remember these names? Look, see what kind of people you're up against.

The final photograph looks like a studio shot. The pretty blonde wears a floral summer dress. The face is familiar. It's Lever's.

Queron's voice in the corridor alerts him, so he closes the file and is returning to his seat when she comes in. Apparently uninterested in the file on the desk, she says: 'Even though this is painful to you, Caroline, I don't want you to close your mind to the real possibility that it could've been drugs. You see what I'm saying?'

'I *hear* what you're saying,' says Caroline. 'But I can't believe it.'

'It happens pretty often, let's face it,' says Queron. 'Is there anything else you two want to ask me?'

'Yes,' says Rosslyn. 'Can you tell me why officers of the FBI and CIA called at my client's home when she was away in Maine?'

'Excuse me?' says Queron.

'Like when I was in Maine,' says Caroline. 'And after Jane's death – some FBI and CIA people called at Moorfield House. They asked questions of our family priest and the local patrolman.'

'Are you sure you're right about that, Caroline?'

'Yes, Ms Queron,' says Caroline. 'I'm very right. The priest wouldn't lie. Neither would the patrolman. I know those people. I've known them all my life. Our family's never had any trouble. Like raised the interest of the CIA and FBI. And there was the woman at the inquest from the British Home Office. From the British security service.'

'Do you think Jane might have done that, Ms Queron?' asks Rosslyn.

'What makes you think she might have?'

'You tell me, Ms Queron. Does the name Wendy Lever mean anything to you?'

'Who is she?'

Caroline seems about to raise her hand. To point at the file on the desk. Before she can speak, Rosslyn says: 'She's an MI5 officer.'

'Is that right?' says Queron. She looks doubtful. 'Lever – no, can't say I've ever heard the name before.'

Rosslyn looks at her. *You're holding out on my client, Ms Queron.*

'If there's anything else I can do before you return home,' Queron says to Caroline, 'feel free to call me, here at the embassy. Any time. Excuse me now, I have a meeting.'

Rosslyn stares at her in silence. *I'd like to speak to you about Wislawa Odone. Only your face is expressionless. Trained to give nothing away.*

Outside the embassy on the pavement Caroline gazes out across Grosvenor Square. At the snow. The tall trees look black and white. The branches stretch to the sky like raw bones. Her lower lip is tucked beneath her teeth. 'They don't want to know, do they?'

'I think you're wrong,' Rosslyn says. 'There's a whole lot they don't want us to know.'

He looks back at the embassy. And in a ground-floor window he recognizes the figure of a woman who's watching them. Queron: speaking on the telephone. 'Don't look now,' he tells Caroline. 'We're being watched. I think we've made an enemy of Ms Queron or the government of the United States.'

'Or the CIA assholes,' says Caroline, who can't resist a glance at the ground floor office window. 'CIA. US government. *Jee-sus.*'

'You said they add up to one and the same thing, didn't you?' says Rosslyn.

'I'm right.'

He flags down a passing cab. Tells the driver to take Caroline to her hotel. 'The Malvern Hotel. Coptic Street.' He holds open the door for her.

'But do you still believe I'm right?' she asks.

'I can't yet say for sure.'

'But do you *believe* in me? Or do you believe in that Queron woman?'

'I don't believe in her,' he says. 'I'm beginning to believe in you.'

She reaches for his hand. 'I need that.'

'Do you want to have dinner with me tonight?' he asks.

'Sure,' she says. 'Call me.'

'I'll pick you up after I've finished at the office.' He wants to get back to ASG now. To check out the names he saw in Queron's file – SECRET TRINITY CHAPTER HUMINT PHOTOGRAPHIC.

Taking a final glance at Queron's window, he sees the blind's been closed.

7

WISLAWA MARIA ODONE United States Secretary of State

Queron is on the telephone to Washington: 'There's no way the inquest will be reopened. It's watertight. There remains the matter of Van Rijn's whereabouts. What will happen at the start of the New Year. If Trinity is thwarted.'

The woman's voice in Washington says: 'I cannot be associated with it.'

'But they've already been responsible for two ritual killings in Trafalgar Square. Who are those sick people?'

'I can't say.'

'You can't or you won't?'

'Both.'

'You realize the situation the British may be facing?'

'Sure.'

'There's the threat of mass murder. There are people in the Chapter who'll stop at nothing. To keep the funds. To ensure the Resurrection scenario. Suppose another element contributes to your exposure?'

'My funds are in my mother's name.'

'What is she going to tell the press?'

'Nothing.'

'Nothing?'

'Right.'

'See, I have to say you're on the rack.'

'I can't agree.'

'Well, I just hope you're right, Secretary of State.'

8

On Rosslyn's return to Strand Chambers, the security guard tells him: 'The chairman wants to see you, Mr Rosslyn. It's urgent.'

'She does? Tell her I'm on my way.'

'You're to go straight to her office.'

'Really?'

'That's what she said to tell you. Straight to —'

'Thanks, I've got the message.'

Of the top-floor offices in Strand Chambers, furnished as a job lot from Harrods, Ruth Swincarron's has the grandest view. Across Trafalgar Square. Nelson's Column. To the National Gallery. St Martin-in-the-Fields.

'Alan, this won't take long,' she says.

The secretary, who has the air of the Princess Royal and is wearing a diamond brooch depicting a horse's head, passes round the coffee. First, at the head of the conference table, to Swincarron. Then to Peter Alexander and Dr Maxine Gertler, the ASG co-founders and principals, sitting either side. Then to Rosslyn. Black. No sugar.

Swincarron's beaky face has the remains of a tan, the trace of her recent pre-Christmas holiday in the Caribbean. The skin has the look of scampi.

'I wasn't entirely sure, Alan,' she says, 'that you'd fit in when you joined us. As you know, I'd made quite a few telephone calls. Sounding out the people you'd worked for. What emerged was that you're a bit of a loner. Nearly everyone agreed that you were a first-class investigation officer. Pretty unflappable. But to put it mildly, your relationships with superiors were difficult.' Rosslyn wonders quite what she's driving at. 'All right perhaps in the public sector,' she says. 'Would you agree with me? Not a good idea in the private sector. Fine, if you have a budget funded by the taxpayer. But not much good when it comes to explaining things to shareholders; what they want is satisfied clients who pay the bills. What finally decided us in your favour was that liking for going out on a limb. Just what we needed at the time. Tell us, are you entirely happy with us here?'

'What makes you think I might not be? You're paying me more than double what I earned at Customs and Excise.'

'That's the point,' says Maxine Gertler. 'What's your present case load?'

'Light,' says Rosslyn. 'A major auction house with a few rotten apples peddling million-dollar art-works whose owners may have obtained them in doubtful circumstances. Merchant banks, some of whose younger people have engaged in unauthor-ized trading.'

'Run of the mill stuff mainly,' says Swincarron. 'Would you think of yourself as something of an underused resource – working, say, at about seventy per cent of your capacity?'

'There's Caroline Moorfield.'

After a moment's silence, Swincarron asks: 'Wouldn't you say, Alan, that the whole affair smacks rather than of a bleeding heart investigation?'

'I believe she may have a case,' says Rosslyn. 'Judging by the general attitude of the women at the US Embassy's American Citizens Services Branch and what they told me.'

'Which is what?' asks Gertler, examining her manicured finger nails. 'What general attitude are we talking about here?'

'Ms Moorfield's convinced her sister may not have died in the way that's been told. That's what she believes.'

Alexander adjusts the knot of his Old Etonian tie. '*Belief*, Alan, is one thing. *Budgetary reality* is quite another. We're not in business to overturn some slipshod coroner's verdict on a drug addict's death. Let's talk fees and income. Actually it's money's that's the bottom line, isn't it?'

'Think she'll continue to be able to afford us, Alan?' asks Gertler. She's looking hard at Rosslyn's clothes. She seems to be pricing his appearance.

'I think she can afford us,' says Rosslyn.

'Haven't you wondered,' asks Alexander, 'if this is worth either the time . . . or the effort that it's likely to cost? The problem is that the face of the investigation doesn't quite fit the ASG house style, does it?'

'For example, we have to ask ourselves whether her sister's death involved criminal use of drugs,' says Gertler.

'That's what was implied,' says Rosslyn. 'On the other hand, Ms Moorfield denies her sister ever did drugs. I'm as sure as can be she's telling me the truth.'

'How can you be so sure, Alan?' asks Swincarron.

'Because I trust her.'

'You *trust* her?' says Alexander with a dry cough. 'God, Alan, that's a little rich from a former Duty Man. This is the real world. Our game isn't about *trust*. Never, please never, *trust* a client.'

'There's an awful lot in what Peter says,' says Swincarron. 'Think about it, Alan. You see, we have to ask ourselves whether Ms Moorfield's sister was involved with the police for any reason?'

'She wasn't,' says Rosslyn.

'But what about the drug abuse?'

'What are you asking me to say to you?' says Rosslyn.

'Rather *suggesting*,' says Swincarron, 'that you must be *absolutely sure* there was no drugs involvement. And why? Because we have the most substantial raft of Arab clients anywhere either side of the Atlantic or in Europe. They have investment interest in us. Far greater than in, say, Kroll or Asmara. So we wouldn't want to offend them, or indeed *any* client with a particular religious belief or racial axe to grind. Christian. Jewish. Muslim. Japanese. Russian. You name it. What we're saying is that this particular case looks like a bleeding heart problem which isn't, frankly, very savoury. And at the end of the day, it's low rent, isn't it? It's not as though the fate of nations hinges upon the outcome.'

'Except that there was a woman from MI5 at the inquest. Intelligence and Resources Operations. So there's a security service interest in the Moorfields. Here and in the States. And when we were at the American embassy we were seen by a CIA officer. A woman called Queron.'

'What did she want?' asks Swincarron.

'She wanted either Ms Moorfield or me to identify some mugshots.'

'She did? Of whom?'

'One was the leader of the cult Jane had been looking at. Another was of the man who claims to have been her friend. Our client maintains her sister would never have got herself mixed up with people like that.'

'How can you be so sure, Alan?'

'Because Ms Moorfield would have been the one person her sister would've confided in if she'd been in any trouble. She had a friend who gave evidence at the inquest. But Ms Moorfield was the one person her sister Jane talked to.'

'Didn't you confront this friend of hers,' Alexander says, 'at the inquest?'

'No, I didn't.'

'Why didn't you?' says Gertler.

'Because it wasn't somehow the appropriate moment. Ms Moorfield was distraught.'

'Fair enough,' says Swincarron. 'Still, at least as far as you know, the sister wasn't short of money?'

'No. She had enough money.'

'What we mean, Alan,' says Alexander, '– and this may be painful to your client – is that Jane Moorfield could've had enough money to support a serious drug habit.'

'I don't believe she ever had a drug habit in the first place.'

'Which really adds up to no more than hearsay, Alan, doesn't it?' says Alexander.

'If you want to think of it like that,' says Rosslyn. 'But I'm sure Ms Moorfield's got things right.'

'So, say again,' says Swincarron, 'what is it exactly that your client is asking us to do for her?'

'She wants to know conclusively whether Jane had been doing drugs. She believes the answer to be no. That the drug overdose was inflicted on her. If she's proven right, then she wants to know who murdered Jane. She wants the proof. She says she wants the killer or killers arrested. Indicted. And prosecuted. I think that's fair enough.'

'I suppose she realizes our services will be expensive?' says Swincarron.

'I've already explained that to her,' says Rosslyn. 'She has no problem with money. You can do a credit check.'

'OK. You've been fair with us,' says Swincarron. 'We'll be fair with you. You want to stay on board this Moorfield case?'

'Yes, I do.'

Swincarron gives a sigh of resignation. 'All right. I suggest you keep on it, shall we say, for a period of limited duration? No more than one month at the most. And ensure that she meets full expenses at the full rate.' She leans back in her chair. 'We mustn't give anyone the impression that ASG services come cheap.'

'On the contrary,' drawls Alexander, who's looking out of the window across Trafalgar Square.

He catches Swincarron's eye. Rosslyn can tell that they seem to have worked the meeting around to delivering the stern warning. Sure enough, it comes from Swincarron. 'And, Alan, just you make very sure,' she says, 'that you don't get on the wrong side of the people at the US Embassy. Or MI5. Or any branch of the security services. Start as you mean to go on. No crossed wires. Bear that in the forefront of your mind.'

Back in his office, mulling over the images he has in mind of those SECRET TRINITY CHAPTER HUMINT PHOTOGRAPHIC pictures, it seems patently clear to Rosslyn that some naked wires have already been crossed. Take:

- **EDWARD AHEARNE** (*see* **VIRGINIA AHEARNE**, MI5 Legal Adviser, London)

Presumably they're involved with the Trinity Chapter in a way that isn't on the level. Otherwise, why are the names on file in the first place? Likewise:

- **WISLAWA MARIA ODONE** United States Secretary of State

Odone really is the big name. The world player. Extensively profiled by the media. But I don't remember reading anywhere that Odone subscribes publicly to any particular religious faith.

Additionally, there are these 'associates' of hers. And remember the annotations in the margins next to the name of that former 'counsel to the Senate Judiciary Committee, now Odone's chief of staff at the State Department'. Even **IRENE MAUSCH**, *Odone's mother.*

Now bear in mind Swincarron's warning. No crossed wires. Seems like already there's some nasty electricity in the air. But equally, Swincarron could have stamped her big foot and told me to drop the Moorfield case. And she didn't. The money, all that crap about the size of the fees, about ASG not coming cheap, it's cock. ASG is flush with cash. Just about the richest firm of private intelligence consultants in the world.

And now, Caroline Moorfield, I'd say the fact is that you're getting out of your depth. In it up to here. And now me too.

9

Caroline needs to talk to someone and telephones Rosslyn from a call box near Goodge Street underground station. She'd just like to hear a friendly voice. The glass walls of the box are covered with cards advertising the services of call girls. Friendly invitations from NEW BLACK BEAUTIES. ORIENTAL NURSES. Invitations to visit dungeons. To join in MILLENNIUM CORRECTION with a NEW AUSTRALIAN BABE. Invitations to Brits in need of disciplinary services.

The woman at Alexander Swincarron Gertler tells her: 'Mr Rosslyn has stepped out of the office. But he's left a message for you to meet him for dinner. Eight o'clock at Chez Moi. 1 Addison Avenue, W11.'

With Moorfield impetuosity she dials the number of the Provident Care and Nursing Agency in Warren Street.

The woman who answers tells her that Marcus

Luke is 'off duty for a few days. I'm afraid we don't have a note of when he'll be back.'

'Can you give me his home phone number?'

'Bear with me one moment . . .' When she comes back on the line she says: 'If you'd call back later.'

So she dials Directory Enquiries. The Irish voice tells her that Marcus Luke's number is ex-directory.

She explores another avenue. Dr Julia Llewellyn.

The man at King's College Cambridge porter's lodge is pleasant. He tells her that Dr Llewellyn is 'presently away'. He offers to have a message delivered to her rooms to await her return. Caroline asks that he tell Dr Llewellyn to call her.

Her final call this afternoon is to the Home Office at 50 Queen's Gate. She asks to be put through to MI5. The telephone operator asks for her name and telephone number. Caroline gives her the details.

'To whom do you wish to talk?'

'To whom – a Ms Wendy Lever.'

'What is the nature of your call, Ms Moorfield?'

'Personal.'

'And which department do you wish to speak to?'

'Intelligence Resources and Operations. Ms Lever.'

'I'm sorry,' the voice tells her, 'there's no such department in the Home Office. And I'm afraid we have no listing of the name you mention. I'm sorry we can't help you further. Perhaps you are mistaken.'

She cannot understand why everyone's so unhelpful.

10

Chez Moi. Dinner for two on the banquette in the alcove at the back of the restaurant. The table favoured by lovers, where you can sit side by side. Number twelve.

Rosslyn tells Caroline he's made preliminary checks on the names he saw in Queron's file. Odone, the US Secretary of State. Her Washington associates. 'If Jane was right about the basic nature of the Trinity Chapter, and if Odone's tangled up in it, then I'm astonished it isn't public knowledge. It's as though the Vice President had links with Scientology he doesn't want anyone to know too much about. The same sort of thing applies to Virginia Ahearne. She's MI5's legal adviser. And Lever works for the department with an interest in extremist religious cults and political factions.'

But Caroline seems somewhere quite different.

She dwells again on the day she heard of her sister's death. It seems to Rosslyn that she's touched by some need to keep her scars of grief open. It doesn't seem to be the time or place to explore in greater depth the connections he's made in his mind between the names he read in Queron's file. Caroline's mood has changed. She seems lost in a nostalgia for home. He lets her do most of the talking. About 'the Cape landscape in the colours of some old embroidery. As Dad used to say: "like a Currier and Ives Christmas card come to life from long ago".' She seems to find solace in this talk of home. She takes some photographs from her shoulder bag and shows them to him. 'These are my designs. The colours of Cape Cod. Woods. Wild flowers. Empty beaches. The ocean. That's where I belong. Yeah. Here's another shot I love.'

The photograph is of a wooden barn. The perspective is distorted. As if it's been flattened by the snowy ridge and the iron sky.

'The barn's the colour of rust,' says Caroline. 'It's like the barn at the back of home. Moorfield House. It's the twin of what I call The Wrist – that's the barn mother had converted for me to use as a pottery studio.'

'Why's it called The Wrist?' Rosslyn asks her.

'From Thoreau's description of Cape Cod: "The bared and bended arm of Massachusetts: the shoulder is at Buzzard's Bay; the elbow, or crazy bone, at Cape Mallebarre; the wrist at Truro; and the sandy fist at Provincetown."' She avoids his eyes. 'I need to get some sleep,' she says.

'I can drop you off at your hotel.'

'No. Really. I can find it on my own.'

'No,' he says. 'Clients have to be protected at all times.'

'You don't say, Mr Rosslyn.'

'Company rules, Miss Moorfield.'

'"Miss Moorfield"?' she says with a smile and takes his hand. 'For Christ's sake, call me Caro, won't you?'

In her bloodshot eyes he sees the pain behind the smile.

Heading for Bloomsbury in the cab, she returns to the subject of Jane: 'You do think the coroner got it wrong, don't you?'

'You mean the police. The doctor. The forensic pathologist *and* the coroner?'

'Yes.'

'Well, we have to face it,' says Rosslyn, 'the police for a start don't care about druggies as human beings any more.'

'There may be an exception out there somewhere,' says Caroline.

'Yes,' says Rosslyn. 'If, let's say, the police officer who was called to the scene found signs of violence. In this case, as the record shows, the police officer concerned didn't. The forensic pathologist would have noticed any signs of violence had they been reported. That's her job. So would the doctor. There's the evidence of experienced witnesses. And not one of them found a sign of violence on Jane's body.' He quotes Dr Lancaster's letter from memory. 'He said he saw "minor contusions to both her wrists". And he recorded them. "No other abnormalities were detected."'

'What about "the awkward sites for injections"? What was it he saw?' She too has committed the remarks to memory: '. . . not the venepuncture sites one normally sees in comatose intravenous drug abusers brought to casualty".'

'That's not unusual,' says Rosslyn. 'Sometimes you see signs of needle penetration in skin over veins in the arms and the thighs and sometimes even in the ankles.'

'You don't think we'll get the inquest reopened, do you, Alan?'

'Truthfully, no I don't. But I don't happen to think that's the whole story.'

Snow covers the steps to his basement flat in Pimlico. Pausing a moment on the pavement at the southern end of Claverton Street, he looks back along the street to see if he's been followed home. The habit of the former undercover Duty Man.

Once inside he neutralizes the burglar alarm. His absentee landlord finally agreed, under protest, to renovate the dingy basement, and the damp has been prevented from rising any higher. He hasn't bothered to paint the raw plaster walls. North African rugs cover the floors and most of the marks left by the builders. There's a constant draught from the cat flap in the front door. A piece of botched DIY, the surrounds of the painted wood and metal flap bear the marks of the several cats kept here by the previous tenant.

Without roots, Rosslyn has lived out of a suitcase for perhaps too long. He remains, as Mary called him, the Basement Man. One of the *one in three* who lives alone in London.

He's making coffee when the telephone rings. The answering control is on. He hears Caroline's voice. It says: 'Alan, if you're there, pick up please.'

'I'm here.'

'Listen,' says Caroline. 'You know that message I put on the Internet – I've had a reply. From some priest in Geneva. He calls himself Father Gian Maria Morandi. He says he's from some organization called the International Family Foundation. What's more, he also says that he knew Jane – he knows all about her work on her thesis.'

'Well, if what he says is true, then obviously it's a clincher, isn't it? Let's face it, there can't have been more than one American student called Jane Moorfield researching into her particular field.'

'I know. I was worried for a moment that I might have wound him up a bit because I even insisted on him describing Jane to me. What's more, there were other things that only a few people could've known. I asked him to give me the name of her tutor in Cambridge. And he came right out with it. Dr Llewellyn. Dr Julia Llewellyn.'

'What else did he tell you?'

'He wasn't about to give me the whole story over the phone, was he?'

Rosslyn waits for her to continue. There's a new

excitement in her voice. 'It's all we've got to go on,' she says. 'Because, as far as I'm concerned, that inquest was total bull.'

'It wasn't. You were there. So was I. You have to ask yourself what possible motive anyone could have for fixing this inquest. You have to be prepared for the possibility that you're wrong and they're right.'

It's as if he's winded her. Somehow punched her in the stomach. There's a sharp intake of breath. 'Alan, just whose side are you on?' The tone has become plaintive almost. She's five years old again. Back in the nursery. Life's a cheat.

'I'm just trying to point out the pitfalls of an investigation like this. It isn't a question of what you believe. It boils down to a question of evidence. You don't think that Jane would ever have taken drugs. But you can't be sure of that. What the inquest found was sufficient for them to return the verdict they did.'

He waits. His experience with clients tells him that the only people who think that they've received justice are the winners. Those who claim a victory for common sense. But if common sense were so clever, the cases wouldn't get to court in the first place.

'I don't understand you, Alan. There has to be something in this Morandi guy.'

'Maybe there is. Maybe there isn't.'

'He wouldn't go to the trouble of answering a

personal ad from Geneva if he didn't think it mattered.'

'Did he mention anything about money, did he ask for any?'

Caroline is becoming angrier. 'No, he didn't ask for money, Alan. And I didn't offer him any. Can't you accept there may even be the possibility that he just wants to help *me*?'

'All right,' he says. He realizes this is one battle he has no chance of winning. 'I don't suppose it'll do any harm if I go to see him.'

'I gave him your number. I told him you're acting for me and he said he would definitely call you tonight.'

After midnight the call comes through.

The voice says, 'Mr Rosslyn? My name's Gian Maria Morandi. I think I can be of help to you. Perhaps we could discuss matters. Face to face, as soon as possible. Here in Geneva.'

'I'm not in a position, Father Morandi, to disclose any particulars about my client without her say-so.'

'You should make it very clear to Caroline Moorfield that she's in danger.'

'In what way?'

'I prefer not to talk further on the phone. All I can tell you at this moment is my opinion. That Caroline Moorfield is right in thinking her sister didn't kill herself.'

'Much as I respect your opinion, Father Morandi,

it still isn't enough to justify my coming to see you in Geneva at such short notice.'

'Mr Rosslyn, I know that in your profession you probably deal with a lot of difficult people – *unstable*. But I need to see you. Surely what matters is the safety of your client. If you have any worry about my credentials I suggest you telephone the London School of Economics. INFORM: the Information Network Focus on Religious Movements. My name is on their registry. Can you see me tomorrow? Shall we say noon tomorrow? Here?'

'Give me the address in Geneva.'

11

Snow and fog delay the British Airways Wednesday morning flight to Geneva. From the Terminal One departure lounge at Heathrow Rosslyn calls INFORM in Houghton Street.

'I need to make an enquiry about a friend,' he says.

'We'll be happy to help,' the assistant tells him. 'In what connection?'

'Does the name Jane Moorfield ring a bell?'

'Yes,' the assistant says. 'An American. I remember her. She worked here briefly some time ago.'

'She was researching the funding of new religious movements.'

'I remember. With special reference to the Trinity Chapter. But she hasn't been back for some time.'

'I'm sorry to have to tell you that she's dead. I'm helping her family with various personal matters.'

'I'm sorry.'

'And I have to see someone who was of help to her. To do with her work. In Geneva. Father Morandi.'

'Morandi,' the assistant at INFORM says. 'The International Family Foundation.'

'I'd really appreciate it if you could tell me something about it briefly.'

The assistant at INFORM sounds guarded. 'All I can tell you is public knowledge. Morandi's set-up is virtually his own creation. He runs it pretty well single-handed.'

'How long's it been in existence?'

'I'd say for about four or five years.'

'And how good's his information?'

'As far as the practices and beliefs of new religious movements go, it's very good. As reliable, I'd say, as anyone's in the Western Hemisphere. He has contacts with what amounts to an international network of NRM ex-members, friends and relatives.'

'Do you know who funds him, or is it confidential?'

'No, it's public knowledge too. Initially his funding was provided by the Catholic Church, a Swiss government agency and US funding sources. The Swiss have continued to provide core funding. But he also receives grants from various charitable foundations, including the Tel Aviv Trust. He'll accept donations from virtually anywhere and he certainly receives them from the grateful families whose relatives he's helped.'

'Do you know if he's accepted money from any cults?'

'No, he hasn't. Definitely not. In fact, he operates a policy of refusing money from any organization that might compromise the results of his research. The Swiss police are on record as having worked closely with him at the time of the Jouret tragedy.'

'Is there anything else you can tell me?'

'That's about it.'

'Thanks for your help,' Rosslyn says.

He hears an announcement about the Geneva flight. At last, the passengers are being asked to board the plane.

12

From Geneva Airport to the Rue St Pierre address, beyond Place du Bourg-de-Four in Geneva's old town, it's a twenty-minute taxi ride in the heavily falling snow. By now Rosslyn's late for his appointment with Father Morandi.

Outside the small apartment house there's nothing to indicate that this is the office of the International Family Foundation. There's no name plate on the entrance.

Morandi opens the door himself. He is a tall, balding Swiss in his early forties. Stooped, with an aquiline nose. The black serge suit hangs loosely. The thick lenses of his glasses accentuate the eyes bruised through lack of sleep. He glances quickly up and down the street and asks Rosslyn for proof of identity: 'Your passport will do.'

Satisfied that his visitor is who he claims to be, Morandi ushers Rosslyn into the quiet ground-floor apartment at the back of the house. At the end of the narrow corridor Rosslyn notices the heavy door to Morandi's inner sanctum: reinforced and bomb-proofed with unpainted steel. Father Morandi unlocks and opens it carefully. The office is protected by bomb-proof shutters which block out the light.

Passive infra-red lights flicker in two corners of the room. The small green light beneath the CCTV camera suggests that Morandi is recording the interview.

'Do you think anyone followed you here?' he asks.

'I don't think so,' says Rosslyn, removing his coat.

'I hope you don't mind me asking,' says Morandi cautiously, 'but apart from your client, who else knows that you've come to see me here?'

'Just some colleagues,' says Rosslyn.

'At your agency, Alexander Swincarron Gertler?' says Morandi. 'It has a considerable reputation.'

'So do you, Father Morandi.'

'Ah, yes,' says Morandi. 'You spoke to INFORM. They're very good people. The only ones doing research into new religious movements that really counts. A pity your government hasn't embraced the need to really do something before. I suppose you people know how to take precautions against unwelcome surveillance?'

'As far as possible, yes. But then even the watchers can be watched.'

'Apart from them, would anyone else happen to know you're here?' asks Morandi, showing Rosslyn to an upright chair.

'I doubt it.'

'Regrettably,' Morandi says, 'in my work I have to be very careful.' He gestures towards the CCTV cameras. 'I hope you don't find them too irritating.'

His face loosening, Morandi settles slowly in the chair behind the wide desk. Beneath a powerful desk light is a copy of Alexander Stille's *Excellent Cadavers* and Andrew Hubback's pamphlet *The Prophets of Doom: The Security Threat of Religious Cults*. The desk is piled high with files. Index card boxes. Telephone directories. Near to them is a laptop computer. Bookshelves line the walls. An open cabinet is filled with newspaper and magazine cuttings. Prominent files are labelled:

- AUM
- HEAVEN'S GATE
- WACO
- SOLAR CHURCH
- SCIENTOLOGY
- DRESDEN'S CALL OF BLOOD
- NATIONAL ALLIANCE/NATIONAL
- VANGUARD
- POSSE COMITATUS
- CHURCH OF THE CREATOR
- OPUS DEI
- KKK

On the mantelpiece, beneath a miniature reproduction of the fifteenth-century terracotta Virgin of the Annunciation in Florence's Museo Bardini, are two framed photographs. One of Giovanni Falcone. The other of Paolo Borsellino.

Rosslyn notes the tell-tale nicotine stains on the first and second fingers of the right hand. These and the precautions taken against bomb attack tell him he's dealing with a frightened man.

Morandi opens a pack of cigarettes. Filipino. Blanco Excelsiors. 'I think before we start, Mr Rosslyn, I'm going to have to introduce a note of criticism. I think I'd have advised your client to have used a method with a rather lower profile in seeking to obtain information about her sister. I'd have advised her against revealing her search for information quite so openly on the Internet. Has she announced it anywhere else?'

'She's placed a personal ad in the *Herald Tribune*.'

His stare falls on Rosslyn darkly. 'You should perhaps have cautioned her against doing that.'

'Father, she's a free agent,' says Rosslyn. 'If she hadn't done that, I wouldn't be here to see you.'

Morandi makes no reply, just inclines his head and opens a file on the desk. He takes out a photograph and hands it across the desk. Rosslyn looks at the photograph, which shows Morandi standing with a good-looking girl in her late twenties. 'Jane Moorfield,' Morandi says.

Rosslyn looks at Jane's face. Good complexion. Big smile. Fine teeth. The resemblance to Caroline is striking. 'I know that Jane was researching into the Trinity Chapter,' he says. 'But how far did she need to go?'

'If you're asking me whether she was a follower or a member, then the answer's a categorical no. As far as I could see, the more she learned about the movement the less she liked it. I know for a fact that she found it increasingly difficult to retain any academic objectivity. We had several conversations about it. I think, Mr Rosslyn, that when I started out I thought I was dealing with just another group of unpleasant sectarians. Misguided, if you like, but nothing more serious than that. It wasn't long before I understood that I was looking at something far more disturbing.' His voice falters. 'The more I looked into it, the more I realized its complexity. It seemed to combine an incredible sophistication on the part of its leader with an almost unbelievable degree of naiveté on the part of his followers.' He flicks cigarette ash from his coat sleeve.

'Surely,' says Rosslyn, 'that's quite a common feature of these organizations?'

'Yes. What makes the Trinity Chapter different, however, is that any followers or members who try to leave have a habit of disappearing without trace.' He stubs out his Blanco Excelsior and leans back in the chair. He muses almost to himself: 'Also, they disappear all too frequently after they've made over large sums of money to the Chapter.'

Rosslyn waits. Morandi is talking generalities. He's being too guarded. After all, people with more money than sense often do drift from place to place. What's more, they don't always leave a forwarding address. Firms like ASG spend a lot of their time tracking down precisely this sort of person. Usually it's at the request of some pretty worried families and relatives. Rosslyn doesn't know too much about these religious movements. But as far as he's concerned they encourage the aimless sort of person. People who seem to have an overwhelming need to attach themselves to someone or something. He watches Morandi's tired and flickering eyes.

'Look, Mr Rosslyn, we both know that there's more to this than I've told you so far.' The bony fingers are trembling. 'You're aware of this precisely because your client, Caroline Moorfield, has told you so. I think what I'd like from you is some indication of just how much you know. I don't expect you to breach any client confidentiality. But I think it would save time if you gave me some indication of how far your enquiries have got you.'

'Not very far. My client has some faxes her sister sent her. And one of them does contain references to offshore banking deposits made by Trinity. Very large sums in fact. And they touch on the likelihood that Trinity Chapter members include what she described as "extremist Anglo-American and European political figures".'

Morandi shakes his head. 'And I suppose your client is interested in them too. Is that what you're saying?'

'Did Jane offer any names?'

'No names as such,' says Morandi. Rosslyn catches the fear and tension in the voice. The breath catching in the chest. The exaggerated clearing of the throat seems to pain him.

'Did she mention the US Secretary of State?' asks Rosslyn. 'In connection with the Trinity Chapter?'

'No, she didn't,' says Morandi.

'You're quite sure?'

'Yes, I'm sure.'

'So tell me about Jane. Give me your impression of her. What, for example, was her state of mind?'

'I didn't see her all that often,' says Morandi, lighting another foul-smelling Filipino cigarette. 'But I find it very hard indeed to believe she ever took drugs of any sort. She even objected to my smoking. She never drank either, or at least never in my presence. We had rather lost touch. I wasn't aware of the tragedy or the inquest until I spoke to her sister and telephoned her.'

'Would you have recognized any signs of drug abuse, Father?'

Morandi pulls a strand of black tobacco from between his lower teeth. 'Perhaps,' he says. 'I have to tell you that I saw no obvious evidence of it as far as Jane was concerned. So I might probably side with your client as far as the verdict is concerned. Do you think the coroner got it wrong? I imagine it wouldn't be the first time, or would it?'

'Probably not,' says Rosslyn. 'But in this instance there was some pretty overwhelming support for the coroner's view. I have to say that I can't see there's any fresh evidence that would overturn the verdict. Unless you can give me something to take home, Father Morandi, we might as well not waste each other's time.'

He allows some time for Morandi to agree. Perhaps he considers the silence to be a threat. Morandi lowers his head, then slowly pushes his glasses up to the bridge of his long nose. 'If I told you that on at least two occasions I've received visits from both the CIA and MI5 trying to get information about the Trinity Chapter, would that make you feel you're making better use of your time?'

Rosslyn looks at him askance. 'Yes, it would. But what I need right now is names.'

Morandi alters the angle of his desk lamp so that it casts a ghostly shadow across his features. 'How about a legal attaché at the American embassy in London? Donna Queron. Do you know her?'

'Yes, I met her with Caroline at the embassy. When did you come across her?'

'I got a call from Queron shortly after I last heard from Jane. She announced herself as a legal attaché and so on.' He rubs the side of his neck. 'I suppose you and I both know that the rank of legal attaché can be pretty much an umbrella term in US diplomatic circles, yes?'

'Yes, I know. But what was it she wanted from you – or didn't she get round to it?'

'She got round to it all right. It didn't take her long to say what she wanted from me. How much had I told Jane about the Trinity Chapter? And what did I think Jane had learned on her own account? She asked me, for example, "Have you named names. If so, which?" And could I give her any information about the Chapter that I might currently be receiving from former members, their families or friends? And could I generally update her?'

'And did you?'

'To a certain degree, yes. But most of the stuff was what I'd received from Jane.'

'What was that to do with?'

Morandi looks uneasy. 'She seemed most interested in the circumstances surrounding the deaths of three American women in London.'

'Who were they?'

'Members of the Chapter.'

'How did they die?'

'Drug overdoses. It seems a check had been made on what happened to them. None of them died in suspicious circumstances.'

'But Jane thought differently.'

'Yes.'

'What did she think?'

Morandi says simply: 'She suspected perhaps that each had been a possible murder and not a suicide. That was her view. A hypothesis. Each was or had until recently been a member of the Chapter. Jane alleged that the Chapter had been either directly or indirectly responsible for the women's deaths. Maybe they had been driven to commit suicide. How was I to tell?'

'She had no concrete way of proving her allegations?'

'None. So there the matter rested. But she maintained that each had made substantial donations to the Chapter. I suggested to her that the allegations were very serious. And she should report them to the British police.'

'And did she?'

'No, she said she couldn't.'

'Why was that?'

'She didn't believe that her evidence was substantial enough.'

'And you agreed?'

'Yes, I did. One had no real alternative.' Morandi seems to be thinking this out carefully. 'What she reckoned was that eventually someone else would show up and verify her allegations. If they did, then no doubt the deaths would be properly investigated by the British police. She had made a start, she told me, by approaching relatives of the dead women. But it seemed that the parents and families had in every case been advised by lawyers not to speak to her. I personally couldn't see what the families had to lose by talking to Jane, as long as presumably their lawyers were present. My instinctive feeling was that somebody else had got to them before Jane. So that's why they wouldn't talk to her.'

'Did you mention this to Queron?'

'Yes,' breathes Morandi, 'I did.'

'And what did she say to that?'

'She said she thought I was being a little paranoid. Families are entitled to discuss what they wish with whom they want. She said it was ultimately a private matter. For the families concerned.'

'You know that family friends of Jane's were visited by the CIA and FBI where she lived in Vernon Hills, Massachusetts?'

'I didn't know,' says Morandi, puzzled. 'But given Queron's interest, I'm not surprised, are you?'

'No. And there was something she *didn't* tell Caroline. That Jane had been in touch with you. And I'd guess Queron thinks Jane never would. That you wouldn't come out of the woodwork. She hadn't reckoned on Caroline placing that message on the Internet. Let alone you seeing it and contacting me.'

Morandi frowns.

'Have you heard again from Queron?' asks Rosslyn.

Morandi takes a deep breath. 'Yes.'

'What happened?'

Morandi draws deeply on his cigarette and coughs. 'Before I heard from her again I received another visit about Jane. From a woman claiming to be a British security service officer with an interest in the Trinity Chapter. A Ms Wendy Lever.'

A Filipino boy who Rosslyn takes to be Morandi's secretary brings in coffee in a thermos. The boy gives Rosslyn a look of suspicious courtesy. The look reserved for some police officer or other who's interrupting a well-established routine with bad news.

Rosslyn continues: 'What was it Lever wanted from you?'

'Very much the same sort of information Queron had asked for.'

'Did you give it to her?'

Morandi is silent for a moment, lost in recollection. 'No, I didn't. I had to explain,' he says at last with a flicker of satisfaction, as if he's taking pride in having done the right thing, 'that I'd already entered into a confidential agreement with another party to supply information.'

'You mean with Queron?'

'Yes. And that I couldn't help her. Lever was just another in a long line of people who seem to want something from me. She talked non-stop. Perhaps you'd care to listen to some of what she had to say?' He indicates a miniature VCR on the side table. Then he speaks in Spanish into what Rosslyn takes to be a hidden microphone. He's asking his secretary to bring him the video recording of his interview with Lever.

Morandi switches on the machine and takes some time to find the relevant passage. Fast-forwards. Rewinds his way through Lever, who's speaking fast. Finally, he finds the section he wants and presses PLAY.

The camera has captured Lever from above –

13

WENDY LEVER: Do you realize, Father Morandi, just how diligent the Trinity Chapter are? They preserve their conviction that the Master's Second Coming will demonstrate to the world that His is the One True Way. It's so much crap, isn't it? They're deeply corrupt. They're trapped. Dangerous. No matter what risks need to be taken. No matter what loss of life ensues – They're seriously evil people and I think you know that. For some reason you're scared. You're protecting someone. And I think I know who that is. YOU. I can tell you that they've got a well-established security apparatus. They're in a constant state of readiness. Whatever they do, it's always with extreme caution. They always manage to cover their tracks.
MORANDI: You have looked into the circumstances of the deaths of those young American women?
WENDY LEVER: We have. The coroner's verdict stands.

– TRANSCRIPT, FR. GIAN MARIA MORANDI/MS WENDY LEVER INTERVIEW, geneva, 1999

Morandi presses STOP.

'Which is untrue,' he says, 'if by *protecting* one takes it Lever meant hiding something. You've looked around here. You can see that there is *protection*. I wondered whether she herself wasn't under some order or other to protect someone. But she didn't enlarge. Instead she went further. She made a very strange request. She went so far as to ask me whether I had noted the parallels with

Christian doctrine. I thought, tell me something I don't already know.'

'And did she?' says Rosslyn.

'Not really. She went on about the fanaticism of the Chapter followers. She didn't need to tell me that their fanaticism matches Trinity's blasphemous claims. That if needs be they will, according to Lever, commit murder – and continue to commit murder until Trinity's so-called Resurrection is achieved. If and when it ever is. Murder, I argued, won't guarantee anything, Mr Rosslyn.'

He watches Morandi toying with the pile of cigarette butts in the ash tray. 'Unless they're covering something up.'

'Did Lever enlarge on this?'

'No,' says Morandi.

'Did you?'

'No.'

'Are you quite sure you didn't?'

'Yes, I said. I have a certain degree of autonomy in my work. I'm not answerable to security service rules and regulations. Finally, I rather firmly showed her the door. And, almost as a parting shot, she said, "*Your life's at risk.*" I could've told her that too. One has to learn to live with threats from lunatics. I expect you wonder whether my view of the world isn't a little too highly coloured. I noticed you looking at the bomb-proofing in here. The emergency escape route. Etcetera. And I suppose you were wondering whether these precautions are really necessary.'

'I was,' says Rosslyn. 'But something you've just told me has made me change my mind. When you came to the bit about Lever. I need to be sure about this. "*Your life's at risk.*" Were those her exact words?'

'Yes, it's something I almost prefer not to think about.'

'*Think* about it, Father Morandi. We both know that when a member of the security services tells you that, you'd better believe it. And when those people take the trouble to make an overseas trip to tell that to a foreign national on foreign territory, a foreign national who's a priest into the bargain, then you can be very sure the warning has more than local implications.'

For the first time this afternoon Morandi's face relaxes. Fear lets up a moment. The guard drops.

Rosslyn uses his smile like a knife. 'You haven't lied to me, Father. By the same token you haven't told me everything.' He watches Morandi reach for another pack of Blanco Excelsiors. 'You have another name or names for me, don't you, Father Morandi? Why not give them to me? Here and now.'

He pauses before opening the pack. 'I have nothing else to tell you, Mr Rosslyn.'

'I don't believe you.'

'I'm afraid,' says Morandi, 'you have no alternative.'

'If you're still worried, I can guarantee you twenty-four-hour protection. We have associates in

Bern who can be here by tonight. Why not let me call them now?'

'It won't be necessary.'

Rosslyn watches him slip the unopened cigarette pack into his pocket. 'I want to know the other names, Father.'

'If you'd allow me time to think it over,' Morandi says. 'As I think I've told you already, in my work I have to be careful.'

He reaches for one of the files on the shelf. One marked PRESS. And takes out a single cutting from the *Guardian*. Handing Rosslyn the cutting, he says: 'You see what I mean –'

Rosslyn reads:

HOME NEWS |7

News in brief

Two dead in Trafalgar Square attack

TWO men believed to be in their twenties were found dead in Trafalgar Square yesterday. The bodies were discovered by police outside the National Gallery at 1.30 am. Police are seeking witnesses to the attack. It is believed members of a religious group may have witnessed the attack which police believe to be a drugs related revenge killing. – *Jacqui Hayden*

'Trafalgar Square suggests,' says Morandi, 'that the witnesses to the attack may have been Trinity followers. The sacred place. On the other hand, of course, there's the issue of drugs.'

'There's no proof of that.'

'But then there wouldn't be,' says Morandi.

'And I have to tell you that killings of that kind in London are pretty commonplace.' Rosslyn hands back the cutting. 'But if you're anxious about your safety, don't forget my offer. Protection. If I were you, I wouldn't leave it too long before you make up your mind.'

He's puzzled. *You're a man in obvious danger. A man who's brought me all the way to Geneva. You tell me my client is in danger too. You show me the cutting about the killings in Trafalgar Square. And you don't take up my offer. I would if I were you.*

'My secretary can call a taxi for you,' says Morandi.

'Thanks,' says Rosslyn. 'What you say about the danger to my client rings true. What I wouldn't want you to do, however, is underestimate the very real danger to yourself.' He shakes Morandi's hand. 'Please don't ignore the offer. If you need to, you can contact me at any time of day or night and we can set up protection for you.'

The Filipino boy is standing in the doorway to the outer small office. 'Your taxi's waiting,' he says. 'But the weather's very bad. There are no more flights out of Geneva tonight.'

Rosslyn declines their offer to help him find a hotel room for the night.

'Thank you for your help,' he says.

'You're welcome,' says Morandi.

Rosslyn crosses the street through the snow. Getting in the waiting taxi, he glances back across the Rue St Pierre. He tells the driver to take him to a hotel near the airport. Who knows, the weather may improve. Morandi's door is already closed against the winter darkness.

14

He dines alone that night in the restaurant of the Hotel Aiglon on Rue Sismondi, writing the record of the interview with Morandi. He's been unable to speak to Caroline, who isn't at the Malvern Hotel. His efforts to contact Lever have met with the same success as Caroline's: the Home Office goes so far as to deny Lever's existence.

He decides to take an early night.

The foyer of the Hotel Aiglon is crowded with stranded passengers. As he heads for the lifts, he looks round. Standing at a telephone desk is a slim woman, crouched sideways as if on a very private call. The poorly-fitted wig catches Rosslyn's attention. She looks worried. The lift doors open. Some men and women chattering in French squeeze in next to him. As the doors close he again catches sight of the woman on the telephone. For a second her gaze holds his. Pinned to her coat is the Trinity Chapter ribbon of white silk folded into three strips: | | |.

The French gasp as the lift pulls up. Laughs of enjoyment, as though they're on a funfair ride. Rosslyn's stomach tightens. *Who was the woman talking to?* The white ribbon seems like a warning.

Almost like the badge of someone infected with the plague whose bacteria he's inhaling.

15

Soldiers held in the Military Corrective Training Centre are not criminals in the sense we understand criminal. Some lack maturity. Lack will. Youths who suffer fractured families do not know the love of parents. Unhappy, unfulfilled souls who lack that centre we the fortunate may consider we possess.

This is true of Morgon Wroth.

Morgon Wroth has never doubted.

His name will truly find the secure place in this Divine Testament. For Brother Morgon has played his part in my protection with that love which passes the love of women.

– TRINITY, THE DIVINE TESTAMENT, LONDON, 1996

Rosslyn, as the priest suggested, is one of several interested parties to have beaten a track to the house on Rue St Pierre. Others have included officers of both the American and British security services. Each determined to open up Morandi's archives. To unpeel the layers of secrecy covering the workings and intentions of the Trinity Chapter. Each persuaded that the cult will commit some atrocity at the dawn of the Millennium. Each has approached Morandi with caution. Sharing a common anxiety, mutually suspicious, unprepared to reveal their hands, each has laid cards on the table. But face down. And that is how they've stayed. Had the discussions been franker, a deal more open, then the pieces of the infernal jigsaw might have been easier to piece together. Together the secret forces of law and order might already have come up with the name of Morgon Wroth.

Had they put a team of legmen on this former Welsh Guardsman the millennial carnage might have been prevented. Surveillance officers could have set off, for a start, on the trail of the bewigged woman with the white ribbon pinned to her lapel. The disguise, to say the least, had been a conspicuously poor one. At home, others might even have succeeded in tracing the call she'd been making to Wroth in London. Had they done so, they'd have heard her tell him that Rosslyn had spent nearly two hours with Morandi. Evidence, as if it were needed, that Morandi and now Rosslyn number high on the list of sworn enemies. Morgon Wroth requires no further convincing that Rosslyn and Caroline Moorfield present an unwarranted and dangerous threat.

Morgon Wroth: veteran of the Falklands campaign, his military career ended as an inmate of the Military Corrective Training Centre, Berechurch Hall Camp, Colchester. The president of the court martial, a dull Grenadier major, described him as 'this dangerous and evil young soldier . . .' and convicted the prisoner in handcuffs to detention.

Two years: the maximum sentence allowed, for the combination of desertion, fraud, theft and extreme physical violence. Held in the 'Collie' D Wing, he appealed against the verdict of the court to the convening officer even before his sentence was confirmed. His appeal was rejected. Then he appealed to the theatre commander at Rhine Army headquarters. To no avail. Then upwards to the Director of Army Service Conditions in the Ministry of Defence.

Appeal dismissed.

Undeterred, aggrieved, Wroth went on. To the Army Board.

Sentence upheld.

Finally he appealed to the Courts Martial Appeals Court, effectively the High Court in all but name. Its word, in short, was that the prisoner Wroth was a sick, dangerous and deluded madman. His legal aid barrister, Ms Naomi Rubinstein QC, pleaded that he be given psychiatric supervision and counselling. Wroth's solicitors, Brady Nassaueur Drummond, proposed counselling by Dr Van Rijn, a natural medicine practitioner.

Outwardly calmed by Dr Van Rijn's fortnightly visits to Colchester, Wroth put himself through a punitive regime of body-building. He expanded and hardened his already formidable eighteen-stone physique. He was built like a cement mixer, and everything about him suggested violence. The jutting jaw. His sense of justice. Punishment was in the blood. When he ate his favourite meats he chewed them like a dog, his large tongue licking the protruding lower lips, breaking the bones of chickens and lamb between his large teeth. Possessed, as it were, of a brooding *gravitas*, he took himself seriously. And complaining about his fate, the sullen Welsh giant – about whom, as a giant, there was nothing remotely gentle – was gently encouraged by Dr Van Rijn to think of 'basic matters spiritual'.

It took a surprisingly short time for the troubled mind, filled as it was with thoughts of revenge against the world, to become the repository of other-worldly thoughts. Mostly, these were of his own importance.

The Great I Am.

The One.

One.

One.

Wroth was born to follow. Born to be led. As it turned out, by Dr Van Rijn.

Once he'd stepped out of the Military Corrective Training Centre on to the streets of Colchester, Wroth took the fast train to Liverpool Street and beat a path to Harley Street. Dr Van Rijn gave him employment as a general caretaker, maintenance man and driver.

It seemed the rehabilitation was complete. The unfortunate was now fortunate. Another of Dr Van Rijn's success stories. Symbol of the good and gentle doctor's altruism, Wroth was appointed to preside over the care and maintenance of Trinity House on the Harrow Road, the derelict apartment block at the boundary of London's largest necropolis, the Kensal Green private cemetery.

All this thanks to Dr Van Rijn.

Tonight at Trinity House, after the call from Geneva, Wroth has marked Rosslyn's card.

Now he waits for the telephone to ring. For the caller to be Dr Van Rijn.

A stickler for timekeeping, his mentor calls at the predetermined minute.

Wroth passes on the intelligence he's gained from the woman in the Hotel Aiglon.

If Dr Van Rijn is surprised to learn that Rosslyn has visited Morandi, he gives no indication of it. Instead, he gives Wroth the instructions the Welshman's been waiting for. To the uninitiated, these instructions might seem obscure: *'First take the delivery in Adinkerke. Make the final payment to KZ. I have just spoken to him in Plzen. Then arrange to make the purchase from Universal Vehicles.'*

The two deliveries Dr Van Rijn is telling Wroth to oversee are clandestine. One involves a 3.5 litre accident and emergency ambulance. This requires Wroth or an associate to travel north by train and taxi to Brighouse in the West Riding of Yorkshire. £50,000 is to be paid for the ambulance.

The other requires Wroth to travel from London to Dover in a downmarket hire car.

He will avoid the Channel Tunnel, taking advantage instead of the Christmas newspaper offers of £1 cross-channel ferry tickets. His journey north from Calais to Adinkerke will be through the bland French countryside. The blander in the winter and the snow. The roads are mostly empty in the pre-Christmas season. In the cheap hire car he will have three folded canvas hold-alls. They will contain silver foil, black plastic waste bags and industrial tape.

The car journey to the Belgian border and the now disused Belgian customs post will take him just over thirty minutes. In Adinkerke, Wroth's cash hand-over will be just another among those arranged, daily, for the purchase of £600,000 worth of tobacco. Sixty per cent of Great Britain's hand-rolling tobacco market is made up from tobacco smuggled out through Adinkerke. Its tobacco outlets are open twenty-four hours each day. The cost to the Exchequer is more than £425 million in lost revenue. It is not, however, tobacco that Wroth will be collecting. His collection will be of a lethal substance.

This means that the main and, indeed, likely enemies that he must avoid are twofold. First: HM Customs Collector for south-east England stationed in Dover. Fortunately for Wroth, Customs Red and Green channels have been abolished. So the Law is little concerned about the flood of hand-rolled tobacco from Belgium. And the authorities in Brussels couldn't care less.

Second: Chief Investigations Officers of the Inspectorate of Belgian customs, the Rijkswacht. Their local officers will be on the QV.

But at this time of year the local Rijkswacht

officers are ill-disposed to stir up animosity among the citizenry of Adinkerke.

With Wroth saying he's en route to restore his grandfather's grave in the Second World War cemetery beyond Adinkerke – where the northern route becomes the coast road beyond Westende – the chances of his being apprehended are, he calculates, about ten to one against. And One, as in | | |, is Wroth's lucky number.

Thus, scrupulously planned and reconnoitred, the clandestine importation strategy of Dr Van Rijn is watertight. It needs to be. For Wroth is to import a final consignment of Czech Republic-manufactured high explosive into the United Kingdom. The last 210 pounds of it.

As Dr Van Rijn has confirmed, it will be delivered to Wroth by KZ – Karel Zieleniec from DV Militar, Plzen, the state armaments manufacturing agency privatized in 1994. Neatly packed in unmarked bags, the lethal high explosive will ensure the future of the Trinity Chapter fortunes. Fortunes which will also ensure Wroth's future in his smallholding in southern Spain. The future in the sun. Certain to be secure. Well deserved. A paradise a million miles away from the Military Corrective Training Centre. Suitable for this good soldier home from the hills, the deserts and the punitive MCTC régime.

The safe haven where Wroth the military man and maker of lists reviews the future on parade – *I*

Wroth, prepared for the springtime and summer of the Millennium. I Wroth, prepared for anything.

Including the outcome of the forecast, which is for heavy snow across northern Europe, the United Kingdom and London.

Once he has understood the instructions from Dr Van Rijn, Wroth unwraps some raw steak. Some of it he will eat himself. Most of it is for his Pride and Joy. His companion. The Rasselaer – P & J. The name chosen by Wroth because P & J is trained to tear out the throats of his master's adversaries. Wroth reckons the combination of his own strength and P & J's represents a fighting machine *sans pareil*. Few would be inclined to disagree. Sometimes, alone at Trinity House, he grills the meat with his blow torch. He chucks in a few vegetables. Scorches the skin of courgettes and onions as he scorched the faces of the youths that midnight in Trafalgar Square. The incident of which the police have been able to make neither head nor tail.

16

Nothing could illustrate the extremism of the Trinity Chapter more effectively than the fundamental proposition it maintains. Namely, that Trinity's Resurrection is a certainty.

I believe, on the basis of my knowledge of the Trinity Chapter, that if his attempt to fulfil his prophecy is thwarted, his followers will ensure that violence is committed on a public scale. On a specific date, as he promised. At a specific time and place such that it will divert and then concentrate the attention of the world's media. Yet of course there exists no concrete or certain proof of my argument. I base it simply on the following:

My assessment of the world's several thousand cults and new religious movements.

My reading of Trinity's mind.

The extent of his followers' devotion.

And, finally, upon the patterns of evidence Ms Moorfield demonstrated to me with such conviction.

I believe that had Ms Moorfield lived to complete her thesis it would have ranked among the most consequential twentieth-century works in the sociology of religion.

– FR. GIAN MARIA MORANDI, INTERNATIONAL FAMILY FOUNDATION, GENEVA, DECEMBER 1999

Victoria Station. Platform 9. The doors of the late-night South London Metro train shut. Caroline is seated in the front carriage. Rosslyn, she feels, will be pleased with the initiatives she's been taking. One has already yielded Morandi for him to see. And she wonders what progress he's made in

Geneva. He hasn't called to report to her on it.

Thanks to the Provident Care and Nursing Agency, she's turned up Marcus Luke's phone number and she's travelling south from Victoria to meet him. Her destination is Gipsy Hill, where Luke has said he'll meet her outside the station.

The train rattles up the slight incline out of Victoria Station. Its wheels grate and whine. The train judders on the tracks. Picks up speed. Empty lager cans roll across the carriage's wet floor. Over the Thames on Grosvenor Bridge, the train gathers speed. Chelsea Bridge to the right. Past the vast white chimneys of the ruined Battersea Power Station.

Feeling safe in the warmth of the train, she watches the blue electric flashes spit across the tracks. Streaks of light flood drab hoardings. The movement relaxes her and she tells herself she can't really believe in Morandi's warning. In what may lie behind the vague threats. That her life's in any danger. And certainly she has no thought for the figure of the woman at the far end of the railway carriage. Ever since she left the Malvern Hotel the woman's been on Caroline's tail.

Holding the copy of the *Evening Standard* open at the page of astrological predictions, the woman has her back to her quarry. Her legs are crossed at the knees. Her winter boots, stained by sand and salt and melted snow, are slightly drawn back beneath the seat. With no interest in whatever future the stars may predict for her, the blue eyes are on the reflection in the nearest window. Blurred images of the few other passengers. Mostly her eyes rest on Caroline. When the train draws into Clapham Junction and the carriage empties, she adjusts the collar of her green waxed jacket to hide her face.

Caroline stares at the sign saying: NETWORK SOUTH EAST WELCOMES YOU TO BRITAIN'S BUSIEST RAILWAY STATION.

She thinks about Marcus Luke. A great deal, she believes, depends on him: on what he can tell her about Jane's life in London.

After Balham, where the station lights are out, the train forks left. The Gatwick Express streaks away to the right, its lights blazing from misted windows. When the train shoots into the tunnel before West Norwood with a kind of pneumatic gasp, she feels she's now committed to some strange race against time. If only, she thinks, she can unravel at least a part of the enigma surrounding Jane's last days before the cremation service tomorrow. Had she not been selecting lines to read for Jane's service (a few short passages from the Book of Revelation), she most probably would have noticed the face of the woman watching her who's paying no attention to those astrological predictions. *And I saw a new heaven and a new earth*, she reads. She's copied the lines in her journal from the bible in the hotel room: *For the first heaven and the first earth were passed away; and there was no more sea.*

First one out of the train at Gipsy Hill, she doesn't notice the woman behind her who's last to make the exit. Keeping at a discreet distance in the cold fog, the woman follows Caroline up the slippery steps. Across the narrow covered bridge. Into the ticket hall, where Caroline recognizes the slim figure in the Burberry mackintosh. The fair curly hair and smiling face. Marcus Luke.

'Are you alone?' he asks her.

She turns. Thinking he's asked her if perhaps she's been followed here.

'Sure,' she says. Looking vaguely around the ticket hall, she sees it's empty. 'I'm alone.' There isn't even a collector on duty to take her ticket.

'There's an Indian restaurant across the road,' Luke says. 'The Mandalay. Vegetarian.' His smile is comforting. 'It stays open until late.'

'Great,' she says. 'You lead the way.' She follows him to the Indian restaurant. The Mandalay. So late at night, they're the only customers.

He's wearing the same dark suit and collarless white shirt he wore at the inquest. He's smaller than she remembers him from the coroner's court. About her own height. The skin is soft and hairless. The full head of hair shiny as if he's just shampooed it. The eyes, with long albino lashes, are a penetrating blue. The angelic features seem somehow full of innocence.

'Did you have an easy journey?' he enquires gently, drawing back a chair for her to sit at the table by the bar.

'Yes,' says Caroline. She notices he sits down carefully. He slowly unfolds the paper table napkin as if it's a precious relic.

'You can never be sure whether there'll be a security alert at Victoria,' he says. 'What would you like to eat?'

'You choose,' she says, watching the waiter light a cheap red candle.

She notices he doesn't consult the menu. Just rattles off various items to the waiter as if he's learned them by heart. She's no idea what they mean. He treats the waiter with extreme politeness, and she notices the Indian seems slightly impressed by his customer's languid accent – taking him, she imagines, to be from the sort of British upper class that rarely, if ever, visits the Mandalay on Gipsy Hill.

'I don't drink,' he says. 'Don't let that stop you though, Miss Moorfield. Would you like some wine, a glass of beer or something?'

'No thanks,' she says. 'And please call me Caroline.'

'Water then?'

'A diet Coke.'

'I'll join you, Caroline,' he says with a wide smile, as if her choice marks some kind of celebration. She notices he has full and very moist lips. Almost like a girl's.

'You know why I've come down here to see you,' she says. 'It's very important to me that you tell me just what happened to Jane.'

[151]

'It was bad, wasn't it,' he says.

'And is everything you said at the inquest really true?'

Luke nods. 'Jane told me that you're, well, sceptical about the world,' he says gently.

'I'm only interested in the *truth*, Marcus. About *her*.'

'How much did she tell you about me?' Luke enquires.

'Nothing.'

'What about her friends?'

'Excuse me, what friends are we talking about, Marcus?'

He frowns. 'People connected with the Chapter, say.'

'She didn't mention any friends like that.'

'Nor how we first met, Jane and I?'

She shakes her head at him, and then smiles: 'Why don't you tell me about that?'

'It's open to misunderstandings,' he says. He falls silent. Caroline recognizes, or thinks she recognizes, the expression of fear in his eyes. Or perhaps the memory of their first meeting is somehow strange. Maybe he was shy of her. Wary of the distance she could quickly put between herself and a man. Especially if he was as attractive as Marcus. Yes, she can see that Jane must have found him appealing.

'Some of what we talked about,' he says, 'Jane and me. I mean . . . when we met, some of it's confidential. I mean professionally. There are things I can't touch on. It's important you understand that, Caroline.'

'If you say so.'

'I wouldn't want you to think I'm being defensive. Evasive even.'

'I don't,' says Caroline. Though of course that's exactly what she's thinking. 'Tell me,' she says, 'and I'll make up my own mind.' She watches him dish out the portions of the mushy Indian food very carefully. 'Why don't you just begin at the beginning, Marcus?'

'She got my name from INFORM,' he says. 'Not that I have anything to do with them. But they're perfectly well-meaning people. Academics mostly. Someone must have told them that I had been a follower of Trinity. A former member of the Chapter.'

She feels he's slipped back into his evasive mode. He's putting up defences. She wants to get straight to the heart of his relationship with Jane. 'I want you to tell me,' she says, 'about Jane.'

'One afternoon, I think last spring, she called in unannounced at the Van Rijn Clinic in Harley Street where I was working. Ostensibly she wanted treatment for a frozen shoulder. Dr Van Rijn proposed a course of acupuncture.'

'But Jane had a phobia about needles.'

'Yes, I know,' says Marcus. 'And Dr Van Rijn

[153]

helped her greatly to overcome it. He's a gentle man.'

'You mean she went through with the treatment?'

He opens his eyes wide. As if he's begging her to believe him. 'Yes, she did. And it was very successful. I can't remember exactly when it was, perhaps some time in September, when she asked me out for a cup of coffee. We laughed a bit about it because I don't use caffeine. Then she came out with it.'

'Came out with what?'

'She asked me directly whether I was still a member of the Chapter. Of course, she already knew the answer from INFORM. So over the next few weeks I was able to help her with her research. I explained, as you probably know, that Trinity had died.'

'How did he die?'

'Quite suddenly, alone and of natural causes. In an Oxford Street hotel. Sadly, he had been ill for some time. He didn't want to talk about his last illness. I personally felt that he had a premonition of death. Bear in mind, in any event, that he had predicted his certain Resurrection which will coincide with the Millennium.'

Caroline shakes her head. 'Do you really believe in that?'

'Let's say I do not disbelieve it. Time alone will prove whether he's right. Or whether he's wrong. I suppose one could say the same of Christ. Trinity, like Christ, was mourned. As you probably know, Trinity's buried in Kensal Green Cemetery.'

He produces some photographs from his wallet

and shows them to her. 'This shows the route through the cemetery to the tomb. Jane and I spent a beautiful afternoon there. One of London's forgotten and most romantic places. Then, some time in November, she sent me these –'

The writing on the two postcards showing angels on tombs in Kensal Green Cemetery is Jane's:

London's hidden places still offer winter sanctuary to the city's wild creatures. For example: grander cemeteries where hedgehogs sleep next to insects in the gaps between monuments to forgotten dignitaries of Empire. Abandoned tunnels: homes to hibernating bats. The narrower tributaries of old Thames. Ponds. Reservoirs. Overgrown canals. Further afield is city heath land where urban foxes hide. And there are those wide park spaces of Richmond or Windsor: deserted winter country for silent herds of deer.

Perhaps the magnetism such places exert for me can be explained by my need for solitude. Mystery. That peace also to be found in London's obscurer churches. That mysterious peace, as some of us when children were taught to pray for, that the earth cannot give. I am not, I must confess, a regular churchgoer these days. But from time to time I find myself repeating that request: 'Lord, give us the peace that the earth cannot give.'

'She copied the lines from a short story called "Happy Christmas Lucy Smith" and told me she found them very beautiful. And so do I. She thought the angels looked like me.'

'Could be,' says Caroline. 'Then what happened?'

'I heard from her less frequently once she got so absorbed in her thesis. About the funding of Millennial New Religious Movements –'

'– with Special Reference to the Trinity Chapter,' says Caroline. 'And did she tell you that she'd found that massive sums of money had been deposited secretly in places like the Seychelles and the Bahamas?'

'She didn't tell me that in so many words,' says Luke. 'True, the Chapter received donations from many sources.'

'If it's so rich, how come then,' she asks, 'that Jane reckoned the Chapter to be in a state of terminal collapse?'

'I wouldn't go so far as to say that. True, after Trinity's death in 1996, the Chapter fragmented. Largely into two groups. Those who left the treatment centres to work elsewhere. And a smaller group of those who continued, and continue still, to pray for his Resurrection and His Life.'

'Did Jane speak to any of them?'

'I can't tell you.'

'You won't – or can't?'

'Well, to be honest, I don't really know. By the time I next saw her, towards the end, she had fallen foul of the drug habit. It was then that she must have sought help. I tried to offer her counselling. And the rest, the inquest, I'm afraid you know about it, don't you?'

'I'm sorry,' says Caroline. She shakes her head regretfully. 'But I do *not* believe she did drugs.' She looks him straight in the eye. 'See?'

'I see. I know you don't. I heard what you said at the inquest. But I'm afraid, Caroline, it's the truth. You have to face the truth.'

'That she killed herself?'

'Yes, she did. In the way they said. And I feel very guilty that I failed to help her. Of course, it could perhaps have been an accident. I think that's what it was really. But it could also have been deliberate. Alas, Caroline, neither you nor I will ever know for sure, will we?'

'I mean to find out.'

'Oh, I hope for the sake of your peace of mind that you do.'

'Could Dr Van Rijn help?' she says, laughing nervously. 'Or was he a member of this God-awful Chapter too?'

'He wasn't a member. No.'

She studies his wide eyes. 'But he was sympathetic to it?' she says, unblinking. 'Come on, tell me. What was it he did?'

'Well, in so far as he assisted at the centres, yes. You could say, in a practical sort of way, he was sympathetic to the Trinity Chapter.'

'But how well did he really know Jane?'

'Only professionally. No more or less than that.'

'Then he can help me, can't he?'

He hesitates and turns away from her searching

eyes. 'No, he won't be able to help you.' He seems tense. 'But believe me, Caroline, I'd like to. If you don't mind me saying so, you're the image of her. Of Jane. And I really hate to see you or anyone else cast quite so low.'

Does he really mean that? It's hard to tell. She'd like to think he's completely blameless. What can she say, except 'I appreciate that, Marcus.'

'I feel rather helpless,' he says. 'If it'll be any consolation to you, I have some photographs of Jane in London at my place. I only live round the corner. A few minutes away. If you like, we can go back to my place. Would you like to see them?'

Oh my. Come up and see my etchings. Let's listen to some music. Why not? 'Yes, sure, I would.'

'OK,' he says with a look of odd vulnerability. 'Why don't I pay the bill then?'

'No, be my guest,' she tells him. 'I'll pay.'

'No, no, I insist. Really, it's on me.'

Looking at his smile, the honesty in his eyes, and feeling a sense of his love for Trinity, she thinks she can understand the leader's magnetism. Something of the essence that's persuaded his followers to believe in Him.

Leaving the restaurant, she thinks of Rosslyn and feels that Marcus Luke will likely be of help.

Anyway, I like him. He's gentle. Passionate even. I like the way he looks. Like an angel who hasn't yet fallen but might. In an interesting way. It's getting late.

But she doesn't care too much that she's probably going to miss the last train back. And on this December night Gipsy Hill is dark and empty.

Empty except for the figure of the woman standing in the shadows of the doorway to the newsagents. She's read about south London prowlers in the British papers. But, anyway, the figure is a woman. So fine. And with Rosslyn away and her knowing no one else in the city, she'd rather not spend the night alone. She'll be quite happy to stay with Marcus in his apartment.

If he asks me. Even to sleep with the believer.

17

Invincible. Immortal. Inviolate. The One True God of Love
Reborn in his Living Flesh as He prophesied for your sakes.
In the first minute. Of the first hour. Of the first day. Of the
New Century. The Century of Trinity. The One-One-One.
Reborn as He prophesied. Reborn in the blood of women.
And so the Followers make preparation for His Second
Coming. As He so sacrificed His life for you, so bow before
Him with oblation. With Him you will change the World.
And with Him you will enter Paradise on Earth.

    – THE TRINITY PRAYER

Marcus Luke's apartment: the entire top storey of
the large quiet house of red brick. Once a Victorian
vicarage, it stands at the apex of the triangle formed
by Gipsy Hill, Westow Hill and Beardell Street.

    The floors are of pinkish maple and the high
windows face north-east. They offer a fine view of
the Crystal Palace transmitter mast, its flashing
lights just visible in the mist: red, then white, then
red again. Caroline is reminded of an artist's studio.
Like ones she'd seen years ago on Boylston Street in
Boston.

    He lights the wood stove with apple logs and the
smell reminds her of Moorfield House. Then he
shows her a dozen or so photographs he'd taken of
Jane in London. Outside Buckingham Palace. The

National Gallery. In Trafalgar Square. Piccadilly. In Kensal Green Cemetery.

The burning wood spits and hisses. Apart from the reflected street light outside and a single desk lamp, it offers the only light in the room. She gazes at the fire while he makes herbal tea. The light from the flames dances and flickers on the walls.

On the way here she'd asked him why he'd left the Trinity Chapter. And he'd said he'd prefer not to discuss the details.

Over the herbal tea, she asks him the question once again. Why he left.

And he starts to explain. In that thoughtful, fluent way she likes: 'Some things don't need saying, Caroline. You see, I bear them no ill will. I keep my promises. And in many significant respects I owe the whole of my spiritual existence to the Chapter and its teachings. Its tenets are wholly good. They do a great deal of selfless good work. Ministering. Caring. Helping lost souls to rebuild their lives. Not hard to see why the Royal Family showed so close an interest. Government ministers. Oxbridge dons. Newspaper proprietors. Celebrated playwrights. Architects. Discipline and mystery is an exciting combination. He has healing hands. He offers consolation. The close relationship with those who follow his teachings. As Christopher Isherwood found fulfilment in Swami Prabhavananda, Huxley in Hinduism and the Vedanta school of philosophy, the Beatles in the Maharishi. He is beyond the New

Age and Mind-Body. He is literally the New Age. Beyond Mind. Beyond Body.

'Then why did you leave?' she persists.

'Because once I'd qualified as a nurse I found that somehow what Trinity had to offer me in the way of spiritual strength wasn't finally what I'd been searching for. I was working for one of their drug rehabilitation centres. Actually, the one in East Grinstead. Basic nursing. Let's just say that, in my case, I found God. I was reborn. I moved on to a different plateau.'

'Was that the only reason you left?'

'It was the most important one,' he says. 'Though one never actually, in so many words, leaves it. Its influence is so very strong. It permeates everything. Had you ever met Trinity and the members of the Inner Chapter, the most formidable of his devotees, you'd understand exactly what I'm saying.'

'Did you know Trinity well?'

'Oh yes, I did.'

'And you were able to help Jane with her research then?'

'Yes.'

'So what was Trinity like?'

'The finest man I ever met. Extraordinarily charismatic. He emanated goodness. I'd have thought Jane might have told you something of him.'

'She told me very little. Who was he?'

'Not all of it's public knowledge. Born Julius Gowrie, Trinity was raised by foster parents in

Oxford and educated at private schools. His life was one of change. As a child, when the teachers found they couldn't handle his violent mood swings, he was taken away from school and taught at home by a series of private tutors. Julius was beautiful. Kind of a loner. Often sick. He suffered from anorexia, migraines and nervous troubles. When he fasted he reached a state of ecstasy. He'd spend weeks not speaking to anyone. And he claimed a miracle of healing had saved him twice from pneumonia. This was a miracle he himself performed.'

'You believe that?'

'So help me God. That's the truth. It's exactly what happened. He went up to Cambridge in the 1970s. Studying medicine, he specialized in endocrinology. He began to read very widely. His models were Buddha, Jesus, Muhammad, Lao Tzu and Jung. During a trip to India, he decided to abandon medicine for meditation and the healing arts. Briefly, he became a disciple of Bhagwan Shree Rajneesh, committed to Rajneesh's fundamental commandment: *Love Oneself*. He engaged in extreme sexual promiscuity, insisting that he only eat food, like rice or vegetables and fruit, that had been in contact with the juices of sexually aroused women.'

'What's that got to do with *goodness*?'

'He was unpeeling layers in his personality. He had a remarkable aura of goodness.'

'What do you mean?'

'It was a long and wonderful process of change. In

India, even the most extreme of Rajneesh's followers, the *sannyasins*, adored him. But when Rajneesh started to believe in his own divinity – when he famously said in New Jersey, "I am the Messiah America has been waiting for," Trinity finally split with him. Abandoned his followers in India, and headed back to Europe to lecture wherever he could find an audience. Mostly to students in university faculties and societies. In Bonn, Paris, Rome, Cambridge. And just as I did, I can imagine how beautiful they found him.'

Caroline finds his quiet passion oddly infectious. She appraises him, wondering at the contrast between his baby face, its innocence and his authoritative tone. He seems to be at one with his idealism. Bolstered by his conviction. Straightforward and strong. Almost like a lover.

'I often listened to him later. Talking about the Joy of Life through homeopathy. The secrets of success and the God Within. Myself. Myself. Myself. What he called the *One-One-One*. "We are One United."'

'How does that square with his sexual promiscuity?'

'Oh, that. It was a thing of the past. As Nietzsche put it: "I tell you, one must have chaos in one to give birth to a dancing star." You see, he based his teaching on "celibacy and the logical ideal of total life transformation". He told me how he endured illness, cured himself and revealed a truth, bringing order where previously everything had been chaos.

His most devoted followers genuinely believed him to be a genius. He gave us hope. We believed him to be very God of very God. The Messiah. One in Three. Three in One. Hence Trinity.'

'The Divine?'

'Yes,' he says. 'Divine.'

It seems to Caroline that it would be inappropriate, almost offensive, to contradict this passionately-held view of Trinity's Divinity. *'Sometimes mad,'* she remembers Jane having written in one of her faxes home, *'sometimes sane gurus. Some are harmless souls. Some are dangerous monsters.'*

Trinity, it seems, doesn't fit either of those categories. Not according to the gospel of Marcus Luke. And she wonders whether those are his real names. And begins to feel she needs him.

He smiles. His teeth sparkle in the dim light. And he takes her hand.

'Were you a bit in love with him?'

'Oh no,' he says. 'Not that.'

'Did he love you?'

'I'm not that way.' He holds her hand just long enough to realize that it's true. And she feels his eyes on her. And thinks he might intend to show her. So she leaves her hand in his and feels a small spasm of arousal.

'What you don't know,' she says, 'is that after she died, there were FBI and CIA people asking about her. They visited my home.'

'What did they want?'

'They wouldn't say. I guess they were making checks. From Boston. Up from Washington even. Something to do with the State Department. I don't know about those people. Maybe it had to do with how she died.'

'What do you think?'

'Maybe they were interested, like . . . after Waco. King Do and Heaven's Gate. Mass suicide. I'm sure she never bought into all that stuff. The end of the world. Witchcraft. Armageddon. Apocalypse. She was too smart to buy into that kind of garbage.'

'The Chapter is very different,' says Luke. 'It serves as a bond against the outside world. The more its members realize the rest of the world may very well deny Trinity's prophesies – his Resurrection at the dawning of the Millennium – the stronger their common bond of victimization and persecution.'

'You don't mean that they *want* to be persecuted?'

'No one does. They just totally believe in Trinity's divinity. For many of them the Chapter gives them the love the world denies them. Believe in Yourself. Believe in Me. Believe in Trinity. For He Is Always With You. The belief finds its expression in their secret prayer. The *ultimate* text of Trinity.'

'What's that?'

'You want me to recite it?'

'Sure. Yeah. Go ahead.'

'*The Trinity Chapter Testament*. Book One Chapter

Seven. *"My children. Be always constant. Remain true. For as it is prophesied and written, the world will witness the Father's Resurrection. When in goodness your Father will surpass Christ himself."'* Here he makes the sign. Across his chest: | | |. Then continues: *'Invincible. Immortal. Inviolate. The One True God of Love Reborn in his Living Flesh as He prophesied for your sakes. In the first minute. Of the first hour. Of the first day. Of the New Century. The Century of Trinity. The One-One-One. Reborn as He prophesied. Reborn in the blood of women. And so the Followers make preparation for His Second Coming. As He so sacrificed His life for you, so bow before Him with oblation. With Him you will change the World. And with Him you will enter Paradise on Earth.'*

'You believed in that?'

'I did. Yes.'

'Well, it kind of scares me.'

'There's nothing to be scared of.'

'And you, Marcus. Doesn't it scare *you*?'

'Why should it?'

'Because the US government has your photograph on file – I've seen it in the embassy. A woman called Queron has it. She's CIA. She asked me to identify it. And I did. And she showed me a picture of Trinity too. And you're not frightened?'

'Not in the slightest,' he says, eyes wide. 'I know they've asked questions about me. They called on Dr Van Rijn. And he put them right. I can't be persecuted for my religious beliefs. I have absolutely nothing to be guilty about. Do you?'

'No,' she says lamely.

'There you are.'

'In fact I feel pretty proud of what Jane was trying to do. Only like totally torn up by the way it ended.'

He moves a little closer to her. 'I'll help you in any way I can.'

'To find out what happened to her in the last days of her life?'

'I've told you all I know. I promise you.' Then he adds, almost as an afterthought: 'Finally, the only people who could really help you find out what happened are the members of the Inner Chapter, wherever they may be. And with those I can't help you. Not from the outside.'

He's sown the seed in her mind. Prompted the idea. *Why not get to them from the inside?*

With you as my lover.

She leans her head on his shoulder and he puts his arm round her. He smells sweet. Maybe of patchouli oil . . . It's almost as though he's waiting for her to ask, just as Jane must have asked him too: 'How did you first join the Chapter?'

He leans forward and puts another log on the fire.

'There are those,' Marcus tells her, 'who were persuaded to consider joining by friends, relatives or people in the workplace – like me – by someone already a member. The Inner Chapter would've already considered the suitability or otherwise of the personal and family background. Of all new recruits, noviciates, those were the most welcome. The Network Friends of Trinity the Master.'

'Like you were?'

'Like I was. Public school educated. Well-off parents. The house in Dorset, another in Tuscany. Dad a commodities broker. Me with a trust fund from my grandmother. Others may be men and women from the worlds of national and international politics, public service, the arts, sciences and academic life. People with solid public reputations. Substantial financial resources. Theirs, like mine, was the fast-track route to final review. Their induction shortest. Then there were the Young Friends of Trinity the Master. Their route was a bit longer than that of the Network Friends. Young Friends, men and women under the age of twenty-five, they were university undergraduate or post-graduate students of proven intellectual ability and promise. Those preferred were usually in their final year at Oxford and Cambridge. I'd say a third were American, one third British, one third of other nationalities. Mostly German and Japanese. Then there was the route taken by the Redeemed Friends. A minority in Trinity Chapter. Like their university counterparts, they were mostly under thirty and had successfully undergone treatment for drug or alcohol abuse, or both, in one or other of the treatment centres established by the Trinity Chapter.'

'Did you recruit any of them?'

'Yes, I did. We monitored them during counselling and therapy. They'd usually severed contact with their immediate family and friends or vice versa.'

'How were they actually recruited?'

'At the end of treatment. By one or other of the doctors in attendance at the centres. Otherwise, recruitment can be either in the hands of the Inner Chapter or those of the some half-dozen Oxbridge tutors who serve the Trinity Chapter as parents.'

'Who were they, these *parents*?'

'Someone who first targets the Young Friend for monitoring. Or vetting. Unbeknown to the Young Friend, a painstaking examination of strengths and weaknesses took place. A detailed picture of the Young Friend's personal and family background was made.'

'Then what happened?'

'A confidential report would be delivered to the Inner Chapter for evaluation of the potential recruit's strengths and weaknesses. The Inner Chapter needs to be sure of the new Friend's spiritual capacity. That I, for example, or you would be capable of understanding the necessary theology. That you'd be capable of living the Master's *Weltanschauung* or world view, which separates His followers from non-believers and unites His believers.'

'In what?'

'In their common purpose and obedience. A new Friend needed to feel. To believe. To totally commit his or her being to the force derived from waiting and preparing in prayer for the Master's Resurrection.'

'Where does the money come in?'

'Well, the Chapter considered it a strength for the new Friend to be free from financial dependency. To have access to enough personal or family capital. To be the beneficiary of some family trust fund to guarantee regular contributions. The new Friend is then parented.'

'What really is this parenting?'

'It's a gradual process. Sometimes it lasts many months, during which the recruiter creates a need in the subject for spirituality. Only if a parent is sure the new Friend is certain to make the leap of faith.'

'So I couldn't like walk in off the street then?'

'No recruit walks in off the street, like a potential Scientologist, to take some form of personality test. No. And to date, none has been recruited like travellers approached by the followers of the Reverend Syn Myung Moon at the San Francisco bus station and Fisherman's Wharf area. Those who do walk in off the street, the "By-Chancers", are treated with courtesy.'

'Courtesy – why?'

'Old-fashioned courtesy's the most effective way of disguising suspicion. Paranoia even.'

'Like yours, Marcus?'

'What do you mean?'

She touches his hair. 'You didn't invite me here just to look at photographs of Jane, did you?' He shrugs. 'Did you, Marcus?'

'There's always the danger of betrayal by anti-cultist moles.'

'What do you *mean*?' she asks.

'Members of some extremist Judaeo-Christian faction bent on subversion. Or a journalist seeking an *exposé*.'

'Or someone like Jane?'

'Someone like Jane,' he agrees. 'But I can't imagine they thought of her as a threat.'

'Or me, Marcus. Do you think of me as a threat?'

'Sorry. You –?'

She leans towards him and kisses his mouth.

The single candle illuminates them. Marcus Luke has left a CD playing on repeat:

> *Just Show Me How to Love You*
> *E ci ridiamo su*
> *gabbiano di scogliera*
> *ma dov'eri nascosto'*
> *dov'eri finora?*

18

Wise men say nothing in dangerous times.

– SIR DICK WHITE, FORMER DIRECTOR GENERAL MI5 AND MI6, TO THE AUTHOR, LONDON, 1962

On the way by car to the crematorium in north London, Rosslyn tells her about Geneva. Morandi. The sight of the bewigged woman in the foyer of the hotel near the airport.

She finds it easier than she'd imagined to lie to him about where she's been and what she's done since they last talked.

No, she thinks. *And I don't feel guilty because he's comforting me. Because of Marcus.* Neither does she feel guilty – *well, guilty's not the right word really, is it?* – about betraying Rosslyn's trust in her.

She feels her night with Marcus is one of life's small betrayals and, anyway, she's Rosslyn's paymaster.

So what should he care anyway? Who I make love to is my business and has nothing to do with the investigation. And I think, in her way, that Jane would have been pleased Marcus made me so happy in his bed.

She notices the long strand of fair hair on her jacket sleeve and she leaves it there like some secret memento of a rite of passage.

Rosslyn's saying: 'I worry about you.'

'What? Oh yeah. Well, this'll be over soon, won't it?'

'I mean about your being at the hotel alone,' he says.

'Is that what Morandi said?'

He throws her a sideways glance. 'It's what *I'm* saying.'

'Then *don't worry*,' she says, more sharply than she'd intended.

'You should make sure those faxes of Jane's are safe.'

'They are.'

'Where are you keeping them?'

'In my journal. With my traveller's cheques.'

'Yes. But where?'

'In the hotel safe, Alan. No more questions, OK? Not now.'

In the crematorium chapel, when the undertaker from Kenyon's asks if she's ready, she tells him: 'Let's do it.'

Besides Rosslyn and Caroline, the only people in the congregation are the young officiating priest, the man from Kenyon's and the crematorium attendant. Caroline has placed a bunch of red roses on the simple coffin. She has fixed the bouquet to the raw wood with a strip of double-sided Scotch tape the crematorium attendant's given her.

The priest begins: 'I am the resurrection and the

life, saith the Lord. He that believeth in me though he were dead, yet shall he live: and whosoever liveth and believeth in me shall never die.'

Sweating, he speaks in a cracked voice, frequently dabbing at his reddened nostrils with a handkerchief. He makes slightly theatrical gestures of despair. Not because he's weeping but because he has a feverish cold. His camp gestures of despair lessen the misery of the dreadful ceremony. He seems relieved when it's Caroline's turn to address the congregation:

'Caroline Moorfield,' he sniffs, 'as her beloved sister Jane would have wished, will now read a chosen extract from the Book of Revelation.'

Caroline stands, her journal in her shaking hands.

As she's told Rosslyn, every item of clothing she's wearing belonged to Jane. She's even styled her hair, French braided it, and applied some make-up to resemble Jane's. Caroline's contrived resemblance to the likeness of Jane he saw in Morandi's office is uncanny.

She reads aloud: 'And I saw a new heaven and a new earth. For the first heaven and the first earth were passed away; and there was no more sea.' She leaves out the passage about John and Jerusalem prepared as a bride for her husband. 'And God shall wipe away all tears from their eyes; and there shall be no more death, neither sorrow, nor crying, neither shall there be any more pain: and the former things are passed away. Amen.'

'Amen,' says Rosslyn. He holds her hand.

The red velvet curtain closes in front of the coffin.

There's a whirring. Caroline shuts her eyes. The coffin sinks into the gas furnace.

'Amen,' she whispers.

Outside the crematorium, the man from Kenyon's approaches her with his hands clasped. 'Your sister's ashes will be ready for collection,' he says, 'this time tomorrow.'

'Thank you.'

'In twenty-four hours, Miss Moorfield,' he says, with a reverential bow. 'Unless of course you wish for them to be scattered or perhaps interred here. Arrangements can be made.'

'No, I know she'd have wished her ashes to be scattered near home.'

'Whatever you wish,' the undertaker says. 'Fortunately, you don't need an Overseas Certificate for their legal exportation. If you wish, so you don't have to be put to any more inconvenience, we can arrange for your sister's ashes to be delivered to whatever address you may be staying at here in London.'

'OK, fine,' says Caroline. She gives the man the address of her hotel.

Their shoes crush the frozen grit and snow as they walk to Rosslyn's BMW.

Caroline takes a last look at the chapel in the bright winter sun.

Blue sky. She imagines the landscape stretching to a different horizon. In Vernon Hills. Fir trees. Pines. Frost in the air. Sun sparkles. Glittering crystals. She holds her breath. Holds back her tears.

Then, staring at the watery sun, she lets out a whimper of pain like some trapped animal.

'Come on,' he says, holding her to him tightly, 'I'll take you back to the hotel.'

At the Malvern Hotel, Caroline tells him she's 'feeling pretty exhausted. I'm going to try and get some sleep.'

'Shall we meet later?' he asks her. He suggests they have some dinner together. 'At my place perhaps?' She seems pleased. 'Around eight?'

'I'll be there,' she says, heading for the lift.

In Room 65 Caroline finds a message. Would she call Father Morandi? The number is in Geneva.

She returns his call. The secretary explains that Father Morandi's on another call and asks Caroline to wait. 'I'll tell him you're waiting.'

When Morandi comes on the line he says: 'I'd like to see you as soon as possible. I usually stay at the Heathrow Hilton. I'd be very grateful.' He breaks off for a moment: 'I'd appreciate it if you'd treat our rendezvous as confidential. I want you to take very seriously my advice about your safety.'

She tells him not to worry.

'Tomorrow? Unless you hear from me otherwise, I'll be in Room 5006. Between noon and one?'

She agrees to meet him there.

Morandi continues: 'An envelope with your name on it will be left for you in the hotel safe – by way of a precaution.'

In the foyer Rosslyn calls up his messages. There are two. Both from Swincarron's secretary, who tells him she'd like him 'to call in as a matter of some urgency'.

On the telephone to ASG, Swincarron's secretary tells Rosslyn 'the Chairman would like to see you.' She won't enlarge further. Her voice is unusually sharp. And no, the Chairman's in a meeting and she isn't taking calls. 'She's asked *me* to tell *you* to come in as soon as you get this message. We've been trying to contact you all morning.'

'Tell her I've been at a funeral.'

'*When* can you get here to see her, Mr Rosslyn?'

About to tell her he can get to the office in half an hour, he sees Caroline leaving the hotel. She's carrying a bouquet of red roses.

'I'll be in this afternoon,' he tells Swincarron's secretary.

He sees Caroline's now out on the street.

The suspicion she's deceiving him prompts him to follow her through the snow. And there is someone else following her. In the direction of King's Cross and St Pancras.

19

He prides himself on being able to spot the legman a mile off.

The security service usually uses a minimum of four people for a street observation operation. An officer may have to stay put and wait in a car for many hours on end. Blending into the background, they may have to dress up or dress down, putting on clothes only to take them off quickly to change their appearance. More often than not it's a woman's job.

He's spotted the tail. The green weatherproof jacket. Lever. She was there when Caroline left the Malvern Hotel on foot. What's odd is that there's no team. No back-up vehicles. None of the usual features that suggest a well-organized operation. Just Lever.

When Rosslyn sees Caroline pass by the derelict building that was once the recreation club of the British Rail Staff Association, Lever's there on the street behind her. When she pauses briefly near the American Car Wash Company, Lever pauses too. Only the car wash and the car body repair workshops in the arches are open for business. Rosslyn catches the tang of spray paint, fibreglass and diesel fumes.

At the crossing of St Pancras Road and Goods-way, Rosslyn hangs back. Across the road, in vast white letters, is the painted legend that seems to be everywhere else on London's walls:

He sees Caroline is waiting for the traffic lights to change. So is Lever. Overhead, crossing one of the two iron-and-steel bridges, a train rumbles north, showering the road with grit and dirty ice fragments. Caroline turns her face aside in the direction of the massive Goodsway gasometers. The shallow-domed containers have sunk low, leaving the hollow iron skeletons looking curiously naked in the dirty mist. And Lever stays fifty yards, perhaps sixty, behind her.

Caroline turns left into Cheney Road and then left again into Battle Bridge Road, a cul-de-sac. In wasteland beyond a scrapyard, Rosslyn watches her lay the roses on the snow. Stepping back, she bows her head in prayer and for almost two minutes stands there motionless. At last, she looks up into the dull sky and sobs.

Lever follows her at a discreet distance back to King's Cross, where she goes into the Great Northern Hotel. Still following her, Rosslyn sees her sit at a table in the hotel's Coffee House. The Coffee

House is decked out for Christmas and the New Year. The neon display above a Millennial Calendar. The Coronation Street Lucky Numbers fruit machine flashes: 2000:2000:2000:2000:2000:2000:2000 – out of sync with the muzak, which is *Andrew Lloyd Webber's Millennial Hits*.

Rosslyn stands watching in the corridor. He sees Lever order a mug of hot chocolate. She settles down to watch the reflection of Caroline mirrored in the window facing the south-western entrances to King's Cross Station.

Lever wears a black cashmere sweater and white silk shirt. Her cheeks are a little flushed. She sits back with her pale blue eyes on the young American reflected in the window. Her long fingers remove traces of dry chocolate powder from the rim of the mug. Tearing open a paper pack of sugar, she's careful to leave the wrapper bearing the name of the hotel in the ashtray. The surveillance officer's habits die hard.

Rosslyn sees the sharp eyes focus on the reflection of the face that still bears the marks of recent tears. Caroline is writing a postcard.

A sound from outside makes Caroline turn her head and, for a moment, stop writing. It's the sound of amplified chanting outside in the station fore-court:

Trin-it-eee
Trin-it-eee
Three in one
One in three

He watches her turn her head. Eyes tightly closed, she's muttering something to herself. Perhaps she's praying. Suddenly she sits up straight, unpeels a roll of Sellotape and seems to stick something carefully to the postcard.

When she eventually calls for her bill Rosslyn notices that Lever's ready to leave. She's already settled her bill.

As Caroline approaches, Lever turns away to avoid her glance. The walking shoes look too heavy for her long and slender legs. Lever gathers up her green waxed coat and scarf from the chair beside her and leaves no tip.

Near a newspaper and magazine kiosk, Rosslyn sees Caroline is buying a postage stamp from the receptionist. She's asking the whereabouts of the nearest post box. The receptionist offers to mail the postcard for her. But Caroline rejects the offer. And the receptionist tells her where she can find a post box in the station. And that's the direction she takes when she leaves the hotel.

Suddenly he's lost sight of Lever. Perhaps she's lost her quarry. Perhaps, thinks Rosslyn, she's spotted me. There's no sign of her either on the icy pavement at the entrance to the Great Northern, with its doorman in his dark-blue and gold-braided overcoat scattering salted sand on the ice.

The wind whips frozen litter against the hotel's southern wall. A disused TV aerial wire flaps across the flickering neon sign GREAT NORTHERN HOTEL: glowing red. The words are barely visible in the dark mist. The clock on the tower of St Pancras chimes the time.

To his left, across the road, Rosslyn sees two police officers watching the small group of men and women chanting:

> *Trin-it-eee*
> *Trin-it-eee*
> *Three in one*
> *One in three*

A shaven-headed man dressed in a white blanket is thrusting pamphlets into the hands of people in a long queue for taxis. Each recipient is blessed with the sign. Three vertical strokes: | | |. Most of the morning travellers drop the pamphlets in the gutter.

A third police officer is giving directions to a tourist. When he peers across the street again he sees the figure dressed in white is fast approaching Lever. Presumably she's picked up Caroline on her way to find the post box.

'Only believe in Him,' he says. 'For according to his divine prophecy,' he announces with great conviction, 'He *will* come.' He thrusts a pamphlet into the legman's hand and smiles. 'Sister, do you believe in Him?'

Rosslyn can't hear Lever's answer.

'*His paradise will be created upon earth. As it is written —*'

Caroline hesitates at the post box. Before mailing the postcard she reads it over:

Dearest Caroline and Marcus
Thank you for last night.
For believing in me and promising to help me.
See what is stuck to this?
One of your hairs and two of mine.
One in Three. Three in One. I I I.
I am inordinately fond of you.
But I won't tell you.
I want to be with you soon.
My love —
Marcus and Caroline
X I X I X I.   ♡ ♡ ♡

Rosslyn next sees Lever emerging from the station. By now she's picked up Caroline's trail. And she's picked up pace, walking briskly northwards along St Pancras Road beneath a hoarding sponsored by British Airways: RING OUT THE OLD — THE 20TH. RING IN THE NEW — THE 21ST.

The last days of the century and everyone's a historian and a partygoer. Mostly the latter. Rosslyn, however, no longer believes in the history he was taught. *Nothing's going to change except the date.*

He closes up on Lever, who's following Caroline into the Old Church cemetery: past the icicles hanging from the painted notice HER MAJESTY'S ST PANCRAS CORONER'S COURT.

It is here that Rosslyn pushes his right hand beneath the hard right elbow and pushes it firmly leftward: 'I think it's time we had a chat, Ms Lever.'

The moment of recognition. One professional to another. The blue eyes do not blink. Her legs are slightly apart, the winter boots solid on the ground. 'Take your hand off me first and then we'll have a conversation.'

Rosslyn releases his grip.

Lever faces him. 'Since you seem to know my name, I'd like to know who *you* are.'

'We'll come to that,' says Rosslyn. 'Let's find somewhere else to talk.'

Lever's face is close to Rosslyn's. 'You'd better have a good reason for this.'

'And so had you,' he says.

'Well, let's get off the street for starters.'

20

Condensation on the café windows obscures the view of the St Pancras Road. The stained mirror catches the reflections of cheap lights flashing from the branches of the plastic Christmas tree. From the tape deck, above the hiss of a coffee-making machine, comes the Christmas song:

Who can know the reason for the season?
It's a happy celebration of His Love.

Rosslyn collects a mug of tea for himself from the Cypriot woman at the counter. Lever's asked for hot chocolate. Two sugars.

They face each other at the window table like a couple in a melancholy painting by Edward Hopper.

The ritual niceties over, Lever asks: 'Where did you get my name from?'

'Just about everybody I meet. Listen. I don't mind you following my client. Let's face it, she needs all the protection she can get. But I'm just curious as to why *you're* so curious about her. Since we're getting on to names, mine's Alan Rosslyn.'

Lever smiles. 'I know that, Mr Rosslyn. Customs. Investigation Division. '83 to '99. Now ASG.'

'And you're from –' says Rosslyn, '– Intelligence Operations and Resources. Home Office. Aka Box. MI5?'

'OK,' says Lever. 'You still haven't told me, though, what this is all about.'

'OK, I'll drop a name. And let's see what happens when you pick it up, all right?'

'Fire away.'

'Let's try Father Gian Maria Morandi and see what happens.'

'I'll say one thing for you –' She clears her throat softly. 'You certainly get about, Rosslyn.'

'That's what my clients pay me to do, isn't it?' he says. 'And guess what?'

'You tell me,' Lever says with half a smile.

'The priest told me he had a little visit from you,' says Rosslyn. 'And what's more, what you said to him worried him considerably.'

'It was meant to,' says Lever. 'Listen, you've been around long enough to know the game. Now, OK, I'll drop a name. And to quote a well-known phrase, let's see what happens when you pick it up. You dropped one. I'm going to drop two. Jane and Caroline Moorfield.' She waits for a moment. 'Caroline Moorfield is your client,' she continues. 'And Jane Moorfield, her sister, happens to be dead. I was at the inquest, along with a few other interested parties. So I heard what the forensic pathologist had to say, and the WPC who gave evidence. Then there was that man Luke, the one who identified the body.

I heard what he had to say for himself. He claimed that a card with his name on it was found on Jane Moorfield. And I was there when the coroner returned the verdict. Death by Misadventure. What do you think this adds up to, then?'

'It adds up to one very dissatisfied client of mine who thinks that someone, somewhere has got their sums slightly wrong. The priest suggested to me, in so many words, that this investigation ought to carry a health warning. Am I right or am I right?'

Lever tilts her hand just above the greasy surface of the table. The movement of a ship unsteady on the seas. Rosslyn notes that she's a nail biter. 'You mean – am I right or am I wrong?' she says, frowning.

'No, right. You had a go at recruiting Morandi, didn't you?' says Rosslyn.

'If he talks as much as that,' says Lever, 'I'm glad we didn't. But I don't want to get into things too much right now. This isn't really the time or place, is it?'

'Then what are you prepared to tell me?'

'That when I went to see Morandi in Geneva to lay it on the line, I wasn't trying to put the frighteners on him. I want him on my side, don't I?'

'You tell me.'

'Because, believe me, this is very heavy shit indeed. That if your client carries on in the same way as she's been doing so far, she's going to be right up to her neck in it. I know you won't welcome this . . . I think you and your client ought to sort out pretty quickly who's actually conducting this investigation of yours. I thought *she* was supposed to be paying *you* to do it. So what's she doing running around London like a cat on hot tiles? Let's say they get to her – I mean, let's say you have a dead client on your hands. That isn't going to look too good for business, is it? Don't say I haven't told you. I say again: you are looking at heavy shit. Street level. The priest must have filled you in on just how dangerous these Trinity people are. You'd think that everybody would be of like mind.'

'Aren't they, then?' says Rosslyn.

'The short answer to your question is no. The very people who should be interested aren't.'

'You mean someone's turning a blind eye?'

'I prefer not to believe it,' says Lever. 'But I keep on coming to that conclusion.'

'Got any names?'

'I don't want to start naming names,' says Lever. 'Not here. Why don't we have a meet on home ground?'

'Whose?' says Rosslyn.

'Mine.'

'Then you have got a rotten apple in the barrel, haven't you, Lever? Let's have it on the up and up, Lever. Do you know who this Luke is? I need to see him.'

'So what's stopping you?'

'He doesn't want to meet,' says Rosslyn.

'You know why not?'

'You tell me.'

'I could tell you. You'd better decide,' she says, 'whose bloody side your client's on.' The blue eyes are penetrating. 'And why the Americans are so interested in her. And you too, Rosslyn. They've been on to you since you first took her on.'

'Are you talking about Queron?'

She smiles. He sees the photograph of her in Queron's file.

'And you too, Lever. I've seen their photo of you. Who are *you* protecting? Is it Ahearne? Don't say you're one of the bloody followers of this crazy cult too.'

'I don't know who you're talking about.'

'Lever, please. Your Legal Adviser. I saw her photograph and her husband's. Along with yours in the CIA file.'

'They showed them to you?'

'No, they didn't show them to me. I took a look at them. While Queron was out of her office.'

'You expect me to believe that?'

The expression is severe, almost neutral. But he sees the mistrust in the blue eyes. She takes up her coat. 'Why not ask her where she spent last night? Check the hotel. I'm telling you, she's one woman who puts it about. Not that you'd think so to look at her, would you?'

He follows her to the door. 'What are you getting at?'

'Here –' She offers Rosslyn her card.

'I don't need it,' he tells her.

'You might,' she says, unfolding the copy of the *Independent*. 'Look at this one . . .'

Rosslyn looks:

news

Blind companion tells of killer who took 'angel'

Antony Hodgkin
Crime Correspondent

Cambridge must have seemed a haven of peace to sightless Jhong-Jha Tsien who fled North Korea five years ago. But yesterday her dream was shattered when her companion Dr Julia Llewellyn, a 60-year-old Theology Tutor at King's College, Cambridge, was brutally assaulted near Ely by a fighting dog.

Yesterday, Ms Tsien gave an emotional press conference, describing the moment she came face to face with the attacker and his dog.

'We had been for a walk in the fens and were returning to our car when I heard the dog,' she said.

At first, she thought the dog was playing games but became increasingly alarmed when she was separated from Dr Llewellyn who began to scream. Ms Tsien tried to strike the dog and its owner.

In broken English, she said: 'I was crouching. Trying to protect myself. I screamed: "What do you want? Stop it." '

Ms Tsien wept as she faced the press. She said she could feel the blood pouring from Dr Llewellyn's face and throat. She tried to grab the man but he escaped. It was more than two hours later when Ms Tsien was found on the Ely to Cambridge road.

Dr Llewellyn was admitted to Addenbrookes Hospital intensive care for emergency surgery, where a hospital spokesman said that it is unlikely doctors will be able to save the victim's sight.

The detective leading the inquiry into the attack, Detective Superintendent Nathalie Curtin, said there was still no clear motive for the attack. Det Supt Curtin said: 'We still don't know why it happened. The victim sustained terrible near-fatal injuries to her face, eyes and throat.'

Police say the man they are looking for was described as between 30 and 40. He speaks with a regional accent. A forensic scientist said the assault was most probably by a Pit Bull terrier.

Ms Tsien appealed to the public: 'At first chance, tell the police, inform the police, tell somebody. We don't know how many people the animal will maim or kill if the dog and owner are not caught by the police.'

Anyone with information should contact the police incident room on 0723-588588.

'Jane's tutor,' says Lever. 'You should stay even closer to Caroline Moorfield,' she says. 'And Luke. The friend. The one at the inquest. You want to know why? Because he's sleeping with her.'

'What the hell are you talking about?'

'You heard it here first. I'll be in touch with you, Rosslyn.' Then, putting her hand on his shoulder rather unexpectedly, she adds: 'You should cover your arse at ASG. We're going to be working on the same side. See if I'm not right. I'll be in touch.'

She steps out into the snow and is gone. And he's very late for his appointment with Swincarron across the frozen city. At Strand Chambers. Overlooking Trafalgar Square.

21

Freckled hand adjusting the position of the telephone beneath her chin, Swincarron tells Rosslyn: 'Pull up a chair, will you?'

He looks past her at the panoramic view of Trafalgar Square. Clear blue sky. The National Gallery. St Martin-in-the-Fields. Nelson's Column. The plume of white steam rising from a distant roof. He can feel the anger in the air.

'I won't be a second,' Swincarron says, jabbing a finger at the mouthpiece. 'Maxine, on the line from Washington.' She continues speaking on the telephone. 'Alan's here with me now, Maxine. Do you want to talk to him about the American problem yourself? . . . No? . . . Right, OK . . . Well, you'd better give me a number where I can reach you . . .' She scribbles the number on a notepad. 'We'll talk later. Thanks.' She sets down the telephone hard and turns to Rosslyn. 'Thanks for coming in, Alan.'

'My pleasure,' says Rosslyn. 'Do we have a problem?'

'Could be,' says Swincarron, deadpan and narrow-eyed. 'This client of yours, Caroline Moorfield – ' She's interrupted by Peter Alexander's arrival. He pads in noiselessly. Slowly takes a seat at an angle to Rosslyn.

'As you can imagine, Alan, as an ASG associate,' says Swincarron, searching for words carefully, '. . . from time to time we're asked by the Americans for the occasional favour. What we call the knight's move.' She reaches for a paperweight and moves it thus: ↑→ to make her point. 'You probably already know the Americans have been showing an interest in her sister's death. Am I right?'

'You mean the FBI and CIA?'

'How much do you know,' asks Alexander, 'about the exact extent of the American involvement?'

'Only,' says Rosslyn, 'that they asked some questions about Jane and one of her contacts with the Trinity Chapter. What exactly are you getting at?'

'We gather they questioned people,' says Swincarron, too smoothly. 'They interviewed people who knew Jane Moorfield in Massachusetts, didn't they?'

'As far as I know, it all seemed to have come to nothing.'

'Well actually, it's come to something,' says Swincarron. 'According to Maxine.' She reaches behind her for the warmth of the radiator. The freckled knuckles are white. 'What would you feel about calling it a day?'

This is goodbye.

'You mean the investigation?' asks Rosslyn. 'Or my job?'

'Just the former, Alan,' says Swincarron. 'The investigation. I mean, as far as Caroline Moorfield's concerned. Suppose you tell her we'll waive our fees. Call it a day. What would you feel about it?'

'I'd be letting her down badly.'

'You would?' asks Alexander as if he has a bad taste in his mouth. 'I mean, if you don't mind me asking, are you a little fond of her?'

Rosslyn's silence seems to be assent.

Swincarron leans back in her chair. 'Oh, I think she'd get over that,' she says with a weary sneer. She could be talking about the dismissal of a junior assistant. 'You wouldn't need to go into too many details with her about it, would you? But, as it were, professionally – let's say from the professional point of view – you could say that we don't really have the resources and expertise to continue effectively any longer. That something else rather important has cropped up. Let's say, you have to leave for the Emirates at short notice. Something along those lines. The call of duty.'

'If you're telling me that my arrangement with her is over,' says Rosslyn, 'then I'd prefer to tell her the truth. That's only fair, isn't it?'

Swincarron does not wait for a reply. 'The truth is, Alan,' she says, 'that we aren't in a position to have the inquest reopened, are we? Even if we wanted to. At the end of the day, the wiser course of action is for Caroline Moorfield to leave this little can of worms unopened. Naturally, it's up to you. But we want to know what you'd feel about taking that sort of line with her?'

'I've told you. To be honest. I'd feel I wasn't being straight or fair towards her.'

'Honesty is one thing, Alan,' says Swincarron very sharply. 'Reality quite another.'

'Except the truth is that I genuinely believe she has a case.'

'By which you mean – am I right? – that you think her sister was murdered?'

'Let's say I don't think,' says Rosslyn, 'that she died in the way claimed at the inquest.'

'And that is a view,' says Swincarron, 'which appears to be creating some awkwardness between us and other interested parties.'

'Like *which* other parties?' asks Rosslyn. '*Who* are you talking about? The Trinity Chapter?'

'Of course, the Trinity Chapter may enter into the equation,' says Swincarron with a detached, almost academic tone. 'But that isn't something we need to worry about at ASG.'

'What else is worrying you?'

'Our friends at Vauxhall Cross,' says Swincarron. 'They're none too happy, Alan. Neither is Thames House. They don't like your investigation. That's the sum total. Bottom line.'

'Enough to say that it's too close to some other unpleasantness that's arisen,' says Alexander.

'Which is what?' asks Rosslyn.

'Something with an American dimension,' says Swincarron.

'You mean the CIA. Is that what Maxine's telling you?'

'Infer what you will,' says Swincarron. 'That's what I was generally talking to Maxine about in Washington, among other things. Her friends in Washington have suggested to her, in a perfectly friendly way, that the investigation be, say, shelved.'

The secretary opens the door as if upon a prearranged signal that the meeting should be closed.

'Shelved, Alan,' says Swincarron. '*Finito*.'

'Your appointment at Kensington Palace,' says the secretary.

'Time to go, Alan,' says Alexander, getting to his feet. 'It's as easy as that. No hard feelings?'

Rosslyn doesn't budge. 'Who's this come from in Washington?' he asks.

There's an awkward pause. The door is open and the secretary has other staff in her office. It's clear that neither Swincarron nor Alexander want the debate to be overheard. 'This whole thing could wreck this firm,' says Rosslyn for the benefit of the people in the outer office.

'We can't expect Maxine to name names, Alan,' says Swincarron. 'You've been around long enough to know she can't do that. Things have a way of developing in a way one can't always foresee. At the end of the day, one name leads to another and so forth. Doors open. Doors close.'

'You won't name names then?' asks Rosslyn.

'Obviously not,' replies Swincarron. 'Not that I know them anyway.'

'Maxine knows them then?' asks Rosslyn.

'Absolutely none that would assist your client's case,' says Swincarron.

'We're talking deals then?' says Rosslyn. 'Why don't you close the door? Let's get this finished with here and now.' Alexander closes the door, giving the staff outside an embarrassed smile. 'You've struck a deal,' says Rosslyn. 'Is that it? And you can't tell me about it?'

Swincarron leans forward to the paperweight and moves it again. This time in the reverse direction: ↓. 'I'm simply passing on Maxine's considered advice. And at the same time asking you to do the wise thing.'

'Even if you leave me out of this,' says Rosslyn, 'Caroline Moorfield certainly isn't giving up on this. She's convinced that the verdict on her sister is wrong. She believes that with total conviction. Despite the fact that she's already been warned that someone may have a go at her, I know she'll continue.'

'Quite,' says Swincarron.

'Then tell me,' says Rosslyn. 'Tell me why the CIA and our people want us to get our noses out. I'm talking Vauxhall Cross and Thames House.'

'If I could expand I would,' says Swincarron. 'Nothing would please me more than to set your mind at rest, Alan. Believe me. But I can't. I'm happy to say I don't know enough about their reasons.'

'Because it's a joint CIA-MI6-MI5 objection?' says Rosslyn harshly. 'I don't want to have to ask you this, but is someone trying to buy our silence?'

Swincarron smiles. Large teeth. Expensive orthodontics. The bright cosmetic smile. The gambler's. Whether it means yes or no, Rosslyn can't be sure.

'You've put your finger on it,' she says. 'We thought you might. This is sunset time. Happy hour. You can indeed infer that a deal's been struck. We're reliably informed that the Trinity Chapter, whatever it may be, this cult your client's sister was researching, is simply a benign kind of freemasonry with global intent, nothing worse –'

'It's a hell of a lot worse,' Rosslyn interrupts. 'Are you really expecting me to believe this? Listen, I've seen the evidence. I've listened to the one man who knows more about the cult than anyone else. Morandi in Geneva. I've listened to others.' He thinks of Lever but doesn't mention her. Thinks of Queron. Doesn't mention her either. 'Let me tell you,' he says, 'there's nothing benign about the Trinity Chapter, its followers or anyone who sympathizes with it –'

'If you'd let me finish,' interrupts Swincarron, her eyes down. When faced with trouble she usually makes out she's the one being interrupted when it's the other way round. 'I can sympathize with your misgivings. Maxine has explained the situation to us. *Her word is the word*. No more needs to be said.' She's restless. 'Maxine has explained.'

Has she just? thinks Rosslyn.

'But remember these misgivings of yours can only be based upon hearsay,' says Swincarron, raising her voice. 'Upon what your client's told you. As I understand it, she says her sister would never have used drugs. But I don't think you'd *ever* find a judge who'd admit that as evidence.'

'You're asking me to turn the blind eye?'

'Not to tread on toes unnecessarily,' says Swincarron.

'And the same applies to the Trinity Chapter?' Rosslyn asks. 'Its membership is secret, isn't it. Why? Because it was clear enough to Jane Moorfield, as it is to Morandi, that more than one high-profile player is – running scared.'

'What is it, do you suppose, these people are actually so scared *of*, Alan?' Alexander asks.

'Exposure, what else?' says Rosslyn. 'Illegal currency dealings. That's only part of it.'

'I thought the line is that they are relatively innocuous?' says Swincarron, shaking her head. 'They'd argue that they're being persecuted because their ideas aren't in the mainstream.'

'Persecuted? Come on, who by?'

'By the media. All of whom claim that the Second Coming, the resurrection of its leader, is simply a massive con trick.'

'Listen,' Rosslyn says. 'These people don't have the slightest doubt that, call it what you will, this resurrection of Trinity will take place when and where he prophesied. They see the rest of us as trying to stop what they want. They see everyone's hand against them.'

'Alan,' says Alexander, 'don't tell me —'

'That I sympathize with it?' Rosslyn says quickly. 'For God's sake, of course I don't . . . What I can't seem to get through to you two is that these people are fanatics, that they don't deserve protection. That they're making a mockery of free speech and the right to demonstrate. That come the Millennium, New Year's Eve, New Year's Day, there'll be a bloodbath.'

'Oh Alan,' says Swincarron, 'please —'

'There's no *please* about it. You're telling me that I should back off from helping Caroline Moorfield. For what reason?'

'I'll tell you.'

'No,' says Alexander loudly, 'I'll tell you —'

'Because someone,' says Rosslyn, talking over him, 'Maxine maybe, has struck a deal with law enforcement agencies in America and God knows who else besides here. MI6. MI5.'

'So what exactly is wrong with that?' asks Swincarron, very quietly, her voice dropping almost to a whisper. 'You seem, Alan, to have extraordinarily strong feelings about it.'

Rosslyn clears his throat. 'I have. Let's face it, the

track record of our friends here and abroad doesn't exactly inspire confidence. When did they ever stop a president being assassinated? The list is bloody endless. So whose arse is being covered? I'm not saying there aren't certain jobs they can do, and do well. But look at Waco! A total miscalculation. I can't believe that there's anyone in the CIA or FBI who knows about the fanatical religious mentality as it applies in this case.'

'The word to us,' says Swincarron, 'is "Don't enter the yellow box unless there's a free exit." Do you follow me, Alan?'

He remains silent a short while, apparently considering this *apologia*.

At last Alexander says: 'My mother's family is familiar with persecution, Alan.'

This is going some, thinks Rosslyn. 'Then do you believe in this so-called persecution of the Trinity Chapter?' he asks.

Arms crossed tightly across her chest, Swincarron says: 'We believe in the importance of our work, Alan. *Our* work. When necessary, we believe in supporting our American friends to the hilt. Life, as it were, is a matter of wisely and very reasonably considering all sides of the question.'

'Then tell me,' asks Rosslyn, 'why don't the London CIA people have a word with Caroline? Why don't they sit her down and explain whatever situation's preventing them from being so wise and reasonable?'

'Because,' says Swincarron quietly, 'they say that if they were to put the matter to Caroline, or have me, you, or anyone else do so, they'd be acting unlawfully.'

'And will the Americans tell *me* the same thing?' asks Rosslyn.

'If you want to know,' says Alexander, 'they've asked us, I quote, "to ensure that she terminates her enquiries as of now". Full stop.'

'If I do what you ask,' Rosslyn says. 'If I and my client abandon our investigation, can you guarantee, with any degree of certainty, that my client's life will no longer be in danger? Can you *guarantee* her safety?'

'In so far as we can guarantee anything,' says Swincarron.

'That's not good enough,' says Rosslyn. 'I'm not saying I'll tell her to clear off back to Massachusetts; in any case, not before I've talked it over with her.'

'What you're saying, Alan,' says Swincarron, turning nasty, 'is that you're not prepared to accept our word.'

'Not as far as my client's safety is concerned. What you say that the CIA and FBI have asked you to do, I can't prove one way or the other. But I know enough to realize that unless I stay very close to my client she could be at serious risk.'

'And this is on the basis of what the priest Morandi told you in Geneva?'

'Yes,' says Rosslyn. 'And other things besides.'

There's a long silence.

And then Swincarron continues: 'I had hoped that this meeting would've helped clear up a few basic misunderstandings, Alan, and that you'd see our point of view. Alas, if anything, it's served to indicate to me at least that we're very close to a parting of the ways.' She turns to Alexander. 'What do you think, Peter?'

Alexander threads his fingers. 'I have to agree, Ruth.' He looks directly at Rosslyn. 'Obviously, I'd like you to reconsider your position. When you joined us I looked forward to a long and fruitful working relationship. But as Ruth has pointed out, our priority, and I'd hoped yours too, is first and last the future of ASG. It's perfectly clear that you're unhappy to accept our decision in this matter.'

'And,' says Swincarron with finality, 'I have to say that, however disappointing it is to us, it's final. Now I really must go. Kensington Palace.'

Rosslyn gets to his feet.

'There's nothing more to say, is there?' He stands erect. 'I'll clear my desk.'

'Regard this as a temporary suspension, Alan,' says Swincarron. 'The cooling-off period. The better to give you time to reconsider your position with us. We can't afford to rock the boat, can we? So no more Caroline Moorfield. End of story.'

It seems a border's been crossed. The barrier lowered. Shut behind him. Once again, he's out in no man's land. Where the normal rules don't apply. Dog eat dog. And these seem rabid. Hungry in the cold.

22

And so at the rising of the sun we will remember them. One world. One people. One true way. The One One One.

In exile we are Divine. Remember the dead. Nurture the dying. Celebrate Life with all your heart and all your soul.
  – Trinity, *The Divine Testament*, London, 1996

Across the frozen border of France with Belgium, Morgon Wroth drives past the statue in the town centre of Adinkerke. The concrete and bronze celebratory image of the town's contribution to the defeat of Hitler. The image of paranoia, the suspicious little Belgian pushing his bicycle has a sack over his shoulder. Belgians, like Czechs, have kept their reputations as the world's greatest smugglers intact. The statue is covered in snow in the blue-grey light of approaching night.

On past the statue, heading out of town, he passes the rows of tobacco stores announcing the latest cut prices on pavement blackboards. £1.90 for a 50 gm wallet of Golden Virginia retailing in the UK for £7.50. These light and compact wallets are sold in cartons of a hundred. Wroth calculates the profit he could make as a tobacco bootlegger. But this is for the small fry. The Brits who've filled their cars with cheap wine in Calais, themselves with cheap beer for Dutch courage and, by the time they've reached Belgium, need to relieve themselves in the gutter. None of them heed the signs in English: PLEASE USE THE TOILET INSIDE!!

The windswept northern coast road is deserted. Wroth's wrist watch is synchronized with the Czech's. Karel Zieleniec from DV Militar, who's driven here from Plzen.

Wroth, outwitter of the authorities, who loves to score one and maybe more against the world he owes no favours, feels the euphoria of the undercover man. His euphoria is tinged, however, with a sense of anxiety. Dr Van Rijn has told him to be wary of a man called Rosslyn. 'Rosslyn knows the territory,' he's warned, 'the former Senior Investigations Officer of Customs and Excise with Alexander Swincarron Gertler. The threat we will have to face. He will know of DV Militar and Zieleniec. Tell the Czech to be wary of questions being asked back in Plzen.'

He sees Zieleniec's Saab parked by the deserted roadside beneath some poplars. A quarter of a mile distant, Wroth raises and lowers the beams of his car's headlights. In response Zieleniec's lights flash twice. The road is clear.

Within two minutes the packs of high explosive are handed over. The sterling passed. And Wroth tells the Czech to keep his ears open for questions being asked by the man Rosslyn. Zieleniec seems more interested in counting the packs of £50 notes.

He mutters something about wanting to get to Paris later in the night.

No words of thanks, no handshakes are proffered by either man.

Best say nothing when you smell danger.

Eyes narrowed, the Czech glances at the deserted road for any approaching cars, then back at Wroth's massive hands secreting the packs of high explosive in four different places beneath the seats above the chassis. He doesn't bother to wipe the grease from his huge fingers tapered like the claws of a bear.

The two cars drive away in opposite directions. The snow on the wind obliterates the tracks.

Wroth watches in his driving mirror as the Saab's red tail lights vanish. Acid rises in his throat. He feels the familiar spasms of hate twist his stomach. Signs of the impurities he despises.

This Caroline. The sick interference. This Rosslyn you've crawled to for help. The role of this sick ASG. Nothing more or less than a terrible betrayal.

He longs to see P & J clamp its jaws into Caroline's face.

Heading south for Calais and the ferry, he flicks through the radio frequencies and settles back to listen to a BBC talk programme that advises him on the road conditions in the south-east of England. The shipping forecast tells him that the sea in the Dover area is calm.

Then he inserts a tape cassette. One of Dr Van Rijn's. Holy music this, to stir the blood. Mahler's Symphony No 2, 'Resurrection':

> *Auferstehn, ja auferstehn wirst du,*
> *Mein Staub, nach kurzter Ruh!*
> *Unsterblich Leben! Unsterblich Leben*
> *Will der dich rief dir geben.**

with the voice of the Master dubbed over it.

> *When I walked amongst the deluded souls,*
> *And there's a pleasure in being mad,*
> *Which none but madmen know!*
> *Speak Byron: Love watching madness with*
> * unalterable mien.*
> *Cry Milton: Demoniac frenzy, moping melancholy,*
> *And moon-struck madness.*
> *Howl Shakespeare: Make mad the guilty, and*
> * appal the free!*

He smiles. Ejects the Mahler tape. Back to the radio.

Good: the voice from the radio tells him there's a work to rule of Customs officers at Dover.

He looks at his filthy hands. They feel sticky against the steering wheel. They don't fit the image of the military man in his dark-blue blazer with shining regimental buttons. His great black shoes

---

* Rise up, yes, you will rise up, / My dust, after short rest! /
  Immortal life! Immortal life / He who called you will give you.

polished so highly he can count his teeth in the reflection of the toecaps. The tweed country cap pulled low across his low blunt forehead.

The state of his hands decides him to stop off in Calais for a few Carlsbergs and chips. He has a lot to thank the whinging Customs officers for. A lot to celebrate when he gets home again to bloody Blighty and P & J.

On the outskirts of Calais, the Prime Minister's voice speaks to him from the radio. The tone of intimacy. The yearning to be loved: *Looking Forward. Born again. New Britain. The Millennial Heartland. The Fresh Face of Youth and Creativity. New Dome . . . The world, I mean, is looking at Britain. You know. I mean. Ours is a once-in-a-lifetime chance to reshape the world's view of Britain.*

Great words. Great man. 'Not your once-in-a-lifetime chance, boyo,' he says, aiming the tip of his boot at a crouching seagull. 'Mine,' he spits.

Adjusting the earphones of his Walkman, he presses PLAY to listen to his private anthem:

> *I will survive*
> *I've got all my love to live*
> *I've got all my love to give*
> *I will survive*

23

I left the roses in the snow. And after I'd said a prayer for you I came back here, and now, in front of me on the table, I have the cardboard box containing the urn with your ashes in it. My left hand is on the box. On you. When this is all over, I'm going to bring you home. Marcus will help us.

I called Father Scott in Vernon Hills. Wished him Happy Christmas. I told him that I'm bringing you home. He said I'd made the right decision. I asked him if those CIA and FBI people had called – if they'd found out anything. He said he hadn't heard again from them.

I've called Marcus but he's not there. And he isn't returning my calls.

– CAROLINE MOORFIELD, JOURNAL, LONDON, 1999

For the third time at his flat that night, Caroline tells him: 'It's my fault. Llewellyn can't see. Can't talk. It's terrible, Alan. Terrible. And things run in threes. Jane. Llewellyn. Now you.'

And once again he tells her: 'It isn't your fault they've suspended me.'

She's sitting cross-legged on the rug before the wood fire. 'Yeah. But it's so *unfair*.' She opens the steel door to the fire. 'Tell me, Alan, do you ever burn this thing?'

He sits at the table. Toying with a cup of coffee, he smiles quizzically. 'No, I don't light it. It's hard to find the right wood.'

'Pity,' she says, looking up at him. 'I like the smell of burning logs, don't you?' She wraps her arms across her chest. 'It's all so *unfair* . . .'

'Not on me,' he says. 'Unfair on you, Caroline. There's a whole lot of business left unfinished. Think of Llewellyn. Mine's only a job.'

'There must be plenty of other firms like ASG who'll give you one.'

His eyes hold hers: 'But yours isn't finished yet, is it?' He's prepared dinner for two. Pot roasted chicken stuffed with nuts, parsley, marjoram, rosemary, egg, lemon and grated parmesan. Seems to have overdone the cinnamon, ginger and nutmeg. If Caroline notices that the sweet-sour spiciness is a bit too much, she doesn't say. There are candles on the table and the large bouquet of flowers she's brought is in a vase. 'I can easily find someone who'll take me on,' he says. 'Come and sit down.'

She gets to her feet agilely. 'I've caused you too much trouble already,' she says. 'Anyway, I'll have to go home soon.' She watches the reaction but can't read it. 'What are you going to do, Alan?'

'That's up to you.'

'I think it's up to you.' The eyes hold his.

'In that case you're right, Caroline. You're well out of it.'

'Well out of what?'

The ingenuousness of the question surprises him. *Do you know what you're playing with?* He manages the uneasy smile. 'Trinity. Morandi. Now Lever. It's heavy shit. And Jane was right, wasn't she? You wouldn't want to be around when the trouble starts. *I'm serious.'*

Over the rest of the dinner by candlelight.

'Do you really believe in this Resurrection?' she asks, toying with the wineglass.

'If I did, we wouldn't be here now, you and I together.' He brings the *zabaglione* to the table. She says it's her favourite dessert.

'No,' he continues, 'Trinity, whoever he may have been, isn't going to leave any kind of mark like that. Oh no. I wouldn't worry about the crap they *believe* in. I'd worry more about what they'll *do*.'

'So what do you really think that is?'

'What they'll *do*? They'll leave his mark with murder.'

'But, Alan, *why*?'

'Out of fear.'

'Fear of *what*?'

'Of failure. Of mockery. Out of hatred for all those who hold them in contempt. Like all the ones who've gone before. Waco. Solar Church. Aum. Heaven's Gate. The easiest way for the megalomaniac to write himself into history overnight is with a bloodbath. In full public view.'

'Is that what Lever's lot believe?'

'Well, she's been taking you seriously, hasn't she? And Jane too. If the security services are taking the threat seriously then there must be some head-searching going on behind closed doors. About who these big shots are who've supported Trinity. About where the funds have gone too, maybe. Most of all, if they turn violent, about what to do to protect people on the night of 31 December. In the first minute of the first hour of the first day of the Millennium. And that's one very good reason why you're wise to be getting the hell out of London.'

'I don't believe anything bad will *really* happen,' she says. She asks again: 'What are you going to do, Alan?'

'See what Lever has to tell me.'

'Will they pay you?' she asks him.

'For doing what?'

'For whatever it is they want from you?'

'I don't know yet what it is they want from me.'

She notices the new tone of bitterness. 'But does it have something to do with Jane,' she asks. 'With me?'

'What else?'

'And Morandi too?'

'I'm pretty sure,' he says. 'Morandi too.'

'Jesus, I'm sorry I've landed you in such shit.'

'You weren't to know. I'm the one who should be sorry. I've sort of let you down. I believe Jane was murdered. I think you have it right. And this is what surprises me about you. That you're not playing ball.'

'*Excuse me?*'

'That you have your own agenda. Come on, Caroline, you have to be open with me.'

[215]

'About what?'

'Marcus Luke.'

'Yeah, Marcus. Oh, what do you want to know? I saw him last evening –'

'And what?'

'And I just wanted to hear from him about Jane. Listen, she was my sister, Alan. I have a right to ask people about her. On my own. It's important to me. You may not like it, Alan. But it's important to me. You have to understand. So let's not talk about it, OK?'

'Why not?'

'Because it was my decision to see him. And because it's my decision, I can change my mind about anything I like. You didn't make up my mind for me. I made it up on my own. Without you. I decided to see him. And it doesn't mean anything. Nothing happened.'

'Maybe you should've talked it over with me first.'

'Maybe,' she says.

'No matter. I think you're right. But I wouldn't like to think I was responsible for something terrible happening to you. Maybe you should take her ashes and go on home.'

Keeping his eyes on hers, Rosslyn smiles.

And she's certain he doesn't mean what he's just said.

'What will you do at home alone,' he asks, 'in, where is it, Vernon Hills?'

'You know where I live, Alan.' She turns away from his smile. Stares at the screen that obscures the view of his bedroom.

The woman in a kimono is watching a couple lovemaking in a Yoshiwara house. The naked woman beneath the naked man on the tatami mat has her legs wound round his back. The eighteenth-century *ukiyo-e* woodblock print by Koryusai.

'If I told you, Alan, you wouldn't believe it anyway.'

'How do you know I wouldn't?'

'Because –'

'You're hiding something, Caroline . . .'

'Do you know what I'm thinking?' She folds and unfolds the table napkin on her lap. 'Why don't you, just the once, call me Caro?'

'Caro,' he says.

When the candles have burned low.

She points to the card on the mantelpiece. The reminder of Rosslyn's Mary. The 1994 Valentine she sent to him. Five years on and the ink has faded.

> *Freedom's just another word*
> *For nothing left to lose*
> *Kris Kristofferson*

10 million people might like to come home to somebody
What about you to me before 2000?

♡ XXX

'I guess that's her handwriting,' she says. There's the hint of resentment, something defensive about the way that 'her' comes out. And to compound the tone she adds: 'I have to tell you Kristofferson's a better actor than a singer. And Rita Coolidge is a better singer than Kristofferson. Do you know that Rita can conduct a choir?'

'Well, I've never thought as much of his philosophy as Mary did. But I like the card. And I like Coolidge.'

'I thought you'd like the London Symphony Orchestra,' she says. 'From 1997. Here.' She takes the CD from her jacket pocket. 'Play this, Alan. Band two. But that isn't all I'm thinking, Alan.'

He plays band two on the hi-fi. She sings along with her own version of the lyric in voice resembling Sarah Brightman's:

> *Just Show Me How to Love You*
> *E ci ridiamo su*
> *gabbiano di scogliera*
> *ma dov'eri nascosto'*
> *dov'eri finora?*

'Tell me then –'

'Alan, I want to pay whatever fees ASG would've got to you. I want you to go on until you find out who murdered Jane and exactly why. I need to know that.'

He's about to speak but she raises her hand. 'I know the risks. To you. To me even.' She reaches across the table for his hand. 'There's a lot else besides I have to tell you.'

He follows her gaze to the screen.

The woman beneath the man on the tatami mat with her legs wound round his back.

'Those two look so happy. And the woman watching, well, I guess she must look a bit like her. Out of respect *E ci ridiamo su / gabbiano di scogliera. Can't you show me*? I can't ask you, can I?'

'What can't you ask me, Caro?'

She kisses him on the mouth. 'Can I stay the night?'

Kneeling in front of the hi-fi, he puts band two on repeat:

> *Just Show Me How to Love You*
> *E ci ridiamo su*
> *gabbiano di scogliera*
> *ma dov'eri nascosto'*
> *dov'eri finora?*

THAMES HOUSE
Millbank
London SW1P 1AE

Top Secret Eyes Only
Director General
Thames House
Millbank
London
SW1P 1AE   *date as signed*

Dear Director General

<u>Holy Ghost</u>

I enclose the Report of the Review of Security as it
relates both to the Service and the perceived threat
from the Trinity Chapter with special reference to
the period 31 December 1999 and 1 January 2000.

I have interpreted the terms of reference widely,
which you encouraged me to do, in order to provide as
comprehensive a picture as possible of the many areas
that could affect security.

I have been at pains to ensure fairness to those who
might feel personally criticized in this report.
Individuals have been named. None has been presented
with any part of this report and none has been given
the opportunity to challenge factual accuracy. The
procedures I have adopted closely follow agreed
Security Service rules. Such procedures have
touched as high as Legal Adviser's Office level,
illustrating that I have endeavoured to identify
where responsibilities have ultimately reached and
where the criticism stops. Of my recommendations
(see Appendix M), in my view, only 12 carry a cost tag.

However, I feel that where additional costs are incurred these are essential for the preservation of Law and Order during the period 31 December 1999 and I January 2000.

I have been put under no pressure from political or religious groups or any security service department to slant this Report or its recommendations in any particular direction.

W. Lever
Intelligence Resources and Operations

Copy: Top Secret Eyes Only Secretary of State for the Home Office

24

In the early hours, in Lever's presence, the Home Secretary says to the Director General of MI5: 'I wish I'd never heard this.'

The DG's dark-complexioned face is simian. The pungent odour of mouthwash hangs about him. His and the Home Secretary's weariness contrast with Lever's energy. The hound sniffing blood.

The windows of the DG's office in Thames House offer a grand view of the river. But now, illuminated by the lights shining from the Thames House windows, the December fog outside seems like a massive floating wall of white.

On the side table, next to copies of *Hansard* and *Who's Who*, there are framed photographs of the DG's wife and children on holiday in Tuscany. On the far wall, lit by ceiling spotlights, is the large-scale map of the British Isles next to the recent photograph of Her Majesty the Queen.

Open on the desk, marked TOP SECRET EYES ONLY DIRECTOR GENERAL is the report entitled HOLY GHOST.

The DG's personal assistant brings coffee and biscuits for two. A paper mug of hot chocolate for Lever.

The long night has left the DG and the Home Secretary in bad humour. The air is stale. Several hours have passed since he finished reading Lever's report, whose stated purpose is: 'To identify the practical clandestine means of sequestering funds adopted by the extremist religious sect or cult, Trinity Chapter.'

Lever has several times heard the DG telling his apparently exasperated wife on the telephone that he has absolutely no idea when he'll be home.

Twice, with his usual air of icy detachment, the Home Secretary has wiped the lens of his glasses with a tissue, asking: 'Are we perfectly sure this record of illegal sequestration will stand up to the inquiry I'll inevitably have to establish?'

And twice Lever has drawn his attention to the technicalities in the paragraph that points the finger at the guilty. 'The detailed evidence is in Appendix B, Minister. The basic allegation's in Paragraph One/One. Look, it's down there in black and white, sir. In front of you.'

1.1 Throughout October and November last, Alexander Swincarron Gertler Ltd (ASG) in association with Leman Nassaueur Brady, Solicitors, were commissioned by the Van Rijn Clinic to transfer funds from the Turkish National Bank, the Agricultural Bank of Greece, and First City Bank (UK) to an intermediary and Swiss resident, Dr Katrina Farenkampf, at 49/H Anwand

Strasse, Zurich, Switzerland, for electronic transfer *within* Switzerland to Schweizerische Bankgesellschaft (Union Bank of Switzerland), Woll und Landau Bank and Schweizerischer Bankverein (the Swiss Bank Corporation).

'And there's the total,' says Lever. 'In One/Two.'

1.2 Further transfers were made to the latter's branch in Le Locle. During the above period total deposits were made in excess of US$18.5 million.

'Who will confirm the transfer process for us?' the Home Secretary asks, hoping perhaps that no one will.

'Dr Alois Bloch of the Swiss Bankers' Association,' says Lever.

'And he will confirm the beneficiary's name?'

'Yes,' says Lever. 'See Paragraph One/Three.'

1.3 The beneficiary of these illicit transactions is Dr Van Rijn.

The Home Secretary repeats the name: 'Van Rijn. *Van Rijn*. You say his whereabouts are "presently unknown"?'

'Yes. He was last heard of in Belgium. The Belgians don't know his whereabouts.'

The DG turns through the pages of the typescript. 'But you say that you saw his assistant, the man Luke, at the inquest into the Moorfield woman's death?'

'I saw him, yes.'

'And you say –' The DG finds another page with its corner turned down sharply. '– that the Harley Street practice has been closed?'

'That's correct. It has been closed, yes.'

'And that absolutely no records of the financial dealings were found?'

'None.'

The Home Secretary sips the foul coffee. 'And absolutely no evidence of a conspiracy to commit violence on 31 December?'

'None that constitutes proof.'

'That's what concerns me.'

'And that this temporary assistant of his, Luke, is a psychiatric nurse?' asks the DG.

'Yes.'

And still the Home Secretary seeks to shoot holes in Lever's argument.

'Wouldn't you agree with me, Ms Lever, that it could be said you're standing on some pretty thin ice?'

'*Standing on thin ice*, Minister?' says Lever. She is possessed of an unnatural calm, and only the veins in her temples betray her inner anger. 'With respect, sir, I'd say we're all on thin ice. And we're not the only ones.'

'We'll come to that again shortly,' says the DG. His weariness and anger seem to have forced him to drop the mask of innocent regret. And though his mind is reputed to be as sharp as a scalpel, it's

Paragraph One/Four that seems to blunt it:

1.4 The evidence contained in this Report reveals the complicity in these transactions of MRS VIRGINIA AHEARNE, CBE: LEGAL ADVISER MI5 and her husband, MR EDWARD AHEARNE.

Their association with this extremist cult is considered to be contrary to the interest of the security service and ultimately damaging to the security of the national interest.

'Tell me, Ms Lever,' the Home Secretary says, a passing look of hurt in his eyes. 'I hope you won't object to my asking a personal question.'

'Go ahead, sir.'

'It might be asked what really lies behind your determination to prove these charges of impropriety against the Legal Adviser. I want to be quite sure it's nothing personal.'

'I have no personal interest in her,' says Lever. 'I was asked to contribute, I quote, a "report of the Review of Security as it relates both to the Service and the perceived threat to law and order from extremist factions in connection with the period 31 December 1999 and 1 January 2000".' She looks into the DG's eyes. 'You asked me to write it, sir.'

The DG turns to the Secretary of State. 'And you, sir, you asked me to provide it as a matter of urgency. Why, because the Commissioner of Police –'

The Home Secretary interrupts. 'I know what you're saying.' He doesn't blink. His eyes seem to be boring into Lever's head: 'There's no need to keep on reminding me. This recommendation of yours, that Mrs Ahearne and her husband, Edward Ahearne, be interviewed as soon as possible –'

'I suggest you have no alternative, sir.'

Lever's insistence engenders a look of abject defeat in the DG's face.

'It may very well be the case,' says the Home Secretary. 'But is it really practicable?' He reads aloud from Lever's report:

> It is desirable for this interview to be undertaken by a senior security officer with the co-operation and assistance of a second party assessor from outside either the security services (including SIS) or the Special Branch or any Metropolitan Police branch. A recommendation for the immediate appointment of such an officer is made in Appendix N.

'This man Rosslyn . . .'

'His CV, sir, is attached in Appendix T.'

The DG says dismissively: 'It's all very well on paper. He's an outsider.'

'We've worked with him in the past,' says Lever. 'He's about the finest interrogator I've come across. Fair. Totally dependable.'

'Except he's no longer with Customs,' says the Home Secretary. And Lever detects a flicker of a smile at the corner of the minister's dry lips.

'He's still subject to the provisions of the Act,'

Lever suggests by way of a recommendation.

'What else?' asks the Home Secretary, playing devil's advocate. 'Don't tell me he has a personal agenda too?'

'Not that I know of.'

The Home Secretary turns to the DG: 'Then why are you so cagey about him?'

'Because you asked me what I think, Minister. And I've told you, sir. I only know of him professionally. What's down on paper here. Customs Investigation Division. Drugs Financial Investigation Branch. Arms and Explosives. Indecent and Obscene Material. Surveillance and Undercover Operations Liaison with us.'

'What else do you need from me?' asks the Home Secretary.

'Your approval, sir,' says Lever. 'Your say-so to use him.'

'Whilst not admitting to it outside the service,' says the DG, 'we have to draw him close.'

'You do?'

'Because he knows too much.'

The Home Secretary pauses a moment to reflect. 'I see. So be it. I also see, to quote: "In January 1999, he joined Alexander Swincarron Gertler Limited as an Associate."'

'And what you don't know is that they've suspended him,' says Lever.

'Why?' asks the Home Secretary. 'For what?'

'Because he won't give up on a client of his,' says

the DG. 'A woman whose sister's death may have been the Trinity Chapter's responsibility.'

'Is that what the police think?' asks the Home Secretary.

'No. They're not involved. A verdict of Death by Misadventure was returned. Connected with drug abuse.'

'Very well,' says the Home Secretary. 'It's *your* recommendation, Lever.'

'But it needs your approval, sir.'

The Home Secretary gives a sigh of impatience. 'I have to say it'll be *your* responsibility. You're the one, as you're so fond of saying, who's put it down in black and white.' He turns to Lever. 'And do you really recommend him?'

'Yes, I do,' says Lever. 'It's important not to rock the boat. To have someone working with us from the outside. Someone who we can control. Who the service isn't that aware of.'

'Then so be it.'

'Why don't you leave us alone for a while?' says the DG. 'Find Mr Rosslyn and get him in here.'

25

With Lever out of the office, the DG tells the Home Secretary that *Holy Ghost* 'raises a further matter that requires action'. He speaks with a new air of formality: 'To bring the attention of the Joint Intelligence Committee and the Americans to the involvement in the Trinity Chapter of the United States Secretary of State.'

'Say again . . .' says the Home Secretary.

The DG says it again. Word for word. 'The United States Secretary of State.'

As he speaks, the blood drains from the Home Secretary's dull features. The expression is fixed. As if by a taxidermist.

'It's here, sir, in black and white.'

The Home Secretary reads the single sheet of paper the DG hands him:

WISLAWA MARIA ODONE **United States** **Secretary of State**

Formerly US Ambassador to Tokyo, Ms Odone, 56-year-old Polish-Italian Catholic refugee was the President's personal choice for appointment to the United States cabinet office of Secretary of State.

Presently on a nine-day tour of ten capitals including Rome, Moscow, Beijing, her tour will climax with her sojourn in London for the New Year.

Background

In 1952 Odone arrived in Boston, an immigrant from Cracow.

Her education culminated in her appointment as a Sloan Fellow of MIT's Alfred P. Sloan School of Management (Massachusetts Institute of Technology, Sloan Building, 50 Memorial Drive, Cambridge, Mass.) in the late 1970s.

Odone's doctoral thesis was on Organization Theory: *An Investigation into the Principles of Top Management Policy-Making in Military Administration*.

Unmarried, she remained a professor at MIT, becoming the close political intimate of the chairman of the Foreign Relations Committee that confirmed her appointment. She has been a legislative assistant in the US Senate.

Like her predecessor at State, Odone cautioned delay in the use of armed force against Iraq after the 1990 Kuwait invasion, advised against aid to the Nicaraguan contras, strongly advocated the nuclear freeze. 'A conviction multilateralist' – a 'hawk' – she has balanced warring factions in the White House's National Security Commission and State Department. She has made relations with China a speciality, seeking to heal the twenty-one-year rifts and tensions between China and the United States.

A close analysis of all her TV and press interviews to date, especially those on NBC's 'Meet the Press', ABC's 'World News Tonight' and CBS's '60 Minutes', shows her to be a woman of deep spirituality. She lives alone with a private domestic staff in Georgetown.

Associates

Her close associates include FELDEN SCHULMANN, foreign policy specialist; Republican lawmaker MONNY LEHTA; DEBORAH MORTON ZATZ, her media gatekeeper; ADRIANNA CORNEL PERCY, formerly a counsel to the Senate Judiciary Committee, now Odone's chief of staff at the State Department; and EVANS MATTHEW, a veteran career State Department officer, known to be seeking a new career in academic administration.

Trinity Chapter Connection

In 1995 Odone made a series of donations to the Trinity Chapter via electronic transfer through two banks in the Bahamas and Geneva under the name of IRENA MAUSCH, her mother's maiden name.

A Polish émigré economist, Mausch is now a resident of Capri (*See* Xeroxes attached). Were Odone's association with this criminal organization to be revealed, it would demolish the authority of the President of the United States and his millennial administration at a single stroke.

'Do the Americans know this?' asks the Home Secretary.

'We think so,' says the DG. 'Because their CIA station head at the embassy is showing an intense interest in the Moorfield woman. And in Rosslyn. The suggestion is that they prefer a blind-eye policy. And matters to be left.'

'What do you advise me to do?' asks the Home Secretary.

'Simply to tell them what we know,' says the DG. 'So that if there is any trouble down the line we will be in a position to say that it was they, and not us, who did nothing. Very neatly it gets us off the hook. The rest of *Holy Ghost* is something we can deal with without too much difficulty. I prefer to delegate the day-to-day responsibilities to Lever. She is the ferret. She takes pleasure in killing rats.'

'I hope you're right,' says the Home Secretary, with a look of distaste.

'I suggest you speak to the woman Queron yourself, sir.'

'Not MI6?' asks the Home Secretary.

'Oh, I'd be inclined to leave them out of this for the time being. The threat from cults, at the end of the day the threat of violence, is our headache.'

26

Although there should be no question of infringing an individual's liberty to follow whatever religion he or she chooses, the security services of democracies should devote resources to collecting intelligence on subversive, anti-social and potentially violent cults and, where appropriate, be prepared to act pre-emptively against them to protect both innocent cult members and the general public from harm.

– ANDREW HUBBACK, THE PROPHETS OF DOOM: THE SECURITY THREAT OF RELIGIOUS CULTS, INSTITUTE FOR EUROPEAN DEFENCE AND STRATEGIC STUDIES

Rosslyn and Caroline are sleeping face to face when the telephone rings in the front room. Her left arm is draped over his shoulders. Trying not to wake her, he lifts it away gently and switches on the shaded bedside light.

The light glows dimly through the screen. It gives a ghostly look to the couple making love in the Yoshiwara house.

Before answering the telephone, he checks the BT Caller Display. The time is 5.13 a.m. The caller's number WITHHELD. 'Rosslyn?' He recognizes Lever's voice.

'Do you know what time it is?'

'I'm sorry to wake you. I need to see you.'

'Now where are you calling from?'

'Thames House. We need to talk.'

'About what?'

Lever hesitates. 'By the way, your client wouldn't happen to be with you, would she? You should be worried. She isn't at the Malvern Hotel. Just so long as she's safe somewhere.'

'She's safe.'

'That's good. Tell her from me to keep it that way. I mean that, Alan. I can pick you up in thirty minutes. I'll be waiting in the street. A Ford Sierra.'

He turns back to the screen. To the woman in the kimono watching. Only now the woman seems to have come to life. As Caroline. 'What time is it?' she asks.

'Around five.'

'God, I'm cold.'

He holds her in his arms. 'I have to go.'

'Go where?'

'Why don't you stay in bed, go back to sleep? You'll be safe here.'

She looks doubtful. 'Who was that on the phone?'

He takes her by the hand. 'A friend.'

'It didn't sound like a friend. Who was it?'

He starts to dress. 'OK, it was Lever. And she wants to see me. At Thames House.'

'Is this about me?'

'I don't know. But I can't think of anything else it'd be about. They must be pretty bloody interested in you to call at five in the morning, don't you think?'

'Your necktie's crooked. Let me fix it. Here.'

She holds the tie at the knot and pulls his mouth to hers. Drawing away from her, he breathes deeply. 'Later, Caroline. Lever's coming over to collect me.'

'I'll fix us some coffee,' she says.

He stoops to tie his shoelaces. By touch. Keeping his eyes on Caroline filling the kettle. Naked. 'Why don't you wear my dressing gown, Caroline?'

'Why don't you fetch it for me, Alan?'

He collects it for her from the bathroom. Smells her scent everywhere. Lauren. She's made a thorough job of spraying the place with it. He feels pleased. But far less sure about the meaning of Lever's early-morning call. 'Leave my answerphone on, OK? Don't pick up unless you hear it's me.' They drink the coffee black. 'And don't answer the door to anyone, right?'

'And what else don't you want me to do?'

'Don't put yourself at unnecessary risk.'

'I won't. Here . . . Kiss me.'

It's thirty minutes, almost to the second, when Lever's Sierra draws up in the street outside.

Freezing fog shrouds London on the short drive to Millbank.

'Perhaps you'd tell me why you're taking me to Thames House at this bloody awful hour,' says Rosslyn.

'Because I want to make a proposition to you.'

'Then I'm right. You've got a bad apple. Is that what the DG thinks?'

'He thinks we should make the knight's move.' Lever draws in the air with her finger thus: ↑→. *Swincarron's gesture*, thinks Rosslyn. 'So do I. Matter of fact, it's my tactic. My strategy. *My* big one.'

'Is this something that's been run across ASG?' he asks.

'On the contrary,' says Lever.

'Why not?'

'You'll see,' she says.

'It involves my client?'

'In so far as it involves you continuing the investigation, yes.'

'I don't suppose you know that my friends at ASG have shown me the door?'

'I do suppose,' she says. 'We *know*. They don't like your investigation, do they? So you can continue it under *our* auspices. That's the germ of the proposition I'm making on the DG's behalf.'

'What's in it for your people?'

'You work with me,' she says. 'We stay close to Caroline. That helps her. Helps you too.'

'In exchange for doing your dirty work?'

'The DG needs someone neutral to conduct an interrogation that can't wait. Someone who hasn't got an axe to grind. I came up with your name.'

'And what's in it for me?'

'You get into the fast track for your client,' says Lever. 'She stays safe. So do you. You get on with life. She gets on with hers. We want the other side to know you're in the game with her. We want them to show their hand.'

'And if I don't agree to this proposition of yours?'

Lever glances sideways at him. 'I wouldn't want to scare you. There'll be blood on hands. Yours. Hers.' She looks back to the road ahead. Beyond the roundabout by Lambeth Bridge. To the Thorney Street turning off Millbank. 'Don't say I didn't warn you.'

Rosslyn averts his eye from the snow and the place where his policewoman lover was shot to death. No grave. No bouquet of roses marks the spot. 'Can't you be more specific?'

'Once you accept the DG's proposition, yes. And, by the way, you can blame me for this.'

'Blame you for what?'

'Coming up with your name.'

'What do I get?'

Lever is almost unbelievably evasive. 'The safer passage,' she says. 'Time to finish your job. I get time to finish mine and bin the bad apple. No more blind eye.'

The steel gates open at the grey entrance to Thames House's Thorney Street underground car park.

Once Lever has parked in the space reserved for her, Rosslyn notices she's removing a tape cassette from the car's hi-fi system. 'New bloody warnings,' she says. 'New game.' She pockets the cassette. 'Warnings of timed explosive devices disguised as cassettes inserted under cover of night in cars belonging to staff. Queen's Regs: "Cassettes will be removed from parked cars." '

Rosslyn follows her up the concrete steps. 'Not much changes in this place,' he says.

He's right: at the best of times an air of menace permeates Thames House. As they head for the lifts, their footsteps echoing on the marble of the ground floor intensify it.

So does the sparseness of Lever's office in Intelligence Resources and Operations on the fourth floor. It's at the far end of the silent corridor.

Now here, in the airless room reinforced against bomb-blast, Rosslyn sits across from Lever at a metal and plastic table. On the wall is a calendar for both 1999 and 2000. A photograph next to it shows Lever hand in hand with an older man who, judging by the likeness between them, Rosslyn takes to be her father.

He listens to her proposition.

'You join with me in the interrogation of the Legal Adviser. Take her apart. Follow the money. Get proof from inside the horse's mouth that the Trinity Chapter is hell-bent on leaving its bloody mark on history.'

Rosslyn sees that 31 December 1999 has been circled in red on the calendar. Lever is starting to open her bag of tricks.

'By the way, two things. One, I'm glad you're here. And two, the Legal Adviser's name is Virginia Ahearne.'

'Virginia Ahearne,' says Lever, 'is a trained and very able lawyer. Educated at St Mary's Ascot and Newnham Cambridge, where she gained a double first, she's our uneasy conscience who's answered the call of duty for the past four years . . .

'She's reckoned to be spiritual. The woman of integrity. The clean pair of hands. Trusted. She can be relied upon to stand above most of the petty squabbles and internecine departmental warfare. The woman of institutions, she's the respecter of the Rule of Law, with a passionate belief in making the United Kingdom a safe haven for future generations. Mostly she's earned the respect and admiration of her peers. Some fear her. No one really likes her. Come the New Year she retires. There's been a lot of speculation about what she'll do then . . .

'Mention's been made of her as a likely candidate for senior college posts at both Oxford and Cambridge. It has been suggested to her that she would make a useful recruiter of Oxbridge students for careers in one or other of the security services, both MI5 and MI6. It'll provide her with a nice little annual bonus to the pension . . .

'The truth, confidentially, as far as her future is concerned, is that she prefers the appointment as a principal with your lot.'

'What, with ASG?'

'Your lot. On balance, she thinks she'll be better suited to giving professional advice to your principals. Remaining on a kind of active service in the private sector. And getting paid a handsome whack for doing so. Not that she's in need of money . . .

'A fortune inherited from her merchant banker father – an art collector and philanthropist – means she's no need to count the pennies. She prefers her husband, Edward, to handle the housekeeping. Given his drinking habits, I'd have thought that unwise. I suppose you'd call it love. Ahearne devotes himself to what he calls 'good works' of a religious and charitable sort. He's the consort. Handbag carrier. Walker. And though he wouldn't like to be described as such, housekeeper. *My Sweet Prince*, she calls him . . .

'The Ahearnes keep the routines of their working and domestic lives separate. Never discuss operational matters. They credit the length of their childless marriage, as she says, "to having pitched their tents apart". Should have pitched them a little nearer. Confided, maybe, in each other a little more. Who know what makes couples like them tick? I have to say I sort of pity her. What with her reputation and career facing deep shit. She may or may not be unaware of her husband's secret life . . .

'And that's what we're going to prise open. You and me together. See if she knows what really happened to Jane Moorfield. See if Caroline's right. At ten this morning. Meanwhile, read this.'

She hands Rosslyn the copy of the report. *Holy Ghost*.

'Here's the bad apple,' she says. 'Ask me questions as you go. Anything you like. She won't be easy going. And one other thing you don't know is that she and her husband, they're friends of the Prime Minister and his wife. So this one hasn't to go wrong.'

Rosslyn opens the report and thinks of Caroline. And what to tell her: *You're right. In your way, I think you've probably been right all along.* And see her smile.

He begins to read the fruits of Lever's researches. *Holy Ghost.*

27

Millennium, literally a period of a thousand years (a pseudo-Latin word formed on the analogy of biennium, triennium, from Lat. *mille*, a thousand and *annus*, year). The term is specially used of the period of 1000 years during which Christ, as has been believed, would return to govern the earth in person. Hence it is used to describe a vague time in the future when all flaws in human existence will have vanished, and perfect goodness and happiness will prevail.

– *Encyclopaedia Britannica: Appendices of Definitions*, London, 1996

If the Legal Adviser Virginia Ahearne is surprised by the vagueness of the DG's introductory remarks about Rosslyn, she shows no sign of it. The interrogation takes place late in the morning. At Lever's suggestion, to cover his role in the private sector, Rosslyn is now *Michael Seifert*.

'Mr *Seifert*, an instructor from Portsmouth. Money laundering. Organized illegal currency deal ing . . .' And Rosslyn's grateful that the DG doesn't elaborate further and simply explains to her that Lever and Seifert 'will appreciate your assistance with an operational matter . . .' and adds airily that 'it's in the way of liaison . . .' *If Lever's got it right*, thinks Rosslyn, *if Ahearne's really got something to hide, she won't be about to question my credentials.*

She's a solid and rather awkward woman. Thick legs. Pasty make-up. Wearing two strands of pearls. Greyish hair. She seems to be suffering pain in her lumbar region. 'I've often lectured MI5 and MI6 trainees at the Portsmouth establishment, Mr Seifert,' she says to Rosslyn. 'I'm sorry I can't quite place you. Haven't we met somewhere in the past?'

Here you go. Questioning the credentials. 'Perhaps,' he says. 'I think we may have.'

I wonder. But the interrogator rarely queries the niceties of the opening round. So we won't start now.

The double doors are closed by the DG's assistant with the firmness that suggests the meeting is not be disturbed. And Ahearne looks round, concerned. Perhaps her pride's been slightly wounded.

The DG slowly opens the file on his desk. *Holy Ghost.* 'Help yourselves to coffee,' he says pleasantly.

Ahearne sits between Lever and Rosslyn. All three face the DG, who's behind his desk. 'I hope I haven't inconvenienced you,' he says. He smiles a little at Ahearne. 'As we know, so many operations begin with the grain of sand that fails to turn into the proverbial pearl.' He nods at Lever. 'If you'd rehearse the background, please.' He looks at the clock on the wall by the door. Then at Lever and the opponent Ahearne. Lever cool. The milkmaid complexion. The pale-blue eyes. Ten or fifteen years younger than Ahearne, the power bureaucrat. Intimate with the movers and shakers. Who has the ear of toffs at the BBC. Member of the government focus groups. You name them, Ahearne knows them. *Habituée* of the River Café. Social fucking climber. Koala bear look, with claws as strong to stay up on the social ladder. The jungle VIP. *Wouldn't fancy your talons around my neck.*

Here's Lever. The woman from the other side of the tracks where we belong. Unimpressed by Ahearne's insider reputation. Cool anger in the eyes. As if opening for the prosecution, she begins: 'Briefly, I will refer to an operation involving major currency fraud, money laundering, murder and conspiracy to murder.'

She's content to name the operation: *Holy Ghost*.

At her request and on Rosslyn's powerful recommendation, the DG has seen to it that all the relevant files have been blocked by the biometric security system newly installed in Thames House. Good old New Labour. We always keep our traps shut. So even if Ahearne survives the interview, she won't learn anything when and if she noses through any records that may refer to *Holy Ghost*.

'The target is an organization called the Trinity Chapter,' Lever continues. 'Ostensibly, it's a secretive religious group, a cult or religious movement. Most probably now reorganized. Having diverted and hidden its capital investments world-wide, it's seeking to preserve them.'

'Do you know anything about the Trinity Chapter?' the DG asks Ahearne. He tries to keep it light.

'You're our statutory theologian, Virginia.'

'Only what one's read in the press,' she says, shifting uneasily.

'Is the disc giving you trouble?' the DG asks her.

'It's the damp, I think, DG . . .' she says. 'This awful cold.'

Rosslyn watches the narrow blue eyes. The mascara a little smudged. The traces of lipstick on the dull upper teeth. There's a silence. It's Rosslyn's first move.

'I thought you might've heard of this Trinity Chapter, Mrs Ahearne,' he says. 'It seems as though it's a distant relation of Scientology or the Reverend Moon's organization. A millennial cult.'

'I haven't heard of it. Is there any reason why I should?'

'The Trinity Chapter is a little secretive,' says the DG. 'Like freemasonry. Along those lines. Only *secretive* is not the word they might use. Private, perhaps. Less pejorative.'

Ahearne says solemnly: 'In my admittedly limited experience, most new religious movements exert, as it were, benign influences.'

'This is a cult,' says Lever bluntly.

'And down the line,' says the DG, 'the operation involves the Americans as well as ourselves. We need to be careful we make appropriate moves.'

Ahearne looks perplexed. 'Why has it landed on our doorstep?' she asks. She looks at Rosslyn. 'Is this to do with money laundering?'

'Yes,' says Rosslyn, 'we've turned up some fairly cogent intelligence connected to substantial money laundering. Diverted and hidden funds. It intersects with several other operations. As Ms Lever's said.'

'Which sources?' she challenges.

'The intelligence circulated on a limited scale,' says Rosslyn. 'From SO10 to SO6 – to the database of the commercial crime intelligence bureau. Then automatically up here to us. Large deposits have been made in –'

'– the Bahamas,' Lever cuts in. 'The Seychelles. British Virgin Islands. Mauritius. The Dutch Antilles. Labuan. Malta and Monaco. Only the Swiss have so far denied them bank facilities. Presumably . . . far from wanting any repetition of Jouret and his Solar Church butchery, they want nothing to do with it. In any case, the powers of the Swiss regulators are limited.'

A look of something like fear twists Ahearne's face. The skin at her throat has reddened.

Rosslyn thinks: *You must know that the World Bank investigators are seeking further powers to investigate banks holding dirty money.*

'May I see a copy of the report?' Ahearne asks.

'At the appropriate moment,' says the DG. 'Suffice it to say, for the time being, that we must discover who's been operating these funds. Where they come from. Where. When. How. Why. Their linkage to national and international political circles. Public service. Industry. Sciences. And academic life. And one of them should be of more than passing interest to the Americans in the Department of State – allegedly one of the remaining members of the Trinity Chapter.'

Beads of sweat have formed in the down on Ahearne's podgy upper lip. 'What proof is there of this?' she says, still giving the impression that she's unsure as to quite why she's being questioned. Rosslyn senses that she's on the verge of taking umbrage. She'll deny everything. Take dire exception. Total denial is the best defence. Say nothing. Protest. Demand to see the written record. Admit nothing. Never apologize.

But Ahearne tries a different tack. She's going to make very sure she'll be reasonable. 'If our friend in the Department of State has certain religious beliefs –'

She attempts to cross her legs. Lumbar pain forces her to abandon the attempt.

'Surely,' she says, 'that's his personal business.'

Good move, thinks Rosslyn. *Bully for you, take the stance on ideology.*

'Oh, of course it's her business,' says the DG.

'Sorry?' says Ahearne. 'You said *"she"* – we're not talking about Wislawa Odone?'

She knows, thinks Rosslyn, *she knows. Bad move to question the gender.* But before he can follow up, the DG throws a soft ball: 'Are you sure that spine, the disc of yours – it really is all right?'

'Of course,' she says. And seems wisely to have

discarded her speculation about the Secretary of State. Rosslyn's clocked it through.

'But you should be aware,' he says, 'that we're looking at the issue of hefty money laundering. And things get more serious down the line. At least two or perhaps three women members of the Trinity Chapter have allegedly been murdered.' He watches her coldly. 'And the Inner Chapter, the remnants of the governing body of the Chapter, may well have been – indeed, most likely *were* – implicated. The deaths were all drugs-related.'

'This isn't really a matter for us, is it?' says Ahearne. 'If you're asking for my advice I'd say we should simply hand it to the police and to the Americans.'

'That's what I wanted to hear you say, Virginia,' says the DG. 'Absolutely right. But you see we have to decide precisely *what* to hand to the Americans. We haven't got the time to deal in generalities.'

'Whatever evidence shows proof of wrongdoing,' says Ahearne. 'Speaking as Chair of the Legal Advisory Committee, as Adviser, it isn't within our legal purview, is it?'

Disappointment furrows the DG's brow. 'Unfortunately,' he says, 'as far as we know, our primary source is missing. So is proof, the evidence. The source was, as it were, the only witness for the prosecution.'

'What source are we talking about, what "prosecution"?'

'A postgraduate student,' says Lever, 'researching cults, sects, new religious movements and so forth.'

'I don't know anything about that,' says Ahearne. 'Who says the six hundred religious movements in the UK are of genuine concern to us? Unless,' she adds rather sourly, 'they present a serious threat to security. And I doubt that. And one would've thought it wiser that we don't allow ourselves to appear overly interested in people's freedom to believe in what they are entitled to believe in. I'd give little credence to the view that a British-based religious organization could translate its beliefs into the American political arena. At any rate, not without us having some prior indication.'

She smiles confidently. The beads of sweat on the upper lip appear to have evaporated.

'What happens,' Rosslyn asks her, 'if, say, fanatical beliefs, translate themselves into extremist action?'

'That, of course, is a different scenario,' she replies. 'One takes it that you're saying there's no proof they will. Purely hypothetical –'

'Say,' asks Lever, 'there's a threat, for example, of some major disruption?'

'How major?'

'Public violence?' asks Lever.

'We've learned a lot about conspiracy to launch chemical attacks from Japan's Public Security Investigation Agency since Aum,' says Ahearne slowly. She's gearing up to make gentle mockery of the interview. 'Are we suggesting that this Trinity

Chapter is to commit a similar atrocity of some sort? If so, no one has discussed either the security aspects of investigating them, or indeed the legal implications with me.'

'Perhaps,' says Lever. She quotes: ' "*Although there should be no question of infringing an individual's liberty to follow whatever religion he or she chooses, the security services of democracies should devote resources to collecting intelligence on subversive, anti-social and potentially violent cults and, where appropriate, be prepared to act pre-emptively against them to protect both innocent cult members and the general public from harm.*" Would you agree with that opinion, Mrs Ahearne?'

'What's your *source?*' she asks, feigning exasperation. She tries, once again without success, to shift her back into a more comfortable position.

'An Institute for European Defence and Strategic Studies paper,' says Rosslyn: '*The Security Threat of Religious Cults.*'

'With respect,' Virginia says, 'they're another pressure group dealing in suppositions. It isn't quite enough, is it?'

The DG glances at the clock on his desk, then at Ahearne. 'I have to make a decision, Virginia. Do we, or do we not, inform the Americans?'

'I think it would be premature,' says Ahearne. 'The Americans very wisely deal in facts, don't they? If there's a basis for prosecution concerning the alleged murders, that's a matter for the police. Not us. As to the allegation of money laundering, that's one aspect that needs to be left until there's evidence to give us a basis for further action. Look at the facts. Figures. The evidence. Unless it all adds up to some threat to national security.'

The DG blows aside the screen of verbiage. 'You're quite sure, Virginia,' he asks directly, 'that you know nothing, absolutely nothing whatsoever, about the Trinity Chapter?'

'Nothing,' she says.

'And your husband,' says Rosslyn. 'Might he perhaps know something about it – something that he hasn't told even you?'

'We never discuss operational matters,' says Ahearne. 'I'll certainly ask him for you, if you wish,' she offers. She smiles with her mouth, not her eyes. 'But I doubt he'll prove to be of help with anything of this nature.'

Rosslyn is scrutinizing her every facial twitch. Each blink. Each frown. 'You wouldn't mind if I asked him a few questions?' he asks her.

'Of course not.' The celebrated conscience is uneasy. 'Absolutely not.' She's turned her face sideways. Away from Lever. Away from Rosslyn. To the DG. Here is the appeal to the top: 'Would you allow me to be present when you see him?'

'I'd prefer it if you weren't,' says Rosslyn.

'In that case,' she says rather tartly, 'perhaps you'll let me know the outcome.'

'I'm sure he'll tell you about it himself,' says the DG.

'We make a point of *never* discussing operational matters.' Getting to her feet, Ahearne looks at him with resignation. 'Why bring Edward into this?'

Good, thinks Rosslyn. *She's taking umbrage.* And as if on cue, she says coldly: 'I don't want to continue with this.'

'I'm sorry,' says the DG, showing her to the door.

Once it's closed behind her, he allows himself a watery smile.

'She's a liar,' says Lever.

The DG has his hand on the *Holy Ghost* report.

'Let's see if she's hooked herself,' says Rosslyn. He taps a coded number on the telephone console: the telephone number of the Ahearnes' house in Richmond-upon-Thames. Presses another tab. An amber light shows. No Reply. Then the amber light turns red. 'She's dialled out,' says Rosslyn. They see the number on the calls screen: 0171-930-8688.

The male voice says: 'Travellers' Club.'

VIRGINIA AHEARNE: I want to speak to my husband, Edward Ahearne, please.

MALE VOICE: He's in the smoking room.

VIRGINIA AHEARNE: Can you get him to a telephone, please? It's urgent.

MALE VOICE: Who shall I say is calling?

VIRGINIA AHEARNE: His wife.

MALE VOICE: If you'd hold on, Mrs Ahearne . . .

The husband eventually picks up.

VIRGINIA AHEARNE: If you receive any telephone calls you'll be very wise not to answer questions.

Edward Ahearne sounds the worse for wear.

EDWARD AHEARNE: What calls? What are you talking about?
VIRGINIA AHEARNE: Calls from here.
EDWARD AHEARNE: Where?
VIRGINIA AHEARNE: I'm at work. Do you know about something called the Trinity Chapter, Edward?
EDWARD AHEARNE: No, I do not . . . Where are you?
VIRGINIA AHEARNE: I've told you. You're pissed. I'm *at work*. Edward, are you perfectly sure you don't know what I'm talking about?
EDWARD AHEARNE: For God's sake, Virginia.
VIRGINIA AHEARNE: Then bloody well remember what I said.

The line goes dead.
'I'll monitor any other calls,' Lever tells Rosslyn. 'Get on the street. Visit Ahearne. 106 Pall Mall.' Handing Rosslyn a slim brown envelope, she adds, 'Show him the dirty photographs. Sleazy manipulative bastard.'
For the first time, Rosslyn clocks the passionate hatred in Lever's voice.
I'm impressed.

28

THE S WORDS

| | |

SIN SPIRIT SACRED SOUL
   – EDWARD AHEARNE, PRIVATELY PRINTED,
RICHMOND-UPON-THAMES, 1999

Rosslyn introduces himself to Edward Ahearne in the front hall of the Travellers' Club in Pall Mall. 'I'm a friend of your wife's.'

'I suppose you realize,' says the ruddy-faced Ahearne beneath his breath, 'that I know nothing about my wife's duties . . . Nothing,' he adds with absolute conviction. 'Mister . . .?'

'Seifert. Michael Seifert. Would you mind if we have a short word in private?'

The breath stinks of whisky. 'About what, Mr Seifert?'

'A personal matter – affecting your wife's career.'

'Well, all right,' says Ahearne, fiddling with the knot of his silk bow tie. 'In the bar?' He nods to the stairs. The actorly fat of his jowls jelly-wobbles.

Seated in a deep leather chair in one corner of the downstairs bar, just within earshot of some other members, Rosslyn says quietly: 'You see, Mr

Ahearne, I have a problem. Are you aware that we've interviewed your wife?'

Ahearne folds his arms across his chest. 'I wouldn't know.'

'She told you nothing about an interview?'

'Certainly not.'

'She didn't phone you about it?'

The drooped eyelids flicker. 'If this concerns an operational matter, I think you'd better talk to Virginia about it, don't you?' He orders a double whisky for himself. Tonic water for Rosslyn. 'I can't enter into details. Anyway, you rather emphatically told me in the entrance hall that this was by way of being a personal matter.'

Get a little man on his home patch. His club. Where he won't want anyone to hear his integrity being challenged. It's best to go straight for the jugular. 'Your wife has confirmed that you are an established member of the Trinity Chapter.'

'Would you mind lowering your voice?'

'She's right, isn't she?'

'I'm afraid, Seifert, you're terribly mistaken.' The whisky glass is shaking in the stubby fingers. *You're a nail biter.* 'I don't know what you're talking about.'

'Would you be prepared to swear that on oath?'

'If you wish. But I'd appreciate it if you would ask my wife to be present.'

'She has her problems,' says Rosslyn. 'She's in pain. It's not surprising, is it – she's got a great deal weighing on her mind.'

'What on earth makes you think that?' Ahearne says. 'Please understand, I really don't want to discuss this Trinity Chapter or anything else in her absence. I can't.'

'You know all about it then?'

'Only what any reasonably well-informed reader of the quality press could tell you.'

'I think you know far more than that, my friend. Are you telling me that you could talk about it if, say, your wife were right here with us now?'

Rosslyn turns to face Ahearne directly. His face is only inches away. 'Fortunately, women aren't allowed in this part of the club,' Ahearne says lamely.

I can smell the lying on your whisky breath. I think you want to tell me what's on your dirty mind.

The webs of broken veins in Ahearne's cheeks are puce.

'You know, Ahearne, about the Trinity Chapter, don't you?' He lets the painful silence tell. 'I put it to you,' Rosslyn continues, 'not only do you know about it, but you're frightened of admitting it, aren't you? What have they sworn you to, Ahearne? What is it you're hiding? Why aren't you prepared to out yourself, to say, "I'm proud to be a member of the Trinity Chapter"? Come on, it isn't an offence, is it? You're a member of its Inner Chapter, aren't you?' He leans in even closer.

'You're very wrong,' Ahearne says, almost in a whisper.

'About what? About you being frightened?'

'I have nothing to be frightened of.'

'Then look at your hands.'

'Please . . . lower your voice . . .' He turns to the bar steward. 'Another whisky. Double. Same again for my visitor here.'

'Is it the Trinity Chapter that's weighing on your mind?'

'I have absolutely nothing to be ashamed of.'

'Good, I've been asked by the Director General to talk to you. I'm on your side.'

'You could've fooled me.'

'Then don't fool with me, Mr Ahearne. You're a long-standing member of the Trinity Chapter. You've kept it a secret for how many years – what is it, five or even six?'

'You're misinformed.'

'I see,' says Rosslyn. 'Then let's think about what we have in common, shall we?' He changes tone. He's counting on his fingers. Stating the obvious: 'I realize it isn't *ipso facto* an offence for any security service officer or his or her close relative or partner to belong to any religious denomination. But, of all people, your wife knows that a failure to disclose any information relating to a current operation will result in disciplinary proceedings being brought against her. To say nothing of criminal proceedings. You must be aware that a tragedy's occurred, that young women have been murdered. There have been drug-related deaths. All connected to the

Trinity Chapter. You are in shit. Do you understand what I'm saying? Shit.'

'I'm very sorry to hear that,' says Ahearne. 'But if you're suggesting that the Trinity Chapter is in any way connected with such matters, you are, I repeat, very much mistaken. You should know they have powerful lawyers here, in Washington and through-out Europe.'

'I'm talking security,' says Rosslyn. 'Humint.'

'What?'

'Human Intelligence. Humint. Friends in the United States State Department. CIA. FBI. Our friends too. No one's mistaken, Ahearne. Except you.' He watches Ahearne flinch. 'Set murder against a proven background of money laundering, extortion, serious fraud and the hell knows what else, and you have to understand that the member-ship of this cult needs to be questioned.'

'Really – but what's your proof?'

'A great deal,' says Rosslyn. His voice is gentler. 'Please don't deceive me, Ahearne. Please don't bother to lie to me.'

'Why should I lie to you?'

'To protect your wife,' says Rosslyn. 'Let me put a suggestion to you. Let's say, to save your wife any further trouble, you make a full personal statement to me . . .'

'I have nothing to say to you,' Ahearne says quickly. 'Nothing.'

'We can do it now,' says Rosslyn. 'Or later. I'd

prefer you to co-operate with me and do it now. Take your time. Obviously, your co-operation will count in your favour. We've no intention of asking your wife to resign. Or of this leading to her prosecution. Or to yours. You should know. She's a trained lawyer, Ahearne. She knows the legal niceties of this situation. So you can help us. It's that easy, isn't it?'

'What are you proposing?'

'Just inviting you to co-operate. Your wife's respected by her peers. By her seniors. Her juniors. She's given devoted support to the service. She's about to enjoy a happy retirement, isn't she? Benefits of a decent pension.' He leans nearer to Ahearne, his hands clasped round his glass of tonic water. Like a bank manager who knows too many personal details of over-spending for his client's comfort. He's offering the deal. 'It'd be a pity to jeopardize your future, wouldn't it? And the alternative – a bit rough, perhaps? No pension, say, no fat prospects of consultancy for the wife in the private sector. No title for her. No DBE. And all because we have one little difficulty to overcome – you. Listen, the proof of serious, even organized, criminal activities within the Trinity Chapter is overwhelming. I don't want to strike against them yet. Not even soon. I want to net the lot. C'mon, Ahearne, is it or is it not true you're a member of the Trinity Chapter?'

Ahearne's lips twitch.

'OK then,' says Rosslyn. From inside his jacket, he produces the envelope. 'Take a look at these. See if you recognize anyone.' Inside the envelope Ahearne finds four photographs. 'The ceremony of initiation, Ahearne. Right, recognize the face?'

Ahearne looks at the photographs. Sees himself – naked on what looks to be a doctor's couch. There's an audience watching what's being done to him. Dressed in white robes with chains around their necks, some gold, some silver. At the end of each is an ornament in the shape of three vertical lines: I I I.

'Has Virginia seen these?' Ahearne asks.

'Not yet,' says Rosslyn.

'The DG?'

'Yes,' says Rosslyn. 'That's what you allowed them to do, isn't it? Pump you full of water and empty your guts of all impurity? Messy, isn't it? Now you just tell me the truth, my friend. Or do you want your wife to explain what all this is about?'

Disconsolate, his defiance broken, Ahearne stares at his empty whisky glass. Across to the bar. Anywhere except at Rosslyn. 'The Chapter,' he says, 'however private it may be, is in no sense whatsoever a criminal organization. On the contrary.'

'What is it then?'

'Our beliefs inspire good works throughout the world. Were it not so, I would never have joined.'

'You weren't coerced?'

'Certainly not.'

'Are you, or have you been, in any way involved in its financial dealings?'

'Certainly not.'

'But you have made donations to it?'

'So what?'

'So how much?'

'Over a period of years,' Ahearne answers, 'some fifteen to twenty per cent of my investments. My wife knows nothing about this. I really must insist you don't bother her with this.'

'If you'll answer my questions, Mr Ahearne.'

'They were my willing contributions.'

'Except it's *her* money you contributed.'

'We are married,' says Ahearne. ' "What's thine is mine." '

'But it's her money?'

'Our money . . .'

'Mostly hers,' says Rosslyn. 'No matter. The court will decide.'

'Are you investigating the bank accounts too?' Ahearne asks. 'What court?'

Rosslyn counters with a different question. Another tack. 'Have you ever been approached by anti-cult investigators?'

'No, of course I haven't. Have you?'

'Don't be facetious.'

'I'm being very serious, Seifert. To the best of my knowledge, you will find no members or indeed ex-members who have received the attentions of anti-cultist zealots. There's nothing to hide.'

'For Christ's sake, Ahearne, how come its membership is so secret then?'

'Not secret. In the nature of things, it's *private*.'

'In the nature of what things? What nature are we talking about, Ahearne?'

'Deeply-held beliefs.'

'Which are what?' asks Rosslyn.

'The teachings of Trinity,' Ahearne says, almost as a boast.

'I see,' says Rosslyn. 'Tell me, does the name Jane Moorfield mean anything to you?'

'I'm sorry,' says Ahearne. 'Who?'

'Jane Moorfield.'

'Never heard of her. And I have to tell you that I'm most certainly not prepared to divulge the names of any of our members.'

'Are you aware that your membership includes several figures who are widely respected in their fields? In politics here and in the States. Academics. Lawyers. Judges. Industrialists and so on.'

'I am not prepared to comment further.'

'And in the American intelligence community?'

'I'm not obliged to tell you anything about fellow believers.'

'Or even about members of our own intelligence community, here in the UK?'

'No comment,' says Ahearne. 'Several distinguished members of the Foreign Service happen to be members of this club.'

'I wouldn't know,' says Rosslyn.

'Really?' says Ahearne. 'I'd have thought some-one in your position would know that sort of thing.'

'Let's try another name,' says Rosslyn. 'Someone who isn't a member of this joint of yours. Morandi – mean anything to you?'

'Nothing.'

'Father Gian Maria Morandi,' says Rosslyn, 'of the International Family Foundation in Geneva?'

'No comment.'

'Ahearne, why do you keep on saying "no comment" . . .?'

'Because I'm afraid these are all matters I can't assist you with.'

Rosslyn clears his throat. 'Does the name Marcus Luke mean anything to you?'

'No comment.'

'Very well,' says Rosslyn. 'Good. Let's call it a day then. For the time being, Ahearne. Perhaps you'll keep yourself in readiness for a fuller discus-sion?'

'About what?'

'The how. The where. The when. You know what I'm talking about, Ahearne.'

'I'm not sure that I do.'

'You will.'

'So you say. I take it,' says Ahearne, 'that none of this will go any further. I'm thinking of Virginia. I don't want to place her in any jeopardy.'

'You already have,' says Rosslyn. 'All I need is your co-operation. The whole truth.'

'Then tell me what I say to Virginia about our discussion.'

'What she'd say to you: "I can't discuss operational matters."'

'You do realize she's the Legal Adviser?'

'Listen,' says Rosslyn, slipping the envelope with the photographs into his inside jacket pocket, 'I don't care if she's Jesus Christ Almighty. Thanks anyway, Ahearne.' He's thinking of Caroline. 'Mind if I use the phone before I go, Ahearne?'

He gives Rosslyn a bitter look: 'You'll find one in the entrance hall.'

Pick up, Caro –

> *Just Show Me How to Love You*
> *E ci ridiamo su*
> *gabbiano di scogliera*
> *ma dov'eri nascosto'*
> *dov'eri finora?*

She doesn't.

So he calls Lever. 'I nailed him,' he tells her. 'He's right in it up to here.'

'Is the wife in it too?' she asks. 'Did he tell you?'

'She could be as well. Only he didn't say so. Not in so many words. It'll get worse before it gets worse.'

'It already has,' says Lever. 'You'd better get in here.'

The tone of Lever's voice troubles him. 'You don't sound pleased,' he says.

'It's Caroline Moorfield.'

'What about her?'

'Where is she?' Lever asks.

'At my place.'

'She isn't, Alan. She's done a runner.'

'What?'

'Up until now, I'd have said we're winning. Now, Alan, your client. Jesus. You should've seen this coming. She has to be one of them too, doesn't she?'

'What are you talking about?'

'You'd better get in here fast, Alan.'

Leaving the Travellers' Club, he turns and sees Ahearne standing there. There's a strange smile on his face. The look that says, *'Got you, Seifert. You maggot. Foreigner.'* Or something worse of a racist nature.

Rosslyn looks straight through him and heads out into Pall Mall and the driving snow.

29

Less than a mile away. Out of the snow. Downing Street.

On the second floor of the Cabinet Office the meeting of the JIC, the Joint Intelligence Committee, nears its end. Exceptionally, it's been delayed and has run over time after the Prime Minister's return from Washington earlier in the morning.

The MI5 DG is waiting for what he thinks of as the appropriate moment to land the dynamite on the lap of the American, Donna Queron, across the table. The simian DG is thankful the JIC Chairman knows nothing about what's on his mind. The DG and the JIC Chairman entertain considerable dislike for each other.

A bullish figure, the Chairman is an experienced Whitehall operator. A personal foreign affairs adviser to the Prime Minister, he's never known to suffer fools gladly. He commands the respect of the two dozen staff members of the JIC around the table. Selected from the Foreign Office, the Ministry of Defence, the Government Communications Headquarters (GCHQ), Secret Intelligence Service (SIS or MI6) and the Security Service (MI5), each would recognize the DG is facing the most serious threat to the credibility of his service in several decades.

He wants, of course, to do the right thing. He feels a sense of confused, somewhat pained gratitude towards Lever. There's no denying the existence of the spreading virus contained in the *Holy Ghost* Report. His mind elsewhere, the DG ticks off the Secret JIC Agenda items as they're dealt with:

- FAR EAST   MIDDLE EAST   EASTERN EUROPE   AFRICA   SOUTH AMERICA

Why not look at what's happening on your doorsteps? There's some waffle about the 'enemy' countries.

- ALGERIA   IRAN   LIBYA   NORTH KOREA   SYRIA

Time drags. Next on the agenda is secret area intelligence:

- NUCLEAR STATUS   ARMS CONTROL   ARMS PROLIFERATION   COMMUNICATIONS   TRADE

A government department requires an intelligence report on several areas. The request is considered, accepted, forwarded to the appropriate Secret Service area desk for action. A local committee, a Current Intelligence Group, is formed. The Chairman names some secret intelligence officers, members of the JIC itself, and then Queron, senior representative from the CIA with diplomatic cover at the US Embassy. The intelligence analysts who contribute to the Current Intelligence Groups are usually officers with a general experience of broad geographical areas. As such they are unanswerable to any political ideology. The DG is well aware that more than a few of the American intelligence community's senior officials, from the Director of Central Intelligence downwards, are political appointees. What, he wonders, will they make of what he has to pass on about *Holy Ghost*? And what will Queron? Queron, who the DG intends to engage in a confidential conversation once the interminable meeting finishes.

She might not care to admit it, but unlike her British counterparts, she's answerable to, or at the least has to be sympathetic to, whatever political agenda her current master may have drawn up in the White House.

Holy Ghost contains a virus the White House can ill afford to ignore.

At last, the end of the meeting. JIC members leave the room in twos and threes.

It seems to come as no particular surprise to Queron when the DG asks her 'for a brief word – two minutes.'

As it happens, he thinks their discussion in the cabinet room office will take rather longer.

'Do have a seat,' he tells her.

Unsmiling, he chooses his words carefully. He can't help sounding patronizing: 'This is simply an informal briefing. A warning, if you like, that we'd like to run across you. I trust it will be helpful. To all of us.'

'Sure, I appreciate that,' says Queron. 'I'm here to help. You tell me what I can do, sir.' The American emphasises 'You tell me' as if she's no man's fool. Certainly not the DG's.

The DG inclines his head. A smile flickers on the dry lips. There's a twitch in the muscles of his receding chin. The eyes remain blank. He knows, in the usual run of things, that paradoxically, the more Queron and her kind offer help, the more guarded they become. But what he has to tell her this morning is not in the usual run of things. He knows Queron once incurred the wrath of General Schwarzkopf, who bitterly complained in public that CIA intelligence briefings during the Gulf War were bureaucratic 'mush'. To her credit, the athletic Queron, American secret world survivor, side-stepped Schwarzkopf's criticism. Now here she is, CIA London station head. No mean player. Sensing trouble. Her narrow eyes, literally the colour of steel, match the dull darkness of the DG's. The only other thing they have in common is mutual distrust. Some say fear lies at the root of it. Succinctly, he puts Queron in the picture about *Holy Ghost.*

'Are you by any chance familiar with the Trinity Chapter?' he asks her.

'No, sir, I am not.'

'It seems it's proving unhealthily attractive to influential networks of consequence.'

'Like what networks?'

'Political networks. Washington. New York.

Houston. Los Angeles. And elsewhere.'

Queron looks sceptical. 'Are you telling me who?' she asks, her broad mouth fixed in a humourless grin.

'Your Secretary of State, Wislawa Odone.'

'Excuse me? What are you saying to me?'

'That we've followed her money.'

'What money are you talking about?'

'Private fund distribution. Electronic transfers under a cover name.'

Queron narrows her eyes. 'From where to where?'

'Washington via the Bahamas and Geneva to the Trinity Inner Chapter.'

'What proof is there of this?' she asks. 'Are you people breaking doors?'

'Yes,' says the DG. 'If that's the correct expression. We already have.'

'What's the basis of this operation – *Holy Ghost*?'

'You sound as if you don't entirely give it credence,' the DG suggests.

She puts her clenched fists on the table. 'Listen, I know Wislawa. You don't. I can tell you. One hundred per cent. We have no problem with her. She's on the level. The finest Secretary of State this century. We have no problem –'

'Oh neither do we,' says the DG. 'Neither do we.'

Queron stretches her powerful neck. A vein behind her left ear throbs visibly. 'You're saying that we do?'

'That isn't a matter for us to comment upon,' says the DG.

'If you can't comment on specifics,' says Queron, 'maybe you can give me parameters. History. Chronology. For Chrissakes, where does this thing go back to?'

'It seems that the difficulty goes back into the past,' says the DG. He gives the American another brief résumé.

'What else have you?' she asks guardedly.

'Not much else.'

'Her religious beliefs are her business.'

Seem to have heard that one before, thinks the DG. *Virginia Ahearne might approve the view.* 'Of course,' he agrees. Unblinking, he fixes Queron's eyes. 'But you should be aware that we're looking at money laundering. More besides. Corruption on a scale that beggars decency.'

'In connection with what source? C'mon!' she challenges him, at the same time getting to her feet and waving her muscular hands in the air. 'This *is* a matter for you people.' She stares at the portrait of Her Majesty the Queen above the fireplace. 'The young American woman who died . . . who was she? What's her name?'

You already know, Ms Queron. I know you know. 'Jane Moorfield,' says the DG. 'You can see, it wasn't something one wished to raise in committee. We simply offer you the information as a favour. We're hoping you'll take on a burden in the investigation. Of course, we appreciate the sensitivity of your position.'

'Thank you,' says Queron. 'I appreciate your consideration for my position.'

'Let's hope it goes no further,' says the DG.

Queron turns the silver bracelet on her wrist. She walks away from the table. 'Thank you,' she says. 'Would you mind leaving it with me?'

'Not at all,' says the DG. 'I'm sorry I took rather longer than two minutes. Thank you for hearing me out.'

'You're welcome,' Queron says. 'Mind if I use the phone?'

'Do,' says the DG. Not that he cares whose telephone she uses. 'By all means.'

She dials the embassy on a secure line. Puts her hand over the receiver. 'Will you mind leaving me alone a minute?'

Just outside in the corridor, the DG glances back at her speaking on the telephone. The tennis player's shoulders. Crumpled in defeat. He'd like to hear what she's saying. Queron seems to have read his suspicious mind. She gives him a look that says, *I bet you would*. Then asks, 'What's the name again of the woman who died – Moorhead?' She seems, for the briefest moment, to be feigning surprise. Of course. *It's as if you don't want me to realize you've recognized the name. Moorhead?* He thinks, *You know it's Moor-bloody-field*.

'Jane Moorfield,' says the DG. 'F – i – e –'

'Yeah, I know. Have you any other details?'

'Yes. She was aged twenty-six. Single. I believe

she came from somewhere in Massachusetts. Cape Code, I think.'

'Any relatives you know about?' asks the American.

Again he senses, *You already know of the sister's existence.* It seems to be a strange game the American's playing out. 'One relative, I think,' he says. 'The younger sister, Caroline Moorfield.'

Queron returns to her telephone call, leaving the door ajar. Lingering within earshot, the DG overhears her repeating Caroline Moorfield's name.

He hears her say, 'We're now talking Level A3A. Get me a copy of the Secretary of State's updated London visit schedule.'

Security Level A3A – the full star treatment. Big-scale damage limitation is beginning. The buck's been well and truly passed. And if the Americans think they can abdicate responsibility, well, they've got another thing coming. This one they can't get out of.

By the time Queron snaps her final order to the office at the embassy, the DG's out of earshot.

So he doesn't hear her final order:

'And have Dr Maxine Gertler from Alexander Swincarron Gertler call by my office today. Before the end of business this afternoon –'

The DG hurries out of Number Ten to find his car and driver.

He needs to make a formal written record of his conversation with Queron, and also needs to speak to Lever. No matter what the White House decides to do about the Secretary of State, he needs to complete the damage limitation in his own house. Thames House. *Staff morale will be maintained, because the man Rosslyn's hell-bent on pursuing the bleeding heart investigation. We'll say: 'Of course, it wasn't Lever who stuck the knife into Ahearne. Oh no. We wouldn't do that. Not to one of ours. Rather it came our way thanks to the man Rosslyn.'* He brushes the snow from his hair. *Rosslyn: disposable as the London snow melting in his fingers. The knight's move. Perfectly executed:* ↑→.

Got him.

30

We may not be believable to outsiders. Only believe. Faith first. We have not been born overnight. We have grown with Nature. Seed. Growth. Death. Seed. Rebirth. We do not speak of Sin. Rather of Forgiveness. Ours is truly New Religion. New Belief. New Way. We are not in conflict with Man. But Man is in conflict with us. We seek only to forgive humanity. As Hubback writes: 'It is not a great leap for cults to adopt a persecution complex which leads us to defend ourselves by pre-emptive strikes against a hostile and uncomprehending world.' Righteousness needs to be defended to the very end. That is our mission. We will neither flinch from fear nor cease the struggle.

     – TRINITY, THE DIVINE TESTAMENT, LONDON, 1996

En route to Heathrow the cab driver has told Caroline there's a security alert at Terminal 4. And at noon, in the foyer of the Heathrow Hilton, she thinks there are plain clothes police officers behind the hotel's reception desk.

She's right. They're inspecting the guest list on the computer. The routine intelligence gathering connected with international travellers and duties governed by the Prevention of Terrorism Act. Duty officers enquiring into the identities of possibly subversive new arrivals. Men and women of interest to the Immigration Service, or the Home Office, or one or other of the Security Services. As part of P

Squad's enquiries, two of their hundred men and women officers stationed at Heathrow are examining the computer screens with the hotel's security staff.

So when she arrives, the task of watching out for suspicious packages, or anyone looking out of place in the ground-floor reception area, is temporarily the responsibility of the hotel's duty doormen. Just another edgy day in a Heathrow hotel. The duty doormen find no reason to ask her about her business.

Skirting piles of luggage belonging to Arab and Japanese guests, she heads for an in-house phone. She notices the reception area is covered by CCTV cameras. Twice she calls Room 5006, but there's no answer from Morandi. She badly wants to know what he has to say. Maybe he's dozed off. *What the hell, I'll wake him.*

The lift travels smoothly through the floors.

In the empty hotel corridors leading to the western side of the building, with their windows facing the airport, she notices the absence of CCTV surveillance cameras. Outside Room 5006 she listens. Inside a TV is blaring.

She rings the bell.

Probably the floor maid's making up the bed.

Except there's a muffled howling. Inhuman. A dog's, perhaps. A whimpering. Then some sound like a low growl.

She goes to the wall phone at the end of the

corridor. Taps in the hotel's number: 0181-759-7755.

'Good afternoon, Heathrow Hilton. How can I help you?'

'Could you put me through to Room 5006, please. Father Morandi?'

'Won't keep you waiting a moment, caller.'

Some Vivaldi plays for about forty-five seconds before the operator's voice comes back on the line. 'I'm sorry, caller,' she says, 'Room 5006 isn't answering.'

'Can you confirm for me that Father Morandi is staying in Room 5006?'

'Yes, he is. Do you want to leave a message for him?'

'No thanks.'

Where are you, Father Morandi? Have you left the room with the TV on? Or has the maid already made up the room? Is she the one who left it on?

When she returns to Room 5006 she finds she was mistaken on both counts. Now silence concentrates her mind: The TV has been turned off, the howling's stopped.

No one's been in or out.

Someone in the room has to have turned the TV off.

Someone who heard the phone ring and for whatever reason didn't pick up.

So she returns to the wall phone.

'Would you put me through to room service, please?' She waits. 'Room service. Will you send up a jug of coffee, please? For two. Room 5006, please.

I'm with Father Morandi. Oh, and a small thing,' she adds vaguely. 'We've temporarily mislaid our card key. Can you ask someone to bring me another till we can get inside the room?'

The woman from room service hands Caroline the card key. She scribbles an illegible signature for the coffee followed by # 5006.

'Would you like me to take it in for you?' the woman asks. Caroline says she can manage on her own. Once the woman's out of sight, she inserts the card. The lock hums and clicks open.

Inside, the lights are on. It's a pleasant room. A lightweight overnight suitcase, unfastened, is on the bed. The curtains are drawn. A light is flashing on the telephones. One's by the double bed. The other's on the desk next to tourist brochures and the hotel's restaurant menus. Next to the menus is a passport.

Caroline looks at the name and photograph: Mgr Gian Maria Morandi. Born 1956, Lugano. The face is narrow. A high forehead. Short hair. Long and rather prominent nose. Aquiline features. A slight birthmark on the right cheek.

Looking around the room, she sees everything else is normal, except that the door to the adjoining suite has been prised open. She looks into the suite next door. In darkness, empty. *Someone's been in here. Someone's left by breaking into the next suite.* She walks into the darkened bedroom.

Once she's successfully fumbled the light switch

she sees how some intruder has made a getaway through another door to a small anteroom. Then to a passage. On to the fire exit. Through the floors. Down the concrete stairs and out.

Whoever has been here made a fast exit. It adds up: I surprised them.

Apart from that: everything's normal, except there's a putrid smell of faeces in Room 5006.

Combining with other unpleasant bodily smells, it's sweet and sickly. It's even stronger outside the bathroom door.

When she pushes it completely open she sees, dangling over the edge of the pale pink bath, a man's leg. The winter shoe's black rubber is wet with blood.

Holding her breath, nauseated, she backs away in shock.

Morandi's corpse lies in the bathtub, twisted on its left side. In death he looks older than his forty years. A stream of saliva runs from the mouth, sideways across the jaw. The left sleeve of his jacket has been partially ripped away. Perhaps, she reckons, slashed by a blade. Protruding from his neck, stuck into an artery, is a syringe and needle.

Sickened, Caroline gazes at Morandi's bloodied face. Into the wide-open sockets where his eyes should be. And the punctured neck and throat. The yawning cavity where the man's Adam's apple should be. *Jesus, those are animal bite marks. Dear God in Heaven, you really did walk into something.*

For nearly a minute, her heart thumping, she stands in the bathroom, staring at the savage wounds. The grotesque contortion of Morandi's butchered head. *God, what kind of people have permitted this to happen?*

Gently, she touches the broken skin of Morandi's forehead. Then his fingers. No *rigor mortis* yet. In fact, the body is still warm. She feels the spasm of anger. The overwhelming wave of pity for him. The sense of guilt that she hadn't arrived here even a few minutes earlier. *Whoever's been here killed you just before I arrived. Who are you? What animal did this?*

Crouching to examine the cream floor tiles, she finds traces of a white powder. *Is this heroin? Were they trying to make out you overdosed like Jane?*

She sees bluish-crimson blood still trickling from the side of Morandi's head. *You didn't die from the heroin, did you? This is how and why you died. Your killer used the knife to cut three times into your head just behind your left ear. And left the warning trademark:* | | |.

Everywhere the puncture marks. The jabbed skin. Bruised and swollen flesh. The signs of haemorrhaging. Incisions. Marks left by human or animal teeth. Abrasions. Lacerations. It's the surgical neatness of the strokes cut into Morandi's skin which chill her to the bone. *I can't take this any longer. I have to get out of here.*

There's a shout: 'OUT!' She realizes it's her own voice and can barely recognize the sound. Back along the corridor. Past the wall telephone. *Call Alan. Call Marcus.* Her hands are shaking. She desperately wants to get out. Out to the fresh air. To breathe. Her heart beats against her ribs. Feels like an iron clamp. Get out. Get out. She thumps the lift button. *Hurry. Please. Let me out of here.* The lift pings. The doors slide open.

Going down. She feels dizzy. Her breaths come in gasps. She feels her lungs will burst. She begins to moan. The lift stops. The doors slide open.

Everything seems so terribly normal.

Looking round wildly for a telephone, she fights to control her nausea and panic.

From the telephone in the foyer she calls the Home Office.

They deny Lever's existence for a second time. They've never heard of anyone called Alan Rosslyn.

And Marcus isn't answering.

She sees that her presence is being recorded by the CCTV cameras. *Will they think I have something to do with this?*

She has a sickening feeling that somehow she has a great deal to do with it, and she can't think of a way to explain her sense of guilt.

The terrible cuts, the | | |, the exposed white flesh, the blackish-red blood are still in her mind when she asks the woman at the reception desk to produce the envelope Morandi had told her he'd leave '. . . as a precaution'. She stammers the 'p'. The brown envelope is padded with plastic bubble-wrap.

She reads her name on it, and as though it's an accusation, she's seized with panic, at any moment expecting someone to shout after her: 'You! Wait!'

She slips the package with her name on inside her coat and walks fast towards the exit and the cold, fresh air.

Where she blinks into the raw cold and bright white light.

Do I call a cab? The driver would recognize me. Maybe I should take the tube instead?

Some shivering Africans in national costume are standing next to a long Mercedes. And when the limousine pulls away, almost unbelieving, she hears the voice: 'Caro!'

And thinks she's hearing things.

'Over here.'

He's standing by a small windowless transit van.

'What the hell are you doing here, Marcus?'

'Come on, get in.' There's a strained urgency in his voice. He has the transit van's rear doors open. She glimpses the figure of a man inside.

'Marcus, how did you know I was here?'

'Rosslyn told me.'

'Alan told you? He can't have done. I haven't told him about us —'

'I did,' says Marcus. 'It's all OK. Come on, angel. Trust me, Caro. Hurry.'

Suddenly she feels almost euphoric. The wave of relief.

He embraces her quickly. 'You look as if you've seen a ghost.'

'It's worse than that. It's Morandi. He's up there, Marcus. They've murdered him –'

'Let me help you in, angel. We have to go. *Quick*.'

'Marcus – Jesus, I've got blood on my shoes. They *must* have seen –'

'Yes,' says Luke. 'Now get inside.'

He pushes her into the back with a force she finds totally unexpected. Looking down at her blood-stained shoes, she sees she's dropped Morandi's package. It's lying in the gutter and Marcus hasn't seen it. 'Marcus!'

'Here,' says the voice in the darkness. The doors slam shut. 'Climb in, girl –'

'Marcus, wait.'

The accent of the man in the darkness is unfamiliar. Welsh or Scots or Irish. She can't be sure. The hand that powerfully clutches hers is large and blistered. She can see the man is wearing dungarees and heavy rubber boots. She can't see his face. But she can smell his pungent sweat. And chained beside him is the crouching dog.

Muzzled, the white jaws are soaked in flesh and blood. Its foul tongue hangs from its mouth. As if the animal's satiated. The stump mouth even seems to wear a smile. Beside it is a miniature blowlamp.

She twists away. Her coat's caught in the door. And when she tries to pull it free, it tears.

'*Jesus*,' she says, crouching. Pulling at the coat.

'Help me!' she shouts. 'Tell Marcus. Turn back. Stop. The envelope from –'

As she's turning round the clenched fist thuds down at the side of her neck. Just beneath her ear.

She thinks she's tripped. Fallen flat on her face. Her cheeks pound against metallic rims. Again and again. She tastes blood in her mouth. The screaming in her ears starts. She kicks and screams against the hammer blows. *He's clubbing me to death.*

The man is hissing: 'Later, P & J – later.'

The transit van is gathering speed. Then the throbbing in her head seems punctured by the stab of the needle driven into her thigh. Deep. The muscle aches. And she thinks of Rosslyn. And starts to pray. Sees white. Then black.

31

↑→

Rosslyn can't raise Lever on his mobile. Instead, he calls her from a call box in Tottenham Court Road. 'Have you found her?'

'Have *we* found her? Alan, we're deep in the proverbial S H figures one T. It's Morandi that's been found. Dead.'

'He what?'

'Murdered, Alan.'

'When?'

'Some time in the last few hours at the Heathrow Hilton. The police have been there all day. They've put out a description. They want to interview your client. They want to interview Caroline.'

His mouth is dry. 'Caroline?'

'The police have been to your place. They've got officers on the door. Officers at the Malvern Hotel. We don't want you tangled up in the murder investigation. We haven't time. SIS are asking questions. The DG's at Downing Street. And I need you in here. So move it.'

Not until I've been to the Malvern Hotel.

32

↑→
↓

Caroline, blindfold and unconscious, is lifted across Wroth's shoulders down the steps of the iron ladder in the darkness. Strapped to his head, like a miner's lamp, is a powerful flashlight. The beam picks out broken brickwork some two feet wide and two feet high.

He lowers her in the foetal position to one side of the square gap in the brickwork, next to the make-shift steel door bolted to the wooden frame.

Backwards, feet first, in a crouch and with some difficulty, he squeezes his eighteen-stone bulk through the gap. Then he drags her towards him. On the other side of the gap he once more heaves Caroline across his shoulders in the fireman's lift.

The powerful flashlight illuminates the easternmost and sloping chambers of the catacombs beneath Kensal Green Cemetery. Other vaults, chambers and the catafalque to the south for lowering and raising coffins, known only to those whose concern is with this arcane branch of industrial archaeology. The disposal of the dead. Here is the dark and damp resting place of several thousand departed souls below ground. The air in these accessible chambers circulates satisfactorily. But the eastern chambers Wroth has opened up are dangerous. Entry to them has long ago been prohibited. The air here is dank and fetid. It smells of drains. Decayed vegetable matter. Rotten wood and fungi. Apart from Wroth, it is doubtful if other human feet have entered these subterranean vaults in living memory.

In here, carefully monitoring the correct temperature and dryness of the transportable wine cellar, he has stored the one tonne of high explosive he's paid for and had delivered to him in Adinkerke by the Czech.

Here is the *matériel* for the light to illuminate the world on 1 January 2000. It comprises a lethal mix of cyclo-trimethylene-trinitramine, pentaerythritoal, and plasticizer. Smaller boxes contain detonating cord: Cordtex, a proprietary brand for the transmission of the detonating wave. On a shelf above the high explosive is a five-foot-long lightweight and waterproof crate containing two high-powered rifles: Barrett M82A1 Light Fifty As.

Wroth has cleared aside some rotten coffins and their gruesome contents. It is beneath a false ceiling of discarded memorial tablets that he has constructed the cell for Caroline. She will be held here blindfold and manacled. To be fed by Wroth like a battery hen. Talked to by Wroth. Her impurities of mind and body flushed out. Until the receipt of final orders from the Divine Master.

During these final heady hours before the dawn of the Millennium.

The flashlight fixed to his head picks out the marble memorial's lengthy carved inscription:

To the Sacred Memory
of
JOHN COOTE MORTIMER
who died of plague on 6th December 1834 aged 26
FREDERICK MORTIMER
who died of plague on 7th December 1834 aged 18
MARY JANE MORTIMER
who died of plague on 5th December 1834 aged 10
Children of the late Colonel Albert Coote Mortimer
Late Senior Member of the Madras Medical Board
who died of plague on the 7th December 1834 aged 54
Gertrude Coote Mortimer of Mary-Le-Bone
who died of plague on 10th December 1834 aged 46
after patient Suffering

Wroth associates the name Mortimer with *mortuary*. *Mort*, as in death. The cell seems to him named with a singular appropriateness.

In this dark and silent space – where the remains of the Mortimers, felled by the plague, have lain undisturbed in peace for over a century and a half – are the remains of dismembered corpses, victims of a more modern plague and interred here in recent times by Wroth in the Name of The Divine.

For the wise murderer always plans ahead. *Time spent in reconnaissance is seldom wasted.* And the police rarely, if ever, dig up cemeteries to look for murder victims.

The dead do not smell sweet. In any case, to excavate here would be sacrilegious. No, the police prefer to search among the living. The dead are innocent. Such are Wroth's conclusions. What he calls his common sense.

33

Uniformed as well as plain clothes police are in the foyer of the Malvern Hotel.

Rosslyn asks to see the manager.

'He's not available,' the receptionist says. 'He's in a meeting.'

'Who with?'

'The police officers.'

'Where?'

'In one of the rooms.'

Number 65, thinks Ahearne. 'I'll speak to his assistant, if he's got one.'

'The assistant manager's in the office over there. May I tell him who wants to see him?'

Rosslyn flashes the ASG ID card. 'Special Branch,' he lies. 'I'd rather you didn't say anything.' He walks round the receptionist's desk and opens the door marked PRIVATE.

The short and rather plump man looks up from behind the Christmas tree on his desk.

'Lever,' says Rosslyn. 'Special Branch.'

The plump man fastens the buttons of his dark double-breasted suit. Before he can speak, Rosslyn says, 'It's to do with Ms Moorfield.'

'Oh yes, of course,' the assistant manager says

gaily. He puts the aerosol of Christmas Sparkling Snow on the desk. 'What can we do to help?'

'My colleagues are in Room 65 –'

'Making a very thorough search, yes?'

'That's what we like to think it is.'

'We saw so little of her,' says the assistant manager. 'Caroline Moorfield. So many questions about Caroline. You know, the sister died of drugs –'

'I know,' says Rosslyn. 'I want to make sure Ms Moorfield didn't leave anything with you in the safe.'

'You do, oh. Such as?'

'Let's take a look, shall we? In the safe?'

'No can do. Sorry, Mr –'

'Lever.'

'No. Oh no. We can only open it in the presence of the manager.' He's eyeing Rosslyn's crotch.

'I'll have to do instead. Let's get it open and have a look-see.'

'Please, do you mind waiting –?'

'Yes, I bloody do mind waiting. This is a murder investigation, chummy. I'm in a hurry. Open the thing. Now.'

The assistant manager stoops down awkwardly. 'I say . . .' He fingers the combination lock. 'What are we looking for then?' he pants. He starts to rummage in the safe.

'Move yourself,' says Rosslyn. He pushes the man aside and looks inside the safe. 'I'll do the looking. Get away. I don't want your fingerprints all over her stuff.'

Sees purses. A few small canvas bags. A Tessier's carrier bag. Jewellery, maybe. A wallet. Traveller's cheques. Then what the assistant manager obviously didn't want him to find. Half a dozen hard porn magazines: *He/She. Transsexual*. Then to the right, at the back, the small black notebook. Inside: Jane's faxes.

'Someone's at the door,' says Rosslyn.

The assistant manager crosses the office to open it. As he does so, Rosslyn slips the journal inside his jacket.

'No one there,' says the assistant manager, sweating. 'Would you believe –'

'Nothing in here either,' says Rosslyn. 'Thanks all the same.'

'You're welcome, I am sure,' says the assistant manager. 'I thought you must be with the porn boys.'

'Whatever takes your fancy.'

'Pardon me?'

'I said . . . I don't like the look of those comics.'

'Don't know what you mean.'

'What's your name, sonny?'

'May we give *your* name to the manager?'

'The name's Lever. Detective Inspector Lever. If I were you, I'd move your mucky comics out of there before my boyfriends find them.'

At the hotel exit he sees three police officers across the foyer, leaving the lift.

He walks fast to the Tottenham Court Road and

waves down a taxi. 'Claverton Street, Pimlico.'

He settles back to flick through the journal. For any sign. Any indication as to what's happened. Why she could conceivably have been a party of any kind to Morandi's death.

And what he sees jumps up off the stage at him in bold. It feels as though she's stuck her fingers in his eyes and she's holding them there –

> *Marcus. I like my own agenda. Not that I've lost faith in Alan Rosslyn. But Marcus as my lover is kind of mine. He's going to help me to approach whatever now may remain of the Trinity Chapter's membership. To offer myself to it. With Marcus's support. As a noviciate. With his guidance I won't be taking any kind of risk.*
>
> *Things to do:*
> - *See Dr Maryon at Guy's Hospital*
> - *See Dr Llewellyn in Cambridge*
> - *Visit Kensal Green Cemetery and the Trinity apartment block*
> - *Take J's ashes home soon*

'Changed my mind,' Rosslyn tells the cab driver. 'Go to Kensal Green.' His voice is shaking. 'The cemetery.'

The driver could be forgiven for thinking his passenger is in pain.

He'd be right.

'Stop on the way at a chemist's,' Rosslyn tells him.

Where he buys some transparent surgical gloves. In a nearby newsagents he makes another purchase:

a pack of small transparent plastic bags and adhesive tape.

Could Caroline have had something to do with Morandi's death? Like she's been running her own agenda. Confusion plagues his mind.

He leaves the cab at the College Road entrance to Kensal Green underground station, where a woman with a small baby is standing in the snow. She's wrapped up in white blankets, like her child, and chants interminably:

> *Trin-it-ee*
> *Trin-it-ee*
> *Three in one*
> *One in three*

She tries to hand Rosslyn a Trinity Calendar. 'He will come,' she says.

'Oh c'mon, girl –'

She reaches out to grab his coat sleeve.

'*Piss off.*'

'Three in One. One in Three,' she calls after him. 'Bless you too.'

These people are everywhere. Maggots. He crosses the Harrow Road towards the Mason's Arms and past the fish seller's cart overturned on the pavement in the snow. Its battered sign blocks Rosslyn's way:

Whelks per 1/2 pint £2·50
＋ Prawns £2·80
Cockles, winkles
jellied eels £1·80 ＃

Overhead, the sign of the Mason's Arms shows two hands, a mallet and a slab of carved marble. It creaks and squeals as it swings in the wind. The Harrow Road traffic is jammed by a heavyweight truck. Its side tarpaulins are emblazoned EXPRESSOTRANS TRANSITARIOS LDA LISBOA. The vehicle's driver is shouting in Portuguese at another manic Trinity follower to get lost quick.

Past the pub, its windows filled with Christmas lights and banners announcing the approach of the Millennium, Rosslyn sees the apartment building.

It's heavily secured against intruders with steel shutters. Two large red and white notices say BEWARE! PATROLLED NIGHT AND DAY BY GUARD DOGS.

Rosslyn sees no sign of them. The nearest neighbours live in the massive, barely visible council blocks to the north of Harrow Road.

An ugly relic of early 1960s architecture, the building overlooks the cemetery's boundary wall. Built of brick and capped with frozen snow, the twelve-foot-high brick wall faces south. It separates the cemetery from the Harrow Road. Bordered by rail and canal routes, the seventy-seven-acre Kensal Green private cemetery is one of the most remarkable anywhere in the world. The great necropolis of tombs, mausolea and catacombs is said to embody the Victorian ideal of the 'sweet breathing space'. The ideal place for contemplative recreation and spiritual enlightenment.

Defaced by Trinity graffiti and signs, the front entrance to the building has a high iron gate in the wall secured by a lock and chains. There's no sign of life from any of the windows. The damp note taped across the defunct entryphone says OUT OF ORDER USE BELL. After two rings a massive figure in dungarees shouts at him through the bars of an upstairs window: 'Who do you want?'

The Trinity follower, who's given up on the Portuguese truck driver, approaches. He stops chanting. 'Bless you,' he yells up at the windows.

'Bless you,' says the man in dungarees. Then to Rosslyn he shouts: 'Who did you say?'

'Marcus Luke,' Rosslyn shouts. 'I'm a friend of his. Who are you?'

'Caretaker. I'll come down.'

Unfastening the chain to the door, he looks at Rosslyn with suspicion.

'Do you know where I can find Luke?' Rosslyn asks.

'Who are you?'

'A friend from work', says Rosslyn stepping inside. 'Is he living here?'

'No further, boyo,' says the caretaker, blocking Rosslyn's way. 'Can't let you in. I have my orders.'

'What orders?' says Rosslyn.

'To keep out visitors.' The accent is Welsh. 'Is Marcus in trouble?'

'He asked me to collect his mail.'

'It's on the floor outside his door,' says the caretaker. 'His place is locked.'

'Mind if you open his flat up for me?'

The caretaker gives him a broken grin. 'I thought you were police.'

'Me?' says Rosslyn. 'No. We're on the same side.'

The caretaker hands Rosslyn a key. 'Top floor.'

'Before I collect his mail,' says Rosslyn, 'can you tell me – has he had any callers recently?'

'None that I know of.'

'In the past at all?'

'Maybe there was a few.'

'Who were they?'

'I wouldn't know who the people were.'

'Or people you don't want to tell me about?' says Rosslyn.

'Like who, man?'

'A girl?' says Rosslyn.

The caretaker fingers the cheap medallion at his tree-trunk neck. 'No. Not Marcus. Religious. No trouble. Pays monthly in advance, like all the others.'

'Which others?'

'People here. They come and go. He comes and

goes. I don't ask questions of the tenants. He goes to prayer meetings and such like.' The suspicion is returning. 'What's your game then, boyo?'

Without replying, Rosslyn walks towards the stairs.

34

By the door to the upstairs flat he draws on the transparent surgical gloves he bought at the chemist's, then squats down to fix a strip of cling film to the soles of his shoes.

He waits a moment, listening to the echoing sounds of the caretaker busying himself somewhere downstairs, in case he might be making an untoward telephone call about the visitor.

He leafs through the junk mail on the floor: Circulars, catalogues, electoral roll enquiries. All of it addressed variously; either to Mr Kamil Anwar, Mrs Chowdhury Ahmed or Dr Mirza Ali. Bangladeshis, assumes Rosslyn. The personal mail, postmarked Quezon City, Philippines, is addressed to Vicente de Jesus. None of it bears Luke's name.

His eyes take in the flat. Stained carpets. Open, tattered curtains. Shabby furniture. Awful early Habitat perhaps. The door to a bedroom is ajar.

He examines a futon with a crumpled nylon sheet and filthy duvet. The kitchen. Old cooking fat. Opens the fridge. There is a carton of milk. Dated a month ago.

Come on, Luke. Speak to me.

What did Caroline say to you. You to her?

This is the place, isn't it? This is where Ahearne went through that noxious ritual.

Come on. Tell me your secret, Caro.

Why, in heaven's name, did you ask him if you could join the cult?

A door to a wardrobe of scratched pine stands open. Lined with dry newspapers, its shelves are empty. *When was this place last lived in – a month or two ago, perhaps?* The newspapers in the wardrobe are three years out of date. *What was going on in here?* There are a few cigarette butts in a tin. Hand-rolled cigarettes. Rizla cigarette paper. Cheap tobacco.

In the main room that faces the cemetery, he lifts the telephone answering machine. It's still connected. He presses the redial button. *Who were you calling, Luke? Is this your little love-nest?* After four or five rings a woman's voice says:

'Malvern Hotel. How can I help you?'

Which surely means that someone has called Caroline from here.

'Malvern Hotel. Hello? I can't hear you . . . please try again later.'

He replaces the telephone receiver without a word. Beneath it is a London street map. Various locations had been circled in felt tip. The area around St Pancras. The Kensal Green Cemetery. The Malvern Hotel. He drops the street map into a small transparent polythene bag. Then he stands very still. Listening. Looking. Taking in the framed reproduction of a Renaissance madonna and child on the wall above the TV and video recorder. On the video recorder's black surface there are finger marks in the dust. Crouching down, he sees a tape is still inserted. He presses EJECT. On the cassette is a label marked in felt tip with the legend: I I I.

Tempted to play it here and now. Unsure of the caretaker, whether he might cut short his examination of the flat, he thinks better of it. He drops the cassette into a second bag. He'll play it later.

The bathroom remains to be examined. His eyes read the bath tub and basin and toilet like a text. Left to right. And back. And there are more recent signs of occupancy and still others, overlooked, of violence.

Someone has bled in the bath.

Where the bath of chipped white enamel joins the floor there are faint streaks of dried blood and others around the rim of the overflow outlet. He searches for any hairs. Unusually, he finds none.

Has it been a day, a week, a month, or longer since the blood was cleaned up in a hurry And who by? If this has been washed down by the caretaker downstairs, he would surely have prevented me seeing these signs of bloodshed. What's this behind the toilet? In this crumpled, bloodied toilet paper?

He unwraps it carefully. He finds a 5cc syringe. Two 25g and one 23g needles. A folded piece of silver paper with traces of a white powder. He sprinkles some of it on his hand. Heroin.

Washing out his mouth, he's still standing by the basin when he's alerted to the faintest sound of what he takes to be the howling of a dog.

Far below. *Maybe in a basement. Or outside in the snow*. Then silence. Until the door opens.

35

The caretaker is wiping his hands on a greasy, red-striped towel. His rubber boots and dungarees are covered in what seems to be cement dust, as if he's just walked off a building site.

'What is it you're not telling me?' Rosslyn asks him. He shows him the bloodstains in the bath and the contents of the bloodied toilet tissues. The needles and the powder traces. 'Who was doing drugs here, then?'

'I don't know, boyo.'

'Do you do drugs?'

'Shit, no.'

The caretaker stares hard at the bloodstains.

'Whose blood's that?' Rosslyn asks.

'I don't know.'

'These visitors of Luke's. Do you remember an American woman?'

'Well, yes. There was an American. I think he showed her the cemetery. I can't be sure of it.'

'Who else came to see him here?'

The caretaker raises his eyes. 'I don't know. But there was another American. A man who came here like you asking for Luke. Must have been two weeks ago. I don't know. Maybe even three.'

'Who was he? Did he tell you his name?'

'I don't know who he was, boyo.'

'What did he look like?'

'Big. Like big. Over six foot. White. I'd say in his forties. In good shape, like a prizefighter or a wrestler or something like that. He asked me if I'd show him in here. Like you asked.' Rosslyn remembers Queron's colleague at the US Embassy.

'And did you let him in here?'

'Yuh.'

'Did you stay with him while he was in here?'

'He asked to be left alone, didn't he?'

'You tell me,' says Rosslyn coldly. 'Take your time. What was he looking for?'

'He said he was looking for someone, a woman.'

'One woman in particular?'

'I dunno.'

'*Think*. What was her name. Was it Jane?'

'Could've been.'

'Could Jane have been Jane Moorfield? Do you think she was Luke's friend?'

'Could've been, couldn't she?'

'I'm asking you.'

'Listen, she could've been his friend. Why don't you find her? Why ask me? Why not ask her yourself?'

'I can't,' says Rosslyn. 'Because she's dead.'

The caretaker opens his eyes wide. 'Luke *is* in shit.'

'Maybe, maybe not,' says Rosslyn with a tone of indifference. 'How long have you worked here?'

'Past few months.'

'So who pays you then?'

Stepping back a little, the caretaker says: 'I don't have to say anything more . . . to do with the religious movement that used this place.'

'The Trinity Chapter?'

'Everyone knows that. They left. I got this job from the pub. One of the barmen was asking if anyone wanted to act as caretaker and I said: "Me. I want to act as caretaker." Then, a few days later, he tells me I've got the job.'

'What is this place, then?'

'It's a shrine to this man they call the Master. He's dead. And they're moving on places. I helped them clear the place. I mean, I think all they wanted was me to come here. Turn on the lights. Make it look as if someone's using the place. Put down the rat poison. I mean, the basement is full, I mean fucking full of rats. Maybe they come from the cemetery or some place. I asked a bit about this man Trinity, seeing as though I'm a believer. A Christian.'

'Who did you ask about Trinity?'

'The barman who got me the job. He told me. He's left too. Otherwise, all I know is that these people kept themselves to themselves. There was this talk of a Second Coming. Do you know about that?'

'I heard. I don't believe in that crap.'

'Me neither,' says the caretaker. He reaches inside his anorak. 'I found this outside the basement.' He hands Rosslyn a crumpled photograph. 'That's his grave. This Master. Trinity. So he's dead and buried. Out there in the cemetery across the road. They said he's "coming again" in the New Year. That's what they say. You're right. They're full of crap.'

Rosslyn looks at the photograph of the tombstone and reads the legend:

Trinity

| | |

In Sure & Certain Hope

of

His Resurrection

'One more thing. You're quite sure you know nothing about those bloodstains in the bath? Someone bled there very heavily. Make no mistake. Someone was cut to pieces in that bath.'

'You have to believe me, man. I don't know about that.'

'If you have any thoughts about it –' Rosslyn writes a telephone number on the back of the photograph. '– call me. And if Luke turns up, call me. Day or night, right? I include those Americans. If they show up here, ask them where they can be reached. Then ring me. Don't say what I've asked you to do. Don't mention my name to them either. That's between you and me.'

He gives the caretaker Lever's telephone number.

The howling. Once again, by the exit, Rosslyn hears the howling.

'Is that a dog?' he asks the caretaker.

'Mine. Probably found a rat.'

'Sounds more like a human to me,' says Rosslyn.

'Only the dog.'

At the door, looking over the caretaker's shoulder, Rosslyn notices the trail of footsteps in the white dust across the floor.

'Are you doing building works?'

'We've had burst pipes.' He puts his fingers between his teeth and gives a piercing whistle. The howling stops.

'See?'

'What's your name?' asks Rosslyn.

'What's it to you?'

'Might be something if you don't tell me,' says Rosslyn. 'I can always get it from the pub.'

'Wroth,' says the caretaker. 'Morgon Wroth.'

36

Reborn as you prophesied.
— TRINITY, THE DIVINE TESTAMENT, LONDON, 1996

Through the snow outside the woman chanter plods towards him. Before she can buttonhole him, he heads away through the snow to a free cab waiting at the gates to Kensal Green Cemetery.

His mind is fixed on the bloodstains in the bath.

Is that what Morandi meant? Are they going to pump Caroline full of heroin too and make out she's a suicide victim like her sister?

He hopes Dr Maryon has a good memory for the faces of the dead she looks at day in, day out. A more open mind than the apelike Wroth.

37

Except for the sound of Wroth's footsteps, the cold interior of the apartment building is now silent. He tells himself he must wash away the traces of his footsteps in the cement dust.

At the back of the building, he unchains the white Pit Bull terrier and takes the stairs from the ground floor to the basement. In the far wall is a double door. The dog stretches its jaws. Wroth unlocks the chain and padlocks and then closes the door behind him. Here a still narrower flight of stone stairs leads steeply downwards from the basement. He calls the dog to follow him.

His flashlight alerts some scurrying rats. The beam illuminates the way across the damp flagstones. Some fifty feet, to where the brick wall has been opened. He squeezes through the gap into what seems to be the underground cell supported by heavy wooden beams. Here he lights a paraffin lamp. Once he's turned up the flame from red to white he can see his spades and shovels. The pile of sand. Water containers. The cement sacks and the progress of his excavation work. 'Foundation work' is how he'd have explained it to the man called Lever who's just made those untoward enquiries.

This *Lever* man, this afternoon's visitor, would not have lived had he come down here. There have been too many people of his sort asking questions here in recent days. None, of course, has been down here. Or has an idea that his 'excavation' is the construction of a tomb extension. The final resting place. Accommodation for disfigured corpses whose identities have been satisfactorily destroyed. Soon enough they will be joined by others. More bodies committed to the rotten London soil and clay.

He lights a cheap cigar to combat the putrid smell of death. *And Marcus says he's bringing something else Marcus won't talk about –*

Suddenly, beyond a heavy door, the howling starts.

If I was Marcus, I'd have killed her already. Why did Marcus change the plan?

Marcus, who knows best – who should by now have reached the north.

38

And so the disciples make preparation for The Second Coming.
– TRINITY, THE DIVINE TESTAMENT, LONDON, 1996

The north. Where Luke sets down the Victoria Wines cardboard box on the desk in the office of Universal Vehicles Group in Brighouse, West Yorkshire. 'Fifty grand in fifties,' he says.

The woman says it's unusual for UVG to receive payment in so large a sum of cash.

'Charity,' says Luke. 'Collected in cash from several charity events in the West End of London. Grosvenor House. The Hilton. The Dorchester.'

The accounts woman seems unimpressed by the high-flown accent. 'Will you be wanting a receipt?' she asks.

'No.'

Unusual, she thinks. *Fifty grand and no receipt*. She looks at the packs of cash fastened with the National Westminster Bank's tape. *The professional touch that*, thinks Luke. *My idea. People feel better if big sums have been wrapped up by the bank.*

'Thanks,' she says, and locks the cash in the company safe. 'If you'd like to come into the yard forecourt. The manager's asked me to show you over the vehicle.' She's a fund of information. 'We construct for services as far off as Australia and South Africa. Normally, like, the vehicle is bought from LDV vans. Used to be Leyland Daf. We do the bodywork and interior fittings. A hundred technicians have worked on your vehicle, Mr. . . Here it is.'

'What's the outside made of, then?'

'Fibreglass front and side and rear panels.' She opens the rear doors. 'Inside we have lino and aluminium. Body insulation. Ventilation system. If you'd like to come inside and have a look-see.' Luke climbs inside the ambulance. 'Attendant seat,' she explains. 'Bulkhead locker and doors. You'll have noticed the decals.'

'What are those?'

'The fluorescent strips on the exterior. So you can be seen the more easily. We've fitted you up with radios and datatrack. In the cab you'll find the automatic vehicle location system. The AVLS. And you have a detachable roof panel. So you can see out of the top. If you want to see out of the top, that is. Say you needed to communicate visually with airborne paramedics or the fire service or the police. You never know. So there you are. I hope this meets your requirements.'

'Has it got a full tank?'

'Oh, yes. Diesel, of course. Will there by any other questions at all then, Mr. . .'

'No, thanks,' he says. 'Time to go.'

To make it back to Kensal Green.

39

Kensal Green.

Listening to Gloria Gaynor at full blast on his Walkman, Wroth, with the thoroughness you'd expect from the former guardsman and military prisoner, removes all tell-tale traces of the former occupant's presence.

The process is watched by P & J who's muzzled and ready to share the late-night meal with his master. The dog will have to wait. Before they dine tonight, Wroth has to attend to the woman below ground. It's slop-out time. To be followed by the provision of her survival rations.

He turns out the lights and heads for the flights of stairs to the lower floors and basement level. Humming as he goes, he performs a little jig, like the prizefighter before the big fight, to the rhythm of *I Will Survive*.

If it'd been his choice he'd already have disposed of the woman prisoner, who lies in chains moaning in the darkness near the Mortimer family tomb. Choice doesn't enter into it. Discipline and devotion to the Divine Master determine that he must wait for the green light some time during these final heady days of the twentieth century. The soldier's impatience can prove fatal. Belief and trust are what the good soldier needs if he is to perform his duty. They make all things possible.

The beam from his torch shows him the way down the steps to where Caroline is lying helpless.

40

Sometimes I feel like a private detective or a spy looking at the leaders of the new religious movements, tracing their funding. None of these men deserves the worship he inspires in his followers. The charismatic leaders are sometimes mad, sometimes sane gurus. Some are harmless souls. Some are dangerous monsters.

    – JANE MOORFIELD TO CAROLINE MOORFIELD, FALL 1999

Caroline sits barefoot in darkness on the cell's damp stone floor. Under the rough blankets she's been provided with, she wears the white shroud. Shaven-headed, wrists manacled, she breathes through the mouth slit in the rubber head mask that's fastened by a strap tight around her neck. The manacles are locked to heavy chains and these are fixed to meat hooks fast in the dank brickwork somewhere above her head. Steel restraints around her ankles make any movement difficult and painful. The restraints only just allow her to heave herself, when the need arises, to the bucket that serves as the toilet.

Above her, there's the small opening in the brickwork. During the hours of winter daylight, from around 8 am to what must be about 3.30 pm, she can see something of the hell-hole. Being able to see, to look at things, somehow prevents her imagination from running completely wild. Otherwise there's the cold. The interminable enforced darkness.

The cell's double doors are like the heavy doors you see in banks. They open only from the outside.

It's in the space between them that she's left food. Mostly take-away. Pizzas. Charred vegetables. Curries. Chinese. Tea. Some fruit. Once a day he leaves hot water in a bucket, soap, paper towels and a second bucket for her to wash with and to use afterwards as a toilet.

The cell is empty – apart from the sound speaker out of reach above the door.

The days seem indistinguishable from the nights.

She alternately screams and weeps. Sometimes she heaves herself as far as possible across the cell and lies for hours wrapped in the blankets near to the gap beneath the iron door. Somewhere outside, the fan heater has been positioned. The whirring is just about the only noise that breaks the silence.

She thinks that the city's winter cold has numbed her senses.

Can't believe they'll kill me. I feel I'm surfing. On the crest of the wave one minute, then down the next.

There's no in-between. Except maybe when she washes in the bucket. Eats. Defecates.

Forcing herself to close her eyes tight, to impose darkness on herself, she counts the seconds. Up to

300 seconds – 5 minutes. At three hundred, she opens her eyes violently, hoping they'll blaze out some beam of illumination. It doesn't work. This is one of the features of existence here she's come to dread. The countless hours. The torture of the dark.

Blackness. Pricked only by the myriad sparks and stars seen when you squeeze the eyes tight. Inducing the nausea. The hallucinatory state.

The silence is terrible. *Do I dream that silence is a kind of noise? The thump-thump-thump. My heart. The blood-beat in my ears? The pain in my wrists. Numb-numb-numb. Thud-thud-thud. How many thuds until Death?*

She thinks she can hear scratching. Mice or rats perhaps. If so, she's glad to be in the company of these innocent creatures and envies them their freedom. As she had envied them when she was a child and tried in vain to communicate with animals in the language of her invention.

For how long have I been here? Can't tell.

Aerobics in chains. She tells herself to exercise. Each limb and joint in turn. Arms. Legs. Stomach. Neck. She lies on her back and, as far as the restraints allow, spreads her legs apart trying to bring her feet together slowly. The movement causes an audible crack in the gristle of her spine.

She sits meditating. Anything to avoid the horror of her predicament. Thinking of the beaches. Watching ocean waves. She brings to mind the Gay Head Cliffs at Martha's Vineyard. The nature trail at Fort Hill Preserve. The remains of the early settlements.

Stone walls. House sites. She retraces Thoreau's first walk to Newcomb Hollow beach. Now she's walking through the desolate sands of the National Seashore at Provincetown. She can see whales in the ocean. Now she's looking out to Minot's Light at Cohasset Harbour. The sea is dead calm. The tide shifts very slowly. The water rocks gently. Just as she rocks for reassurance. Like a troubled child. Forward. Back. Forward. Back.

Other times she has a film show in her mind. Her father's video of *The 400 Blows*. The end of *The 400 Blows*. She's Jean-Pierre Léaud's Antonie Doinel. She runs along a road. Past hedges. Road signs. Orchards. Open fields. Farm buildings. A parked truck. It's dusk. She rushes down the side of a hill to an inlet.

There are two boats and a narrow jetty. The jetty stretches into the far distance; the open ocean is at the end of it.

I descend a huge open stairway. Reach the beach and run toward the ocean. The tide is out and the beach is long and flat. I'm alone.

*I reach the surf. Walk into the water. It circles around my shoes and I look down, surprised. I turn. Walk in the water parallel to the beach. Taking a look over my shoulder at the sea. I turn my back to the shore. The camera approaches me and the shot freezes into a still —
Caroline Moorfield.*

The ocean behind me —
Fade to black.

She makes mental lists of THINGS I DON'T DO: *Dream. Scream. Sweat. Think of sex.*

Think of the Trinity bastards as people with names, particularly M— L—.

THINGS I DO: *Rock. Suck my thumb. Bite my nails. Weep.*

THINGS I ACHE FOR: *A mirror. A hot bath. To see a smiling face. Salt. To see the sun. Freedom. Life.*

THINGS I'M PROUD OF: *Nothing.*

THINGS I FEEL: *Guilt and shame. Self-hatred. Fear of madness. Sore veins. Puncture marks. Cramp. Hunger. Dirty. Fear of fear. The beating of my heart.*

She hears the footsteps beyond the door and the growling of the dog.

Jesus Christ. Help Me. The voice is saying, 'Food's up, Caroline.' *I can hear the dog howling.*

41

Dr Maryon's office is at the end of the dusty institutional corridors that lead to the Department of Forensic Medicine in Guy's Hospital.

Judging by the equipment in the bright red gym bag, Dr Maryon keeps in shape. A smell of disinfectant mixed with a cheap floral bouquet pervades her office. She offers Rosslyn a chair beside her desk. He notices the CD next to the hi-fi. Mahler's Symphony No. 2, 'Resurrection'.

'I'd like to be able to say I can remember all the details of Jane's examination,' Dr Maryon tells him. 'But you must realize that one performs something like a thousand *post mortems* each year across a very wide area of London. In addition to one's teaching duties it's a heavy load. All I can say is that the report I gave under oath to the coroner is the full record as required by law. Such deaths by drug abuse are all too tragically common and are on the increase. One deals with at least three hundred every year. I'm afraid that's the world we inhabit.'

'Not the one I inhabit,' says Rosslyn.

She looks quizzically at Rosslyn. The dark-brown eyes veiled by the split fringe of black hair. 'Is it that you feel there may be something wrong about the inquest?'

'My client thinks so. You see, her late sister never did drugs.'

'I'm sorry to have to say, however painful it may be for her to face, that according to the record of my examination, she most certainly did. Heroin.'

'Well, I'm sorry, but my client thinks otherwise. So do I.'

'I'm not sure how I can convince you,' she says, as though he's one of her recalcitrant students.

'I want to know the truth, Dr Maryon.'

'Very well then,' she says. She goes to a wall of steel filing cabinets holding case history files. 'In the circumstances, strictly off the record, I'll break the Home Office rules.' She pulls open a drawer and thumbs the files. She hands Rosslyn a xerox. 'That's the letter from the doctor who certified her sister's death.'

Rosslyn reads the letter that had been provided by Dr Ryan Lancaster in evidence to the inquest. He notices three sections have been highlighted:

Alongside the woman were a 5cc syringe, and two 25g and one 23g needles, a folded piece of paper to which traces of a powder were adherent. They brought these with the patient.

I remember thinking these were rather awkward sites for self-administered intravenous injections. These were not the venepuncture sites one normally sees in comatose intravenous drug abusers brought to our casualty.

However, given the physical findings and the presence of the syringe, needles and folded sheet of paper with powder traces, I thought the most likely cause of coma was an intravenous drug overdose, almost certainly an opiate, and I therefore administered a dose of the narcotic antagonist naloxone through the existing IV line.

As there was no immediate response to the naloxone, I intubated her and ventilated her by hand and accompanied her to the intensive care unit.

She arrested at approximately 2.26 am and was successfully defibrillated. However, shortly thereafter she became asystolic – a form of cardiac arrest – and failed to respond to resuscitation.

Efforts to resuscitate her continued for forty minutes. But she was pronounced dead at 3.23 am.

The laboratory returned samples of diamorphine in the peripheral blood and urine.

'These paragraphs,' says Rosslyn. 'Why have you selected them in particular?'

'Because one made as sure as one could that the traces of heroin were consistent with what I found. I always double-check.'

'But I have to tell you that Jane didn't take heroin.'

Dr Maryon smiles sympathetically. 'Please don't for a moment think I'm being unnecessarily harsh. But your client's reaction seems to be the entirely normal one of a close and loving relative. Grief so often produces disbelief. I sometimes think the two words belong, in a way, to the same family. Grief and Disbelief. It's really that she simply doesn't want to believe her sister was an addict.'

'I need you to convince me, Dr Maryon. I need you to convince me Jane Moorfield wasn't murdered.'

'Well, what can I best say to you? Perhaps what I tell my students when I lecture them on Drug-Related Death and Concealed Homicide. Namely, that it's extraordinarily rare for the connection to be made, for the very obvious reasons connected with the nature of the victims.'

You are prevaricating, Rosslyn thinks.

'The habit,' Dr Maryon continues in her lecturer's manner, 'the drug habit usually starts around the age of thirteen. It continues until death. And death occurs, most often, some ten years or so later. On the other hand, victims like Jane Moorfield, who have overdosed in the earlier stages of their addiction, are a frequent and depressing feature of one's work. At the end of the day, one has to learn to live with such a death and everything sordid that surrounds it. Perhaps you can smell the mortuary disinfectant in here?'

'I can smell it, doctor.' He looks around her office. At the folded divan. 'Do you sleep over then?'

'Sometimes.'

'Anyone else use this office?'

'Only colleagues,' she says. 'I operate an open door policy.'

'Doesn't get rid of the smell, then?'

'No. You see, Mr Rosslyn, that's about the only element of my work I am inured to. The smell of the disinfectant. My sense of smell was dulled a long time ago. To tell you the truth, I can't even smell the mortuary disinfectant any more. But most of my colleagues can. I think that's why there are too many chain-smokers among forensic pathologists. I am the only one out of the six pathologists in our department who is a non-smoker. You see, the smell of death is always unpleasant. There's no other smell quite like it. Yes. It lingers. It's nasty. To say nothing of the nastiness one has to look at.'

'I can understand.'

'Then to reassure you. Just as we smell death, we're all too familiar with its many causes. You see, drug-related deaths rarely trigger suspicion of murder. If they did, one would discuss the matter with one's colleagues. Similarly with the police and the coroner. So there are plenty of fail-safes. Why weren't doubts raised?'

'Why weren't they then?' Rosslyn asks. 'You tell me.'

'The reason's perfectly clear. A drug addict's death would not in itself immediately, *qua* drug death, raise their suspicions. It's a brutal fact. The police have grown too used to finding junkies' corpses. In death as in life, I'm afraid to say familiarity breeds contempt. As I've said, we're all too familiar with drug-related deaths.'

'Is that really the truth?'

'Yes, it is,' says Dr Maryon.

'Except the doctor, Dr Lancaster, saw "minor contusions of both her wrists".'

'Yes, he did,' says Dr Maryon. 'And very properly he recorded them.'

'Bruises?'

'Yes. Bruises,' says Dr Maryon. 'Listen to what Dr Lancaster tells us. I quote: "No other abnormalities were detected." So you see, Dr Lancaster's constitutes a very thorough report.'

'What about "the awkward sites for injections"?'

'Let me quote again,' says Dr Maryon. ' "These were not the venepuncture sites one normally sees in comatose intravenous drug abusers brought to our casualty." Is there anything else you want to know?'

'Listen, Dr Maryon, Caroline is her only surviving relative. She has to be satisfied that Jane died as the inquest said she did. That's what I'm helping her to find out. Because she's my client. And she's in one whole lot of trouble. If there was any kind of mistake it might not look too good for you.'

He watches her eyes. She's looking past him, at the door to the office. *What's she thinking?*

'Perhaps you'd better talk to the police.'

'I'd like to see the files on Jane. On any other American women like her who died in similar circumstances and whose *post mortems* you carried out.'

'That's impossible, Mr Rosslyn.'

'I'm prepared to stay here all night looking at them if necessary.'

'You may be. But I'm not. And they're strictly confidential.'

'Then who else do you suggest I approach?'

'The coroner's court officers, perhaps?'

'Who else besides?'

'Or the witness at the inquest who identified your client's sister.'

'Anyone else?'

'Like who?'

'Jane Moorfield's friend.'

'It shouldn't be too hard to find Marcus Luke.'

'Sorry?'

'I said, Mr Rosslyn, it shouldn't be very hard for you to find Marcus Luke.'

'You know where he is?'

'No, why should I?'

'You've got a very fine memory for names, Dr Maryon. So you can instantly turn up the name of a witness out of all those thousands of inquests you attend each year. Or Luke's etched himself in your memory for some other reason.'

'I said "hundreds".'

'Hundreds. Thousands. Whatever. So what are you hiding from me?'

'I've got absolutely nothing whatsoever to hide from you or anyone else.'

'I'm not interested in anyone else, Dr Maryon. I'm suddenly very interested in how you know this Marcus Luke.'

'I don't know him.'

'It sounds to me that you do. Come on. You know Marcus Luke. You know him, don't you?'

'I do not know him. I just remember his name. It's unusual.'

'It's a bloody sight more usual than yours or mine. How come you know it after all this time?'

'Let's not quarrel,' she says.

'Then show me your files.'

'Let me see you out, Mr Rosslyn. If you wouldn't mind, please. I've got a great deal of work to finish.'

'So have I.'

'Then I'll show you the way out.'

'I found my way here, Dr Maryon,' he says. 'Do you know where Caroline Moorfield is, Dr Maryon?'

'Mr Rosslyn, get out of here.'

In the corridor he pauses. He has his fingers on the door handle when he hears the voice.

This is a different and ferocious Dr Maryon. She's on the telephone. He hears the shouting:

'What the hell d'you mean, it doesn't bloody matter? Her sister's sent some private detective here to see me – he's asking to see the files.' There's a pause. 'For Christ's sake, I can't bloody do that!'

He hears her slam the phone down. He needs to get hold of Lever. And Caroline. *What is it you can't bloody do? Destroy your files?*

He waits in the snow on Borough High Street for a cab. Still wondering who she could have been speaking to. With his back to the Job Centre along from the branch of the Turkish Bank UK, he looks up at her office window. He sees Dr Maryon's on the phone again. She has her back to him. Twice he sees her punch the air in fury.

I don't believe you, Dr Maryon. I never gave you Luke's name. You gave me his name. You know Luke. You KNOW Luke. He tries to make the connections. Between Jane, Luke, Dr Maryon – Luke and Caroline he prefers not to think about. And the howling heard somewhere in the derelict apartment block opposite the cemetery. *Who the hell's she talking to? Who are you protecting, doctor?*

He calls Lever's number. *Pick up, Wendy.* There's no reply.

Early evening darkness has closed in as he approaches the flat in Claverton Street, Pimlico. He stops in his tracks. Inside, the lights are on, the curtains partially drawn. *Maybe this is Caroline.* No one else, apart from ASG security, has keys. He peers over the railings. Instead of Caroline, through the gap in the curtains he sees a figure move.

Outside the door, as a precaution against any chance intruder taking the plastic bags containing the marked London street map and the video cassette, he shoves them beneath a rubbish bin. Then he rings the bell once, steps back and waits.

The blind in the window is twisted aside a fraction. He hears a key inserted in the lock. The door chain drops.

The woman's voice behind the door says: 'Come in, Alan.'

42

Maxine Gertler is standing in the passageway. 'I apologize for having let myself in like this,' she says.

Rosslyn takes off his coat. 'What's your problem, Maxine?'

'Can we join the others in the living room?' she says casually.

'What others?'

Leaning round the door, he sees Swincarron and Alexander. Both on their feet. As if they've already decided it's time to go. Wearing their overcoats. Sheepish. Looking out of place. Like criminals. 'Made ourselves at home, have we?' Rosslyn says.

Swincarron gives a hollow laugh. 'Forgive us, Alan.'

'Are we in more trouble?' asks Rosslyn, without bothering to hide his contempt.

'Maybe,' says Swincarron, dead-eyed.

'Why's that?'

'Caroline Moorfield –' she says.

'What about her?' Rosslyn snaps.

'There's a minor complication –'

'There is?' says Rosslyn, his voice rising in anger. 'You come in here without asking. And you stand there telling me there's only a *minor* complication. Oh *please*.'

'Don't point the finger at us, Alan,' says Gertler.

'Do you know where she is?'

'No, we don't,' says Swincarron. 'The police seem to think you might know. They've been asking some pretty awkward questions at Strand Chambers. About your client. And you too.'

'They can always come here and ask me face to face.'

'And what will you tell them about her disappearance?'

'That I don't know anything about it.'

'That could be very awkward for you,' says Gertler. 'In view of what happened to that friend of yours at Heathrow, poor bastard. Morandi, wasn't it? Here –' She's holding out the late edition of the *Evening Standard* folded at an inside page.

Rosslyn stares at the photograph of Caroline above a short article describing how –

> The body of Swiss priest Fr. Gian Maria
> Morandi was found earlier today at the
> Heathrow Hilton. Police are seeking
> the whereabouts of a young American,
> Caroline Moorfield, in connection with
> the murder victim.

Swincarron reaches for the *A to Z* on the table and moves it thus: ↑→ – the knight's move, to make the point. 'In the circumstances,' she says, 'you may be wondering not so much why the police have been to

see us, but rather why they have been to see *you*,
Alan.'

'I have the feeling you're about to tell me.'

'And you'd be feeling correctly,' says Swincarron.

'Vauxhall Cross,' says Gertler.

'And the Americans?'

'And the Americans,' says Swincarron. She's
fingering the face-lift scar near her right ear. It
seems to be giving her grief.

'What are you trying to say?' asks Rosslyn.

'We're not here to name names,' Swincarron says.
'We're talking deals.'

'Otherwise I wouldn't be here,' says Gertler.

'Where would you be, Maxine?'

'As a matter of fact it's my evening to be at the
gun club.'

'Still shooting hand-guns, are we?' says Rosslyn.
'Still breaking rules – you shouldn't admit to it,
Maxine. Stick to the clay pigeons.'

'You should keep your hand in,' says Alexander.
'Maxine's got a new little Browning. Waiting in your
safe at Strand Chambers, isn't it, Maxine?'

'You haven't come here to talk about shooting
practice,' says Rosslyn.

'No,' says Gertler, 'Maybe we should talk basics.'

'Like what?'

The reply is slow in coming. Eventually, it's
Swincarron who says: 'Alan, we're here as friends,
to suggest it'd be wise for you to go to ground – at
any rate, shall we say, for the time being.'

'Who says?' asks Rosslyn politely.

'Friends,' drawls Alexander.

'You know who we're talking about?' Gertler adds.

'I may,' says Rosslyn helpfully. 'But I'm sure as hell not sure *what* they're talking about.'

'Caroline Moorfield,' drawls Alexander as if he's talking to a simpleton.

'It's important,' says Gertler, as if she's running out of oil for the troubled water. She leans forward to the *A to Z* and moves it. This time in the reverse direction: ↓.

'We're not here to discuss Caroline,' says Alexander slowly.

'Can you guarantee Caroline's safety?' Rosslyn asks them.

'In so far as we can guarantee anything,' says Swincarron, tight faced.

'That's not enough,' snaps Rosslyn. 'You should know me well enough by now to realize that I'm not saying I'll tell her to clear off to the States. Not before I've talked it over with her —'

'I think we can rely on you,' Gertler puts in. 'We know your mind. You're the Duty Man.'

'Meanwhile,' says Swincarron, 'as a gesture of trust, here are the keys to this little love nest of yours.'

You think I don't know you'll have had them copied. Or that I won't change the locks?

'Always the Duty Man,' says Alexander, turning

up the collar of his cashmere coat. 'You know we're on your side.'

'I said I think you'd better leave,' says Rosslyn. He shows them outside.

'I know we can rely on you to stop your client doing anything stupid,' says Swincarron, by way of a parting shot. 'Meanwhile, if there's anything we can do to help, you've only got to telephone. Oh and by the by,' she adds on the doorstep, 'we've left a little Christmas box in your bedroom. *Une quelque-chose*. Are we spending Christmas with her?'

'Seems not,' says Rosslyn.

'Sorry about that,' Swincarron says quietly, bleeping the car alarm of the BMW parked across the street. 'We are on your side, Alan. Unfortunately, you're on your own. Unless of course you count your friend Lever. Don't you understand? Your loyalty's with ASG. With us. She's in it too. The whole bloody lot of them. In it too. Up to here.'

Once the BMW's out of sight, Rosslyn retrieves the plastic bags he brought from the flat in Kensal Green.

Back inside his flat, in his bedroom, he sees the oblong Nicole Farhi box on his bed. It's been carefully sealed with Sellotape. When he opens it, he finds it packed with wads of new £50 notes. The plastic seals say Coutts Bank. He calculates they've tried to buy his silence with several grand.

Underneath the plastic packs of notes, wrapped in

tissue paper and sheets of Swincarron's blue writing paper – from Smythson's of Bond Street and embossed with her Fitzroy Square address – is Swincarron's idea of a *quelquechose*. A handgun and lightweight holster. The Ruger Mark 4B.22 pistol. The grip frame holds the ten-shot loaded magazine. The overall length is just about eight inches.

Taking the Ruger with him, he goes into the bedroom to play the video.

43

He watches the semi-skilled video compilation of talking heads. Filmed in what seems to be a deliberately unidentified setting, it reminds him of a tape issued by extremists seeking ransom for political hostages. The first person to talk directly to camera is Jane. Her face framed in a white shawl, she's chanting:

For it is written, I am your child. Constant. True. For as it is prophesied and written, the world will witness your Resurrection. When in goodness you will surpass Christ himself . . .

Here she raises her right hand.

Invincible. Immortal. Inviolate.

She makes the sign: | | |.

You, the one true god of love, will be reborn in living flesh as he prophesied for our sakes. In the first minute. Of the first hour. Of the first day. Of the new century. The century of Trinity. The One-One-One.

A second time she solemnly makes the sign: | | |.

Her eyes brim with tears.

And with you we will enter Paradise on Earth . . .

Either this is good acting – *or you really believed it.*

The second appearance is by a middle-aged man. Motionless and blurred, the image of him could be from a still photograph.

The voice-over intones:

You the righteous believe in my certain resurrection. In the first minute of the first hour of the first day of the next century. The faithful will ask for every world leader of state and church to ring out the bells from every church and tower at noon on Saturday, 1 January 2000. The time of the two-thousandth anniversary of the birth of Christ and My Resurrection to walk among you here on Earth. I give you strength to await my certain second coming. When, in my name, you will be rewarded as Christ's disciples with Immortality.

Very slowly he raises his right hand to make the sign: | | |. And continues:

The Holy Ritual. Beloved sister in Trinity, for acceptance mind and body need to be one. For purity makes all things possible. Ozone as well as hydrotherapy for the colon is this blessed act of purification. And the sacred acidopholus to reseed the colon with flora that may have been lost during the evacuation of all former impurity. Three blessed stainless steel speculums. Blessed to administer the entry of pure water. Do you feel the water entering you?

Another voice is singing in the background:

> *Wieder aufzublühn wirst du gesät!*
> *Der Herr der Ernte geht*
> *Und sammelt Garben*
> *Uns ein, die starben!**

---

* You are sown to bloom again! / The Lord of the Harvest goes / And gathers the sheaves, / Even us who died!

Take it or leave it, Rosslyn thinks. *Mostly leave it*.

He lifts the telephone to Lever.

She picks up.

'Don't move,' she tells him. 'Just wait till I arrive.'

'Where's Caroline?'

'I wish I knew,' says Lever. 'More's the pity, Alan. She's done a runner, and the police don't like it. The rest of it is that the police have a package addressed to her.'

'Who from? That bastard Luke?'

'Leaving him aside, Alan –'

'He's a bastard. Where the hell has Caroline gone?'

'I don't know,' says Lever. 'The package is from Morandi. Addressed to Caroline.'

'What's in it?'

'You'll see,' says Lever. 'Wait there, I'm coming over now. And one more thing. Before I get there, if anyone tries to call you . . . buy you –'

'They already have.'

'You're being stitched up, Alan. The police are about to raid your place. That's why I've been told to get you here. To see the DG. And the Commissioner. And the Home Secretary. With a party in from Vauxhall Cross. They're in a meeting. They want us here together.'

'For what?'

'To follow the Home Secretary's orders. Everyone's following orders. Like you and me too.'

'Before you leave, I want to get a forensic expert out of bed. I've found stuff at Kensal Green I need testing. Traces of Jane Moorfield. And we need to get after Maryon. But get on to forensics.'

'Alan, you know what time it is?'

'I know. Just get someone from forensic out of bed. I need someone to see this stuff. And now.'

'As you say, Alan. And now I'm taking you to see a corpse.'

44

Rosslyn hears the rumbling of the night train gathering speed over the bridge near the Lambeth mortuary at the corner of Pratt Walk and Juxon Street. Stark light illuminates the windowless, eighty-foot-square room. The distant rumble of the train accompanies the opening of the refrigeration room doors.

The mortuary assistant, in green overalls, cap and face mask, is wheeling in the body. He leaves the trolley next to the central porcelain slab. At the foot of the trolley is a small printed notice in a plastic cover: Number. Name. Description of the body.

Once the train's out of earshot, the only sound is the hum of the ventilation system.

The pathologist wears a face mask, disposable gown and white rubber wellingtons of the same kind loaned to Rosslyn and Lever. Fixing the velcro strap of what looks like a caver's or miner's light around his head, he says: 'I'm required to ask you if you're both immunized. Against tuberculosis, hepatitis B and tetanus.' They nod in confirmation. 'I should warn you that the face of this sort of death is very nasty. If either of you feel you want to leave . . . you've only got to say.'

Lever, her teeth clenched hard behind the mask, makes a sound suggesting she wants to get it over with fast.

'Talk us through it,' says Rosslyn.

'Before I do . . .' says the pathologist, 'not that you'll *want* to touch the victim, but formality requires me to warn you not to touch. Bones are very sharp. As you see, I'm wearing double rubber gloves. There's faecal matter. The most common danger is from immunodeficiency syndrome – AIDS . . .' He peels the plastic sheet off Morandi's corpse. 'Here we are. We gather he was Swiss . . . a priest, I believe . . . *Rigor mortis* is beginning to disappear. Twenty-four hours from now it won't be present. Don't be too perturbed by the odour . . . some San-Veino, or chloroform, used to kill maggots. Happily, it also arrests tissue gas. Fortunately, refrigeration has anyway somewhat decreased the stench of decomposition. The victim is categorized as a "floater", the term we apply to a corpse that has been in the water, no matter what the cause of death. Now this, I expect, is what you've come to see . . . I'll tell you what I'm doing. One must be careful not to damage tissues. I must first prise open the jaw . . .' He carefully inserts a skull key. 'We're in the retromolar space and . . . if I twist, very gently, steady she goes . . . I can insert this mouth prop . . . Want to take a closer look?'

They peer inside Morandi's mouth.

'What you're looking at is very unusual. Bite

marks. Inside the mouth. You'll already have noticed the deep cuts to the flesh, somewhat discoloured by now, of course. Those three straight lines. He's been sort of flayed open. It's like a ritual cutting of some kind. I'd say a small carving knife was used. Very sharp indeed. You'll also have seen the numerous puncture marks. Bite marks. One has to classify bite marks according to whether human or non-human teeth produced them. In this case we have signs of both. We've already taken swabs within the area of the bites. There's some evidence of saliva transfer. But given he was found sub-merged in a bath, very little. You can see bruising. Abrasion. Scratching. Some penetration of the skin to subcutaneous tissue. And, of course, those incised wounds. What shows us inhuman or dog bites are the anterior segments. A dog's anterior segment is narrower than a human's. The dog's central incisors are narrower than the lateral. You can see punctures to the tongue and gums of a conical, somewhat curved pattern . . .'

Lever backs away.

'All right?' the pathologist asks her. She isn't. She heads for the exit in silence.

'What are you saying killed him?' asks Rosslyn.

'I'd say the lacerations, those vertical slashes, were most probably made after death. At any rate, let's say Father whatever-his-name-is . . .' He looks at the plastic label. '*Gian Maria Morandi* . . . probably never knew anything about them. But the teeth marks are

[343]

another matter. It was an attack of great ferocity. I'd say a Pit Bull terrier or some such most probably bit him to death. And there are these scorch marks. A very high heat has been applied. A flame.'

Shaking his head, Rosslyn lets out a long breath.

'Would you like a glass of water,' asks the pathologist, 'or perhaps a cup of coffee?'

'No thanks.'

'Do you mind me asking, are you also from the security services?'

'No, why do you ask?'

'There's been a whole procession of them in here to look at this. If it's any comfort to you, you're the only visitor who's stuck the course without vomiting. With the exception of one of my colleagues. You seem to have seen such things before.'

'Too often,' says Rosslyn. 'Only none as terrible as this. And not someone I knew and respected. Tell me, was your colleague who looked at Morandi –'

'Elizabeth Maryon,' says the pathologist. 'Do you know her?'

'Vaguely.'

'One of the best in Europe.'

'So I'm told.'

'I'm sorry about your friend Morandi,' says the pathologist.

'It's a terrible sight.'

'Yes,' says the pathologist, his rubber wellingtons squeaking on the wet floor. 'Believe me, the handiwork of a pervert. You never get quite used to what they do. In life . . . that's one thing. In death, another.'

'I can understand that,' says Rosslyn, following him to the door.

Maryon. Like the rest. The bacteria floating in the air.

'Thames House,' Lever tells the woman driver. 'One of us may need you later on.'

The car heads through the deserted streets for Lambeth Bridge and Millbank.

There's word that the Home Secretary, no less, is at Thames House tonight. Along with the Commissioner. Women from Vauxhall Cross. Some junior ministers even. Quite a Christmas circus. There are even dark suggestions that heads are going to roll. And nasty rumours about a millennial atrocity. Emergency security plans to be in operation across London. But then there would be anyway, and they've somehow got lost in the mounting euphoria about the last Christmas of the century. The volcano of enjoyment that will erupt across the world as the Millennium dawns. There's been talk of little else for the past twelve months. The whole world is hell-bent on celebration.

Hell would seem to be the operative noun. Rosslyn couldn't be less interested in the nation's wild mood. The planned extravaganzas. He's thinking of Morandi. Of Caroline. Trying to tell himself not to allow personal feelings to get in the way of connecting Marcus Luke to her disappearance. He has a list as long as his arm of visits to be made. Back to Wroth at the Kensal Green apartment block. Back to Dr Maryon. On to Dr Llewellyn in Cambridge. And someone must turn up Dr Rijn for good measure. Wherever he may be, in Belgium or elsewhere.

Lever, though, won't let the Ahearnes take a back seat. It really seems as if she has a personal score to settle. The sight of Morandi has left her in a foul mood. The extent of her bitterness matches her determination to break Ahearne. 'I have a mind to arrest him myself,' she says as the car crosses Lambeth Bridge. 'If I'm not allowed to nail him and his fat-arsed wife, I'm handing in my resignation.'

'Why's it so *very* personal?' asks Rosslyn.

She brushes aside the hair from her forehead. Shows the scar. 'My ex did that. With a bottle opener. Pissed. You know what Ahearne's reaction was when she read the doctor's papers?'

'No, but I think you're going to tell me.'

'She said, "I rather think you're a born victim. I see I made a note to that effect at your last promotions board." So I suppose, as much as anything, I'm trying to prove her wrong. Which is what she is. Wrong and wrong and wrong. And thinks she's right-right-right. Now it's her or me.' She tells the driver to drop them off at the main entrance.

'Let's see which category applies to the Home Secretary,' says Rosslyn.

Since I saw Mr Rosslyn here in Geneva I have received anonymous threats to my life. These, so I am warned, will only cease if I am prepared to hand over my files on the Trinity Chapter. Together with the comprehensive record of the information I supplied to Jane, to Mr Rosslyn and to Ms Lever.

I refused to co-operate with Ms Lever, knowing that members of the British security services are members of the Trinity Chapter. I find no reason whatsoever to trust Ms Lever. Fearing for my safety, as I fear for Caroline Moorfield's, I contacted Ms Queron by telephone at the United States Embassy in London. She told me that she would be pleased if I would agree to hand over the necessary papers so that her office could identify whosoever was issuing these threats to my life. And who is in control of the Trinity Chapter funds.

Subsequently, under the instructions of Ms Queron, I agreed with the anonymous caller to hand over my records at a rendezvous in Torino. Ms Queron was not present.

Some six men and women, whom I believe to be Italian plain clothes police and officials from the

British or American embassies in Rome, witnessed the handover.

After my return to Geneva, the threatening calls began again. Again I was being asked to provide the caller with whatever information I had on the Trinity Chapter, the contents of Ms Moorfield's researches and the information I supplied to Ms Lever and to Mr Rosslyn. This time the caller was a woman.

I asked a police adviser to the International Family Foundation to have my calls monitored. He was able to trace the call to a public telephone in Cambridge, England. But, unfortunately, and for reasons he was not prepared to discuss with me, he was not prepared to provide me with the precise location of its origin. Or who made the call.

When the calls persisted, I again informed Ms Queron that I intended to report the matter to the Swiss police. I told her that the calls had been traced to Cambridge, England.

Ms Queron asked me not to approach the Swiss police or any other authority. She would, she said, be in touch. I heard again from Ms Queron, who urged me to make no contact with anyone purporting to be investigating Ms Moorfield's death. Namely, Mr Rosslyn and Ms Lever.

Ms Queron made it very clear to me that not only was I still in danger, either from members of the Trinity Chapter or anti-cultists; but that, if I were to make contact with anyone purporting to be investigating Ms Moorfield's death, other lives would in turn also be placed in jeopardy. Ms Queron insisted that I do not travel outside Geneva and that I should report to her again if the threatening calls persisted.

She also reassured me that, in conjunction with the Swiss authorities, she had arranged for officials of the United States Embassy in Berne to begin a surveillance operation which would also provide me with a measure of protection.

It is entirely on my own initiative, before the surveillance operation is in place, that I have to go to London in order to explain the situation I have recorded here and to request, from Ms Queron, some form of protection and anonymity.

— FR GIAN MARIA MORANDI, TAPE TRANSCRIPT, GENEVA, DECEMBER 1999

45

In the Thames House conference room Morandi's last tape is viewed in silence for the second time tonight. While Morandi speaks to camera, the Home Secretary takes notes. Rosslyn's mind is mostly on Caroline. The Home Secretary's felt-tip pen moves even faster when Morandi reaches his posthumous conclusion. In capitals. Like a warning telegram. The pen squeaking like the pathologist's boots on the mortuary floor:

HIS FOLLOWERS WILL ENSURE THAT VIO-
LENCE IS COMMITTED ON A PUBIC SCALE.
THE PATTERN WILL BE MUCH THE SAME AS
IT WAS WITH AUM: A SPECIFIC DATE AT A
SPECIFIC TIME AND PLACE.

Lever's chief, the head of Operations and Resources, hits the STOP button. There's a long silence round the table. From the Home Secretary. Junior Minister. Three women assistant directors from SIS. Faces Rosslyn can't put names to. The Commissioner of Police. The Commander of the anti-terrorist branch, SO13. Several other officers. Some in uniform. Others in plain clothes. And all in a row, the deputy and assistant director-generals of MI5.

Also, there are agendas from the series of earlier meetings on the table. Rosslyn, unnoticed, idly casts an eye over the nearest copies. The annotated maps of Trafalgar Square and London's West End. The copies of the TOP SECRET MI5 Memorandum from Operation Resources and Intelligence, describing in detail 'the Joint Security Service/Scotland Yard Public Order Forward Planning Unit Emergency Plans, Ref. 31 December 1999.'

London's massive New Year's Eve celebrations. The night of the sacred dawn of the Millennium bringing rebirth and hope to the troubled world. Like hell.

The TOP SECRET MI5 Memorandum showing that the POFPU comprises a chief inspector, three inspectors and an auxiliary staff of three. Rosslyn reads fast:

On the night of 31 December 1999, in the event of a major disaster, police and security service officers will follow the mnemonic or memory aid CHALET:

- C – Casualties: approximate number
- H – Hazards: present and potential
- A – Access routes for emergency services
- L – Location of incident: exact
- E – Emergency services present and required
- T – Type of incident: chemical, major hazard, crash, explosion, bomb attack etc.

And here are the up-to-date operational details of the arcane and most secret organization of the 'Central Communications Complex. Scotland Yard.

Territorial Support Group and Special Operations Room (Radio Call Sign – Mother 2 Golf Tango)'. The units gathering intelligence to co-ordinate the emergency response to major incidents.

The ranking system to be adopted for the police command structure on the night of Resurrection:

- Gold = Strategy
- Silver = Tactics
- Bronze = Operational functions

'I'd say he seems to have been a man possessed,' is all the Home Secretary can say of Morandi.

Some epitaph, thinks Rosslyn.

Male secretaries hand round paper cups of coffee from the refreshments trolley.

'Who,' asks the Home Secretary, 'murdered him?'

'We don't know yet, sir,' says the Commissioner of Police, looking hard at Rosslyn. 'Perhaps Mr Rosslyn's Caroline Moorfield will tell us, sir. Or the Americans. Or even Mr Rosslyn himself –'

Low blow, thinks Rosslyn. 'With respect, why don't we ask the Americans?' he says. 'Queron at the embassy, for a start?'

'We've already spoken to her,' says the DG.

'We want to talk to your client, Moorfield,' says the Commissioner.

'In my judgement, she had nothing to do with it,' says Rosslyn.

The Commissioner leans forward across the table. Eyeball to eyeball. 'Mr Rosslyn, with respect, her fingerprints were all over the hotel room. Traces of *her* footprints were found in the blood. In the bathroom. In the bedroom. On the exit route to the fire escape. She was there. She was not unaccompanied. She was there with someone else.'

'What are you suggesting, sir?' Rosslyn asks.

'She had the opportunity. The means. And the motive. We want to talk to her. And we're going to get there. And I advise you to put nothing, I mean nothing, in our way.'

'I think it's a good idea you find her,' says Rosslyn. 'I don't like to think I might have lost a client.'

A look of something like disapproval for Rosslyn's view clouds the Home Secretary's face. Then, like a teacher producing the smile of sarcasm, the Home Secretary's lips flicker. He clearly approves of the Commissioner's resolution and cold belligerence.

Rosslyn senses the meeting's closing ranks. Against himself and Lever. For the first time, Rosslyn notices Lever's pale blue eyes are bloodshot. She looks disconsolate. She must be sensing the direction of the unspoken opposition.

Rosslyn catches the Home Secretary's eye. 'Sir, may I, through you, ask the Commissioner what motive he is describing? Are we to believe that Father Morandi was involved in Jane Moorfield's killing too?'

'We've been through that case before,' says the Commissioner.

Really? thinks Rosslyn. *You have? . . . How come? . . . When?*

'It wasn't a killing, Mr Rosslyn. You were at the inquest. You and Ms Lever both. You heard the verdict. The evidence is cast iron. Let's not waste the Secretary of State's valuable time discussing that inquest, right? I understand your interest in the Moorfield woman's case. It's a private commission. Private interest. We're discussing the national interest, Mr Rosslyn.'

Rosslyn glowers at him. 'That's why we're here, isn't it?'

'Through you, sir, Secretary of State,' says the Commissioner. 'I don't think we need reminding by a private security executive why we're here. Let's focus on Morandi's killing.'

'Would you mind, Mr Rosslyn?' says the Home Secretary. 'Commissioner?'

The Commissioner continues: 'I have to tell you, Mr Rosslyn, I saw the corpse and it wasn't nice. You didn't see it. I did. You haven't been there. So don't you start lecturing me about motive.'

Rosslyn remembers Lever's warning: *Don't let them know we saw the corpse.* 'I'm totally convinced she didn't kill him,' says Rosslyn.

'I see,' says the Commissioner with venom. 'Then you have to explain to me here and now why she's vanished?'

'Who says she has?' asks Rosslyn.

'We do,' says the Commissioner. 'She was last

seen at the Heathrow Hilton early this afternoon. She took the package containing the video with the victim's statement on it. She then crossed the reception area. She went outside. The driver of a limousine remembers seeing her. She was carrying the package. Then she was seen walking away to a truck, a van of some description. Then she vanished. When the van left there was the package lying in the gutter. With your friend Morandi's tape inside. So obviously she'd been to Morandi's room. Number 5006. She stole the package.'

If they've already been over this, why is he telling me this? What's he trying to convince me of?

'How come her name was on it?'

'Because she wrote it on the package herself. In case she was stopped, right? It's the oldest trick.'

'If you'll allow me to say so, I don't believe it was a trick.'

'Rosslyn,' says the Commissioner with mounting rage. 'Stop deceiving yourself. You saw Morandi in Geneva. You heard what he had to say. This happens to be my problem. The Secretary of State's problem. Everyone's problem. You heard it: "–violence committed on a public scale – the pattern will be much the same as it was with Aum, this time on a specific date, as he promised, at a specific time and place. I base my argument simply on a reading of his intellect and the patterns of evidence Ms Moorfield told me –" You've known about this, Rosslyn. You've said nothing. The Americans have firmly denied any dealings with Morandi. If I may say so, Secretary of State, it's really rather unwise of our observer here, Mr Rosslyn, to sit here solemnly trying to tell us these people aren't dangerous, insane –'

The Home Secretary interrupts: 'A minute, Commissioner, let Mr Rosslyn explain the contrary view.'

'I'd like to, sir,' says Rosslyn. He turns to stare at the Commissioner. 'I have not said I don't take these threats seriously. On the contrary, I believe Morandi. I believe that the cult Jane Moorfield was researching most likely murdered at least three women. That the inquests were at the best inadequate or at the worst, fixed. You have to ask yourself why that might be, Commissioner? To use your own approach, let's try motive, opportunity, means. The only basic reason has to be that someone out there is covering for this cult.'

'I'm saying, Secretary of State, that's exactly what we believe the Moorfield sisters were doing.'

'And I'm saying totally the opposite,' says Rosslyn. 'Caroline Moorfield believes her sister was murdered. Now look at how they did for Morandi. A 5cc syringe. Two 25g and one 23g needles. The smack. The stab wounds. The One-One-Ones. Same people. Ask forensics. Only in addition, there were dog bites. He was bitten to death, Commissioner. And three scorch marks. You should connect those with the two killings in Trafalgar Square. Only you haven't got one single lead on those yet, Commissioner, have you? So now your officers have to tell me why Dr Maryon suddenly can't find the *post mortem* photos of Jane Moorfield. Or are you going to tell me she isn't up to her neck in it too? You tell me – what's she hiding?'

'You've seen Morandi's corpse?' says the Commissioner.

'One thing at a time,' says Rosslyn. 'Dr Maryon first.'

The Commissioner smiles, leans down to the briefcase open beside his chair. 'Here.' He slides some photographs across the table to Rosslyn. 'We had these, Rosslyn. We wanted to look at them. We told the doctor not to say we'd got them. She's totally in the clear. And you waltzed into Guy's Hospital and accused her of being a liar. Well, I have to tell you she's about the best forensic pathologist in the country. You just overreacted. You don't know the half of it.'

'What don't I know the half of, Commissioner?'

Rosslyn looks at the photographs of Jane Moorfield's corpse. The Commissioner gives a slight grin. 'You want to throw in some other names, Mr Rosslyn?'

'Ahearne,' says Rosslyn. 'Mr and Mrs Ahearne. Marcus Luke. The caretaker at that apartment block in Kensal Green where I found traces of blood. The man Wroth. More of the same needles and a syringe, Commissioner. A 5cc syringe. Two 25g and one 23g needles. Smack. Along the same lines as what was found near Jane Moorfield the night she died. Read the inquest transcript. Make your connections. Jane Moorfield. Trinity Chapter. Marcus Luke. Ahearne. Caroline Moorfield's disappearance. More besides – you should find Van Rijn in Belgium. And someone needs to question this woman. This United States Secretary of State.'

'They already have, Mr Rosslyn,' says the Home Secretary. 'She's totally in the clear.'

Rosslyn flinches. *The blind eye.*

'Then may I tell the Commissioner, sir, that he's entitled to question my view? But he hasn't got a shred of hard evidence, one to suggest that Caroline Moorfield and her sister were implicated in this cult, and two that there will not, I say again, will NOT be some violent form of demonstration coinciding with the millennial celebrations. You haven't even begun, Commissioner . . . you haven't even begun.'

The Commissioner is ashen. 'Secretary of State, Director General, I think we should get to the heart of this,' he says impatiently. 'Do you want me to disabuse Mr Rosslyn?'

The Home Secretary hands the DG the scrap of paper with his notes on it:

HIS FOLLOWERS WILL ENSURE THAT VIO-
LENCE IS COMMITTED ON A PUBLIC SCALE.

'Mr Rosslyn,' says the Home Secretary, 'a video recording showing Jane Moorfield participating in activity to do with this cult was found in your flat.'

The Commissioner is smiling. *You bastard –* Lever's right *– You're stitching me up.*

'There are charges pending, Mr Rosslyn,' says the Commissioner.

'Then make them,' Rosslyn says.

'That's not a matter for me,' says the Home Secretary. 'But tell the meeting in your own words, Mr Rosslyn, what it is you believe they actually want?'

'If they're thwarted,' says Rosslyn, 'if they're pinned down, prevented from getting the money out of the banks – that's when they'll go haywire. If you want to know what they want, the Commissioner here, or the Director General even, could have asked them. But you've held back. They're on the run. It's happened before. It'll happen again. They won't be stopped. They don't want to be stopped. That's what they want.'

'The banks have already denied they have their funds,' says the DG.

'Then you should bust them,' says Rosslyn. 'Find out who's been asking for it.'

'Like who?'

'Whoever's taken Caroline. Who's holding her . . .'

'There's no evidence she's been taken hostage,' says the DG. 'None.'

'In fact,' says the Commissioner, as if he's delivering the winning punch 'we think she's most likely already returned to America. Using an assumed name. And this is where your involvement ends.'

'It only ends if she's dead,' says Rosslyn. 'And I don't believe she is. She's no use to them dead. But if she's being held somewhere – that puts a very different spin on things.'

There's a silence. Lever's looking at him. Her looks seem to say, *You've a bloody nerve.* She looks away to a secretary, who hands her a note. The look of defeat spreads across her face. She closes her eyes. Very slowly.

When Rosslyn catches up with her as the meeting breaks up, she shows him the note the secretary gave her.

Marked URGENT, it says: 'Dr Llewellyn died 5 a.m. in Cambridge.'

46

Downcast, Lever is slumped behind her office desk. It's strewn with faxes. Some with green stickers attached for filing. Most have red stickers attached: FOR IMMEDIATE ACTION. She glances at a single page. Unpeels the red sticker from it. 'The police are searching for Caroline. They're looking for Luke and Wroth.'

'But they haven't spoken to me,' says Rosslyn.

'They will,' she says. 'If only Dr Llewellyn had told me the whole story. Without her, without Morandi, I don't see we have anywhere else left to go.'

'Why not go to Cambridge? Speak to the detective who was looking for Llewellyn's attacker. See what he has. It's a murder investigation now.'

She searches among her faxes. 'He's already given me what he has. It adds up to nothing. No one knows anything. Not even Llewellyn's girlfriend, Dr Tsien. And she's blind. So what's she going to tell us?'

'Then why not go to the Americans? Pin Queron down about Morandi and Caroline. Ask the DG to intervene. Let's just take the action. Just do it.'

'OK, hang about, Alan. You heard what he had to say. He's already dealt with the Americans. They don't want to know about the Moorfields. They don't want *you* to know, Alan. They don't want to know. Full stop. They want you neutralized. That's why Maxine Gertler planted that gun on you. And that's where Gertler got it from. They've used you. Have you ever asked Caroline how come she employed your services in the first place?'

'On the advice of the local priest, she spoke to Susan Isiskind at the embassy. She filed a report to Donna Queron. As she would. And Queron called Gertler.'

'Don't you see it, Alan?' Lever says. 'If they hadn't gone to ASG, then we wouldn't be here together now, would we?'

'The gun came from Queron?' asks Rosslyn.

'Yes.'

'How do you know?'

'You should've looked at the registration number,' says Lever. 'It's US Air Force Special Forces from Mildenhall. We traced it through Washington. Now they're crying out to get the thing back. And I'm not going to let them have it until we're through.'

'Then turn out the stables,' says Rosslyn. 'Nick Ahearne for starters.'

'I want to wait.'

'And wait for Maryon too? Why not bring her in? Now. Bang her up. A night in Holloway and she'll talk.'

She shakes her head. 'Same applies. No, best to wait.'

'And Morandi? Did he leave word in Geneva – before leaving for London – about the reason for his journey?'

'I called his assistant,' she says. 'The Filipino. He says Morandi was terrified for his safety. And he was right to be, poor sod, wasn't he?'

'Christ, I hate this,' says Rosslyn. 'You can't let it rest here. You have to move.'

'I don't want to make it worse,' says Lever. 'You saw Morandi's corpse. What they did to him. I don't think it was a punishment killing, do you? Let's not pretend it was some random murder. He'd hardly unpacked his bloody bag. He wasn't expecting anyone else. Only Caroline. More, I suspect, some-one was making sure that he wouldn't talk to us or anyone else interested in the fucking Chapter. You saw the wounds – the One-One-Ones.'

'I advise that we focus entirely on Caroline,' says Rosslyn. 'Keep her in mind to the exclusion of all the rest.'

'But I thought you said you wanted me to nick Ahearne?'

'Of course,' says Rosslyn. 'We have to get at him again. Who else do we have? No Morandi. No Llewellyn. We don't have anyone who counts as a real suspect. As far as we know, the police aren't even investigating the Trinity Chapter. Your DG won't come out into the open until the other side kills again. That's his way. Do it by the book. Do nothing active until he has to. Same goes for the

Chapter. Otherwise, why did they kill Morandi? You know why?'

'They don't want their strategy exposed.'

Rosslyn nods. 'We have to imagine what it is they want, what it is they're trying to protect. All we have now is the idea that the Chapter's trying to preserve itself. And other than what Jane Moorfield told us from the grave, we don't even know anything about the so-called Inner Chapter. If Morandi's killing means that someone *was* seeking punishment or retribution, then our job might be easier. I don't believe they were. They were trying to silence him, and they succeeded. I think whoever killed Morandi killed Jane and the other women. Someone in that apartment block haemorrhaged very badly in that bath. Look at the parallel with Morandi's death. So who was it who bled in the Kensal Green apartment?'

'Forensic will tell us,' says Lever. 'I'm sure as hell not walking into one of those traps. Believe me, I've been there before. These people hate you, Alan. Like they must have hated Jane. One more thing.' She swivels in his chair to open the unlocked safe door. 'The police have given us this.'

He raises the cardboard box.

'Her ashes,' she says. 'And this –' It's a video cassette she's holding. 'From the Heathrow Hilton. The CCTV recordings. You don't need to see it now. It's of Caroline. The point is that she was looking into the CCTV camera lenses. The sign of someone who doesn't give a shit whether she's been video recorded or whether she hasn't. Whoever murdered Morandi went there with a specific purpose in mind. He or she went there with the heroin and the needles and the knife that cut into the back of his head. The blade that made the three slashes. The One-One-Ones. And on that basis, I wouldn't say that we're looking for a professional killer. The hired hand. There are easier ways of doing it. The sort of man who gets five grand for bumping someone off isn't going to do it in a hotel. The professional isn't going to make it look as if it were amateur night. No. Whoever did it knows what Morandi was all about.'

'I have the feeling that they also know what we're about,' says Rosslyn. 'The press will pick up on the murder. Morandi will be news for a day, not much longer. Until one day the police arrest a suspect and after, say, ten months down the road, there's a trial. By that time the world will be a different place altogether. I believe Morandi. He paid for telling the truth.'

'How can you be so sure?' asks Lever.

'Too long on the game,' says Rosslyn. 'Too long for peace of mind. You get to read their moves like a chess player.'

He thinks of the ASG principals lording it over him in his flat, and Maxine Gertler making her knight's moves: ↑→↓. 'They're predictable. I want all of them to think they're reading our minds. And that yours is the open book. You stay put in here, right?'

'Until when?'

'Until I tell you I've got the truth. Let me tell you what my old chief used to say when we had a really nasty investigation going. Say, against some IRA wild card murdering bastard – the scum woman who shot dead my Mary. Or the bastards manufacturing paedophile pornography. Leaving out the evil. Leaving that aside. Just remember the lengths they'll go to. Not just to achieve their aims. But to protect themselves. That's what those old farts in that meeting can't imagine. It's a question of doing something unspeakable to your grandmother, if you get my drift. It's worse than that. It's the sheer disposability of life that shocks you. Take Morandi. That's what you never get over. That's why you fight. Anyway, my boss the Sea Captain used to say: "Alan, don't treat an investigation like a battle. Treat it like war. It's either you. Or it's them. Forget that and you're dead meat." Well, I don't mean to be. I'm going to talk to the friend of the tutor in Cambridge. If they haven't stitched her up too. Then Wroth again. And find Caroline. The rest of them can go home and start thinking about Christmas and this god-awful Millennium.'

Lever gets out of her chair and crosses the office to her wall safe. 'You'd better take this, Alan. You see, you should know I've been told to back off the Ahearnes. To back off them altogether. So keep this as a souvenir. Only don't tell the cops I gave it back to you.' She hands him the loaded Ruger. 'We got it away from the cops.'

Rosslyn takes the hand gun.

'Here,' she says. 'Use this too.' She hands him the holster.

'You've read my mind?' he asks.

'Yes, you're going to Kensal Green?'

'After I've seen Lancaster. The doctor who examined Jane. And he's one doctor who'd better tell me the truth.'

'After that?'

'Once I've heard from your forensic man. Kensal Green.'

'You'll need a warrant. I've told forensic to put the tests in the fast track,' she says.

'You should see Llewellyn's woman friend. One of us has to – what's her name?'

'Jhong-Jha Tsien.'

'She'll talk to you maybe,' says Rosslyn. 'Unless the Americans have got to her first. All they want is for Odone to stay looking sweet and squeaky clean. And she isn't.'

Lever gets up from her desk. 'Alan?' she asks. Drawing near to him, she hesitates.

'What's the problem?' he asks.

'Nothing, Alan. You see Lancaster. Then Kensal Green. Only don't stir things. Please. I have a job to keep, right. We've overstepped the limit already.'

'So what's biting you, Wendy?'

She smiles. 'It doesn't matter –'

'What doesn't matter, Wendy?'

'You realize you've started calling me Wendy. No, it's not urgent. It can wait. I like you calling me by my name.'

'Wendy,' he says. 'I'll remember that.'

'You are a very hard case, Mr Rosslyn.'

'If you say so.'

She watches him leave. Stooped now. Drained. Prepared to face Kensal Green on his own. She'd like to have kissed him good luck. Held him. Kissed him. But here and now doesn't seem to be the place or time. Anyway, she wants to nail the Ahearnes. Once and for all.

And the telephone is ringing.

He's waiting by the lift when he hears the running footsteps. The lift doors open.

'Alan, wait!'

He shoves his foot in the door to allow her to squeeze in.

'Forensic have matched those items from Kensal Green. You're looking at Jane and Caroline. She's been there too.'

She leans close against him. Looks into his eyes. 'What else I had to say to you, Alan. Well, it's not urgent.'

'Say.'

She hits the lift's STOP button. 'I've been wondering,' she says, 'what it is you really believe?'

'What do I believe? You're asking me now.'

'Yes.'

'That everyone else knows best, right. The Queen. The Prime Minister. The Home Secretary. DG this. DG that. Anyone you like to name. Anyone who runs us. And that's everyone. I believe they want us to believe in them. And they call it freedom. Well, fuck them. I don't call it any kind of justice. And freedom – forget it. Do you understand?'

'No.'

'Tough. That's the sum of it. I'd like to believe in God, wouldn't you? I suppose I believe in doubt. The open mind. That the sun'll come out tomorrow, maybe. Yes, I believe in Maybe. Maybe is what I believe in, Wendy Lever.'

He feels her knee move gently between his legs.

'Are you in love with Caroline?' she asks.

'What do you think?' he says.

She kisses him hard and long on the mouth. They hold each other.

'That's the answer,' he says.

'I'd hoped as much.'

She presses the button for the lift to finish its descent. 'And now you know where you are with me, Rosslyn. Although why you've never guessed beats me.'

The lift slows.

'One another leads to a thing,' he says with a smile.

'That a threat?' she asks. 'Isn't it the wrong way around?'

'Yes. It's the wrong way around. And it's a promise, Wendy Lever.'

'I'll hold you to it,' she says. 'You wait.'

'Good,' he says. 'I'll wait.'

The doors open on to the foyer of Thames House and several irritated people who've been waiting for the lift.

47

I believe in The Faith. My Faith. It bridges all faiths and creates a common humanity. The oneness of humankind.

— EDWARD AHEARNE, NOTEBOOK, RICHMOND-UPON-THAMES, 1999

Edward Ahearne's mind is plagued. Late at night, clutching at straws, he's *en route* by cab for the rendezvous he's made at the apartment block in Kensal Green. Matters with the Chapter need straightening.

My life is on the brink of ruination. To say nothing of this paradise on earth and whatever else may lie in the Great or not so Great Beyond.

He must issue firm warnings. Set matters straight – *very straight indeed.*

If they can't offer a proper explanation, he'll confess things to Virginia. Ask forgiveness for causing this turmoil.

This is The Future. Our future.

He imagines her motherly tones: 'It's all right really, Edward, My Little Prince.'

He takes some comfort that she isn't involved in these allegations.

Should I come straight out with it? Do I go down on my

knees and say: 'Look, among those figures of consequence' – I don't quite know how to put this – 'I am one among many. I've even contemplated a moment when I could tell you about Trinity. The certain sense of calm. Ecstasy of true belief. I'd like to interest you in the faith that sustains me.' What do I have to confess to? Nothing. I believe in The Faith. My Faith. It bridges all faiths and creates a common humanity. The oneness of humankind.

He's feeling sick. Is tasting acid in his saliva.

His mind spins –

Why should I confess to good? Evil, yes of course. But good? How does one actually CONFESS TO GOOD? Why does the man Seifert need to be so destructive? So why not, if this is what I believe, come out with it? And say I have devoted my soul to the service and to the Trinity Chapter. It has offered me sustenance. Mine is a modest and decent secrecy. For years I have followed the paths of enlightenment. I have found the source of civilization's destruction. We worshippers are a secret band. Knights of the Round Table. So many so young, so spiritually and physically attractive young people. Youth. No sad bible bashers. No God Squad. Not us. Search the letters of Paul to the Romans, Corinthians, Galatians, Ephesians, Philippians and Thessalonians. You will find the miracles. Healing. Prophecy. Are not Trinity's healing centres the place of miracles? For the first time in my life Trinity has brought me Peace. A Peace that does not pass Understanding. I UNDER-STAND IT. Is it now to be taken from me? Suppose there is an iota of truth in these allegations –

The curse forms in his mind. To stop himself saying it out loud, he makes the sign: | | |.

Soiled. I am Unfaithful. Of course, the Trinity Chapter is not without its persecutors. Enemies. Debunkers. Anti-cultist fanatics. Established churches. Glib and irreligious cynics who believe in NOTHING. Truly self-righteous atheists.

'Blessed Trinity,' he prays, 'Beloved Master, fill me with Your Spirit. Be always constant. Remain true. For as it is prophesied and written, the world will witness the Father's Resurrection. When in goodness your Father will surpass Christ himself. Amen. Invincible. Immortal. Inviolate. The one true god of love. Forgive all those who do not understand your goodness. Give me strength. Amen.'

He pays off the minicab driver some distance from the deserted yard at the rear of the derelict apartment block in Kensal Green.

48

Outside the Ahearnes' house in Richmond-upon-Thames. The London Emergency and Accident Service ambulance draws up in the darkness.

Virginia Ahearne is unaware of its arrival in the street, or of the two figures who open the garden gate beside the house. They are dressed in scarves and heavy winter coats. To protect their faces against the cold, as well as their identities, they wear the Patra black balaclavas of thermal silk favoured by mountain rescue teams.

Past the frozen beds of old-fashioned roses, beyond the mossy lawn now covered in a crust of snow, to where Virginia is fuelling the raging bonfire beneath the beech and horse chestnut trees. The smoke from her husband's numerous private papers drifts skywards in a plume of sparks.

Throughout the night she's turned out his desk, his filing cabinets, wardrobes, even box files he'd secreted in the attic. Piece by piece, chapter by chapter, she's learned of her husband's spiritual journey. Into what she considers a dreadful darkness.

The secret past: From the fanatical undergraduate Anglo-Catholicism she knew about and imagined to have been discarded as the post-adolescent neurosis of a lonely soul. To the outpourings in the diaries. Meanderings. Cloying confessions to himself about guilt. Inadequacy. How bafflement at her successes turned to resentment. Finally hatred. Then suddenly – Damascus. For Edward, her Little Prince, the light had come in, of all places, Venice. One rainy Easter in the early 1990s. Dazzled in the otherwise melancholy gloom, he turned his back on organized religion. 'I am Wounded Christian,' he confided to himself. Then, quite suddenly, his life began to blossom.

Virginia discovered that he set off on what he called 'the Journey of My Inner Landscape'. *'My soul is Revelation,'* he has written to himself. *'I am CLEANSED.'*

Astonished, amused, repelled by the intimacy of her husband's voyage, she's pored over the accounts of his bizarre and secret sexual predilection for colonic irrigation at the hands of the women of the Trinity Chapter.

What he calls 'the ecstasy of Cleansing and Confessional'. Harmless stuff in itself, maybe. Psycho mumbo-jumbo of the sort she more readily associated with the chattering classes, even with minor and not-so-minor royals. But far less harmless, more damaging, indeed insulting, has been the squandering of *this Money – MY MONEY*.

Spent on this vile organization which has apparently for so long, unknown to me, held you in its spell. Those nights at the Travellers' Club. Praying in Mgr Gilbey's chapel. So you said. Why had I never realized it?

'Dined with fellow members. Sympathetic souls –'

Garbage. Look at this: you were at Trinity Chapter gatherings at Trinity House in Kensal Green and God alone knows where else. Searching, so your squalid little diaries record, 'FOR THE SACRED IN MY LIFE'.

What is she to make of the secret obsession with the imminent Millennium?

She stares at the slowly rising bonfire smoke. The curled black paper fragments dancing overhead, sparkling in the freezing air. The remnants of the secret seem to mock her.

And she begins to weep again as she wept earlier.

Earlier that afternoon, when she'd wept quietly to herself. Realizing a kind of truth. *Where are you, Edward? Have you left me alone? Gone to join these dreadful people. Never to return?* Knowing *that my life has been built properly and logically on facts.* Dwelling *on the evil in other people's lives I am so astute in seeing. For the benefit of the DG. The Prime Minister. Home Secretary. The Nation. The machinery of State. And I never saw evil when it stared me in the face.* Vowing *Edward, when you return I will demand that you undergo rehabilitation counselling until every last shred and vestige of your disgusting beliefs and betrayals is obliterated. By God, you will repay every last penny of mine that you've squandered on these repulsive people.*

She kicks the last of Edward's papers into the blaze. The cloud of acrid smoke puffs into her face. It stings her eyes and she rubs them, smearing her face with black ash.

She is stooping over the fire when the gloved hand closes over her mouth.

Twisting, she looks helplessly at the hideous face covered in the balaclava mask. Metal handcuffs are slipped around her wrists and fastened. The canvas bag is placed over her head. The cord tightens into her oesophagus. Bites into her neck. Kicking, trying to scream, she is lifted across the man's shoulders and carried quickly to the quiet street where the ambulance is waiting. She has an impression of the man's immense strength. He smells dank. Of wet earth and rotten vegetables.

She screams: 'Edward Edward Edward, help me.'

And chokes.

49

The yard behind the apartment block in Kensal Green is lit by a yellowish glow of lights from the adjacent street. To gain access to it Edward Ahearne passes two giant skips overloaded with smashed office furniture. Beyond it is a car wreck. He pauses uneasily by the wreck. There's a strong smell of petrol in the air. Ahead of him stands the single steel door. To one side of the door is a small bell. *Someone's here in this godforsaken place. A prowler. Mugger. Not now, please.* Somewhere in the distance he hears a muffled howling. *A dog perhaps.* Fear rises in his chest. 'Is anyone there?' he calls. His heart thumps. Who or what is there he cannot tell.

As he reaches the door, his suspicion is confirmed. *Something, someone is moving in the car wreck. Someone is there.*

When he turns his back to the apartment building to take a look he's stopped in his tracks. A length of steel chain whips around his neck.

I'm being mugged –

He tries to scream for help.

I'm bleeding – Lifting his hands to grab the chain, he overbalances backwards and begins to fall, choking, face down into the snow, and is dragged away towards a pile of unused garbage bags and a raw wood crate like a coffin. Dust and grit blind him.

He tries to shout. To scream. His mouth fills with blood and snow.

Hands in fireproof gloves seize his throat. He twists his head this way and that, at the same time kicking out at his assailant.

A second later the small gas blowlamp is lit. The butane-propane mix turns blue. The flame coughs, spits. Carefully adjusted, it hisses evenly into his face. Scorches.

Once the blue flame is extinguished, his body, limp and unconscious, is dragged towards the car wreck reeking of petrol fumes.

The violence of the explosion stops his watch at precisely 10.30 p.m. on Christmas Eve, 1999.

○

Full Moon

50

Christmas Day.

The DG's Bell 222 helicopter sets down at Chequers, near Wendover in Buckinghamshire. Spewing a cloud of snow across the south park, it comes to rest next to the Prime Minister's Westland and the United States Air Force Chinook helicopter that's transported two armoured limousines to Chequers.

For the DG, the Chinook's presence is an uncomfortable reminder of the arrival here in one hour's time of the United States Ambassador's party. The guest of honour will be the US Secretary of State, Ms Wislawa Odone.

The Thames Valley police officer escorts the DG on the few hundred yards' walk to the front entrance, where a Wren shows him into the Jacobean-panelled Stone Hall. The DG slips slightly on the Bokhara rug. He passes the visitors' book he won't be asked to sign.

He stands awkwardly in the two-storey Great Hall beneath the brass chandelier with its eighteen candle lamps. The Great Hall smells of furniture polish and the sickly scent of the lilies in the vases. Warming his hands at the log fire burning in the hearth, he reads the Christmas cards on the alabaster mantelpiece. Secretarial signatures have been scrawled below fulsome messages of Peace and Good Will to All Men with best wishes for 2000 from heads of state and the closest members of his cabinet.

Naval and Air Force domestic staffs are making final and silent preparation for the arrival of the United States Ambassador and the US Secretary of State.

Near the Christmas tree from the park, two US Secret Service agents are engaging in conversation with the retired woman Naval Commander who's the Chequers curator and the chief steward, a woman RAF Wing Commander. The DG knows the schedule and the details of the high-security arrangements. The United States Ambassador and United States Secretary of State are travelling to Mildenhall. They will then make the rest of their journey by helicopter to Chequers. Together with the Prime Minister and his wife, they will lunch in the dining room, at the round table in the window recess with its view of the rose garden in the snow. The snow-capped topiary. The oak tree planted by Stanley Baldwin. After lunch of smoked salmon and roast beef, the US Ambassador and the Secretary of State will visit the American Cemetery at Madingley outside Cambridge. At some point *Holy Ghost* will *have* to be discussed.

A steward tells the DG the Prime Minister would

like to see him. The PM is waiting outside with the Home Secretary on the South Front terrace.

The DG would welcome a cup of coffee. He would prefer to stay in the warmth. However, the Prime Minister has other ideas. He wants to talk in privacy. The gardens will have to do. In the South Garden Hall, the steward points him in the direction of the South Terrace.

The gardens. Where the Prime Minister, with the Home Secretary, Deputy Prime Minister and the DG in tow, leads the way from the South Garden Hall on to the South Front's broad paved terrace. The leather soles of the DG's shoes are already damp. He loses his footing on the ice of the flagstones. He steadies himself by reaching for the arm of a wooden garden seat.

Snow covers the lavender hedges. Grass walk-ways The sunken Elizabethan knot-garden. Watched by armed protection officers in the distance.

The DG sees the apologetic and almost sad smile on the Prime Minister's face. The operation *Holy Ghost*, a running sore that refuses to heal, is creating difficulties in their dealings. Neither much likes the other and the sullen presence of the Deputy Prime Minister makes matters worse. The simian DG's intuition, a sixth sense, his quiet cunning, warns him that they're about to use *Holy Ghost* to cut his throat.

Near the lime tree planted by Lady Thatcher, the DG sees the Prime Minister's unctuous smile vanish. 'I suppose you've got a fairly good idea,' the Prime Minister says, 'of the extremely unpleasant warning we've been given by Washington.'

The DG turns to the Home Secretary, whose features are red and blue with cold. He averts his eyes. 'I haven't seen the latest reports,' the DG says, hoping to be put into the picture.

'You're implying,' the Prime Minister says, 'that it would have been a good thing if you had been shown them?'

'Yes,' says the DG. 'If, as I imagine, they affect *Holy Ghost*.'

'That's because they've only been given to us,' the Home Secretary puts in. 'Only the Prime Minister and myself have seen them. As well as Her Majesty and DG SIS.'

'That's why you haven't been shown them,' the Prime Minister emphasizes for the DG's benefit. 'The Americans have implied that a deal's been done. It suggests immunity from prosecution.'

'Whose immunity? What prosecution?'

The Prime Minister gives a smile that suggests he prefers to leave the DG's question unanswered.

'We've been advised,' he continues, 'that the Inner Chapter of this godforsaken cult plans a major atrocity to coincide with the Millennium. We have been advised to close the West End of London. That's what the Americans have produced for us to be concerned about.'

'I can understand your concern,' says the DG

solicitously, almost like a doctor. 'I'd like to know exactly what's been said. What concerns you.'

'It's the White House that's concerned,' says the Prime Minister.

'And so am I,' says the Home Secretary.

'Surely it's a matter for the Commissioner,' says the DG.

'And the Palace,' says the Prime Minister. 'The Queen won't tolerate any interruption in Millennium celebrations. She won't hear of cancelling her appearance on the Palace balcony. Or of forbidding entry to the Mall, Trafalgar Square and the West End.'

'That, if I may say so with respect, is unwise,' the DG says slowly. 'The husband of my Legal Adviser is to be interrogated a second time today about his involvement in this cult. I've no doubt whatsoever that he'll tell me what I need to know.'

'Your Legal Adviser isn't involved *as well*, is she?' asks the Deputy Prime Minister.

'That's what I need to be sure about,' says the DG. 'So far it's only the husband.'

'Is she or isn't she?' the Home Secretary asks.

'I need firm proof of it,' says the DG.

'What are you going to do if she is?' asks the Prime Minister.

'Institute disciplinary procedures,' says the DG. 'Press for her immediate resignation and so forth. I mean –'

The Home Secretary shrugs. 'And finally hand in

yours too? If we have senior security service personnel up to their necks in corruption, money laundering, murder and conspiracy to murder, then we're facing a situation that will totally destroy the credibility of the service. And you're the one who's responsible.'

'It's far too early for me to comment,' says the DG.

The Home Secretary's voice is flat. 'I just have commented. You heard me. Fail to clean the stables and you go.'

'It's a problem that can be solved,' says the DG.

'One you have to solve as soon as possible,' says the Prime Minister. 'I mean, to say nothing of whether or not we go against Her Majesty's wishes. Whether we have to give the warning the maximum news coverage. And say we have to keep people, God knows how many, out of the West End. You know, I mean –'

'I understand your dilemma, sir.'

'My dilemma. I'll tell you what I understand,' says the Home Secretary. 'I *understand* that you personally gave the operation to the Americans after the Joint Intelligence Committee. They took it as a guarantee that in no circumstances would we be a party to embarrassing the President or any of his associates. Now the whole bloody thing's blowing up in our faces. Thanks to you. It almost feels like a deliberate balls-up.'

'Nothing could have been further from my mind,' the DG says. 'I made it abundantly clear to our

American friends that we were handing over substantive intelligence to their people. Both as a duty and as a favour.'

'And yet you're continuing to run *Holy Ghost*,' says the Home Secretary. 'And you stand here saying your Legal Adviser isn't herself compromised. Are you seriously saying that she of all people doesn't know what her husband's involved in? What the hell is this planned atrocity *about*?'

'Everything that requires to be done is being done,' says the DG.

'Yet you tell us,' says the Home Secretary, 'that you haven't the faintest idea where her husband is?'

'All I've been told is that he left home some time yesterday,' says the DG. 'He left no word as to where he was going. He hasn't been heard of since.'

'What about his bloody wife?' says the Deputy Prime Minister.

'Naturally, his wife is very worried.'

'He's done a runner,' says the Home Secretary. 'My God, you'd better find him and fast. Who is the officer in charge of this *Holy Ghost* – what's her name?'

'Lever.'

'Who you solemnly say has got no serious evidence of what the Americans are telling us?'

'She's one of our best officers.'

'And yet,' says the Home Secretary, 'it's *your* view that these people are party to murder and conspiracy to murder.'

'I mean, you know, is that really the whole truth?' asks the Prime Minister.

'I've already said, sir, we need to establish the truth,' says the DG.

'You mean *you* need to,' says the Home Secretary.

'I can't afford to have my Legal Adviser compromised by her husband's lack of judgement,' says the DG.

'What you can't afford,' says the Prime Minister, 'I mean, is to put us in the position of having to overrule the Palace.'

'So what's your woman Lever going to do about it?' asks the Home Secretary.

The DG stiffens: 'Her duty.'

'Don't stand there talking about duty,' says the Home Secretary. 'For Christ's sake, I want an arrest. Prosecution.'

'There isn't yet enough evidence to justify a successful prosecution.'

'Then I think you'd better redouble your efforts,' says the Prime Minister. 'How much longer have we got?'

'As long as it takes to find Ahearne,' says the DG.

'Very well,' says the Prime Minister. 'Go back to London. Find him.'

'Meanwhile, in plain language,' says the Home Secretary: 'You dug the hole. Now get us out of it. Do I need to remind you of how long you've got?'

The DG doesn't need reminding of the days left to the dawn of the Millennium.

He finds his way alone to his helicopter for the short flight back to snowbound London. His feet are numb with cold. This last-of-century Christmas seems to offer no comfort. And the prospect of the New Year is chilling.

51

Mars in conjunction with Moon. Mars 3° North

Caroline thinks: the rumble sounded like some small explosion you hear in a distant quarry. Shaking the house to the foundations, the explosion had echoed in her head and she felt the dust fall in a cloud from the ceiling. *Hey, good,* she'd thought. *The fire and police people will investigate. They'll come. They'll find me.* She'd heard the police sirens in the distance and the very faint sound of voices in the building. *Say it was a bomb?* Her heart leapt with hope. *They'll have to search this place. They'll find me.* So she'd tried to scream. And the voices went away. The noise of the explosion beat in her head. She wondered if her tormentor had been hurt? Taken away? *Christ, they've taken him away and now, after all of this, I'll starve to death –*

She thinks of ways of ending everything. Slowly picking at the fabric of a blanket. To tear it into strips. To make the noose and hang herself. *I could just do it. If only the inner door didn't lock from the outside.* She believes she can fix the noose around her neck and fall forwards. *How long will I have to dangle before I lose consciousness and go?*

There's a total absence of anything in her cell that

would help her end everything. No knife, no fork. She eats with her fingers and licks them clean like a cat.

They want to keep me alive. To kill me in their own good time. Blackness. The darkness that doesn't descend. It collapses on me. I touch my face all over. Are my fingers feeling the skin of my eyelids, nose and lips? Or is my face feeling the skin of my fingers? I often lose the feeling in my legs. My wrists are numb and seem to have expanded to a monstrous size.

She's shivering. Her throat is dry and sore. The circulation in her feet and hands seems blocked, her eyelids stuck together. The glands behind her ears and in her neck have swollen.

CAROLINE: Hello? Please. Who is it?
WROTH: There are five days left – four days until the Resurrection.
Today must be December 26th?
CAROLINE: What will happen to me?
WROTH: It has to be done.

There's no light from beneath the door. She calls out for the man to return. But he doesn't.

The silence brings despair and loneliness she's never known or ever thought she'd know.

Later she thinks she hears a radio playing Gloria Gaynor: 'I will survive.'
Or is it inside her head?
Please God. Help me.

[393]

52

The early hours of 28 December 1999: Rosslyn stands watching Dr Ryan Lancaster in his office at University College Hospital. Lancaster, head to toe in white, taps away at his computer keyboard. Leaning against the wall is the lightweight racing bike he rides to work. On the saddle is a yellow helmet. Next to his computer is the photograph of his wife and family and the holiday house Rosslyn takes to be somewhere in north Cornwall. There's another of a much younger Lancaster as the Cambridge middleweight boxing blue. The doctor keys in **American. Female. Age**. In their 20s. **Jane Moorfield**. Copies of his letters to the **St Pancras Coroner**. Hits FIND. 'Print?' he asks.

'Please.'

'I'll do two.' Lancaster leans back in his desk chair. 'I was at Oundle with the last but one Legal Adviser to MI5,' he says. 'Did you know him?'

'No.'

'Pompous little twerp,' says Lancaster. 'Wanted to be an architect. Always was a duffer. Architect. Here's your tackle.' He scans the printed sheets. 'I have to say there's a rather uncanny similarity between the deaths. I see the same: *"5cc syringe*

and two 25g and one 23g needles, a folded piece of paper
to which traces of a powder were adherent". And –
"The patient was a young, thin, fair-haired Caucasian
woman. I estimated her age as between twenty-five and
thirty."'

Almost word for word the same as the letter he
sent the coroner:

I remember thinking these were rather awkward sites for self-
administered intravenous injections. These were not the
venepuncture sites one normally sees in comatose intravenous
drug abusers brought to our casualty.

'It's the same story,' says Rosslyn. 'And the
forensic pathologist. Was it Dr Maryon?'

Lancaster taps the keys. Up comes **Dr Elizabeth
Maryon**. 'Mind you,' says Lancaster, 'nothing
necessarily unusual in that. We're looking at her
territory. Mine too, for that matter.'

'Then do you mind if we try the name Trinity?'

'Not at all.'

In goes **Trinity**.

Rosslyn watches the screen.

'My God,' says Lancaster. 'She did him too.'

'It figures,' says Rosslyn. 'Mind if I use your
phone?'

Rosslyn calls Lever: 'Turn up the HOLMES file on
Marcus Luke. Find out if he identified the body said
to be that of Trinity at the inquest. Call me back on
this number.'

Two minutes later, Lever is on the line: 'Luke

identified Trinity. Real name Julius Gowrie. More's following.'

Rosslyn gives her the names of the three other American women.

'Wait out,' says Lever.

When she comes back on the line again, she says simply: 'Yes, the same. Luke identified all three at the inquests in St Pancras. I have the dates. Maryon did the *post mortems* on all three American women. Each verdict was Death by Misadventure. Drugs-related. In the King's Cross and St Pancras area. And Trinity, who was found at the hotel in Oxford Street.'

'See,' says Rosslyn. 'Maryon's part of the whole thing. She's the link. She's the only one who could've faked the *post mortem* on Trinity. He isn't going to resurrect, because he isn't dead. It has to have been some other poor nameless sod who died. Hold Maryon till I've been back to Kensal Green tomorrow morning.'

'Forgive me,' Lancaster says as Rosslyn's leaving, 'I couldn't helping overhearing – you have a problem with Dr Maryon?'

'She may be the one with the problem. Only you didn't hear that, right?'

'Of course I didn't,' the doctor says. 'But I'd be happy to help.'

'Then one question. Suppose you wanted to murder someone. How would you do it?'

The doctor doesn't hesitate to offer an opinion. 'Easy. Create a drug dependency situation. Easy enough with the alcoholic, socialite or manic depressive. London's awash with drugs. The murder dose would be solid stuff. Not flour and sugar plus drug substance. No substitutes. Use a location near a hospital. Say a disused church, cemetery or patch of wasteland.'

'St Pancras or King's Cross, say?'

'Ideal. The police bag up the body and take it to the Tropical Diseases Hospital that happens to be round the corner from the mortuary and Coroner's Court. Let's call the forensic pathologist Dr X. Out of every one thousand *post mortems* Dr X does each year, at least six remain unidentified in perpetuity. In this case fingerprints are checked with the CRO. Dental impressions are examined and checked. Known addicts in the area are talked to by one or other of the coroner's court officers.'

'How long would it take?'

'Say nine months to a year. The body is bagged and put in the fridge. The records are held on a computer. Usually Windows-based on a local area network.'

'Not a watertight system, then?'

'Leaks like a sieve.'

'Forensic pathologist Dr X,' says Rosslyn, 'can alter the identity of a body with impunity.'

'Naturally. She has six a year to choose from, doesn't she?'

'So in other words, if you have a bent forensic pathologist at work –?'

'Easy,' the doctor interrupts. 'Easiest thing in the world. It's all part of London culture. Rotten to the core. Corpses don't ask questions. The police couldn't give a shit for druggies. Forensic pathologists don't see people. They see corpses. They're inured to death in all its forms. That's why the discipline attracts some pretty odd sods.'

'You haven't told me any of this, have you?' says Rosslyn. 'We haven't mentioned Dr Maryon, have we?'

'Dog doesn't eat dog,' says the doctor. 'And dogs don't talk. Frankly, I'm none too keen to get involved. I simply mentioned Dr X. You look as if you could use some sleep.'

'I could,' says Rosslyn, drawing on his coat. Thinking he has about five hours to get the sleep he needs.

53

As Rosslyn heads south for Claverton Street, Caroline lies awake in the subterranean cell in Kensal Green.

Earlier, at feeding time, the voice beyond the iron doors had said: 'You're to be moved.'

She didn't reply to him. Just let the silence hang.

He shouted: *'You will be moved!'*

Finally Caroline said: 'Oh yeah – what's new, jerk?'

And she heard the footsteps retreat.

She talks to herself: *I haven't eaten anything for how long? Maybe twenty, maybe thirty hours. But the wind whispers: 'Eat-eat-eat-eat.'*

54

Rosslyn is dreaming of voices in his head when the radio alarm wakes him at 7.35 am. The newsman is saying there are three days to go and some crazy from the Armageddon 2000 Society is saying that she's fleeing to the highest point in the United Kingdom to be nearer to the Maker.

Shaving, he listens to some architect blathering on about the 'vision of Greenwich' and 'the importance of Sex, Food and Architecture'. Steam clouds the mirror.

The phone rings. It's Lever saying she has copies of the inquest transcripts. The record confirms the hypothesis Rosslyn had encouraged Dr Lancaster to construct the night before.

'The question is,' says Lever, 'where are Trinity, Luke and Caroline?'

'We have to start at Kensal Green,' says Rosslyn.

'I'll pick you up,' Lever says. 'Give me half an hour.'

The wind drives the snow in the Harrow Road against the wall of the cemetery and the buildings opposite.

Rosslyn checks the front entrance. Someone's done

a workmanlike job of boarding up the front entrance. It'd need a sledge-hammer and crowbar to smash them open.

The rear entrance door of steel is chained and padlocked. But it's the state of the yard that concentrates Rosslyn's mind. There's been a junk blaze here within the last few days. It seems to have been caused by the charred car wreck. Maybe some villain's tried to dispose of a vehicle. Some of the metal seems to have been wrenched apart. Rough and serrated edges of raw metal suggest the car was blown up. Perhaps by a minor explosion. Say the fuel tank went up. He can't be sure of it; or whether the blast was assisted by a small high-explosives charge. What's odd is that the old service area has been cleaned up. There are no telltale signs of charred clothing.

'We'll get inside,' he tells Lever, who's been ringing the bell to no avail.

He pushes a wheelie bin towards the side of the building. 'Let's try the window.'

The window ledge is covered in patches of ice and grease. With his second attempt to heave himself up, he manages to get a grip on the window frame. Pulling his coat sleeve over his clenched fist, he punches at the window. The third punch splits the glass. More hits create an opening. He leans down to grasp Lever's wrist. She jumps once and can't make it. Next time she succeeds, and the recoil of her jump shoves back the wheelie bin so hard that its cover opens. Rosslyn pulls her up to the ledge. With

Rosslyn leading the way, they lower themselves inside.

Only the moaning of the wind breaks the silence inside the building.

'This place has changed,' says Rosslyn. 'It's been totally cleaned out.'

'Of what?'

'Like spring-cleaned.'

The two of them look at each other, almost fearful. A steel hawser slams against the brick exterior. It sets up a twanging echo. Rosslyn feels his stomach shrinking. 'I know she was here. She must have been.'

'Forensic says so.'

'I know. I feel it.'

Lever sniffs. 'Where's the fucking caretaker then?'

'Hello?' Rosslyn shouts. Silence.

The air smells of white spirit and disinfectant.

The upper floor confirms Rosslyn's view. So does the ground floor: there are smears on the floor-boards as if someone's wiped away cement and sand in a hurry.

They cross to the steps leading to the basement. The stair well is dark and the mains electricity supply is dead. He kicks the door open.

'I should have brought a torch,' says Rosslyn.

'My fault,' she says.

'No,' he says. 'Mine.'

He takes her hand. 'Mind the steps. They're slippery.'

He can hear Lever breathing close behind him. 'Leave the door open.'

There's enough light now to make out the dank stairs leading down from the near side of the basement. Already there's a vile stench of rottenness.

'Anyone here?' Rosslyn shouts. His voice echoes. There's no reply. 'Why have they bothered to clear this God-awful hole out?'

'Someone's left in one big hurry,' says Lever.

'They have to have left something behind.'

'There's dogshit,' she says. 'And, Christ, a rat.' She kicks out wildly. 'I hate you fuckers.'

In the basement Rosslyn stretches out his arms in front of him like a blind man. Lever holds on to the folds of his coat. He's feeling his way across the damp flagstones, some fifty feet. He stops. 'There's a newly bricked-up section here . . . cement's not dry . . . Stand back a second.' He kicks hard and heavily, flat-footed, at the brickwork. 'Stand back more,' he tells her. Panting, he takes a three-pace run and launches a savage kick at the brickwork with all his strength. There's a thud. The section of bricks falls away on the other side. Twice more he kicks. Flays at the edge of the hole. Now there's a gap in the wall large enough to get through. He hears Lever inhale and cough out the fumes of putrefaction and decay and drains.

'It's human flesh,' she says. 'Jesus, Alan. You can smell the shit. Don't go any further.'

'We have to look.'

'I can't see,' she says.

'Feel. Just feel . . .' He feels the sweat, warm and sticky on his forehead. Somewhere in the tunnels far off he hears a howl. It's animal. Not human. *A fox? Not here, now? The howl of death. Like the voices that had woken him this morning. Only they were from the radio.*

'I can't stand the stench,' she says. 'Alan, I tell you it's human.'

'If I touch a corpse . . . I'll tell you. Hang about.' His fingers close around manacles. The length of chain fixed to the wall. He crouches down. Feels white blankets. Suddenly he freezes.

There's a clank.

'It's me, Alan,' says Lever, terrified. 'It's like I'm holding a waste bin or something. Fuck. It's a toilet. Ugh. Fuck.'

'This is like someone's S and M gear,' Rosslyn says. 'Restraints. Chains. Manacles. What the hell's gone on in here? Perverts.'

He feels Lever pulling at his coat. 'I want to get the fuck out of here,' she says. Her voice is terrified. Cold. Shaking.

Rosslyn feels his lips fixed. Drawn back in his head. His teeth bared. 'Wendy, stay where you are. I'll keep talking so you know where I am.'

'Alan, don't leave me.'

'I can feel another opening . . .' He shakes her

hand free. Then he edges forwards. There's a large slab. He's touching the shape of a massive tomb-stone. His hands run along the carved inscription. His finger traces:

MORTIMER

'Mortimer,' he says.

'What?'

'That's the name on this godforsaken slab.'

He steps beyond. Feeling. Feeling.

Now he sees a small green glow.

'I can see something. Like luminous. A glow.'

'Alan, let's get out of here. Please.'

'And God, this is a watch . . . I'm holding a hand.' He wishes he'd brought rubber gloves. 'Rigid. Cold. Can't get them off. Pearls. The two-strand pearl necklace.'

'Don't do it, Alan. Leave her. C'mon, please.'

'It's Virginia Ahearne. Has to be Virginia Ahearne –'

He gropes his way still further on. Deeper into the darkness. He feels remnants of marble. Something slimy like a slug seems to attach itself to the back of his hand. He flicks it off. His lips and tongue are completely dry. He can feel his nipples rubbing against a shirt button or something. In his mind's eye he sees Caroline. *The dead face. Open mouthed. Without features.* He knows any second he'll reach out and touch her face.

But he doesn't. There's no more rubble. Just a long

passage. He reaches down and his fingers touch a pebble. He swings his arm. Throws the pebble ahead of him. It rattles. Echoes. The passage ahead has to be very long. Beyond that there's the wall of darkness and there's no point going further.

'Alan, talk to me,' says Lever.

'OK, I'm coming back. Someone else'll have to come in here fast and see where Caroline is.' He pauses. 'Keep on talking, Wendy. So I can find you.'

She begins to chant. Like a dirge. Slowly. 'Alan. Alan. Alan. Alan. One two three four five six . . .'

By the time she's reached twenty-five he's holding her hand. Leading her back the way they've come. Across the basement to the stairs and out.

Fresh air has never smelled so good. They have some difficulty in avoiding the splinters of the window Rosslyn smashed to gain entry. Lowering themselves from the window ledge is equally awkward, because Lever had kicked the wheelie bin away and the lid is open. Rosslyn goes first and sinks into the piles of garbage. His foot splits a bag and the wind lifts the charred remnants of some printed brochure. He helps Lever down. Then looks at the remains of one of the brochures that's stuck to his feet. Once they're both on firm ground he glances through its pages.

'This is who's been here,' he says. 'Take a look.'

She reads over his shoulder: VAN RIJN CLINIC FOR NATURAL HEALTH MEDICINE.

'Gowrie,' he says. 'Trinity. Wroth. Marcus Luke. But no Caroline.'

'No Caroline,' she says. 'The police should search that place down there.'

'No,' he says. 'Let's wait.'

'You have to see if she's down there.'

'If she's there, she's dead. He looks at Edward Ahearne's watch. His tie. 'You recognize the neck-lace?'

'Virginia Ahearne's. Yes.'

'If Caroline's not there, she's alive. Has to be alive.'

'How can you be sure?'

'If not, it's over. Bar the Resurrection. Bar the killing. More of what I touched. The bloodbath.'

She frowns at him. The colour's returning to her cheeks. 'You think –?'

'If,' he says, 'you're thinking what I'm thinking, the answer's yes. You're right-right-right. I think he'll do it on New Year's Eve. And God help anyone who's near him at the time.'

Returning to the car they find the woman and child Rosslyn had seen when he'd first called at the apartment building. She's chanting. The same old dirge.

'He is coming,' she says.

'I know,' says Rosslyn. 'But who left?'

'Believers,' she says. 'Believers.'

'Who?'

'They left because someone was taken ill.'

'Who?'

'I don't know, brother. We do good works.'

'How, when did they leave?'

'I don't know,' she says. 'Only believe, brother. They'd called an ambulance.'

'An ambulance?'

'So whoever was taken ill will be cured and saved. I think it was an ambulance.'

'You think. What did you see?'

'A white van.'

'A van. Not an ambulance?'

'I can't be sure. No. Perhaps. Yes. It was a van. A little bus. Thanks to the Divinity of Trinity. Brother and Sister. He who will come.'

'Yes,' says Rosslyn.

The disciple makes the sign: | | |.

In the warmth of the car.

'That bloody visionary,' he says, 'wouldn't know a number 9 bus if it hit her in the face. We have to run a hospital check. But I don't hold out much hope. Caroline's no use to them in hospital. Look. Trinity isn't dead. But if he's going to achieve the Resurrection, he'll have to remain in hiding until the last minute. And now we've met the major players – except the one who's conspicuous by his absence. Van Rijn. He's the one who has to be Trinity. If so, we have to test the hypothesis. We'll take a leaf out of Caroline's book. Place a personal ad. In the Deaths columns. *The Times* for starters. Smoke the bastards out. Maryon, Wroth and Marcus Luke. All three. Isolate Van Rijn.'

'What's the wording of the ad?' she asks.

'We'll word it at my place. Then take a break until tomorrow morning.'

'You're going to cook me dinner?'

'We'll fix it together. Or go out. A date. Which?'

'I need a bath. I've nothing to wear.'

'You'll do.'

Leaving tyre marks on the ice, she drives off and away.

55

The single light illuminates the large reproduction of the eighteenth-century *ukiyo-e* woodblock by Koryusai. The screen that obscures the view of the bedroom. The woman in the kimono is watching the couple lovemaking in the Yoshiwara house. The woman beneath the man on the tatami mat has her legs wound round his back. The chaos of the bed reveals something of the lovemaking that's taken place not long before.

The draft *Times* ad on the table reads:

> VAN RIJN. Dr J. Van Rijn, aged 57 years, on 15 December 1999, previously director of the Van Rijn Clinic, Harley Street, suddenly but peacefully at Adinkerke, Belgium. A kind and gentle man. Donations to the Trinity Chapter, Trinity House, Kensal Green, London W10.

56

I must Create a System, or be enslav'd by another Man's;
I will not Reason and Compare: my business is to Create.
  — WILLIAM BLAKE, JERUSALEM

The Isle of Dogs. Next day, 2 pm. Five times during
the afternoon, Luke has listened to the woman's
voice: 'The Vodaphone number you have called is
switched off. Please try again later.'

Maryon hasn't shown up. She isn't answering his
calls. He'll call her again in a few minutes.

He stands on the walkway staring at the deserted
street. The muzzled Rasselaer, P & J, squats at his
feet. *Where are you, Maryon?*

The suspicion is growing that she may have
formed some other plan. He remembers her rage.
The result of the visit she received from Rosslyn.

*Have you . . . have you gone over to the other side?
Have you taken a look at the bank accounts? Have you
even taken funds? Could you have done a runner?
Betrayed us before the chimes of midnight?*

The 3.5 litre Accident and Emergency ambulance
stands in a lock-up garage next to the unoccupied
warehouse.

Inside, Wroth sits on the attendant's seat watching Caroline. She is strapped to the stretcher base, her arms and legs tied. The rubber head mask has been removed. She's free to talk. To breathe. But not to move.

'Please don't hurt me any more,' she says. And Wroth, as he's said over and over again, is doing his best 'to keep you comfortable'.

'Let me go. Please.'

'You're safe here.'

'Please –'

'Let me teach you. We are at war with the infidels. Ours is the divine and upper hand. Ours the Inner Life. Let me show you the relics. The travelling treasures. Armament. For the holy war against the infidels.'

She sees an assortment of medical and electronic equipment.

'The pride and joy,' says Wroth.

He checks names, dates, places and the myriad secret details of Trinity's scientific researches: 'Medical. Traditional Chinese Medicine. Technological. Electronic. Forensic. Philosophical. Theological. Says the Master: "Knowledge is Power. Power is Knowledge. My power. My knowledge."'

Wrapped in tissue are syringes. In small plastic bags and silver foil is a substantial quantity of white powder.

'Diamorphine,' says Wroth.

He rummages among the few dull clothes,

clean and neatly folded. '*His* research material.'

Caroline watches him sort through the collection: The video cassettes in plastic boxes labelled BBC GUIDE TO ENGLAND'S HISTORIC MONUMENTS AND GARDENS, or LONDON'S ARCHAEOLOGY. Annotated maps of Trafalgar Square and London's West End. Copies of the TOP SECRET *MI5 Memorandum from Operation Resources and Intelligence.* She reads over Wroth's shoulder: *The Joint Security Service/Scotland Yard Public Order Forward Planning Unit Emergency Plans: Ref. 31 December 1999.*

'What is all this for?' she asks.

'The night of the sacred dawn,' he says. 'Of the Millennium, bringing Rebirth and Hope to the troubled world. And this is mine. See. Look. Mine.'

She sees the small ring-binder.

'My notes,' he says with pride. 'On the layout and workings of the north London Colehurst Green crematorium. Oil and gas supply tanks manufactured in Frankfurt am Main. The great furnaces from Essen. Marvels of dispatch. For the future. Yes, the future. For the years ahead. For the followers to free themselves from the infidels. Let me show you things. As Trinity showed me.'

He opens a small cardboard box lying in the second suitcase. She sees the blowtorch and the gas canisters that power the torch's flame.

'The Holy Flame.'

Next to the torch and canisters is a paperback instruction manual.

'Armament against the infidel. So that the heathen will not prevent the Second Coming.'

In English, German, French and Spanish, its title is *High Explosives*.

Leafed inside the manual's pages are photographs of scorched, disfigured faces.

Wroth says quietly: 'They died because they did not believe.'

'You –' she says, 'you did that?'

'Necessarily.'

'What do you mean?'

'It was necessary,' he smiles.

'You enjoyed it?'

'Whatever,' he grins, 'is done in the Master's name is necessary.'

'You're *sick*.'

'Not sick. Saved. Ours is the dedication to the service of all mankind. To the care of the sad, the distressed, the empty souls who seek natural harmony. Poor demented creatures.'

'Don't talk to me any more,' she says.

'Oh, but you must know. You must understand the mind of Van Rijn. See how Trinity is made. By Divine movement. Like the chess master's move. Do you play chess?'

'I used to.'

His vast and hairy fingers describe the knight's move: ←↑.

'From Van Rijn to Trinity to rebirth. The Divine Master who died to be reborn. To resurrect in full human form on earth as Trinity.'

'You people are mad.'

'No, wise. We are wise. We had celebrities from the worlds of the arts. The world of movies, television and the Royal National Theatre. Here –' He shows her the colour photo of a beaming Wislawa Odone. 'All of them grateful to the Master.'

She reads the bold handwritten expressions of gratitude and apparent familiarity from hapless patients of the Van Rijn Clinic.

'Listen to the music,' he says. 'The Master's choice.'

Once more plays the tape of Mahler's Resurrection Symphony:

> *Aufersteh'n, ja aufersteh'n wirst du,*
> *Mein Staub, nach kurzter Ruh!*
> *Unsterblich Leben! Unsterblich Leben*
> *Will der dich rief dir geben.**

And whispers:

> *Speak Byron: Love watching madness with unalter-*
> *able mien.*
> *Cry Milton: Demoniac frenzy, moping melancholy,*
> *And moon-struck madness.*
> *Howl Shakespeare: Make mad the guilty, and appal*
> *the free!*

She sees the veins bulge at the side of his forehead.

---

* Rise up, yes, you will rise up, / My dust, after short rest! / Immortal life! Immortal life / He who called you will give you.

He reaches to the floor for a paper cup and slowly raises it to her lips like holy water. 'Drink,' he says.

She sips the liquid. Cold and bitter herbal tea.

'And I want you to listen to the voice of the Son.'

He plays a new tape. The taped monologue is delivered by Marcus Luke.

'The voice of Son Redeemed,' Wroth adds.

> *Mother, Son and Holy Ghost.*
> *The Epistle of Son to Trinity.*
> *In your name, Father. For Your sake.*
>
> *As I have been wont to perform in all humility.*
> *The infidel Moorfield is passed over.*
> *As You commanded.*

The sound of Marcus Luke's voice sickens her. 'I don't want to hear this crap,' she says.

'But you must.'

The tape of Luke's voice continues:

The world bears witness now to Death by Misadventure.
As it was written by You. In deed. And word.
We remain inviolate.
My Love for You is undimmed.
Guided by Your Light and in Your Mercy, with sacred offerings to the Inner Chapter, now in Your Name we make all things possible.
I, Your humble servant, seek only to hear the word of Your Coming.
I pray that You, in all goodness, will show me the way of salvation and give me, Your loving son, to be revealed.

*My filial devotion. Your strength to complete Your task
at the dawn of the Millennium now approaching, so all
people will bear witness to Your Resurrection. In Your
Name, Amen.*

'Whose redeemed son is he?'

'The Master's son.'

'Trinity's?'

Marcus Luke is Trinity's Son?

'Trinity's?' she repeats.

He smiles.

'Where is he?' she asks.

'He will come.'

'Why's it taking him so long?'

'He is waiting for his mother.'

'Mother?'

'Yes. So we may be united. In three. In Trinity.
Mother, Son and Holy Ghost.'

'Where are we going?'

'Into the Master's immortal hands.'

She sees he's touching the photographs of the
women's disfigured faces. Caressing them. Whispering: 'You who laid down your lives for His Name's
Sake. That He might be reborn at the moment of One
One One. In the first minute. Of the first hour. Of the
first day. As it is promised. So Thy Will be done. Let
us continue to perform our Bounden Duty. Let them
thwart us, and the world will witness the death of
one hundred souls and mourn the dead and
mutilated for a thousand years.'

He increases the volume of the music:

> *O glaube,*
> *Du warst nicht umsonst geboren!*
> *Hast nicht umsonst gelebt.*
> *Gelitten!**

'Death and resurrection,' he says. And makes the sign: | | |.

> *Was entstanden ist,*
> *Das muss vergehen!*
> *Was vergangen, aufersteh'n!*
> *Hör' auf zu beben!*
> *Bereite dich zu leben!* †

'Look, Caroline.' He shows her a page from a Filofax.

He has it open at the page headed R. She sees: ROSSLYN, Alan. And next to it: WENDY LEVER. Home Office, c/o Box 3255, Intelligence Resources and Operations, Thames House, Millbank, London SW1P 1AE.

'He will purify them in death,' says Wroth. 'Come the night.'

She wonders exactly what he means.

He reaches up into one of the overhead lockers. She can smell his stale sweat. 'This is the Master's,'

---

* O believe. / You were not born in vain! / Have not lived, suffered / In vain!

† All that is created / Must perish! / What dies must rise again! / Tremble no more! / Prepare yourself to live!

he says. He lifts down a cardboard box and shows her a medical-looking gadget.

'Portable machine for colonic irrigation,' he explains. 'Adapted to provide ozone as well as hydrotherapy.' He shows her the small polythene jar. 'Acidopholus to be taken to reseed the colon with flora that may have been lost during evacuation of the bowel ducts.' And there's the slender box of wood. The varnish scratched. 'In this are stainless steel speculums. Do you know what they are for?'

'No.'

'For the pumping of water into the bowel.'

'For what?'

'The cleansing. Each tube has a protruding rim. Do you know why?'

'No.'

'To prevent the tube being introduced too far inside.'

'Inside what?'

'The rear channel.'

'Whose rear channel?'

'Yours.'

'Mine?'

'Yes, yours.'

'And then –?'

'Be patient, Caroline.'

'What happens then?'

'Trust me.'

'Are you going to –?'

'You mean that?'

'Assault me?'

'Oh no,' he says. 'Not that. No, I have been celibate all my life.'

'I don't believe anything you say. You're full of shit.'

'Please, Caroline. No words like that in the presence of His relics.'

'Fuck them.'

'No.'

'Fuck you. I hope you rot in hell. Motherfucker. You're sick, sick, sick.'

She feels her nails. Long. Sharp. Looks at the veins in his forehead. Wonders if she has the strength to draw blood from his massive neck and hairy throat.

Marcus Luke buys a copy of the *Daily Mail*. Goes to a café. Orders an all-day breakfast. He flips through the pages of the *Mail*. Spits out his scrambled egg. Returns to the newsagents. Buys four other dailies. Turns up Deaths in *The Times*.

Reads, stunned and fearful:

> VAN RIJN. Dr J. Van Rijn, aged 57 years, on 15 December 1999, previously director of the Van Rijn Clinic, Harley Street, suddenly but peacefully at Adinkerke, Belgium. A kind and gentle man. Donations to the Trinity Chapter, Trinity House, Kensal Green, London W10.

57

30 December 1999. Her Majesty's Prison for women, Holloway. The false silence hangs over the modern buildings of dirty brick. On E Wing's fourth floor, in the sparsely-furnished room set aside for Dr Maryon's interrogation, the wall clock says 12.15 pm. Before Maryon's brought in, Rosslyn tells Lever: 'I want the full confession. How she covered the deaths. The whole Trinity Chapter strategy for the first minutes of the Millennium in Trafalgar Square. So the Prime Minister can decide what to do about the People's Celebration. Whether to go on TV. Confess to everyone just why hundreds of thousands of people should stay clear of Trafalgar Square on New Year's Eve. "The whole world will be watching." Some crap like that.'

'There's Caroline to think about,' says Lever. She toys with the plastic mug of tepid tea in front of her. 'We can run more checks on hospital admissions throughout the Greater London area.' No patient's answered to the name of Caroline Moorfield.

'It's a scam,' says Rosslyn.

'And what if Maryon stays stumm?'

'We'll hear what she has to say. Let's go for her. Tell the screw. Get her in here.'

Is it fear or rage that churns his stomach? Or anxiety about Caroline? The pulse always quickens before the one-shot interrogation. This is not just another suspect. This a broken woman in paper overalls. Stripped of dignity. A pathetic sight. Drawn and exhausted. Full of self-pity. Or is this the guise, the front that says: *Please have pity on me. I am harmless. Use your eyes. They don't deceive you. Can't you see —?*

'Take a seat, Dr Maryon,' he says. 'Would you like a cup of tea?'

'No, thank you.'

'Coffee then?'

She shakes her head. 'No.'

He sets Lever's tape recorder on the table between them. 'How are you?' he asks.

'Hmm,' she says.

'You know what this is about, Dr Maryon?' he asks.

'I suppose you want to ask me more questions about the Moorfield woman, the inquest?'

'No,' he says genially.

Let her think I'm not here to break her for fixing the inquests. Engineering the 'death' of Trinity. Fabricating the evidence that led to the verdicts of Death By Misadventure on the three murdered American women. No. We'll make this easy for you, Maryon. Concede a point for starters. And see how you play it from there on.

'I'm satisfied,' he lies to her, 'that you performed

[422]

your duty in the correct manner. We don't have a problem with the inquest.'

'Then perhaps you'd explain why I'm here?' she says slowly. 'Why I haven't been allowed to telephone my lawyer?'

'Because there isn't time, Dr Maryon. You know why there isn't time.' He looks at the wall clock. 'We have less than thirty-six hours until midnight on the 31st. And you and I both know what that means.'

'It's my right to have my lawyer present.'

'Yes, I know all that,' he says. 'It's also our right to make a tape recording of this interview. Mind if we begin?'

'If you insist.' She brushes the split fringe from her eyes. 'I've never been questioned like this by the police. In prison. I've nothing to hide from you or anyone else.'

'We aren't the police,' says Lever.

'Well, whoever you are.'

'I think you know who we are, Dr Maryon,' says Rosslyn. He starts the tape recorder. 'Right. We're in an interview room on the fourth floor of HM Prison Holloway. There are certain things I have to say to you first, Dr Maryon. Can you tell me your full name?'

'Elizabeth Camilla Maryon.'

'And your age.'

'Fifty-four.'

'Address.'

'Care of Guy's Hospital, London.'

'That'll do. My name's Alan Rosslyn. And my colleague from the security service is Wendy Lever here.'

'I am Wendy Lever,' Lever interjects for the taped record so her voice can be identified.

'I don't think you'll mind if we call you Elizabeth,' says Rosslyn. 'Is that all right?'

'Go ahead.'

'By my watch it's twelve thirty-six,' he says. 'And it's 30 December 1999. Elizabeth, this interview is authorized by the security service. There may be investigations that result in the establishment of criminal offences. I have to tell you that this interview is after caution and that you don't have to say anything you don't want to. And that what you say may be given in evidence. I want you to understand that I am authorized to let you walk out of here with us at any time. If –' He lets the silence hang like a temptation. Draws the sign: | | |

'If what?' asks Maryon.

'If you'd tell us the whereabouts of Dr Van Rijn. We can help him. If –'

'Dr Van Rijn,' she says with a supercilious look. 'Oh yes, if you people don't know it already, he's dead, Mr Rosslyn.'

'Who told you that, Elizabeth?'

'I read it in *The Times*, didn't I?'

'I think you know he's alive,' says Rosslyn. 'That someone unknown placed that announcement in *The Times* using a false name, address and call-back number.'

'I don't know what you're talking about.'

'Then how come you read the announcement of his death?' He gives her the boyish smile.

She shrugs. 'We have a little joke in the department,' she says. 'We all read the personal columns in *The Times*. The deaths. I very clearly recall someone somewhere talking about the man Van Rijn's Harley Street clinic. It's the sort of thing one remembers in one's profession. No more than sheer coincidence.'

'Coincidence?'

'Just as death is so often coincidental, Mr Rosslyn. Shall we say misadventure, to coin a phrase. I wouldn't let it strain your imagination too greatly.' She gives him the girlish smile. 'So you see, just as I was before, I'm being perfectly frank with you now. That's what you want me to be, isn't it. You see, there's a perfectly adequate explanation for everything. Everything. With the sole exception being what on earth you think you're doing keeping me in here.'

'For your own safety, Elizabeth,' says Lever.

'Oh, really? Thank you *very* much.'

'You're welcome,' Rosslyn counters.

'So what else do you want me to tell you?'

'Where Marcus Luke is.'

'I haven't a clue,' she says. 'Look, is there really any point in going on with this?'

'Only if you want to walk out of here a free woman. With full protection from the people in the Trinity Chapter who want to kill you. Like they killed Jane Moorfield. The three other American women like her. Father Morandi and the Ahearnes. Like you, they've all had one thing in common. The Trinity Chapter. Who'll be next? You tell me. Let's hear it, Dr Maryon. Who?'

'I don't know what you're talking about.'

'You should realize one thing, Elizabeth,' he says. 'You'll be next. Have no doubt of that. Look, we can keep you banged up in here for as long as we like. Or we can let you out with protection. Or we can let you out without protection. And then the hounds'll be on to you – the same people in the Chapter who've got Trinity's funds. Van Rijn's funds. We're talking very serious money. You know that. If Van Rijn's dead, if there's no bloody Trinity Resurrection, then they're away. Out of it. Safe and sound. And then you'll never get your cut. We're talking six, maybe seven figures. In Switzerland, Turkey and wherever else. If he's alive – if he's as driven as you know he is – if he's driven by mania like Marcus Luke and the man Wroth, then there'll be the bloodbath in Trafalgar Square you know about, don't you? Whichever way, you lose out. You need us. Without us, you're dead meat. And without us, I have to tell you, Elizabeth, I don't give a pile of monkey's shit for what happens to you. Now tell me, do you get my drift. Or don't you?'

'I have nothing to tell you.'

'I think that's not true.'

She gives him the girlish smile.

'You can smirk as much as you like. You should know that what will happen in Trafalgar Square is of interest to one hell of a lot of people. And here we sit, Elizabeth – us three, in the slammer – and we'll be responsible for the deaths of how many people?'

Her reddened and exhausted eyes brim with tears.

'You're safe in here, Elizabeth. But what about the hundreds of thousands in Trafalgar Square tomorrow night.'

'We believe,' she says with ghastly conviction. 'New life. New dawn. New – we believe. Marcus will welcome the Divinity to London. Please, I beg you protect them. We are the chosen. Find them, please. Tell them I am safe.'

'We're looking for them. They're not there, Dr Maryon.'

'Find them.'

'Where?' says Rosslyn. 'Where?'

'In the place of the skull.'

'What's that?'

She is weeping profusely. 'Protect the tomb.' She chokes back a sob.

Lever hands her the plastic mug of cold tea she hasn't drunk.

'You know. The tomb.'

'Yes,' Rosslyn lies, momentarily baffled. He sees Lever's looking at her watch.

'Only protect the Mortimer tomb.'

'Say again.'

'Mortimer.'

'What's that? What's Mortimer?' Rosslyn asks, leading her on. 'Is that where Caroline is?'

'She was. That's where she was.'

'And you'd say she's alive?'

'I don't know. And I want –'

'What do you want, Elizabeth?'

'Marcus to stay alive.'

'Is that his real name?'

'I can't tell you.'

'Why can't you tell us his real name? Or don't you know it?'

She begins to weep.

'His father –'

'What about his father?'

'You should've spoken to Julia.'

'Julia Llewellyn?'

'Yes.'

'She's dead. Do you know who killed her?'

'Morgon Wroth.'

'Like he killed Jane?'

'Yes.'

'And what about Julia Llewellyn's friend, Ms Tsien? What can she tell us?'

'Nothing.'

'We're going to see her.'

'You're wasting your time.'

Which must mean we won't be. Rosslyn lets the silence hang a moment.

'So what else can you tell us, Elizabeth?'

'I can't tell you anything.'

'Will Ms Tsien?'

'I don't know.'

'So what are we talking about here, Dr Maryon? The sacred time of death?'

She buries her face in her hands. 'Please go, Mr Rosslyn. Can't you see the damage you've done?'

'I can see the damage you've done, Dr Maryon. To Jane Moorfield and the other women. We're looking at murder and conspiracy to murder. And you're not helping yourself by covering up for the others. What's it to you? Van Rijn's dead. It's all over for you and this lousy Chapter of ours. Can't you understand it isn't too late to stop the others?'

'It's too late, Mr Rosslyn.'

'It's not too late, Elizabeth.'

She looks him directly in eyes. 'You see, I can't help myself –'

'What d'you mean?'

'You'll see, Mr Rosslyn. You'll see. You're the one who's guilty.'

'C'mon.'

'You are destroying innocence. No infidel will deny the Resurrection of Trinity. There will be the sacred bath of blood in Trafalgar Square. The blood of Woman. His Believers. Purified in His Name. The Divinity will stand amongst us. Let those who cast the first stone cast it. He will forgive the blasphemers. Like you, they know not what they do.'

'I think that's where we differ, Elizabeth. I happen

to know exactly what I'm doing. And you don't.' He gets to his feet. 'Happy New Year. From now on you're on your own. Your conscience should worry you.'

'I don't need lessons in conscience from you.'

'No,' says Rosslyn. 'Maybe you don't.'

Lever says: 'The time is one fifteen pm. Date 30 December 1999. End of interview.'

She presses STOP.

'If you think of anything else,' says Lever, 'ask for permission to call me.' She writes the telephone number on the card and leaves it on the table.

■■ ▪ ▫ ▫

Wendy Lever
Home Office
Intelligence and Resources Operations
Thames House
Millbank
London SW1P 1AE

It's in the courtyard car park outside the prison that they get the news.

Lever listens to the voice from Thames House, then draws Rosslyn to one side. Her breath is visible on the cold air.

'There's an inferno in Kensal Green. The apartment building gutted. There's been a major explosion underground. Somewhere in the basement of the apartment block maybe. The whole area's sealed off. They don't know whether it's an IRA arms cache, timed HE device or what the shit. The bomb squad think the house, the street and the underground passages at the circumference of the cemetery are in danger of collapse. It's a miracle the gasometers the other side of the canal didn't go up too. So they say.'

'Any dead?'

'They don't know.'

Rosslyn stares at the sky. His eyelids seem frozen. Where the sun should be there's a blur. The raw wind takes his breath away. He's smiling through it.

'I think they're swallowing the hook,' he says. 'Call Thames House. Get an armed protection team to Cambridge for Ms Tsien now and fast. I want her to know it's in place when we get there.'

58

Cambridge. The rooms in King's College occupied until recently by Dr Julia Llewellyn are on the second floor of the eighteenth-century Gibbs Building.

The high windows either side of the floor-to-ceiling bookshelves offer a melancholy winter view across the deserted Great Court to Wilkins's screen and the gatehouse entrance from King's Parade.

Reproductions of William Blake prints from the Fitzwilliam Museum line the walls of the main room. Among them is the framed reproduction of Rubens' exuberant *Adoration of the Magi*. The seventeenth-century altarpiece painted for a nunnery in Louvain and now uncomfortably installed in the college chapel. Above the mantelpiece is an oil painting. A minor Victorian picture by Sir Joshua Smedley, RA. Some vision of the Living Christ. Beneath it is the framed text. The verse from William Blake:

> *And now the time returns again;*
> *Our souls exult, and London's towers*
> *Receive the Lamb of God to dwell*
> *In England's green and pleasant bowers.*

Sir Joshua's fantastical vision is of Christ resurrected. He's walking among the crowds in Trafalgar Square. Next to the Smedley is a painting of a young oriental woman in her late twenties. The small black and gold label on the silver frame says Jhong-Jha Tsien. Barefoot, she stands on some tropical beach. The high cheek bones and wide face suggest she's Korean. Next to the framed photograph is another, showing Dr Llewellyn seated at a Boulevard St Germain café in high summer. The picture of tenderness. Jhong-Jha Tsien, her long hair plaited, dressed in white silk, is holding Dr Llewellyn's hand. Even the florid, chinless waiter setting down the Pernod glasses seems a little touched by the love in the women's faces. The scenes in the photographs seem a million miles away from the winter draughts of King's.

Rosslyn and Lever sit on a sofa opposite Tsien.

'I'll try my best to be of use to you,' she tells them. 'Would you help yourselves to a drink perhaps?' The bottle of Madeira stands on the table in the centre of the room. 'It's very sad you never met Jane Moorfield,' she says.

'Yes,' says Rosslyn, 'I wish I had. Though I feel I know her.'

'A dreadful tragedy,' says Tsien. 'So unexpected, wasn't it? Not at all, as it were, in character, I have to say. No, it came as a very real shock.'

'As Dr Llewellyn's must have been to you.

You have my sympathy, Ms Tsien.'

'Thank you,' she says.

'If Dr Llewellyn were with us here now, we'd ask her how much she knows about the Trinity Chapter. How much credence did she give to it?'

'She gave weight, shall we say, to its influence. But it's not always what you find credible, Mr Rosslyn, rather let's say what counts is the intensity with which you believe.'

'In self-fulfilling prophecy?'

Tsien smiles distantly. 'Not a phrase one would entertain. But I know what you may be thinking.'

'That Dr Llewellyn's and Jane's deaths may have been connected with their work. Specifically with Trinity?'

Tsien's fine hand, slowly feeling for the glass of Madeira, hesitates in mid-air. 'Let's say that as far as Jane's death was concerned, Julia had no idea what else it could've been connected with.'

'Can you tell us how much Jane discovered that was, say, sensitive? Deep and sensitive information that could've caused the Chapter to kill her?'

'You'd have to put that question to the members of the Chapter. As it were from the inside track.'

'Is that what Jane did, Ms Tsien? Do you think that she had tried to infiltrate the cult by joining it?'

'What makes you imagine she'd have been so foolish?'

'I have a video of the initiation ceremony. She was there. She went through the ritual. She stepped over the boundary. Either she was smitten with the thing. Seduced by it. And finally decided to join it. Or she joined it like an undercover agent. To get at it from the inside. That she knew a whole lot of sad and twisted people supported it. That they got too deep into it before realizing how evil the thing is. Then as they saw the light, they realized they'd got themselves in the yellow box and there was no exit. They maybe tried, and maybe failed to cover their traces.'

'What's led you to that hypothesis?' Tsien asks.

'Because that's what she told her sister, Caroline. To quote, if I remember it right, she wrote to her sister: "As for the Trinity Chapter, some are extremist Anglo-American and European political figures. The Trinity Chapter's proved increasingly attractive to networks of influential figures. New York. Houston. Los Angeles. Hollywood even. In Washington. The State Department's been mentioned."

'I think she was after names,' Rosslyn continues. 'Maybe she'd got them. And then instead of getting in further, she levelled a few unwise accusations. As good as signed her own death warrant. And the cult murdered her. You see, we have to ask ourselves what her intention was. She had the motive. She had the opportunity. These people are evil, Ms Tsien, you know that. Granted, of the six hundred or so cults or new religious movements in this country, few are malevolent. But as our American friends have learned to their cost, there are exceptions. Waco. Heaven's Gate. The rest. Don't forget the

Japanese Aum. Don't forget we're in the last days before the Millennium. And the so-called millennial climate has raised the temperature to boiling point. Would you agree?'

'Yes.'

'And as you may or may not know, the Chapter is extraordinarily well funded. That is certainly something that Jane discovered. And she was terribly suspicious about the Chapter's financial dealings. About the main players. Did she tell Dr Llewellyn who the main players were, Ms Tsien? The main investors and so on. Did she ever once mention any names of those people – "extremist Anglo-American and European political figures. . . . networks of influential figures"?'

'Not really.'

'What do you mean, Ms Tsien, "not really"?'

'I mean, Mr Rosslyn, no she didn't. Though I was Julia's research assistant, some things she kept very much to herself. So did Jane – Jane was rather, shall we say, secretive by nature. Outgoing in many ways. But on the inside she kept things rather to herself.'

'That didn't stop her talking at length to Father Gian Maria Morandi in Geneva about the Chapter. The International Family Foundation. He was rather important to her work, wasn't he? She talked to him. You know who I mean – Father Morandi?'

'Yes, of course.'

'And I saw him myself in Geneva. And I'm afraid

I have to tell you that Father Morandi's been murdered.'

'I know.'

'We very much need your help. With several aspects. One is linked to what Jane was researching.'

'Which is what exactly?' she asks awkwardly.

Rosslyn looks to Lever to answer.

'Their financial arrangements among other things,' says Lever.

Rosslyn thinks: *I don't believe your awkwardness is genuine. You must know what I'm talking about. Who or what are you hiding from?*

'In several cases,' says Lever, 'they've been illegal. We think the funds may be being used for means that are unacceptable. And over and above that, there is the suggestion that the ends the Chapter has in mind may well be violent ones. Those are two good reasons why we need to know what you think. Also what Jane thought. What she told Dr Llewellyn. How well she'd got to know the Chapter. She was especially interested in Trinity himself, wasn't she?'

'Yes. I can't help you make a moral judgement of any kind. Not in so far as they may be using funds in some way that's illegal. But she was by no means alone in realizing that violence underlies their belief. And she was very interested in Trinity himself. As a man. As a phenomenon. The man of persuasion. The charismatic leader.'

'How well did she understand him?' Lever asks.

'I'd say,' says Tsien, 'that if anyone got Trinity's

psychopathology right, Jane did. I think Julia would have said the same to you. And Jane Moorfield felt, I think, that he was driven to commit violence on some massive scale. We, Julia and I, did sometimes think that her enthusiasm occasionally got the better of her. She was very passionate about it. She felt that his influence was, as she used to say, "infected and infectious".'

'Why did she think they're going to commit violence?' Lever asks.

'Her view was that it would be retribution for some deep injury. To seek their place in history. To become immortal. Important. God only wise. And as Eliot says, something Jane frequently quoted with approval: "Half of the harm that is done in this world – Is due to people who want to feel important."'

'OK, but did she believe in the promise of violence?'

'Yes, she did believe they would. Yes.'

'We're looking at tomorrow night,' says Rosslyn. 'Did Dr Llewellyn believe in it?'

'Yes, she did.'

'And did she ever tell you that she believed Trinity might still be alive?' Rosslyn asks.

'Not in so many words.'

'Or that Trinity is a man called Van Rijn. Originally born John Julius Gowrie?'

Tsien hesitates.

'What are you suggesting?' she asks.

'That say he reappears the day after tomorrow. On New Year's Day, as he promised. And then every journalist in the world starts investigating that story of his death in the hotel room. How long can he last out before he's shown to be a fraudster and a killer? A day? A week? So what is it he wants?'

'What do you think, Mr Rosslyn?'

'Don't you worry too much about what I think, Ms Tsien. We're here to find out what you think. Whether on the basis of anything Jane told Dr Llewellyn or you that if Trinity and his followers are thwarted, they'll kill and go on killing until they're stopped.'

'We want to know,' says Lever, 'who exactly "they" are. We don't mean the sad crazies chanting in the streets. We mean the serious ones. The core believers. We want to know about the scenario they really have for New Year's Eve and New Year's Day. Whether there's cogent evidence, any proof, that'll enable us to walk into Scotland Yard and say, "You have to be prepared for slaughter on a massive scale." That's what Morandi told us. Or is this just the raving of a lunatic?'

'Lunatic or not,' says Tsien, 'in either case, it seems to me you'd be wise to take it very seriously.' She seems to blink. Squints. The right eyelash is giving trouble.

Rosslyn takes advantage of her discomfort. 'Is there anything you want to tell me, Ms Tsien? Anything that's preying on your mind?'

'What makes you think there might be?'

'Because, you see, the Chapter hasn't tried to put the arm on you. It surprises me a little, that. Dr Llewellyn was obviously a threat, wasn't she? Who else eliminated her except Trinity's people?'

Tsien seems lost in some painful recollection.

Rosslyn stands up. Stretches his legs. Crosses the room to the window. A floorboard creaks beneath his feet. Looking out across Great Court he sees it is no longer deserted. There are three figures down there. Dim shadows. Waiting. They're neither dons nor students. The armed protection squad is in place. 'Your name isn't in the air,' says Rosslyn quietly, trying to prompt her to continue. 'Has someone offered you immunity or something? Protection even. Your name isn't being talked about, is it?'

'Why on earth should it be?' Tsien asks sharply.

'Because, along with Dr Llewellyn, you have to have been privy to Jane's information. Have the Americans been in touch with you? About Jane Moorfield. Morandi?'

Tsien flinches. 'No comment.'

Rosslyn glances at Lever.

'About Van Rijn?' Lever asks.

'I don't know anyone by that name.'

Rosslyn shoots another name: 'Marcus Luke?'

'I've never heard of him.'

'But, Ms Tsien,' says Lever, 'Marcus Luke was Jane's friend.'

'Then that was her business. Not mine.'

'What about a Dr Maryon?' asks Lever. 'Does the name Dr Elizabeth Maryon mean anything to you?'

'No,' says Tsien.

'Let's see if the name Ahearne means anything,' Lever asks.

'No.'

'Then let's try the United States Embassy,' says Lever. 'Listen, we liaise with them. We're on the same side. Doesn't the name of one of their legal attachés mean something to you – Donna Queron?'

'If you are, as you say, in liaison with them, then you'll already know I have had several confidential interviews with Donna Queron the legal attaché.'

'She's a CIA officer, Ms Tsien.'

'Yes, Donna Queron is a CIA officer. All I can tell you is that she wanted to know if I knew the names of any Chapter members who might compromise their own positions in government or law enforcement agencies. It was a perfectly civil and reasonable approach. She's perfectly well aware that I travelled with Julia and that she lectured a great deal in the United States and Canada. As well as in the Far East. One was privy to a great deal of confidential information. As it happens, most of it trivial. Of little consequence.'

'What did you tell Queron?' Rosslyn asks.

'I simply steered her in Morandi's direction, to Geneva. I simply told Queron that the Chapter feels itself to be caught in some terrible, truly awful dilemma.'

'What other advice did you give to the Americans?'

'Simply not to prevent the ghastly show of his resurrection.'

'And do what instead?' says Lever. 'Have us arrest him?'

'To let him be.'

'Ms Tsien,' says Rosslyn, 'we need your help in trying to find him.'

Shaking her head, she says: 'I'm afraid I gave Donna Queron my word that I'd keep the whole matter confidential.'

'Why? What deal did you make with them?'

That rankles. Tsien's hostility rises. 'No deal at all.'

'You realize that by not helping us, you could be signing Caroline Moorfield's death warrant?'

Tsien turns away. She faces the window. The light of the bluish reflected snow gives her a haunted look. 'I wouldn't want to risk her safety.'

'Then why not take the risk?' says Lever. 'Risk telling me about this deal of yours with Queron. Between these four walls.'

Again the long hesitation. At last Tsien says: 'I have a life to lead. So do you.'

'What are you suggesting?' asks Rosslyn.

'Suggesting that I am advising you, if you'd be so good, to leave. To pursue this liaison arrangement you say you have with your friends at the American Embassy. But I do rather gain the impression that you may have been lying to me about it. Perhaps you'll find your own way out.'

'Before we leave,' says Lever, 'we have to tell you that Trinity's alive and out there somewhere. Preparing to show his face. As he promised. Don't you understand the neatness of it? Don't you see that if you don't tell us the full story, you're dead meat? You have a choice to make, Ms Tsien. Co-operate with us and you have armed protection until further notice. If you don't, then you're on your own.'

Tsien stays motionless. Hands crossed. Head bowed. Silent. It's impossible to read the expression.

'This has to be the most important moment in your life,' says Rosslyn. 'Maybe bar one. The time you met and fell in love with Dr Llewellyn. And she with you. And now she's dead. And your silence says to me that you don't want her killers to go free. Is that what it says? So just tell us, for Julia Llewellyn's sake. Tell us the truth. You help us. And we'll help you.'

Jhong-Jha Tsien has begun to weep.

Her sightless eyes seem to be staring into the distance. 'I assume this discussion,' she says, 'is strictly confidential? If I were to tell you that my interest is a very personal one, would you be prepared, as it were – as I think you suggested – to see that my interest is protected?'

'We've already put protection in place,' says Lever. 'We'll explain the technicalities before we go.'

'Very well. I don't know how much you know about Julius Gowrie.'

'You tell us,' says Rosslyn.

'Thirty years ago he was up here at Cambridge. He specialized in endocrinology, the study of hormone-secreting glands. He dabbled in Maoism in the early seventies. As you may know, he went to India in the eighties and became, for better or worse, a disciple of Krishna Macharia and absorbed himself in the idea of transcendence. Then, when he returned to Europe, he showed up as a one-night-stand lecturer to university societies here and in Oxford, Edinburgh and other places. He was a brilliant speaker. Charismatic. Students, particularly women, adored him. Some almost literally fell at his feet. Under his spell. He was then advocating homeopathic treatments and meditation. It seemed, somehow, the result of a natural progression when he began to advocate a life programme for success. Based on a notion of the God Within.'

'Dr Llewellyn subscribed to this?'

'Yes. With something of a passion. She told me that he had a wonderfully logical and clear mind. The sort of intellect you can't ignore. Arrogant but always logical. Utterly cold. Many women found the combination of the logical and the visionary seductive. He was a very sexual man. With the aura of danger. That never stopped quite a number of women falling in love with him.'

'Including Dr Llewellyn?'

'Yes.'

'She loved him?'

'So she told me. Yes, she loved him.'

'Did she live with him?'

'No.'

'So how far did the relationship go?'

'As far as it could,' she says. 'She had a child by him.'

'What happened to him?'

'I don't know exactly.'

'Did she keep in contact with him?'

'Not as far as I know.'

'When did she last see him?'

'At Trinity's funeral. She told me it was the most painful moment of her life.' She turns her face away from him. Clenches her fists. 'The boy didn't want to know her. Someone at the funeral, I can't quite remember who Julia said it was – someone who didn't know of their relationship – pointed him out to Julia. The woman asked Julia if she knew that the boy had been in trouble with the police and was undergoing psychiatric treatment. Perhaps she really did know who Julia was. Who the boy was. That he was her son. Very angry, Julia said she knew *nothing* whatsoever about it. Given the nature of the occasion, the woman's observation seemed wholly inappropriate. One which caused Julia great hurt.'

'You don't know who this woman was?'

She gives the smile of satisfaction Rosslyn saw before. 'Yes, of course I do.'

'Who?'

'Trinity's last lover. The forensic pathologist – she was Trinity's lover.'

'You're certain of that?'

'Yes, I am. Not, I suspect, that he was ever faithful to her. Rather, I suspect, it was based on some sexual obsession on her part.'

'What did he get out of it?'

'Given her profession, I imagine her contact with the dead excited him, don't you?'

'You tell us.'

'Julia said that he always had that terribly dark side to him. A sort of conflict between purity of mind and body on the one side and, on the other, depravity and morbidity. Somewhere in the middle lay a kind of madness. It persuaded him he was the centre of the universe. The one true giver of life and light. That his was the right way for the world to follow. He entertained ideas of world influence. He made brilliant studies of propaganda. Endlessly, obsessively, he expounded on the propaganda techniques of Goebbels, Franco, Mao. Even studied secret police techniques and procedures. Those of the Stasi engrossed him. He began to believe that the only way democracies could be properly organized was if they were policed by secret services. And over the years he employed several private firms of intelligence consultants to preserve the innermost workings of the Trinity Chapter.'

'Do you know who these firms were?'

'No. Julia said that, paradoxically, Trinity was more open to her about his friends in the world of secret intelligence. He even used to expound his theories to them. Not a few of them seemed rather impressed by his mind.'

'Who were they?'

'Mainly recruiters for MI5 and MI6 here in Cambridge. All of them, as far as I know, have now retired. Some were even his followers.'

'Tell me about these followers,' says Lever.

'More than one of them joined one or other of the security services. He recruited several bright Americans, including two Rhodes Scholars. One of them, I remember, a suicide victim, was the close friend of the American president. Trinity took enormous pride in having followers among the powerful. The rich. Public figures in industry and politics. Of course, not all remained loyal to him. A few did see the light and got out before their membership became a matter of public knowledge. Many, particularly among the young and impressionable, parted with substantial fortunes to him. Even Julia admitted that, however evil his practices and misguided his philosophy and beliefs, he had a fine financial brain. She never doubted that somewhere the Trinity Chapter investments must have multiplied. Thanks to him. And Julia never forgot the son. Never. I'm surprised you didn't see it.'

'What's his name?' asks Rosslyn.

'His name's Marcus Luke.'

We have the Name of the Mother and the Son. And somewhere, coming tomorrow night, the Holy Ghost.

'You realize I've never told anyone this before,' says Tsien. 'Were Julia alive, well, it would all have been so very different.'

'We appreciate your help,' says Rosslyn. 'We're concerned for your safety in the immediate future. We've arranged for some protection officers who'll deter unwelcome visitors.'

'For how long?' Tsien asks him.

'Until Luke, Wroth and Van Rijn no longer pose a threat to you.' He turns to Lever. 'Ms Lever here will explain the security arrangements.'

A clock begins to chime the hour.

59

As Rosslyn and Lever return to London:

Marcus Luke takes a window seat in the Audley
at 41 Mount Street, Mayfair. A short walk from the
United States Embassy, it is the pub favoured by the
embassy staff drivers after duty. This evening the
Audley is doing a roaring trade with much talk,
American talk, of some dinner to be held upstairs in
the panelled dining room. Luke, wearing a dapper
suit, his hair slicked down, turns to the two men
seated at the bar next to him. 'Are you from the US
Embassy?' he asks.

'Sure,' says the man next to Luke.

'I'm supposed to meet one of your legal attachés
here,' says Luke. 'Only it seems she hasn't shown up.'

'Who are you meeting?'

'Donna Queron.'

'Yeah?'

'You know her?'

'Sure. You could call her office.'

'I already have. She's left.'

'That's too bad.'

'I don't understand,' says Luke, above the din.

'What's that?'

'I don't understand,' Luke repeats loudly. 'She's supposed to meet me with a car and driver.'

'You could ask Kwiatkowski,' says the American. 'He's the bald guy over there. See, at the table beneath the chandelier. That's big Dan. Ms Queron's driver.'

'I'll see what he knows,' says Luke. 'Thanks for your help.'

'You're welcome.'

Luke squeezes through the crowd of drinkers to where the bald man with the large stomach is seated with two female companions.

'Dan?' Luke says.

The bald man with the big stomach looks up. 'Yeah, that's me.'

Luke smiles pleasantly into the narrow eyes. Introduces himself as: 'Lewis Mattheson. I have an appointment with you.'

'Sorry?'

'I was supposed to meet Ms Queron here at seven.'

'You were?'

'With a car and driver.'

'Is that right? Not with me.'

'She didn't tell you?'

'Nope.'

'There has to be some mistake,' says Luke.

'There sure does, Mr Mattheson. I'm not on duty until tomorrow. If you don't mind me asking, who are you from?'

'Box.'

'Is it you she has the meeting with tomorrow?'

'I thought it was today.'

'No, must be some kind of mistake. It's tomorrow. Nine am. Thames House. I take her from the embassy to Millbank and then to the Ambassador's reception at Wingfield House. And I guess that's it for the century, right?'

The two women smile at him.

'I'm sorry I bothered you, Dan,' says Luke.

'No problem. Like a beer?'

'No thanks,' says Luke. 'I appreciate your help.'

'You're welcome, Mr Mattheson. Happy New Year.'

'You too.'

Outside the Audley, Luke heads off through the snow for Pimlico.

There, unseen in Claverton Street, slips an envelope through the letter box of the basement flat.

It's marked: PRIVATE. FOR PERSONAL ATTENTION. ALAN ROSSLYN.

Smiling at the pain the contents of the envelope will cause, he turns once, just to make sure he hasn't been observed. Or that he isn't being tailed *en route* to the West End and Trafalgar Square.

60

Luke surveys the scene outside Buckingham Palace. Like people who queue for the best places at the Last Night of The Proms, men and women have already assembled on the pavements by the railings of the palace, as if there's a Coronation or Royal Wedding balcony appearance to be witnessed. On his way down the Mall towards Admiralty Arch and Trafalgar Square, he passes more groups of people heading for the palace.

When he reaches Trafalgar Square, Luke sees that the first of the millennial partygoers are reserving positions for the spectacular tomorrow night. Trinity's followers are in evidence. Chanting, they've positioned themselves on the steps of St Martin-in-the-Fields. Watched by police showing little interest in them, they're wrapped in white blankets against the freezing wind.

Of the others in the square on this bitter evening, there are New Agers and holy people. Happy clappers, self-appointed visionaries and sundry crackpots with placards announcing: REPENT YE – THE END OF THE WORLD IS NIGH.

He sees that the Trinity followers seem to be the most peaceful. Non-religious revellers include men and women in sleeping bags. Happy families singing patriotic hymns.

And protected by bright yellow overalls against the cold, technicians are setting up the equipment for the laser displays that will illuminate the sky at Zero Hour. In spite of the cold, preparations for the massive celebration seem to be on schedule.

Luke shares something of the mounting expectation. He'd like to see Rosslyn's face when he reads the note at the flat in Claverton Street.

61

On Lever's desk in Thames House there are the MI5
and Special Branch reports on the two hundred and
eight followers of Trinity who have been questioned.
Rosslyn and Lever read the names and addresses
listed. The statements taken. The identities checked
against existing data on HOLMES and the MI5
computers. There are several dozen men the age of
Wroth and many more who are the age of Luke.

They read through the reports from the forensic
teams who have scoured the deserted apartment at
the apex of Gipsy Hill, Westow Hill and Beardell
Street in south London. Strands of hair were found
in the bed. They match those of Caroline's taken
from Rosslyn's flat and others from Room 65 at the
Malvern Hotel. Her fingerprints are also found in
all three places, and they match those taken from
Room 5006 at the Heathrow Hilton.

Then there's the report of the trawl among lists of
owners of dangerous dogs. One's turned up at a
veterinary surgery in the Westbourne Grove area,
where the vet treated Wroth's dog, the Rasselaer P &
J, for a broken tooth.

There is a tart *addendum* to the memorandum
from Special Branch, suggesting that Lever should

have returned to Gipsy Hill after she'd established that Caroline had made tracks to Luke's place. As midnight comes, as Thursday the 30th passes and Friday the 31st begins, the suggestion by the police that is critical of Lever gets a cold and combative reaction from the DG at Thames House.

No one has a single sensible idea of the whereabouts of the main players.

Lever and Rosslyn review the disgraced military career of Wroth.

From service in the Welsh Guards to the Falklands, to the French Foreign Legion. The verdict of the president of the court martial: 'This dangerous and evil soldier . . .' The sentence of two years for the combination of offences. Desertion. Fraud. Theft. Violence. There's a note from a junior in Intelligence and Resources Operations that Wroth's solicitors, Brady, Nassaueur Drummond, were the people apparently responsible for Wroth's initial association with Dr Van Rijn. The association that led to Wroth's appointment as caretaker of Trinity House on the Harrow Road.

'The place is burned out,' says Lever. 'The basement and all adjacent areas have been sealed off.'

'Who the hell did it?' Rosslyn asks.

'*The preliminary assessment,*' she reads aloud, '*by the explosives officers suggests the use of HE manufactured in the Czech Republic at DV Plzen, the state armaments manufacturing agency privatized in 1994 –*'

'So that's taking me back to Custom House,' says Rosslyn. 'Out of hours.'

Forty minutes later, he's on his former stamping ground. Custom House on Lower Thames Street. He's crouched over the computer in the new basement offices of CEDRIC: the Customs and Excise Departmental Reference and Information Computer. The TOP SECRET records of suspected illegal arms and explosives movements. Files 1990 to 1999 to date. *UK to Europe. Europe to the UK.* Up on the screen is the photofit of one **Karel Zieleniec** – under surveillance. There's the log of telephone calls made from Adinkerke. To Harley Street. To West London, Kensal Green. The footnote to the last address is marked *See* **Wroth**. And when he turns up **Wroth**, he finds the record of the military career that ended in disgrace. The record Lever has earlier outlined to the meeting in Thames House.

He thinks hard about Van Rijn. *Who are you?* About Marcus Luke.

He'd advise everyone: 'Take them out.' *But take them out from where?*

He thinks of Caroline. And prays she hasn't fallen victim to the blast in Kensal Green.

He calls Lever: 'Find out how much HE was used at Kensal Green. Whether there's more to come.'

'Makes no difference, Alan,' she says. 'They're not going to close off Trafalgar Square tonight.'

'Who says?'

'The DG.'

'He's pissing in the air. Isn't there *anything* on Caroline?'

'Sorry, Alan, nothing. You have to prepare for the worst in that direction. There's to be a final meeting here. Nine am today. Your presence is requested. Joint SIS. Us. CIA, maybe that's your friend Queron. Police. Home Secretary. Quite the little celebration party. There's no more we can do. That's what they tell me.' She pauses. Then in a whisper, as if there's someone in the room with her, she adds bitterly. 'God help them.'

'You want to stay over at my place?' he asks.

'I thought you'd never ask,' she says. 'See you there. Say in about an hour.'

He shuts down the computer.

Tonight. New Year's Eve. Millennium. Trinity's Resurrection and bloodbath.

Eyes stinging with exhaustion, in the early hours he goes home alone to Claverton Street through the snow. Sees no watchers on the street. No lights on in the basement. The hand gun in its ill-fitting holster has rubbed the skin of his collarbone sore. No matter. He wants a long hot shower. And sleep. A lot of sleep. Before the final meeting. Before, along with the rest of the world, he stays up to see in the Millennium.

Nothing's changed in the basement flat. Except for one thing. There's the envelope on the floor just

inside the door: PRIVATE. FOR PERSONAL ATTEN-
TION. ALAN ROSSLYN.

Inside the envelope the single page. No date. He
recognizes Caroline's handwriting. His heart lifts.
Then he reads:

> *Dearest Caroline and Marcus*
> *Thank you for last night.*
> *For believing in me and promising to help*
> *me.*
> *See what is stuck to this?*
> *One of your hairs and two of mine.*
> *One in Three. Three in One. | | |*
> *I am inordinately fond of you.*
> *But I won't tell you.*
> *I want to be with you soon.*
> *My love —*
> *Marcus and Caroline*
> *X | X | X | ♡ ♡ ♡*

What kind of sick bastard's faked this one then?

But something dreadful tells him it's the real
thing. The evidence of conversion. The final
betrayal. Of everything they've fought for. And it's
personal.

The bell's ringing. Lever's at the door.

62

Just wait. Till tonight. – MARCUS LUKE, 31 DECEMBER 1999

Other than the fact that it concerns money, Caroline can make little sense of the argument raging between Luke and Wroth throughout the early hours of 31 December. The Rasselaer sleeps through it at Caroline's feet. Wroth is in the driving seat of the ambulance. Luke is next to him. Of the two men, Wroth is the more agitated. It's Maryon's absence that enrages him.

'She isn't coming,' Wroth says. 'The hell she isn't coming. Without her we don't get the money.'

'I can handle it,' says Marcus Luke calmly.

'And if He doesn't come?' Wroth says. 'I mean, look what's in the papers – use your eyes.'

'He will. You know He will. Take no notice of what the papers said. It isn't true.'

'How the hell do you know?'

'Trust me.'

'But the money – she's the only one with access to the banks.'

Luke is matter-of-fact. 'Wrong. Others have access.'

'They do? Who?'

'You don't need to know.'

'You tell me what it is I'm not to know. Bloody tell me.'

'Just trust me. That's the neatness of it. Trinity values loyalty. Just as he values you. He really does.'

There's an ominous silence.

Caroline hears Wroth muttering.

'Are you complaining?' asks Luke.

'I want to see Maryon.'

'We both do. There'll be a logical explanation for why she hasn't shown up.'

Caroline listens to Wroth grumbling on. She has the powerful sense that Wroth's trust in Luke is fading.

'You should get some sleep,' says Luke. 'The war isn't over yet. They're the same as us. Except they don't believe, do they? We have that. Belief. Everything. They have nothing. Nothing. Nothing.'

Later Caroline hears Wroth call out: 'Caroline?'

She doesn't answer.

'Caroline?' he repeats.

'She's asleep,' says Luke.

She hears Wroth say slowly: 'Why not get it over with now?'

'Because the Master needs to set His eyes on her.'

'Is He going to be the one to slit her throat then?' asks Wroth.

Caroline winces.

'I want to do it now,' says Wroth.

Caroline's breathing comes in gasps.

'I understand,' says Luke. 'But no, it's too early. Wait. It's warm blood the Master needs. Just wait. Till tonight.'

63

TOP SECRET
Washington DC
4.30 a.m. today's date
SUBJECT: US Secretary of State Wislawa Odone

0855 hours. The final New Year's Eve of the twentieth century. In the Thames House conference room there's only one item on the agenda: TOP SECRET meeting – *Holy Ghost.*

Rosslyn, the only person there not in public service, looks out of the window. Sees the thin winter mist across the Thames. The view of the river is reminiscent of one of Whistler's gloomier paintings. Silver streaks. Greys. Dark watery blues. The river is the colour of pewter and only the headlights from the few cars crossing Lambeth Bridge break the stillness. The melancholy cityscape contrasts with the conference room mood of breezy menace.

The sole item on the agenda is whether to recommend what no one wants. Tonight of all nights: whether to declare Trafalgar Square a no-go area. Whether to close most of the West End of London to the expected crowds of some one hundred thousand revellers. Scotland Yard has issued a statement of what it calls 'encouragement': 'We accept that there has always been a tradition of large crowds of people gathering in Trafalgar Square on New Year's Eve. But this is a New Year's Eve like no other. However, we would advise them that events have been organized elsewhere.'

No one of right mind believes that the tradition won't be followed. Tradition suggests that the crowds will start building up in the square after 10.30 p.m., the majority entering from the accessible underground stations to the north-west. More than five hundred British Transport Police officers backed by reinforcements from the Metropolitan Police will be on duty, ostensibly to prevent drunkenness and vandalism.

Why not?

The rest of the world is steadying itself for the great party. Newspaper commentators have predicted that two billion people world-wide are expected to celebrate the advent of the new century. Millions are travelling to the Great Pyramids, the Taj Mahal, Macchu Picchu, Stonehenge. In Madrid, half a million will be filling the Puerto del Sol with bags of twelve grapes, which they'll eat with each strike of the clock for good luck. 120,000 are expected at the Brandenburger Tor, the focus of New Year celebrations since the wall came down in 1989. Crowds will fill Vienna's St Stefan's Square gulping champagne-like *Sekt*. Christmas trees will be chucked on the New Year bonfires in Amsterdam.

Tens of thousands of people, maybe more, will fill the Champs Elysées in Paris to watch the digital clock on Avenue George V tick away the final seconds. Why should anyone reasonably expect the British to avoid Trafalgar Square?

The truth is that the early morning Thames House meeting has been convened for the record: to place on record the secret aspects of the whitewash plans for public safety. The overall security of the millennial celebrations. So if anything does go wrong, the Home Secretary can go down in history as having said: 'See. It's down in writing. We took the very best advice available. The United Kingdom has the best police service in the world and we're justly proud of it. We did our level best. Ours is the responsibility.'

In other words: *'Don't blame me, mate. I did it my way. Now all clap hands.'*

The meeting is his show.

Here he is, working the room with forced charm, offering the same old exhausted soundbites. One for all. All for one. Millennium Government is Open Government. Freedom to Enjoy within the Law. Lack of Interference. Working for the Second Term. The irony that he's imposing his will behind closed doors seems to have escaped him. Even before the formal proceedings get under way, the Home Secretary is giving the impression he doesn't wish to create the mood of panic, public ill-will or anger that draconian last-minute security measures will inevitably incite.

Rosslyn's seen it here before. As a serving Customs

and Excise Investigation Officer. When the IRA killer McKeague found a way to penetrate Thames House. 'He really does believe nothing will go wrong tonight,' Rosslyn tells Lever beneath his breath. Lack of sleep has made him edgy. 'Look at him,' he tells Lever. 'I know his sort. Covering his rear.'

They watch the Home Secretary continuing his rounds. The squeeze of the elbow. Sounding out. Asking what everyone thinks. The solicitous listener. 'You're right,' he says. 'Right.' You don't disagree with this Home Secretary. To do so would suggest one is contradicting oneself. Everyone seems to be in the picture. Except Rosslyn and Lever.

Rosslyn wonders what to infer from his summons to be present at the meeting. He overhears the Home Secretary asking the public servants, in the manner of a hairdresser: 'What are you doing tonight?' Without listening to the replies, he says, 'Have a good time. You deserve it.' It's as if he's the host of the greatest party in history. And it might just as well have already started. More than ever verbose, he's high on confidence. Trotting out the usual guff about 'the people at ease with themselves at the Dawn of the New Century'.

Rosslyn's heard it before.

He stands back from the others, in the corner of the room with Lever. They've been unable to trace the source of the love letter Caroline sent Marcus; or to come up with any useful idea as to what really lies behind it. Lever says it's maybe one more sick result of the government making the security service just that bit more accessible to the public. The move's encouraged nutters. Copper's narks and the habitual writers of anonymous letters. Mostly the hate mail originates in south London. Poorly spelled. Written in spidery capitals. The letters invariably end up in the shredder. She shrugs off the Caroline-Marcus letter. No matter that it's caused him pain. Says again it could in any case be a fake. Rosslyn takes the rather more sanguine view: 'Someone wants us to believe she's alive. They're taunting us. It's like they want us to show our hand against them. I think we'll hear from them again. Sooner than we think.'

'I wouldn't be so sure,' says Lever. 'You have to face *the fact*.'

The fact she's mentioned is that she thinks Caroline's almost certainly already dead. But when it comes to deciding what emergency measures to put in place tonight, she says she's glad it's not her responsibility to decide one way or the other. 'You have to consider that the HE that blew up in Kensal Green is probably all they had. Now the only people who care if Trinity resurrects are his rag-bag followers. Alan, the rest of the world has other things to enjoy. The count-down's diverted attention. There's no going back. You can't stop the bloody clock.'

Which, as Rosslyn says, is what Trinity may be wanting. 'No, you have to think yourself into *his* shoes. And Marcus Luke's. Think of the money we failed to follow up on. Whether Trinity makes his appearance or whether he doesn't, they stand to get it. I'm still convinced Jane Moorfield and Morandi had it right. The man's possessed. We aren't looking at a rational mind. And I still believe Caroline's alive.'

'Please yourself. Belief's out of fashion, Alan,' says Lever. 'You should know.'

'Oh, yes?' says Rosslyn. 'The worst feature is that no one's heard from them. They've taken every precaution they need to pull it off. They've gone too bloody silent. It's as if they've disappeared behind the moon. And they're waiting. That's what they're doing. Waiting. The big diversion tonight.' He draws in the grime of the double-glazed window: →↓. 'The big diversion.'

'The only hope is that the bastards died in the blast,' says Lever. 'Then there's nothing anyone need worry about. But see, I don't think they did. I don't believe it.'

'But I think they're still alive and waiting. And I have the gut feeling the Home Secretary takes the other view. He's not about to look for trouble. Must think it's now in the hands of God. Am I right? What does he believe in?'

'God,' says Lever. 'Like the PM.'

The meeting's being called to order. Seats are being taken around the conference table. The room falls silent.

It turns out Rosslyn's at least got the Home

Secretary mostly right. In the face of the inevitable, this is going to be a masterly demonstration of →↓.

'This needn't take long,' the Home Secretary says with unusual informality to everyone and no one in particular. 'We all have loved ones to go to.'

There's a Mexican wave smile around the table. Smile to smile. The grinning family men and women. From the DG MI5 and his Deputy Director-Generals to the DG SIS and the two cadaverous women in suits, presumably SIS department heads. On around the table. To the Commissioner. To other senior police officers Rosslyn doesn't recognize. And to Queron, accompanied by the CIA officer with the wrestler's shoulders that Rosslyn last saw at the United States Embassy after the inquest. The head round the door of the American Citizens Services Branch office calling Queron to take the telephone call from Langley.

'First,' says the Home Secretary, 'I'd like to say that there's no new substantive evidence that we face a situation requiring the closure of Trafalgar Square and the West End at any time before midnight. You will be familiar with the joint report of the Space Syntax Laboratory at the Bartlett School of Graduate Studies, University College, London. The advice of Westminster City Council, Royal Parks Agency, Department of National Heritage. And, of course, the Metropolitan Police.

'Given the estimate of some 100,000 persons in the area, the Trafalgar Square fountains will be cordoned off. Likewise Nelson's Column and the Christmas tree. Should the square need to be evacuated, the cordoned-off part will be the holding area, affording safety to some six thousand. The main exit routes will be to the Strand, Whitehall and the Mall. Children, the disabled and the elderly will be advised to stay away.

'The lesson was learned as long ago as 1983 when two women were trampled to death when panic gripped the crowd. Checks will be made to make sure no alcohol or fireworks are brought into the square. Additional crowd-control barriers will be in place. There will be extensive medical and ambulance service assistance. Some four dozen ambulances from the London, Prince of Wales District and others, along with St John's Ambulance Brigade vehicles, will be in place.

'I am advised that we do not face a situation that might lead me to think we should sensibly commit ourselves to an on-the-ground deployment of security forces. It's felt, and in my judgement wisely, that any such presence of the security forces might eventually lead to untoward public hostility. The safety of the crowds, which will be very considerable, will be preserved in the usual manner by the police. To them we're very grateful. And I have to say I have every confidence that the celebrations will thus pass without incident.'

This is received with gratified smiles by the senior police officers.

The Home Secretary coughs dryly and takes a sip of water from the tumbler in front of him.

'There will also be those present,' he continues, 'who wish to know what the joint investigation into the main source of anxiety, the Trinity Chapter, has finally yielded. I'm referring, of course to *Holy Ghost*. I say finally because the perceived threat is contained within a time frame. It has a time window. The threat of violence at midnight. The threat is one thing. The evidence of the threat, if there is any, is another. The government is in no position to act in response to beliefs, albeit of a secretive kind, beliefs that are held by fringe new religious movements. We were elected to serve on a fundamental basis: the freedom of people to believe in what they will.'

There's the rustling of papers. Like the reformed alcoholic endlessly returning to the substance of his denial, the Minister can't help returning to the hobby horse. Other people's beliefs. The right to believe in what they will, so long as it vaguely coincides with his own.

'We have to thank a colleague for having seen to the interrogation of a suspect.' All eyes turn towards Rosslyn, who doesn't flinch. 'We now have the medical report on the woman detained in Holloway. The report shows her, in short, to be of unsound mind.

'It may be said by some that our colleagues have to some degree overstepped the mark. I do not intend to engage in some sort of scapegoating exercise. Rather I wish to thank all those who, with good will, co-operated with this investigation. I have asked DG MI5 to talk personally to those people at the end of this meeting.'

Rosslyn briefly recalls the mood of the Home Secretary at all the other meetings that took place earlier at Thames House. What is it, he wonders, that's caused the Home Secretary to take quite such a different view? *What's up your sleeve?* He sees the Home Secretary give Donna Queron a deferential look.

'I'd now like to allow our colleague, Ms Donna Queron, to make a few remarks which I feel sure will relieve us of any lingering suspicions as to the extent of the Trinity Chapter's perceived danger. Ms Queron –?'

'Home Secretary, sir,' she says, 'thank you. I'm specifically requested by the Director of CIA to convey appreciation for the co-operative effort made concerning Operation *Holy Ghost*. As you know, the agency has conducted an extensive investigation into allegations concerning the membership of this religious group. Membership said to involve senior United States government officials.

'And as many of you are aware, agents successfully pursued these investigations throughout Europe with local government approval at all stages. At all stages we were successful. And moreover, we achieved substantial levels of successful protection to benefit our informers.

'I am able to confirm, categorically, that there is no substantive truth whatsoever in the allegation that Secretary of State Odone was at any time connected with the cult named. The record remains as it was at the start of this operation. And it is largely due, Home Secretary, to the efforts of the British security services, that this remains the case. I am formally requested by Chief of Staff at the White House to convey to you the sincere personal thanks of the President of the United States at this historic moment in time.'

Get you.

Beneath the table, he feels Lever's hand hold his. He returns the squeeze. She's drawing on her notepad: | | |.

'Thank you very much indeed, Ms Queron,' says the Home Secretary. 'I can confirm that the Prime Minister has personally spoken to the President this morning and reciprocated thanks.'

'Thank you, sir,' says Queron, getting to her feet. 'If you'd forgive me, we have the millennial reception at Wingfield House to get to.'

'I look forward to seeing you there shortly,' says the Home Secretary.

All smile at Donna Queron. Except Rosslyn and Lever. Expressionless, they keep their eyes fixed straight ahead. They don't watch Queron leave.

Her deputy station head throws a foul look in Rosslyn's direction. Mute confirmation that what makes the special relationship so special is mistrust and hidden hate.

Queron slings her leather bag across her shoulder. Shoulders back. Head up. Ms Fix-it 2000. She who's fixed it.

'May I turn,' says the Home Secretary, 'to the minutes of our previous joint liaison meeting at which the outline was presented of security arrangements for today's date.'

There's a rustling of the papers on the table.

'With special reference,' the Home Secretary continues, 'to the West End of London and Trafalgar Square. I am advised by Director-Generals of both MI5 and SIS and by the Commissioner that the arrangements remain unaltered. The Terrorist Support Group will maintain a low profile. It is now foreseen that after both the accident at Kensal Green and the discovery of bodies in Kensal Green, there is no longer a need to consider what may have been a substantive threat from the followers of the cult as described in *Holy Ghost*.'

Bodies?

Rosslyn scribbles on Lever's notepad: BODIES?

The Home Secretary drones on: 'The Prime Minister is pleased to have advised Her Majesty of the situation –' while Lever writes for Rosslyn's benefit:

Poem
by
Wendy Lever aged 5

Bits-Bits-Bits
A finger here
A leg there
Bits bloody everywhere

The Home Secretary continues: 'And similarly, the Prime Minister has suggested that no untoward, shall we say 'offensive-style', precautions need to be taken that might impede the public celebration that will take place in just over twelve hours from now. The main feature – indeed, what amounts to the sole *public* feature of security – will be surveillance by the Metropolitan Police Air Support Unit as the conventional support to anti-terrorism and the preservation of public order. We can be proud of this.'

Public, thinks Rosslyn. *What's this emphasis on public? What that hides is that there'll be an armed presence out there tonight. Officers with guns. Somewhere high on the buildings surrounding Trafalgar Square.*

The Home Secretary, the believer who believes in nothing much, lists facts, a stream of facts. He announces, with the tone of a puffed-up auctioneer inflating the value of a dodgy work of art: 'One. The Bell 222 helicopter offers versatile surveillance of criminal activities even from heights of 1000 feet or more above the city and its environs . . .'

'Whose bits is he talking about?' writes Rosslyn.

The meeting's growing restless.

Now it's the Commissioner's turn: 'The Bell 222 will carry experienced senior police officers. Observer One.' He nods at the woman inspector. 'Effectively, sir, the helicopter will be an airborne command post. Liaising with DG MI5 positioned at the Canada House rooftop observation point. The whole communications network to Cabinet Office will be co-ordinated.'

It's the helicopter the Home Secretary likes hearing about. 'Commissioner, would you explain the specificity of Observer One's role?'

'Yes, sir,' says the Commissioner. 'Observer One's task will be to control the aircraft's radios and co-ordinate communication. She'll also be chief navigator. Required, at all times, to maintain the helicopter on its airborne course. She'll allow the view of Trafalgar Square to be kept on the right-hand side of the aircraft. And will proceed according to plan.'

'Observer Two,' says the Commissioner, 'will be seated behind the pilot in the right-hand seat. Observer Two will be the Commander of the anti-terrorist branch, SO13 – in command of the overall surveillance task.' He looks down the table to the Commander. 'You will be equipped with the stabiscope.'

'Commander?' says the Home Secretary. 'A word or two on that, if you wouldn't mind?'

'Yes, Home Secretary, Commissioner, sir. As the Commissioner has indicated, the stabiscope is the high-technology telescope on a gyroscopic base which cancels out the effect of the Bell 222's considerable airframe vibrations. It enables me to ascertain an accurate picture of any suspects' movements on the ground. It also allows me to identify individual criminal suspects with great accuracy.'

'That's how it all comes together,' says the Home Secretary. 'And the chopper will at all times be in direct radio contact with New Scotland Yard's Central Communications Complex (TO25). It's a watertight situation . . .'

Rosslyn points to Lever's note of the scribbled question: *'Whose bits?'* She writes in reply: *'Must be the Ahearnes. Otherwise, the fuck knows.'*

The supply of xeroxes runs out by the time they reach Rosslyn and Lever. They share a copy:

TOP SECRET

EXTRACT

Counter-Terrorist Briefing Papers
Metropolitan Police
London 1999

Rosslyn breaks off reading here and writes for Lever's benefit: *'Do you want to call in at the ASG party tonight? You'll get a great view of the Square from Strand Chambers.'* She writes: *'Thanks. You're on.'*

'It only remains, ladies and gentlemen,' says the

Home Secretary, 'for me to thank you for the time and effort you have put in to avert what would, without doubt, have been a tragedy. May I wish you and your families and partners a very happy and prosperous Millennium.' There's the muttered chorus of self-congratulatory thanks around the table. The Home Secretary wears a smile of self-satisfaction. 'You have every good reason to be proud,' he concludes, tidying his papers. 'Thank you. And a very good afternoon.'

'Strand Chambers,' says Rosslyn. 'Nine for nine-thirty. The drink's on ASG. Champagne and some Italian crap for food.'

'On behalf of the Home Secretary,' the DG says to Rosslyn in the doorway, 'I want to thank you personally for all you've done. I've spoken to Ruth Swincarron. A *pro rata* fee payment is being made to ASG for the time you've put in. And I must tell you how sorry I am about the fate of your client.'

'I'm still looking for her,' says Rosslyn.

'*Que sera sera,*' the DG says, adding rather sharply for Lever's benefit, 'I'm afraid Ms Lever can't be of further assistance in that department.'

'As you wish,' says Rosslyn. 'I seem to be the only one here who's in disagreement with the Minister.'

'I wouldn't take it too hard,' says the DG. 'At the end of the day this isn't a political issue, is it? You've done bloody well, Rosslyn.'

'A few days ago I don't think you'd have put it that way.'

'It's a matter of putting the lid on things,' says the DG. 'And you did well with the Ahearnes. You should be proud.'

'Maybe they'll be even more dangerous from the grave,' says Rosslyn. 'Maybe you'll never get to the bottom of it.'

'I wouldn't worry yourself about that from now on,' says the DG. 'Get on with life.'

'You mean you've left the problem in the lap of the Americans?'

'I've every confidence they can handle it,' says the DG. 'You heard what Queron said.'

'I wouldn't trust her further than I could kick her.'

'Somehow,' says the DG, 'I'd never have expected you to say otherwise. Let's be charitable.'

Glancing past the simian features of the DG, Rosslyn sees Lever standing in the conference room doorway.

'Let's stay in touch,' the DG's saying. 'Tomorrow's just another day.'

'I wouldn't be too sure of that,' says Rosslyn.

'There we are,' says the DG.

Lever reads the note she's just been handed by her research assistant. Rosslyn sees the colour drain from her face.

She looks at Rosslyn. Folds the note. Hands it to him. 'You need to know this, Alan. I hate to tell you, but it seems you're the only one who's got it right, doesn't it?'

Rosslyn reads:

TOP SECRET   Washington DC
                              4.30 a.m. today's date

SUBJECT: US Secretary of State Wislawa Odone

ODONE FOUND DEAD IN GEORGETOWN AREA
DEATH THE RESULT OF FATAL GUNSHOT WOUNDS
FBI BELIEVE SHE SHOT HERSELF SOMETIME LAST
NIGHT

64

Use of surprise to circumvent countermeasures is one way terrorists try to attack hardened targets. Even though there are guards, detection devices, and increased perimeter security, the element of surprise can be employed to undermine the hardware and overwhelm the human factor in a fortified security system.

— FRANK BOLZ JR, KENNETH J. DUDONIS AND DAVID P. SCHULZ, THE COUNTER-TERRORISM HANDBOOK: TACTICS, PROCEDURES AND TECHNIQUES, 1990

The United States Embassy car has been dispatched to take Queron from Thames House to the American ambassador's reception at Wingfield House. It's stationary in the snow at the junction of Monck Street and Horseferry Road. The car's windows are misted over. Closer inspection of the embassy driver's window would reveal smears of blood in the mist on the glass. The interior of the car is already cold. It smells sickly sweet of blood.

Held fast by the safety belt, the bald driver lies sideways.

One side of the driver's head, from just above the left ear and down the side of the pulped jaw to the throat below, has been chewed clean away.

Queron is waiting for the car to arrive at Thames

House. It is her misfortune that she's been unable to raise the embassy car pool. She's a little too proud to call up the Director-General's office on the fifth floor above – to ask the British security service to ferry her to Wingfield House. She's Ms Can-Do and she's not about to ask MI5 for a lift. *God, and the car'll need clearance at Wingfield House gates.* She's furious, but had the mixture of temper and pride not got the better of her she might have foiled the plan of those responsible for the death of her driver. Nonetheless, she approaches the senior of the two duty security guards. She asks him for a small favour. Would he mind calling her a cab?

Little chance of getting one today, he tells her.

But as luck has it, there's a black cab drawing up outside on Millbank. The security guard is good enough to brave the driving snow without complaint. And on Queron's behalf, he asks the driver to take the passenger to Regent's Park and the residence of the United States ambassador. Queron is delighted. Ms Can-Do is Ms Fix-It too. She's vindicated after all. She wishes the guard: 'A Happy 2000.'

The black cab sets off with Queron along Millbank in the direction of Parliament Square. But before it turns left, the ambulance overtakes it. Cuts in. Brakes. Stops. Skidding, the cab slams into the back of the ambulance accompanied by the sound of shattering glass.

The cab driver is getting out when the short hammer-blow thuds against his neck. He stumbles backwards. Sinks unconscious into the road, one leg awkwardly caught up beneath the other. At the same time, the passenger door is jerked open.

Donna Queron, mute with fear, sees the masked face. The eyes in the slits. Stares at the hand gun pointed directly into her wide open mouth.

65

How shall we extol thee, who are born of thee?
Wider still and wider shall thy bounds be set:
God who made thee mighty, make thee mightier yet.
— ARTHUR CHRISTOPHER BENSON, SONG FROM POMP
AND CIRCUMSTANCE, OP. 39, NO. 1, BY EDWARD ELGAR

Noon. With twelve hours to go, Rosslyn and Lever are together in Trafalgar Square in the hope of finding some tell-tale sign of Trinity's plan for tonight. Rosslyn's mind rings with a chant in time to the chimes of the St Martin-in-the-Fields clock, distorted by the wind. *Find him. Find him. Find him.*

From the portico of the National Gallery he watches the unloading of the steel crowd-control barriers in the snow. A flock of pigeons takes off above the empty fountains and banks steeply in front of the Christmas tree already cordoned off. The

> **THIS TREE GIVEN BY THE CITY OF OSLO**
> **AS A TOKEN OF NORWEGIAN GRATITUDE TO**
> **THE PEOPLE OF LONDON FOR THEIR**
> **ASSISTANCE DURING THE YEARS 1940–45.**
> **A TREE HAS BEEN GIVEN ANNUALLY**
> **SINCE THEN.**

birds gather briefly at the foot of the tree, where a sign lies on its back:

Then take off for the signs propped against Landseer's eleven-foot-high lions:

```
METROPOLITAN POLICE
NO FIREWORKS, CANS,
AEROSOLS, BOTTLES
ALLOWED IN
TRAFALGAR SQUARE
```

The birds fly upwards in an arc, towards the temporary scaffolding erected around the reliefs at the base of Nelson's Column. At the top of the scaffolding is an illuminated digital sign in red:

TEST: MESSAGE: METROPOLITAN: POLICE: HAPPY: NEW: YEAR

Steam rises from the hamburger van marked in giant letters LUIGIBURGERS: EALING VENEZIA SEVEN DIALS & PALERMO. Police officers are telling Luigi to move on.

There are the groups of New Age crazies. The Union Jacks are everywhere. Furtive lovers touch the Landseer lions for good luck and that done, step back, set their camera on automatic flash, beam to the lens, and kiss again mouth to mouth. A pair of police officers search a couple with painted faces.

To Rosslyn's right, at the entrance to the National

Gallery's Sainsbury Wing, a woman vicar repeats her announcement: 'This is The Birth of Jesus Saviour,' pausing only to snatch a breath before she plays some modernist hymn on her harmonica.

Trafalgar Square is already filling with the curious and the aimless. Gathering as if drawn by a magnet to witness the passing minutes. And the seconds pass to the thudding beat of the Rastafarian drummer at the entrance to South Africa House. Then he too receives an order from the police to move on.

Rosslyn's eyes are lined with weariness. Nothing Lever says lessens the tension in his face. 'We're back where we started,' he says. 'Somewhere out there, somewhere in the city, there's Luke and Wroth and Caroline. We don't know where they are. But they'll be here tonight. And no one wants to stop them. Now no one can.'

'Maybe,' says Lever, 'the whole thing's been called off anyway.' Rosslyn wants to believe that. But he doesn't.

'I feel he's out here somewhere,' he says. 'I *feel* I *believe* in what he's going to do. Look at the faces. Yes, we could be looking at Van Rijn down there. Is he there already? Which one is he?'

Lever shrugs. She taps numbers on her mobile phone. Speaks to the duty desk officer at Thames House. The voice tells her that there's been no trace of anyone called Van Rijn at any UK airport, rail or bus terminus.

'Anyway, if he's in London, he'll be through the net by now,' she tells Rosslyn.

'If there ever was a net,' he says.

Ten minutes later the figure of the man they want to see leaves the Eurostar at Waterloo station.

Rested and relaxed, he carries no luggage with him. He wears a black Italian winter coat and fashionable fake fur hat. Beneath the coat he's dressed head to foot in white. Walking slowly, he joins his fellow arrivals in the queue for a cab.

From Waterloo station he takes the cab to the Strand and gets out near the entrance to Somerset House. From there it's a short walk to the Raj Strand Hotel, the cheap boarding house that occupies the top two floors, about the last hotel today to be displaying the sign VACANCIES.

Telling the manager that he's expecting a visitor, he signs in as Julian Gow and pays for the room in cash.

Alone in his room he doesn't bother to watch the countdown programmes on TV while he waits for his visitor to arrive. Had he done so he would have seen that the visitor wasn't about to show up here this afternoon. Or any other afternoon.

Rosslyn and Lever stare blankly at the TV screen in Christopher's American Grill in Wellington Street.

The news item that mesmerizes them is the penultimate one on Sky News: 'A woman prisoner was found dead in the secure unit of Holloway Prison early this morning. A Prison Service spokesman has named the dead woman as Dr Elizabeth Maryon, a prisoner on remand. She is believed to have taken her own life.

'And now for the weather. Snow —'

In the offices of ASG the same newscast is seen by Maxine Gertler. Ashen, she goes to her wall safe and takes out the Browning hand gun. Then she makes the call to the Raj Strand Hotel.

'Put me through to Mr Gow's room, please.'

Drumming her nails on the surface of her desk, she stares out of the window. To the crowds gathering in the square. To the plume of steam from the hamburger van marked LUIGIBURGERS. Police officers are once more telling the owner to be on his way.

'We need to talk,' she says into the telephone. '*Now.*'

66

THE EXPLOSIVE DEVICE

The explosive device should always be regarded as
unreliable.
It is essentially a mechanical device. And yet, in so far as
we are concerned with massive human destruction, there is
a cogent argument for suggesting the device is intimately
connected to human nature.

The effective usage of high explosives requires that the
constructor have insight into the methods, psychology and
actions of the enemy.

The effective device requires explosive, the detonator or
blasting cap. What we may call the blasting cap is no more
than a compound of low explosive. It is connected by the
constructor to the high explosive, the aim being to set the
latter off. The following steps should be followed:

1 Push the fuse into the hollow end of the blasting cap.
   Ensure it is pressed home.
2 Take the hollow metal end. Crimp it around the fuse with
   care.
3 Insert the whole into the high explosive.

The following is the sequence of events that will occur:

1 Burning of the fuse.
2 Ignition of the flash charge.
3 Explosion of the priming device.
4 Detonation of the base charge.
5 Creation of high temperature to ignite the charge of high
   explosive.

SAFETY PRECAUTIONS MUST BE FOLLOWED AT ALL
TIMES
1 High explosive to be stored with maximum security.
   Observe hygiene precautions. Keep wires clean. Do not
   smoke.
   Do not use weapons in the vicinity of high explosive.
2 High explosive to be stored separately from primers and
   away from electrical and blasting caps.
3 Do not store material near heat sources or metals.
4 When transporting high explosive do not use vehicles
   with metal floor coverings.
5 At all times allow enough time for preparation and
   construction in an area free of static electricity.
6 Use only wood or non-metal tools.
7 In emergency disconnect all electrical circuits.

For timed high explosive device construction follow the
basic lay-out. This is a work of sacred art and will be treated
with respect.

THE TRINITY MEMORANDUM TO MORGON WROTH
FOR 31 DECEMBER 1999 ǀ ǀ ǀ

Wroth drives the ambulance into the Gerrard Street

car park at 3.30 p.m. He parks in one of the several dozen spaces reserved exceptionally today for the Red Cross and St John's Ambulance Brigade.

In the front section of the ambulance, Luke dresses in the paramedic's white overalls, and Wroth moves into the rear section of the vehicle.

There he crouches next to the gagged and blind-folded figures of Caroline and Queron. Side by side, bound with heavy industrial tape to the stretcher units, the two women have been injected by Luke with phetoroantcetymol. The timed sedative will keep them in a deep sleep until the final rituals of purification take place during the last hour of the year 1999.

Breathing heavily, Wroth crouches in silence over the slim cases containing the detonator, timing device and high explosive. He slowly constructs the high explosive device according to the instructions in Trinity's memorandum. The procedure is simple. And the proximity of so great a quantity of lethal substance brings an unusual flush to the dark cheeks. This is as near as he ever gets to the achievement of sexual excitement. The slow process of construction gives him the sense of power over humanity. Trinity is the designer of the power. *I, Wroth, am the Engineer*.

Some time before 4 p.m. he tells Luke: 'The device is live and ticking.'

It is just after 4 p.m. Van Rijn receives the visitor in his room at the Raj Strand Hotel and hears that

Maryon has taken her own life in Holloway.

Sitting on a small chair beside the bed, Maxine Gertler says: 'I doubt she will have talked . . .'

Looking doubtful, his hands clasped behind his back, Van Rijn stands by the window staring at the sky.

'Do you . . .' Gertler continues hesitantly, '. . . do you think that without her you should go down there in the square?'

'What are the security arrangements?' he asks.

'The word is that they'll be no more than normal.'

'I never expected otherwise,' he says. 'Have you heard the weather forecast?'

'A clear night's expected.'

'Come here,' he says. 'Look at the sky. I wonder whether you're right.'

She seems nervous of his criticism.

'See the sky,' he says. 'That looks like snow on the way to me.'

'Yes,' she says.

'Forgive me one second,' he says. 'While I fetch a glass of water from the bathroom.'

By the door he says to her: 'I find it cold in here. Would you turn up the radiator please?'

And as she stoops to find the knob, he drops the door latch.

'And Marcus?' asks Gertler. 'Do you know where he is?'

From the bathroom he calls back: 'You don't need to know.'

'You know . . . where they are?'

Returning with the tumbler of water, he looks at his wristwatch. 'They will be in place. Oh and did you have any difficulty transferring the funds. From Milan to Geneva?'

'None,' she says. 'It's been seen to.'

'Good. And when did you do it?'

'As you asked. On the twenty-second.'

'All of it?'

'Yes,' she says nervously.

'Good,' he says. 'Good.' But he knows she is the consummate liar.

I was in Milan ten minutes before closing time on 23 December when the accounts executive received your instructions. Neither you nor anyone else at ASG intended the funds be transferred into my account. Rather you told the bank to hold them in ASG's account.

With five minutes left until the closing hour, he had calmly made a counter-move and outmanoeuvred them. He had the fortune changed into Swiss francs and the cash sent securely by road to Lugano.

'Then things are complete,' he said. 'You need have no worry now.'

'Except there has been no word from Queron,' she says.

'Why should there be a word from her? She has nothing to fear.' His eyes are hidden in the shadow behind the table light. 'Have you brought me the hand gun?'

'Yes.' She takes the package wrapped in a cashmere shawl from her shoulder bag.

'Leave it on the bed, if you'd be so kind.'

Her hands are shaking.

'Why are you so scared?' he asks her with a smile.

'We're concerned for your safety,' she says.

'I'm grateful to all of you at ASG. But there is no need for concern on my behalf. You've done all that you promised. In My Name.'

She gets to her feet uneasily. 'I have to go now.'

'As you wish.'

She moves to the door. But when she tries to open it, she finds of course that it's locked against her. She turns to see him shaking the cashmere shawl and the steel wrench falling from it to the carpet.

Still she pulls at the door handle with one hand. And with the other she reaches inside the shoulder bag for the Browning hand gun.

Van Rijn moves.

He takes two fast steps towards her with the glass tumbler in his outstretched hand and with tremendous force drives it into her face. Her eyes fill with blood. He stoops over her, pressing his thumbs deep into her oesophagus. And holds them there.

Drawing on disposable rubber gloves, he surveys the scene. Then he cleans up methodically.

He has to use his considerable strength to drag the body into the bathroom. Opening the window, he looks down four storeys to the empty yard below.

From the inside pocket of his black Italian coat he takes out the syringe, needle, tourniquet, and the large quantity of powder in the folded sheet of paper. Once he's administered the diamorphine overdose intravenously, he leaves the syringe sunk deep inside the wrist. Then he heaves the body on to the window ledge. Places the shoulder bag on top of it. Then he pushes.

Even before she strikes the ground head first, destroying the vestiges of his attack, he's slammed the window shut against the cold.

67

Humanity faces the final moment of the critical juncture.
On one side, the dawn of the glorious new era.
On the other, the husk of past and present.
Man can adapt to either.
   —Trinity, *The Divine Testament*, London, 1996

New Year's Eve; 6.15 p.m. The governor's office at
Her Majesty's Prison, Holloway. Rosslyn and Lever
read the short note found in Dr Maryon's cell.
Pinned to Lever's business card is Maryon's last and
final note: *'They will be driving an LDV 3.5 litre Laser.
The Leyland Daf Customline ambulance in service with
the London Ambulance and Emergency Service.'*

Rosslyn uses the governor's personal outside line
to dial directory enquiries. He notes the number of
the London Ambulance Service. When the duty desk
operator comes on the line, he asks who manufac-
tures their ambulances. There's a short wait. 'Say
again? UVG – what's that stand for? Say again –
"Universal Vehicles Group, Brighouse, West Yorkshire." Give me the phone number.'

He dials the Brighouse number.

The heavy voice says: 'Brighouse Security Partners.'

'Police,' says Rosslyn. 'Superintendent Rosslyn.

Metropolitan Police.' I need to speak to the UVG managing director, please. It's urgent.'

'Wait a minute. I'll get the home number.'

The number is in the Wakefield area. Rosslyn can tell from the background noise that he's interrupted the managing director's millennial party. 'I need to know the names of any purchasers of one of your vehicles during the last month.'

'Given the Christmas period. What with the New Year. The Millen –'

'Please, sir, this is an emergency. Please give me the names.'

'There's only been one this month.'

'I need to know who bought the vehicle.'

'Funny you should ask. We none of us know who he was. There was this cash buyer. Paid fifty thousand. Cash. Didn't even ask for a receipt. He took delivery himself. Didn't even give a name. He spoke to my accounts manageress. Hold on.'

Rosslyn hears the company representative give a name he doesn't catch. Then some muffled questions.

The woman, the accounts manageress, comes on the line.

'The man who took delivery of the ambulance,' says Rosslyn. 'I want you to think back, right. Think hard. What did he look like? Was he, say, medium height?'

'Yes.'

'Late twenties, say? White. Fair hair. Feminine

features. Cultured accent. Does any of that fit the description of the man you saw?'

'Right enough,' she says. 'He looked, well, sort of angel-faced. A baby face.' She pauses. 'I can give you the registration number.'

Rosslyn writes it down in bold. 'Thanks,' he says to the deputy governor. 'I appreciate your help.'

He turns to Lever. Taking the note of the registration number with him, he tells her, 'We're on the way. Let's phone the number in.'

(

Millennium &
Last Quarter

68

Should auld acquaintance be forgot,
And never brought to mind?
  — ROBERT BURNS, AULD LANG SYNE

The near gridlock condition of the New Year's Eve traffic delays their arrival in Trafalgar Square. The traffic jams on all the roads in the West End area have forced them to leave the car in Gower Street and head the rest of the way to Trafalgar Square on foot.

The London night already seems to be turning into Happy New Year's Day. And Trafalgar Square with two hours to go is now, arguably, the heart of the greatest celebration in the history of the capital.

On their way to the offices of ASG, Rosslyn and Lever make slow progress. They shove their way through the dancers. Drug takers. Drug dealers. Pickpockets. Chanters. Boozers. There's the tidal Mexican wave. The packed crowd is spaced out. Witless. '*In excess,*' the uniformed police spokesman is shouting at the TV cameras, '*of three hundred thousand revellers are in the West End of London area.*'

Laser beams sweep the sky. Form pyramids. Parallels. Towers. Intersecting lines and lines apparently converging at infinity.

The seconds and minutes crawl their way around the Metropolitan Police illuminated message display system. Each changing minute is greeted with massive yells. Trumpet blasts. Klaxons.

The countdown to 2000 ticks on.

They see the giant screen sponsored by a TV company beneath hangings of red and gold and the Union Jack. It shows a sweating pop star. The old star's TV make-up is blotched. Mascara has started to run down the haggard cheeks. The viewers watching the performance believe he's crying with emotion.

Vastly amplified, the singing knight's ageing voice is no match for the swaying braying crowd. *'This patriotic chorus,'* as the TV person shouts to camera, *'has to be the high point of a long, distinguished and deeply-loved career.'* The majority of the star's audience wasn't even born when his career began. Waving Union Jacks, stamping to the broadcast drumbeat and blaring brass instruments of the Grenadier Guards Regimental Band's Dance Orchestra, they shout: *'Land of Hope and Glory, Mother of the Free'*.

The relayed broadcast from elsewhere in London has been planned by the Department of Culture, Media and Sport bureaucrats. They have been advised by the quango of elderly and ennobled millionaire architects, designers and style gurus. The show is matchless in its lack of style and taste. It's devoid of wit or imagination and is running late.

'*Enjoy, Enjoy, Enjoy,*' a man in football strip yells into a giant fibreglass megaphone.

The detachment of the Salvation Army leads the prayers on the steps of St Martin-in-the-Fields, asking Almighty God 'for better nights and days tomorrow, In the Name of Our Saviour God Almighty'.

'Amen, amen,' sing out the happy clapper youths in suits.

Amen to the Sally Army's entreaties.

They pass the phalanxes of TV cameras pointing at the charity workers wearing funny face masks and bright red noses who are shoving their cans in people's faces outside South Africa House, like villains threatening robbery with menace.

Outside the Royal Bank of Scotland building, they see the bagpiper blowing an accompaniment for the benefit of ranks of men in kilts who're singing the season's number one syncopated hit:

> *We twa hae run about the braes,*
> *And pu'd the gowans fine.*
> *We'll tak a right gude-willie waught*
> *For auld lang syne.*

The crowds press against the cordons of police officers.

Away from Rosslyn and Lever's view from the right of Admiralty Arch, outside Uganda House – at the corner of Spring Gardens and the Mall – stands the group of some two hundred men and women dressed in white blankets.

Their excitement is perhaps the most intense of anyone's in Trafalgar Square. With shaven heads, they've daubed their foreheads in white greasepaint with the three vertical lines: | | |.

Eyes fixed on the digital clock on Nelson's Column, chanting without cease, they hand out pamphlets to uninterested revellers:

> Trin-it-eee
> Trin-it-eee
> Three in one
> One in three

Near the chanting Trinity Chapter figures the parked ambulance goes unremarked.

Hovering above the faithful two hundred followers of Trinity and the ambulance is the police helicopter, the Bell 222. Flying perilously below the five-hundred-foot limit, the crew has a clear view of the followers of Trinity and the glistening white top of the ambulance.

As the countdown continues and the noise becomes still more deafening, it's the ambulances around the square that seem to be giving the senior police officers aboard the droning helicopter cause for concern.

The Commander's eyes focus on the white ambulance: the LDV 3.5 litre Laser. It should be just one of three hundred and fifty Leyland Daf Custom-line ambulances in service with the London Ambulance and Emergency Service that are on stand-by. Just one of the four dozen or so now lined up ready for an emergency.

There's no proper confirmation that the ambulance has been given permission to enter Trafalgar Square. So much for the stabiscope. In short, no one seems to know why it's positioned there. The number doesn't tally with the one Rosslyn's phoned through.

The ambulance radio isn't answering to offer any explanation.

69

In the offices of ASG on the fifth floor of Strand Chambers, the millennial party's in full swing. No one's told Rosslyn it's a fancy-dress do. The theme is Rain Forests/Endangered Species. The guests wear masks and surreal animal outfits. The gorillas out-number all the rest. Manic chatterers compete with the thudding of the disco. Staff and guests are packed round the windows and the blaring TV screens showing the celebrations world-wide.

Left out of it all, Rosslyn and Lever stand on the sidelines by the main windows, ready if needs be to make an unobtrusive exit before the century ends. Both are watching the crowd of two hundred figures in white near Admiralty Arch.

It's the Bell 222 helicopter that catches Rosslyn's eye. Lever's seen it too. 'It's flying too low,' says Rosslyn. 'There's something bloody wrong down there.'

Now the millennial dancing's really got going. Led by a flushed and shirt-sleeved Alexander, it's a kind of mambo hokey-cokey. Maxine Gertler is conspicuous by her absence.

Swincarron, dressed as the Phantom of the Opera, approaches Rosslyn for the dance. She's all dreadful mask. Rhinestone blouse. Sheer silk dress. High heels. Sun tan, teeth and smile. 'Join, honey?'

'Later, Ruthie,' Rosslyn says. *Bat-face*. He puts his arm around Lever. 'Later.'

Getting the message, Swincarron sucks her teeth and looks elsewhere for a likely man.

Rosslyn turns back to the view. 'Just look at that chopper,' he says to Lever. 'What the hell is it doing holding in there so low? What's the reason?'

'Let's dance,' says Lever.

And they join the hokey-cokey.

70

10:46 says the digital clock on Nelson's Column when the police officers are shown up to the fifth floor of Strand Chambers. Led by the ground-floor security guard, the uniformed WPC and detective constable in plain clothes push their way through the jam-packed dancers to Ruth Swincarron. Lever draws Rosslyn's attention to the new arrivals. 'Plod's here,' she says.

Rosslyn sees Swincarron suddenly freeze. She starts to unpeel the Velcro straps of her Phantom mask. She shakes her head at what the police show her. In disbelief, beetle-eyed, she stares at Gertler's shoulder bag. Now Alexander sidles over to the police.

Rosslyn sees him head out and away with the police officers in the general direction of Gertler's office. Alexander is fiddling with his bunch of safe keys.

Swincarron turns. Her eyes connect with Rosslyn's. The arrogance seems to have evaporated. She looks puzzled, perhaps wounded, as if betrayed. Dumping the awful mask in the bowl of melted millennial choco-chip ice cream, she approaches Rosslyn with her long and sun-tanned arm stretched out. Looking straight through Lever, she says: 'Alan, we have to talk.' She grips his arm as only she can do. She has the look of practised grief. 'My office, OK.' He looks into the hang-dog eyes and can tell that Ruth Swincarron is staring at something like disaster.

No sooner has she closed the door to her office than the telephone starts ringing on the desk. She touches the SP-Phone button. 'Ruth.'

Rosslyn hears a cautious Alexander say: 'The, er, item in Maxine's safe has gone.'

'Can the cops hear this?' Swincarron asks.

'No.'

'Don't tell them.'

'No.'

'How did she actually die?' Swincarron asks.

'Self-administered drug overdose,' says Alexander. 'Diamorphine most probably.'

'Self-administered. You're sure?'

'That's the initial view. It seems the officers here are looking for a man who checked into a hotel nearby. Then left. A man calling himself Gow, who'd paid for the room Maxine visited this afternoon.'

'Gow?'

'Yes.'

'Do we know anyone called Gow, Peter? Who's Gow?'

'No, Ruthie, we don't know anyone called Gow.

And the officers here would like to talk to you and me together.'

'In just a second,' Swincarron says. She glances at her watch. Kills the call. Turns to Rosslyn. 'Alan, I don't have too much time. I have to tell you something you were never to know. Maxine, Peter, me. We three administered the funds of the Trinity Chapter. We've known of Odone's involvement. We've done everything we could to help Washington. We've always had this really close relationship with Donna Queron. She's on our side. You see, honey, we have nothing to be worried about.' The sudden urge. Some vestigial pride forces out the declaration: 'We are innocent of any malpractice.'

'Is that right?' he says, shaking his head. 'I don't think so. Your watertight world's started to leak like a cracked toilet, hasn't it? You've covered for Van Rijn. You even helped your friends in Washington to cover for Odone. Except she couldn't stand the heat, could she? Humiliation by the world's press. What sort of White House have you now?'

'What are you saying?'

'I wonder what you've been paid for all of this. What's the Inner Chapter consist of then? Van Rijn. Wroth. Luke. Maryon. Gertler too?'

'What are you saying?'

'God knows, there were the poor bloody Ahearnes too. And now the whole thing's winding up to some fucking showdown down there in the square. So what's the score? Wroth spills blood out there. Causes a massacre. Puts paid to Van Rijn and you take the money. He does a runner and you pay him off down the line. It all boils down to money in the end, Ruth. That's what the whole lousy outfit's all about. Am I right or am I right?'

'Wrong, Alan.'

'No. *Right*. You've been protecting a whole rank of stinking arses.'

'You're talking bullshit.'

'Where's Caroline Moorfield?'

'For Christ's sake.'

'Where is she?'

'I've no idea.'

'That had better be the truth. And what about Llewellyn? Mother, Son and Holy Ghost. Were you party to her murder too? She knew too much, didn't she? Like Jane Moorfield knew too much. Take the wool from my eyes, Ruth.'

'Come on, honey babe.'

'No more honey babe. Let's hear it.'

'That's the truth.'

'What truth?'

She has her hand on the telephone. 'There are no witnesses,' she says. 'No trace of the fund transfers. We acted on behalf of Trinity to our best endeavours.' The eyes are drawn tight. They flick across Rosslyn's.

'What is it Trinity wants from this Resurrection?' Rosslyn says.

'What?'

'Don't tell me you believe in it too – or do you just want to have hedged your bets? He resurrects. He becomes the Second Christ. Or he becomes the most notorious guru in the history of the world. The great millennial celebrity. What can you tell me to prove I have it wrong, then?'

'I can tell you the whole truth, Alan. Right on. You've heard it here tonight.'

'What would you say,' he asks her, 'if I told you that the way Gertler seems to have died is a dead match for the other deaths? For Jane's. Morandi. The other innocent Americans who Trinity's sick acolytes murdered. What would you say to that, Ruthie? And this "item" that you and Alexander are talking of. The item in Gertler's safe. It was a hand gun, right?'

'That's what you say.'

'I do say. Not the same class of weapon that you tried to stitch me up with along with the little cash advance. No. The ladies' stick. The Browning. And it's not there any more. Why not?'

'I don't know what the fuck you're talking about.'

'I'll tell you what the fuck I'm talking about. The cops haven't found the gun, have they?'

'I don't know.'

'Well, I dare say you're about to find out. I'd say Gertler took the gun and called on Van Rijn. Trinity. Gow. Gowrie. And she went to meet him alone, with the sole purpose of killing him. Maybe she'd transferred the funds into the ASG account. But I can't believe that Trinity would fall for that move.

No. He will have taken the leaf out of your lousy book, won't he? The good old knight's move and, given the timing's right, he moved the funds again himself. You're talking money.'

'I don't follow.'

'C'mon, Ruthie. Follow. Follow it. Follow the fucking money. You'll follow when the banks open up for business next week or whenever. We'll see who moved the money. It's too fucking late. There's nothing you can do. The pieces are off the board. This isn't a game. It's fucking war.'

She sits cross-legged on her desk. 'We need to continue,' she says.

'We do?' says Rosslyn. 'With what?'

'With you, Alan. We need to continue as before. You're part of this. You're on our team. You don't want to stay stuck with the little people, do you? The bums out there yelling and pissing in the fucking square. You don't want to be like them, do you?'

She's ranting.

'What the hell are you talking about?' says Rosslyn.

'We're the new people now,' she says. 'Look around the party guests. Whose millennial party has *Tatler*, *Harpers & Queen*? Trustees of the Royal Opera House. People from Heritage. National Trust. Diplomats. A member of the Royal Household. An ennobled architect. Dome people. Editors of the national papers. A knighted artist and a governor of the BBC.'

Rant on.

'The movers and shakers. This is where you should belong. With us. It's us now. Not them. Get real, Alan. Get millennial.'

'Just what the hell are you saying, Ruthie?'

She's shaking. 'What's your price, Alan?' She gives him the little-girl-lost look. 'What do you want?'

'Trinity. I want Trinity and now. Where is he?'

'I don't give a fuck for him,' she says. 'I care about us. About you.'

'Please. I don't think you give a monkey's toss for anything except yourself.'

'Alan,' she says, turning up the smile. 'You know?'

'I know what?' he says.

'There's a way out of this.'

'Then you'd better find it on your own,' he says. 'You and Alexander both.'

'If you wish. It's your baby.'

'It's a fuck of a sight more than that.'

'You care so much, don't you?' she says. 'You live on your emotions. It's a mistake, Alan. It's our game now. But. And but, Alan. One thing, honey, I've never understood about you. *Just what the fuck is it you want?'*

He feels the rage rising in his chest.

'Tell me,' she purrs, 'honey. What do you *really-really-really* want? Don't fool any more with me.'

Eyeball to eyeball, Rosslyn says quietly: 'I'll tell it

to you in the face.' He points to his right shoe. 'I want to see you and everything you stand for under this. The greed. The patronizing snobbery. The Who You Know and not who you might be as a human being. The You Do What I Do and You'll Be OK. Only Do What I Do. This whole God-awful lousy outfit. I want to see and *feel* you lot beneath my foot.'

'I see, honey,' she says. 'OK, don't stamp your little foot at me. OK?' She walks past him. 'I guess that's it.' Touches him on the shoulder. 'You'll live to regret what you've just said, honey.'

'You think so?' he says. '*You* can decide what *you* regret, Ruthie *honey*, when you're sitting alone in the slammer charged with conspiracy to murder and what the hell ever else.'

'I'll see you in court, babe,' she says.

'Yes, you will. And that's my price. And you know who's going to pay it. You are. You're going to pay it, Ruthie. *Babe*.'

71

Red Alert in Rosslyn's office. Lever's being asked to call in to Thames House as a matter of urgency. With Rosslyn watching the descending helicopter, she calls Thames House. She listens briefly. 'Red Alert,' she says, almost to herself. One hand covering the telephone, she turns. '*Holy Ghost* is red. There's an ambulance – it's suss. It's brand-new. They've no trace of it. They don't know where it came from. They want me down there now. Alan, they can't find out what the fuck it's doing down there.' She's pulling on her coat. 'Let's get out of here. They've busted the Czech. He was dealing in high explosives with Wroth. And it's one whole lot more than blew up the place in Kensal Green. It has to be them. They want me out there now.'

Before they leave the office, the bleeper sounds again. 'Hold it,' Lever says to Rosslyn. She pauses. Listens. Turns back to Rosslyn. 'Call this number. The DG wants to speak to you.'

Rosslyn's call is put through to the command post on the roof of Canada House. The communications officer tells him to stay on the line. 'Wait out.' DG MI5 is on another line. He asks Rosslyn where he's speaking from. Rosslyn tells him he's in the offices of ASG.

'The shit's on the doorstep,' Rosslyn tells Lever. 'ASG has shot itself in the foot. Tried to stamp on mine. They're in it up to here. Tried to relieve Trinity of his funds.'

She looks stunned. 'ASG?'

'It's a tug-of-war,' he says. 'Now I think the rope has snapped. We're still on our feet. Swincarron and Alexander are on their fucking backs with the coppers the other side of this wall here –'

Before he can elaborate further, the DG comes on the line to Rosslyn. 'Confirm your earlier call,' the DG snaps at him down the line.

'You've got at least two of the major players in the vehicle,' Rosslyn tells him. 'The white male, late twenties, early thirties. Marcus Luke. The second white male, forties, maybe older. Morgon Wroth.'

'The Welsh voice?'

'You can hear him?'

'The Welshman, yes. We now have audio surveillance in place. The Welshman then –'

'That's Wroth.'

'The others?' asks the DG. 'There are two women in the vehicle. Both American. One we think we know.'

'And the vehicle,' says Rosslyn, 'is most likely carrying one very large explosive device. Do you have any idea of that?'

'If the report from Kensal Green tallies with the Czech's then it may well be confirmed. We're looking at an estimate in excess of figures one point five tonnes of HE. It's your name that's being mentioned in there, Rosslyn. And Lever's. Where is she?'

'Here.'

'With you?'

'With me.'

'I want you both over here now.'

Rosslyn looks at the digital clock flashing on Nelson's Column.

'The DG adds quickly: 'I have to say, Rosslyn, I owe you something of an apology.'

Less than one hour until Millennium. Until inferno.

'Later,' Rosslyn snaps back.

The door to his office has been opened. The police officer in plain clothes is looking unsteady on his feet. 'Mr Rosslyn, I need to talk to you.'

'Later.'

'Sir, we've asked your colleagues, Ms, er, Swincarron and Mr Alexander, to accompany us to the station.'

'Good for you.'

'We'd like to talk to you now, sir. To help us with investigations into the death of Maxine Gertler.'

'She committed suicide,' says Rosslyn.

'We've reason to believe she didn't,' says the plain clothes officer.

'Then you'd better ask those two about that,' says Rosslyn.

'I'm sorry, Mr Rosslyn, sir, I have to ask you to accompany –'

Lever moves fast. She thrusts the ID into the officer's face. 'I'm MI5. Get out of the fucking way or I'll book you for obstructing me in the line of duty. Move yourself.'

The plain clothes officer steps aside.

'Later,' says Rosslyn. 'No offence meant.'

'It is meant,' says Lever. 'We're out of here. Move it.'

72

The Day of Resurrection.
Mine is the God Within.
Myself. Myself. Myself. The One. One. One.
When Birth will be Given to the Dancing Star.
Immortal. Invincible. Inviolate.
With Him you will change the world.
And with Him you will enter Paradise on Earth.
The Grace of Trinity be with us this night. And Evermore.
Amen.

Caroline wakes with no idea of where she is or how long she's been lying here curled up sideways, still a prisoner. She is heavily sedated; her head seems to tilt involuntarily and she breathes audibly and very slowly. Her mouth is parched. Her throat sore. It's as if she's waking from an anaesthetic. Her limbs feel unnaturally heavy. Her head feels strangely cold and swollen and when she turns it with a great effort, she realizes it's been completely shaven. Little by little she makes out the enormous figures of Wroth and then Marcus Luke. They are moving about in what seems to be the dim and greenish light of an ambulance's interior. The air smells of powerful disinfectant. She tightens her buttocks. *There's moisture. Am I dreaming about this water flowing out of me? Or the throbbing noise outside?* She listens. *This must be night.* She hears the distorted voices. *Someone is calling from a bad phone or cheap radio.* The voice from the speaker asks her if she's 'found the sacrament uncomfortable'? *I will not answer.* Squinting, bringing moisture to her eyelids, she tries to focus on the face of the person lying opposite her. The face of the shaven head. *Is this, could this, could you – Queron? Queron. Maybe together we could fight them.* Then she feels the restraints. Her wrists and ankles are tied tight. Her head is swimming. Weak with hunger, she feels nauseous. Something like seasickness.

The voice says: 'This is the sacred ritual. The sacrament from Trinity.'

She sees Marcus Luke. Staring blankly in contemplative silence through the darkened window. On the phone he's saying: '. . . to the branch of the Turkish Bank UK to company Occidental Ankara. Then back to Liechtenstein and the TC Anstalt. To Milan.' It makes no sense to her.

She feels the acid rising from chest to throat. Familiar spasms of hate twisting in the stomach. And there's Wroth. Toying with the hefty rifle in his lap. He's lifting the small volume bound in leather. Repeating to himself *ad nauseam*: 'The Grace of Trinity be with us this night. And Evermore. Amen.'

Three times the bear's hairy hand makes the sign across the chest: | | |.

'Do you hear me?' Luke asks. He's kneeling close to Queron. His voice is calm. 'The fruits of Mahler's drinking from Dostoievsky and Nietzsche and *Des*

Knaben Wunderhorn. Do you know his tomb in Vienna's Grinzing Cemetery, Donna?'

'Yes, I hear you.'

It's Queron.

'Are you *virgo intacta*?'

'Let me out of here,' Queron howls.

'Be calm,' says Luke. 'At peace. Quieten, yes.'

'For God's sake, let me outta here.'

'As it is written, yes. Talk to me, talk to me now. Describe to me the cleansing of the inner waters.'

'You're sick,' says Queron. 'Sick. Sick.'

'Tell me,' he says. 'Have we said our prayers, no? Say after me: "You who laid down your lives for His Name's Sake. That he might be reborn at the moment of One One One".'

As if hallucinating, Luke begins to hum. 'Unum. Unum. *Ooooo-nummmm.*'

'No,' says Queron.

'For you will resurrect with Him in blood – in the first minute. Of the first hour. Of the first day. As it is promised. So Thy Will be done.'

'No.'

'Or your sister will die. Ooooo-nummmm.' The humming continues. A noise in the ears. 'Sempiternam. Communio-o-o-o-o.'

'No,' says Queron.

'As it is written: "New People. The People of Death will visit you and all her kind in the fullness of my time." It comes to us all, doesn't it, my child? There is no more salvation. No rebirth. Other than through Trinity the Divine. Speak to me, no. Talk to me of love.'

'You're sick.'

Caroline admires her fellow captive's tone of defiance.

> *Ich bin von Gott und will wieder zu Gott!*
> *Der liebe Gott wird mir ein*
> *Lichtchen geben,*
> *Wird leuchten mir bis an das ewig*
> *selig Leben!**

Caroline is certain she will die. She prays: 'Please help me, God.'

* I am from God and to God I shall return! / Dear God will give me / A little light, / Will light me on the way / To joyful eternal life!

73

The Day of Resurrection.
Mine is the God Within.
Myself. Myself. Myself. The One. One. One.
When Birth will be Given to the Dancing Star.
Immortal. Invincible. Inviolate.

Upright. Calm. The tall man is dressed from head to foot in white. He leaves the Strand at the western exit. Exposed beneath the hem of his white robe is the only sign of a precaution he's taken if anything might go wrong: if he has to escape trouble, he will cast off the robes and leave dressed as a paramedic. No more than an inch of the nylon trousers of a paramedic's uniform are visible above his shoes.

He approaches Trafalgar Square through the throng with an air of considerable dignity. Perhaps he is expecting the crowds to part like the waves of an ocean. The miracle that will show He is at last amongst them. His progress is slow. 'Forgive me,' he says to those who unwittingly block his progress. 'Excuse me, please.' Passing the cordoned bronze statue of King Charles I by Hubert Le Sueur, he seems drawn to the gathering of the two hundred figures in white near Admiralty Arch.

'For I am among you,' he says unheeded. 'I am coming. I am coming to you.'

74

One point five tonnes of HE. Half as much again as the bomb that blew apart the City in '93. Shattered the six-hundred-foot NatWest Tower. Did £1 billion of destruction. The blast heard six miles distant across London. Planted in the lorry across the road from the Hong Kong & Shanghai Bank and the NatWest Tower. The bomb hurled the diesel engine fifty yards up the road. Metal fragments had been blown away to twice that distance. Left a crater of twelve square metres. That was a quiet Saturday. This too is Saturday. The heart of the City had been almost deserted.

— DIRECTOR GENERAL MI5, TRANSCRIPT OF TELE-
PHONE CALL, 31 DECEMBER 1999

23.48: Rosslyn looks up into the night sky. In the direction of the hovering Bell 222. Blinks at the buildings overlooking Trafalgar Square. The DG's words echo in his head: 'We're looking at an estimate in excess of figures —'

If the metal shards cut into this crowd, will any of these people be able to survive intact? How many won't survive at all? The crucial factor that determines the power of destruction of the explosion is where the device is placed and directed.

He looks at the floodlit buildings: *Some have windows of blast-resistant glass. Glass laminated with layers of translucent poly-vinyl-butyral each some 1.5 mm thick. The panes will bulge and not shatter. But few of the buildings have been protected like this. If the ambulance moves nearer the crowds – if the ambulance moves out – if the bomb ricochets – and the storm of shattered fragments shoots into the limbs, torsos –*

'What's with you?' a man yells. 'Bastard, you pushed me.' Rosslyn sees a police officer toying with his baton. The officer is shaking his head in warning. As if to say: 'If I was you, I'd watch it.'

The entrance to Canada House is a few final steps distant.

75

OBSERVER ONE: It's the Commissioner on the line, sir,
complaining that Americans are involved.
COMMANDER: Which Americans?
OBSERVER ONE: CIA.
COMMANDER: What's their problem? DG, *I need names.*
  – MI5 TRANSCRIPT, 31 DECEMBER 1999

23.50: Rosslyn and Lever step outside on to the
Canada House roof overlooking Trafalgar Square.
Seen from here: above, the converging beams of
searchlights; below, the frightening size of the
crowd. To the north and west: most faces are turned
towards the TV screens mounted on trucks. On the
night wind: the noise of the mass is distorted, crude
and deafening. Music thumps out. Facing police
officers in their yellow jackets, swaying sections of
the crowd have linked arms.

Rosslyn sees the silhouettes of the figures
bunched perilously close to the parapet. Wrapped
up against the cold, the DG has high-powered field
glasses raised to his eyes. Communications officers
and technicians beside him man the small TV
monitors and radio links.

Rosslyn crosses the slippery roof space to where
the DG is standing. Rosslyn's voice is mordant: 'You

realize those people probably don't even care if they kill themselves?'

'I hear what you say,' the DG says. 'We have less than ten minutes. Plus one, maybe. *Maybe.*' He touches one of the technicians on the shoulder. 'Their radio –?'

'It's still dead, sir,' says the communications officer.

'Keep on trying,' says the Commander. 'Where's the negotiator?'

'Held up in Park Lane,' a voice says. 'Traffic at Hyde Park Corner.'

'Get me on line to the helicopter,' says the DG. For the benefit of Rosslyn, he adds: 'You'll hear what this is about. The why you're here.' He asks the technician to give Rosslyn a set of headphones. 'Listen in.'

Rosslyn listens to the talk coming through the crackle. Clipped signals cutting in and out. Voices talking over each other. Usual radio communication procedures mostly ignored. The Commander's voice comes on line the clearest:

COMMANDER: To negotiate I need the names. *We must do it on the ground.* In five minutes we start talking. We have to land. The Palace, say, or Green Park.

PILOT: Too dangerous. The lasers are restricting visibility.

COMMANDER: *We have to land.*

ANOTHER VOICE: If we can't get a line into the vehicle, use SkyShout.

Over the radio the DG says to the Commander: 'The position is as follows. The identity of one hostage is confirmed. Female. White. Late twenties. Caroline Moorfield. American. We confirm HE device contains excess of 1000 lb Semtex, American C4, or UK manufactured PE4. Gunman or gunmen heavily armed. Definitely one gunman inside the vehicle, maybe even two.'

The Commander cuts in: 'We get any lower than this and we'll be negotiating as a fixed target.'

'Assuming they're armed —'

'We go up. They have figures one point five tonnes of HE in the vehicle. We blow up. I can't risk dropping a fireball into the crowd.'

'You want to move out?' asks the DG.

'Yes and no,' says the Commander. 'Do we have someone talk to them, or do we sit it out past the deadline? Do I do the talking?'

Rosslyn sees the DG is listening to another signal he can't hear.

'Wait out,' says the DG. 'Identify yourself, please. I have that — yes, stay on line.' He tells the Commander: 'We're starting talking. Get over here above us now. Give our man SkyShout.'

The DG turns to Rosslyn: 'We've got them now on the radio. They say the only person they'll deal with is you. I want them out alive. They'll negotiate with you. No one else.'

'OK. But why don't you have the square evacuated?'

'We can't.'

'Why not?'

'Because the crowd in Leicester Square's shoulder to shoulder. And some stupid bastard's set fire to the cut-price ticket booth. St Martin's Lane and the Strand are blocked and we have the bomb blocking the exit to the Mall.'

'You got the crowd control warning wrong. There's no way out, is there?'

'It's not my responsibility, Rosslyn.'

Rosslyn looks up at the sky. The helicopter turns. Lifts up above Canada House and steadies. Being positioned to winch him up aboard.

'Who says I'm the only person they'll negotiate with?' Rosslyn asks.

'Caroline Moorfield,' says the DG.

76

The laser beams criss-cross the London sky with giant webs of light. In the square, the crowds seem to be swarming: drawn to some false light of the future, celebrating celebration, bearing witness to some idea that the world will change with this imminent single flick of time. Will it be different, will it be better? *Que sera sera.*

Above Rosslyn the Bell 222, its white undercarriage edged with reflected light, lowers towards the top of Canada House.

Caroline seems to be drawing him to her. *And I'm the fly.*

The fly sent to try and reason with the spider.

From the belly of the helicopter the hawser's lowered. The harness is at its end, to be adjusted and clipped in place to raise him skywards. He's never felt so frightened.

The MI5 communications officers are receiving a barrage of communications. Rosslyn catches the frantic tone of the shouting, confused confirmation of what no one wants to hear. *All surrounding rooftops have been checked. The parapets of Trafalgar*

*Square. The office windows. The National Gallery. St
Martin-in-the-Fields. South Africa House. Admiralty
Arch. The base of Nelson's Column. The exit routes are
jam-packed with crowds. At a total standstill.*

The voices on the radios continue to announce
those who want to have their say:

UNIDENTIFIED: The Cabinet Office Briefing Room
   at the Home Office is on the line.

Given that the woman hostage in the ambulance
is American, the Cabinet Office Briefing Room is
apparently asking whether or not 'some different
intervention force might be necessary – even
military, say?'

'What for?' asks the DG. 'I see no real reason.'
Mumbling, he raises his glasses to his eyes and
points them vaguely at the sky. The DG's Nelson
touch.

Gloved hands hurriedly fasten the harness straps
around Rosslyn's chest. There's the click-clack of
clips and fasteners. Once everything's in place, the
gloved hands make the final checks. He's ready to
be lifted to the helicopter. The voices on the radio
confirm what's happening:

UNIDENTIFIED: Cable lowering. Figures fifty. Forty.
   Thirty. Twenty. Ten feet. Give them SkyShout
   voice. Cut the radio. Tell them he's on his way . . .
UNIDENTIFIED: We have EXPO on the ground.
UNIDENTIFIED: Buckingham Palace. Home

Secretary can authorize special forces, SAS to take action. Home Secretary has told Commissioner: 'Wait and see.'

'Tell him,' shouts the Commander, his voice distorted, 'tell him we're negotiating. WE ARE NEGOTIATING. Our man is taking the responsibility. EXPO to wait. Out.'

The harness takes the strain. Rosslyn is raised skywards. Up to the Bell 222 and the deafening beat of the roaring rotors.

Dangling above Trafalgar Square, his is now the most spectacular view of this unholy climax.

77

Watching the ambulance, the Metropolitan Police Explosives Officer, EXPO, stands in the small delivery bay at the back of Canada House. By now he's ready to neutralize the massive explosive device that's inside the ambulance, and he has just about as much on his mind as he can stand. He's donned helmet and protective bomb suit and he's made ready the explosive ordnance disposal unit, a kind of robotic wheelbarrow. This is equipped with lightweight tools, X-ray and cutting equipment, and the television camera to assist him in his task. On his very troubled mind: *If only the ambulance was an abandoned vehicle. If only the three, four or even five people weren't inside, I could cut my way into the vehicle. Insert an explosive pig stick and either neutralize the device or failing that, blow the whole thing to kingdom come. If only* – Biding his time, he listens in to the radio signals.

'Wait out,' Observer One is saying.

'Sir,' EXPO says over the ground-to-air line: 'I'd appreciate it if you –'

The Commander interrupts: '*Wait.*'

'Sir,' says Observer One, 'the US legal attaché claims one of the people inside the vehicle is a member of the US Diplomatic Corps. Another legal attaché. Stay on line. He wants to speak to you in person.'

'Put him on,' says the Commander.

The Commander hears the voice of this legal attaché, the CIA deputy station head.

CIA DEPUTY STATION HEAD: I have confirmation that our station head, Donna Queron, is being held hostage in the vehicle you have under air surveillance. We do not, repeat not, want any press or media coverage of this situation.

COMMANDER: There isn't any.

CIA DEPUTY STATION HEAD: We have to emphatically insist on that point.

COMMANDER: With respect, this is wasting time.

CIA DEPUTY STATION HEAD: With respect, you, sir, have to appreciate that this executive order is from the Secretary of State with the authority of the President of the United States. It is also approved by your Home Secretary.

COMMANDER: May I remind you we have a job to do up here. This is my responsibility. *Mine alone*.

CIA DEPUTY STATION HEAD: You listen to me, officer, sir. Ms Queron must be brought out of that vehicle alive.

COMMANDER: We don't have positive ID that they're holding a United States diplomat.

CIA DEPUTY STATION HEAD: I am giving it to you,

officer. I am formally informing you, sir, that she is in there. In danger of her life. Your only job is to get her out of there alive.

COMMANDER: My duty is to ensure that we have no casualties here.

CIA DEPUTY STATION HEAD: I wish to visit the scene, sir.

The Commander ends the call dead as Rosslyn is finally lifted on board the helicopter. 'CIA. Dear God,' the Commander is heard saying, 'who the hell do they think they are?'

No one has the answer. Except Observer One, whose face, even in the green and red reflected light from the control panels, is greyish. 'Sir, the Prime Minister is waiting on the line. He wants to speak personally to you, sir.'

Now the Commander hears the voice of the Prime Minister saying: 'You will do everything you can to save the lives of those hostages and bring the gunmen out unharmed.'

'We're doing our level best, sir.'

'Just do it.'

'Yes, sir.'

'And ensure that none of your scene-of-crime officers speaks to anyone. Not to families. Not to the press. No one.'

'They never do, sir.'

'Do not refer to any one of those you may have heard named.'

'They never do, sir.'

'The Home Secretary has prepared a statement to say we believe the atrocity bears all the hallmarks of either an IRA splinter group or Muslim, possibly Iranian, fundamentalists.'

How does he know there's going to be an atrocity? And why not now simply tell the truth?

'DG MI5 has been informed,' says the Prime Minister. 'Do you understand?'

'Yes, I believe that to be the case, sir.'

'Your efforts in all of this will not go unrewarded,' says the Prime Minister.

The Commander fails to disguise an uncharacteristic note of sarcasm: 'Thank you very much, sir.'

Not another word from the Prime Minister. No 'Good luck'. Nothing.

Below, by Admiralty Arch, EXPO in protective gear is on the link line to the helicopter: 'We've no idea what kind of timer, detonator, battery, circuits or main charge is being used – whether the latter is Semtex or dynamite or a mixture of sugar and chemical fertilizer – no idea how or where it's been placed in the ambulance.'

'Sir,' says Observer One. 'DG MI5 waiting –'

The DG is about to speak over the radio link when he's cut short by the SO19 officer: 'Commander, we have an exit to the rear.'

'Down,' the Commander orders the pilot. 'Sky-Shout active.'

'SkyShout active,' says the pilot. 'We're going down.'

The Bell 222 lowers into the danger zone.

With dreadful calm the computerized female voice in the pilot's earphones is repeating its automatic safety warnings *ad nauseam*: 'Pull up . . . pull up . . . pull up . . . pull up.'

Now on board, Rosslyn sees the digital clock on Nelson's Column flip near to zero hour.

The Commander hands over the SkyShout microphone: 'It's up to you now, Mr Rosslyn.'

Below, the legion of Trinity's followers are chanting with still greater intensity. The manic rhythm of their utterance is menacing. There's a madness about it, an edge of panic to it, which contrasts with the more innocent joy in the cheering of the crowds. This troubling sense of ugliness now registers in the concerned mind of EXPO, and it shows clearly in the eyes of the police officers surrounding the ranks of figures dressed in white and on the faces of the mounted officers seeking to reassure their mounts.

78

From his vantage point in the helicopter, Rosslyn sees the tell-tale movement of what could mean progress. On the ground below, the rear doors of the Laser ambulance begin to open.

They're coming out. We're on our way.

He sees the terrified figure illuminated in the brilliant pool of Nitesun light. It is wrapped in a white blanket, and the head is shaven. He sees the unidentifiable occupant stumble out of the ambulance. All that's visible by way of identification is the back of the shaven head. *Caucasian. Surely female. Thirties or forties.*

He can see the police officers are having to use greater force to restrain the crowd and that the Trinity followers are resisting the instructions to stay put. Some yelling drunks are now being wrestled by police officers. The Trinity followers are refusing to make way for the police. Some of them are staring up at the helicopter open-mouthed, arms raised to shield their eyes from the Nitesun's glare.

But it's the ambulance and the mesmerized and pathetic shaven figure that concentrate Rosslyn's mind as the SkyShout carries his voice downwards:

'Police. Stay where you are. Do not move. Thank

you. Please. Slowly. Please. Raise your right arm if you hear me clearly.'

The naked arm is slowly raised from the white blanket. The hand twitches.

'Thank you. Please now crawl on all fours clear of the vehicle until I say stop.'

Impeded by the blanket wrapped around her, the woman begins to crawl away from the ambulance.

'Watch the nearside window, Mr Rosslyn,' warns the Commander coldly. 'Watch the nearside window.'

Now Rosslyn sees the weapon. The Barrett M82A1 Light Fifty A that can at any moment shoot the helicopter out of the sky.

The pilot must have seen it too. He's being warned by that disembodied computer voice: 'Pull up . . . Pull up . . . Pull up.' The helicopter rotors suddenly increase power. The sudden acceleration makes Rosslyn's stomach rise.

The figure of the woman below seems frozen to the ground. *Is this pathetic creature Queron?* And even before the digital clock on Nelson's Column approaches the hour of midnight, two rounds are fired in quick succession. They seem at first to be warning shots.

Rosslyn hears the Commander bellowing to him: 'Tell them to hold fire.'

'Hold fire!'

Now the spotlight on the ambulance is turned on

full beam. It swivels. Searches. Settles and illuminates the yellow jackets of the police officers standing at the edge of Admiralty Arch's central pillar. Rosslyn sees one of the officers break into a run, zigzag, towards the ambulance. Immediately three rapid-fire rounds from the Barrett M82A1 Light Fifty A strike the police officer in both legs, just below the knees, and cut him to the ground. The legs buckle crazily. The fourth round hits him in the chest and it hurls him sideways and backwards to the ground.

Almost as one, the crowd begins to scream.

Near the ambulance the white blanket has dropped from the figure, who's now started running for the shelter of the nearest doorway. The helicopter's Nitesun beam shows the figure is definitely female. She's now naked and she has her arms in front of her face. She stumbles, wheels and falls.

It's Queron. She's out.

The Nitesun beam now illuminates another woman who's leaving the pavement and is running, arms wide, to help the fallen, naked figure.

Rosslyn sees that the woman running from the crowd towards the fallen Queron is Wendy Lever.

His voice thunders down: **'Take cover!'**

There's another shot. And another. The fusillade breaks open the skull of the police officer in a red mist.

The crowds in the vicinity of Admiralty Arch press close, pushing in the direction away from the

arch. Some of them have started to run into the Mall.
Rosslyn can see Lever at the edge of the crowd, and
she's looking upwards.

Wendy, don't you know you're a sitting target?

Again his voice thunders down: '**Take cover!**'

Rosslyn turns to the Commander. 'Lower me down
there.'

'No.' The Commander's concentration seems
gripped by the signals on the radio lines. 'No,' he
repeats. Rosslyn grabs at the Commander's field
glasses. Head close to the Commander's, he focuses
on the ground below. 'The naked woman's Queron.'

He sees Lever drag her towards the crowd. Then
the police officers shield her and she's carried away
out of sight.

'Put me down in there,' Rosslyn tells the Commander.

The Commander shakes his head.

Rosslyn sees the yellowish pallor of the Commander's skin. The dry lips. His sudden inhalations of
air. It seems as if he's about to vomit. 'No.'

In the brief moment of chaos that follows, the
chimes from Big Ben sound out.

Rosslyn's moved in a crouch to the helicopter's
exit. He straps the harness back in place. 'Lower,' he
shouts. 'Now. Move it.'

The Commander is asking: 'Should we evacuate?'

'It's too late,' Rosslyn tells him. 'Fly directly
overhead the vehicle.'

'We're not going down to look,' says the Commander. 'We have orders. We're waiting. Until it goes up.'

'There are still people alive in there,' Rosslyn yells at him. 'For Chrissakes! Lever's a sitting target. She's on the ground.'

The Commander is speaking to the MI5 DG, whose voice is now clearer on the radio link. 'What else do you know about them?'

Before the DG can offer a reply, Rosslyn hears the mounting cacophony of radio voices:'United States Embassy. Washington. Langley. Vauxhall Cross. Box. Friends.' And: 'Is that Donna Queron?'

A voice yells: 'GET THE FUCK OFF THE LINE!'

The American voice replies: 'Excuse me?'

'All we can do is wait,' says the Commander with false calm.

'No. Put me down there.' Rosslyn insists.

'Give it five more minutes,' the Commander says. 'Alert assault teams.' He asks whether or not the Bell 222 is flying at a safe height.

'What's happening inside it?' a voice asks.

'Get me down in there,' Rosslyn shouts.

His demand is lost in the explosions of the first giant Millennial Skyblast rockets. They shoot upwards, followed by a sound like the tearing of a cotton sheet and whistling from between a million teeth. The sparkling flowers drop stars down towards the thousands of faces turned to the sky above Trafalgar Square.

'Right,' says Rosslyn. He raises his hand gun to the Commander's face. 'Fucking do it.'

Struggling to gain control, the Commander nods, gives the order coolly. 'Put him down.'

Checking his hand gun, Rosslyn says: 'Get in low.' He releases the safety catch. Secures it in the holster.

The Commander turns away and retches. Out of sight from Rosslyn, whose descent begins. Down to the ambulance.

The gigantic **2000** lights the sky.

The falling stars of fireworks can be seen almost everywhere across London's 600 square miles. The sky changes from white to red to blue to false daylight.

In Trafalgar Square, the sound system thumps and pounds and wrenches the jumping crowd. The monster TV screens show sweeping shots from Westminster by the river to Hyde Park. From Kensington in the west to King's Cross. Regent's Park. Hampstead. St Paul's Cathedral. The Tower of London. Now the airborne camera sweeps past Blackheath to Greenwich and the floodlit Dome.

Above the others, a sound system blares out:

> *Just Show Me How to Love You*
> *E ci ridiamo su*
> *gabbiano di scogliera*
> *ma dov'eri nascosto'*
> *dov'eri finora?*

Accompanying the eruptions in the London sky: **2000**

The white light is blinding.

In mid-air, Rosslyn struggles to steady himself. Squinting. Looking down at the tide of more than a hundred thousand people. Then at the two figures who seem to be leaving the ambulance. He blinks. Tries to focus. Can't identify them. Can't see them. Just the white faces of the crowd. Bleached by the white light of the **2000**.

Hitting the ground, he frees himself from the harness.

Dangling above him, the harness is rewound into the Bell 222. Now the helicopter leans steeply at an angle. Bound for the allocated landing point out of immediate danger, it heads away to the floodlit courtyard of Somerset House. Away from the *Red Alert* here at the south-west corner of Trafalgar Square.

79

And now the time returns again;
Our souls exult, and London's towers
Receive the Lamb of God to dwell
In England's green and pleasant bowers.
  — WILLIAM BLAKE

Drawn to witness the growing trouble in this corner of the Square, the crowd changes shape. It's pressing the police officers attempting to form a protective cordon around the ambulance. Some additional protection is afforded by the barrier of mounted police officers, whose horses don't like the explosions in the sky and seem to sense the menace around them. And the arrival here of the called-for police reinforcements is impeded by the swelling numbers.

Sickened by what can be seen of blood and injury, some of the nearest revellers have backed away from the mounted police, only to be trapped by the almost hysterical phalanx of Trinity followers in white.

To the north, on the other side of the square, where the celebration continues, another section of the crowd tries to head off against the tide to the pubs, clubs and cafés in Soho and elsewhere in the West End where the serious binge is beginning. They don't want whatever's happening near the Arch to spoil the rest of the Big Night Out. The Big 2000. But for the time being there are simply too many people out on the streets of the West End to make movement possible. This northern section of the crowd finds the exit routes are jammed.

No one pays attention to the figure of the man in the white robes who's pushing his way forwards to the two hundred Trinity followers. Their dirge is primitive and frightening in its intensity:

> *Trin-it-ee*
> *Trin-it-ee*
> *Three in One*
> *One in three*

The man in white follows a group of police reinforcements. Penetrating deep into the crowd, he worms his way towards Admiralty Arch, where the chanting is loudest. He ignores the craning faces in the windows, the baroque display of fireworks in the sky, the bawling crowds. More and more people are appearing at the perimeter of the square. Pressing and jostling against the crowd-control barriers. Celebrating the celebration, the crowd seems filled with a sense of the brilliance of the occasion and their role in this unforgettable night of nights.

They really couldn't be less interested in this man in white, who is repeatedly making the holy gesture:
| | |.

Behind the cordon of stretched plastic tape, armed police officers are discreetly assuming fire positions. They're covering Rosslyn's approach to the front windows of the vehicle. The fact must be obvious to them: covering fire will be virtually useless. They're under orders to stay at what they believe to be a safe distance. Even EXPO's been ordered to stay put. On standby. That's where the forces of law and order stay. Put at a safe distance. Unsure of what to do next. Waiting as if trapped by the surging tide of people, whose mood of joy and celebration is frustrated. Resentful, the crowd is gradually beginning to sour, to turn ugly, simmering on the edge of violence.

The figure in white now assumes the stance of Christ Resurrected in the minor Victorian picture by Sir Joshua Smedley RA. A vision of the Living Christ.

Squeezing through the crowds towards Admiralty Arch, eyes gleaming, the Divine walks upright and ignored. If a few do notice Him, they do not recognize Him. The two hundred chanting figures sway and roll to the sound of the great chant.

'I am among you,' says the figure.

'We are resurrected,' say the nearest figures all in white.

And the chant changes from:

> *Trin-it-ee*
> *Trin-it-ee*
> *Three in One*
> *One in three*

to:

> *WE are resurrected*
> *WE are resurrected*
> *WE are resurrected*

The figure in white tries to make his way through the throng to what he believes to be the centre of the chanting army of His followers.

'I am with you,' he says.

If the centre will only hold. If, indeed, there is a centre.

The Victorian vision of forgotten Smedley bears scant relation to the violence of the chanting and the anger it seems to generate among the police officers. It's as if they're being taunted. It's belligerence and fear that's now registering in their faces. As if they're thinking, with good reason: *Bugger off, we've got better things to do.* This is looking really ugly. And it's getting worse. The army of people in white seems to present a solid wall. The ambulance is standing there in the dazzling light and the exit routes are jammed solid. There is no way out. And no one is in a position to take control.

Once on the ground, Rosslyn walks to the driver's window of the ambulance and tentatively peers inside.

As he recognizes the bulk of Wroth slumped sideways on the floor, the SkyShout thunders from above:

'Mr Rosslyn, we have Ms Queron secure. Signal immediately you need EXPO.'

Rosslyn can see: *Wroth's bulk is rigid. The dead eyes staring. Is Caroline really here inside? Is Luke here too? Where's the explosive device?*

Do I step away and alert EXPO?

That will let Luke know that the bomb man is coming over to render the device harmless, and Luke won't hesitate, will he? He'll kill us all.

Alone. This is the worst time. The approach. Watched by the chanting army. And the device. You'd rather it went off cleanly. The sudden death. Not the maiming. Blinded. Deafened. The amputee. This is when you forget those rudimentary instructions. It's It. Or You. You have to force yourself to look. Steady. Breathe regularly.

In his hand the gun is cold and hard and seems frozen to his skin.

The Nitesun beams down. So bright it feels as if the heat is burning his eyes.

He can see the rear doors of the ambulance are slightly open. Rosslyn nudges them a little further apart. Just the necessary few inches to see in.

Then he stops in his tracks. The interior stinks of faeces and vomit. Inside, he sees the explosive device is just beneath the rear bench. Beyond that is what seems to be a bulky, heavy-duty plastic body bag. *And something or someone inside it is definitely moving.*

'Don't move,' he shouts inside. 'Do not move.' His mouth is dry. *'Repeat. Do not move – Luke?'*

There's no reply. Rosslyn sees no sign of him. *Marcus Luke must already have got away.*

The body bag now lies still.

But the dog is in there.

The front passenger door of the ambulance opens. Marcus Luke, wearing the overalls of the paramedic, slips out. Calmly he walks towards the crowd, which parts to allow a way through for this paramedic with the fair curly hair. With the look of a chorister, he's unremarked by the sea of eyes staring skywards. He squeezes carefully into the crowd, mouthing apologies to the accompaniment of the thunderous and vain appeals from the SkyShout:

'Stay calm. Do not move. Please.'

Unobserved, Marcus Luke makes his exit into the crowds and is gone.

Rosslyn turns. He glimpses the animal's bared teeth. Bulging eyes. The bull neck. Muscles stretched and bulging, it flays at Rosslyn in mid-air. It tries to get the paw grip. To bite flesh. It twists. The force behind the leap drives it down and out of the vehicle.

Legs splayed, it hits the road. Poised for one split second, as if about to launch a return attack, it suddenly charges at the wall of mounted police officers and the followers of Trinity.

One of the horses seems to rear. The crowd pulls back in desperation. It parts suddenly. Staggering, the rearing horse slams several of the howling figures in white robes against the crowd-control barriers. Several are trampled beneath the horse's flaying hooves, screaming. Others try to clamber over the barriers, over each other, only to collapse, unable to get free. Those at the bottom of the heap have their faces pressed against the barrier. They choke and start to suffocate.

'Rosslyn hears the mounting screams of panic. And sees those in the front rank of Trinity's followers. Some are struck by flying hooves. There's a broken face. Bloodied flesh. Twisted arms. The relentless screams of panic.

The turmoil of the crowd parts to reveal the man with his eyes fixed open. The white robes splashed with blood. The prominent features. Rosslyn recognizes Trinity.

For a fraction of a second, the staring eyes seem to fix Rosslyn's.

Diverted, Rosslyn freezes until he sees the dog. It's turning. Pent up and panting, its bloodied jaws open, it charges straight for him.

Rosslyn lifts the Ruger and fires carefully: once into the animal's bloodied mouth and then twice between the eyes.

80

The edge of the Nitesun beam shows Rosslyn the construction of the explosive device. The tangle of the wires. *And what looks to be the detonator.* Then an oblong plastic shape. *Has to be the timer.* No bigger than his own shaking fist. His eyes and fingers check the circuitry. Again the body bag moves and he thinks he hears a moan.

Of someone alive inside it. Or is it from outside? It's louder now. No time to get whoever's there clear before the device goes off. So cut the wire then. But if the circuit collapses? Oblivion. Cut the wire. If the relay's closed? Current will zip into the detonator. Oblivion. The detonator's shock wave blasts into the main explosive charge. Oblivion.

The breath in his nostrils sounds like the whistling of a baited, cornered animal. He leans forward to the wire. Nausea rises in his throat. Bares his teeth. Locks his jaw. Bites and snaps the wire. The wire cuts deep into his lips and gums. He spits metal strands. Listens. Tastes his blood. *Must hear. Must hear. Now the timer –*

He clambers further into the ambulance. A voice from outside is screaming: 'Please! Please! Please! We have injured people out there.'

Stretching, he reaches behind him to close the vehicle's doors. Soundproof against the relentless din of panic. Now he hears what he wants to hear. *The timer's ticking.* Tinny. Metallic. The warning tick-tick-tick taunts him.

One-One-One. The | | |.

Nearer. Louder. Ticking on. Like a maddened pulse. The ticking of the Memo-Park timer. Time's up.

The wire's cut.

The ticking's stopped.

Spitting blood, he leans backwards and kicks the doors open.

'Get a doctor in here,' he shouts to the nearest police officer. 'It's safe.'

Outside, he sees the twisted faces of the dead and dying. The white shrouds stained with blood. The bodies watched by ghoulish faces. Mouths open. The pavement is awash with blood. And there's no more chanting. Horrified, people are trying to back away from the pile of crushed corpses.

Tearing at the body bag, he stretches and rips away the shining black plastic. Yanks and pulls in desperation at the industrial tape.

The shaven head is Caroline's. The eyes are open wide. 'I have no clothes,' she says. 'I have no clothes.' And she starts to moan.

He carries her wrapped in the remains of the body bag into the foyer of Canada House.

The DG is on the ground floor. He's standing next to the corpse. 'You recognize him?' he asks Rosslyn.

Rosslyn looks at the face.

'Yes.'

He stares into the DG's bloodshot eyes. It's as if they're saying: *We never expected you to come out of it alive.* They flicker. Rosslyn will remember the flicker for a long time. He can't be sure. But it's as if it's saying: *It might be more convenient if you hadn't.*

Am I right? Or am I right?

'Van Rijn,' the DG says in a matter-of-fact tone. 'Van Rijn. Your man.'

Rosslyn looks into the dead eyes of Trinity the Divine.

'Someone bag the bugger up,' the DG says. 'What happened to the dog?'

'I shot it.'

'You *shot* it?'

The flicker of regret in the DG's face suggests it may not be quite the done thing to shoot a dog.

Rosslyn is cradling Caroline in his arms when he hears the voice behind him. The familiar voice is saying: 'Alan?'

He looks up into the eyes of Wendy Lever. She stoops down and touches his shoulder. 'You've cut your mouth,' she says.

He wipes the blood from his jaw.

'I'm impressed,' she says.

New Year's Day

Venus, brilliant in the evening hours,
will be seen in the south-western skies.
The crescent moon will be seen near Venus.

They admitted nothing. They just rowed. Quarrelled. Endlessly rowed. About the money.
— CAROLINE MOORFIELD, LONDON, 1 JANUARY 2000

The first morning of 2000: the single light illuminates the large reproduction of the eighteenth-
century *ukiyo-e* woodblock by Koryusai. The screen
that obscures the view of the bedroom. The woman
in the kimono is watching the couple lovemaking in
the Yoshiwara house. The woman beneath the man
on the tatami mat has her legs wound round his
back.

Rain falls across London. The teams of City of
Westminster garbage collectors gather more sodden
rubbish than they would expect to scoop up in a
month.

Police officers in waterproofs stand about near the
killing ground by Admiralty Arch. Watery chalk
marks on the pavement show where some of the
thirty-six followers of Trinity were trampled to
death in the early hours.

Damp pages of

block the drain outside Uganda House.

The early TV news bulletins suggest that the deaths should never have been allowed to happen. The junior minister from the Home Office says it is 'the personal wish' of the Prime Minister that the full enquiry take place immediately.

He quotes the Prime Minister as saying he's 'completely satisfied that everything possible was done in the interests of public safety. The tragedy was the result of a spontaneous demonstration that no one could have foreseen. He sends his profound sympathy to the relatives of those who died. They can be assured that the government will seek out those who persecute religious minorities and grant them no sanctuary. The government and people are united in their resolve to allow believers to pursue their faiths.'

Past noon, Rosslyn wakes next to Wendy Lever. Sleep presses behind his eyes. Not for long.

The doorbell's ringing.

The unannounced visitor on the doorstep is the MI5 DG.

'Mind if I come in, Rosslyn?'

'By all means.'

Rosslyn leads him into the kitchen. 'Coffee?'

'That's be nice. No sugar. Milk.'

'I'm afraid I have no milk.'

'Black'll do then,' the DG says. 'I hope you're rested.'

'Fine, thanks.'

'You must be pretty shaken up.'

'Yes,' says Rosslyn. 'How can I help you?'

They sit at the kitchen table. 'It's a question of debriefing Ms Moorfield,' the DG says, adding with a tone of patronage: 'I'd like you present when we do it.'

'Fine by me.'

'Shall we say in two or three days time?' says the DG. 'Unless you have prior commitments at ASG.'

'As a matter of fact I won't be going in there again.'

'Ah, really? I think that's probably the wise decision. Off the record and by the way, your erstwhile colleagues Swincarron and Alexander will in no circumstances be granted bail.'

'I think that's probably the wise decision too,' says Rosslyn. 'How's Caroline?'

'Perfectly satisfactory in the circumstances,' says the DG. 'Queron too, considering. They're both pretty shaken. But you can take it from me that they're as well as can be expected. In the circs. Oh and the forensic people are still working on the identities of the dead. There were thirty-six at the last count.'

'So many?'

'Yes. But then panic, the horses and so forth.'

'It could've been worse,' Rosslyn interrupts.

'Exactly,' says the DG.

Rosslyn brings the coffee to the table. 'And what about Luke?'

'He's no great loss.'

'He's dead?'

'Yes.'

'Who identified him?'

'Queron.'

'Really. Queron did?'

'Yes, indeed. The embassy have handed over the evidence such as it is. We have photographs of the key players. That kind of thing. There we are. Good riddance. The Americans want to get Queron home at the earliest opportunity. Can't say I blame them.'

'Will your people get a chance to question her?'

'Out of courtesy, the Secretary of State's decided to leave that to Washington. Good move, I think.' He takes the envelope from his coat pocket. 'Here. This is for you.'

Rosslyn opens it and reads the unfamiliar handwriting:

Embassy of the United States of America
24 Grosvenor Square London W1A 1AE

Mr Alan Rosslyn   January 1, 2000

Dear Alan Rosslyn,

I'd like to express my gratitude for your co-operation
with Holy Ghost.

These have not been easy days. There has been much
unnecessary violence and death.

I trust you will be proud of all you did on my behalf
and on that of Ms Moorfield. I have no doubt that
you are responsible for having saved our lives. No
words can express my gratitude in full.

With sincere wishes for the future and a peaceful
Millennium.
Sincerely yours,

D Q

Donna Queron
Legal Attaché

'That's nice,' says Rosslyn. 'And where's the body of Van Rijn?'

'Police Mortuary. Juxon Street. I'm going to take a look at him this afternoon.'

'And Luke too?'

'Yes. Do you want to see them, as it were, personally?'

'Why do you ask?'

'Thought you might be curious.'

'Thanks all the same, I'm not *that* curious.'

'There we are. I suppose Luke thought he'd get away in the crowds.'

'Did you find the gun, the Barrett?' Rosslyn asks.

'No. We're still looking for it. Anyway, he probably intended to collect the Trinity funds in Italy or something. That's Ms Queron's initial view. When they believed Van Rijn was dead and with no Maryon on the scene, I suppose Luke thought he was home and dry. Why else would he have shot the man Wroth?'

'He shot Wroth?' says Rosslyn.

'Yes, indeed he did. For the same reason Wroth killed Morandi. For the same general principle according to which Jane Moorfield died. Let's say it's the principle that three can keep a secret if two are dead. But one's inclined to ask oneself, as it were, why the bomb? Shall we say that if they were thwarted they'd have punished the world? Do you share my view? What do you believe?'

'That it has to have been theirs,' says Rosslyn. 'That's what I believe.'

'I suppose it doesn't matter what you believe,' says the DG. 'It only matters that you believe. That's what the Prime Minister told me.'

'Then if I were you, I'd tell him who else said that.'

The DG's simian face lights up with a smile. 'I will. Who?'

'Dr Goebbels.'

The smile vanishes. 'Yes, well. Anyway, Queron's assessment is that Luke wanted the device disarmed. But Wroth didn't. Division within the ranks. They'd heard nothing from Van Rijn. Wroth believed he'd been deceived. He really wanted to go ahead with it. But Luke. No. It seems he was a rather different kettle of fish. Played the role of the pacifier. What he wanted was the money. I suppose you could say it usually boils down to that in the end. Money. And Moorfield and Queron. Well, I suppose you could say they were terribly lucky to get away with it.'

'I don't quite see it like that,' says Rosslyn 'They'll be damaged for life. And I wouldn't trust Queron further than I could kick her.'

'She has her job to do,' the DG says. He looks at the coffee in the mug. 'There we are. By the way, three more small things. Caroline Moorfield for a start. One: she's asked me to thank you. Two: she wants you to know that she'll be paying you in full. Not ASG.'

'Say thanks to her.'

'Thanks to you, Rosslyn.'

It's all over. She'll be all right. He wants to find it in him to feel sorry for her. *She did the wrong thing for the right reasons. I have to admire her resilience. Unlike Queron and her cronies, who you could say did much the opposite. They had their jobs to do. Queron will soon be shipped off to some comfy posting.*

'And –' the DG places a folded £20 note on the kitchen table. 'Three: Queron asks rather thoughtfully if you'd personally be kind enough to place a bunch of roses on the spot where Jane Moorfield is believed to have died. I think you know where that is.'

'Yes.'

'King's Cross St Pancras, isn't it?'

'More or less.'

'I'd appreciate it. By the way,' the DG adds, looking rather sheepishly at the erotic screen print. 'I suppose Lever's not at her place.'

'No, she isn't.'

'Do you happen to know where she is?'

'She's here. Asleep.'

'Really? Ah well. Good. I thought as much. In the circumstances.'

Strange, thinks Rosslyn. *Her clothes are on that chair next to you. But I suppose you wouldn't recognize the black silk underwear.*

'And the last thing I have to tell you,' says the DG. 'I suppose you realize the importance of saying nothing, I mean absolutely nothing, to the press or TV. Nothing to anyone. It's on the Prime Minister's personal insistence. One has to be so very careful who one trusts.'

'It's OK by me.'

'Good,' the DG says, getting to his feet. 'I think I'll be on my way. Thanks for the coffee. Rather better than at Thames House, I'm bound to say.'

'There we are,' says Rosslyn. He shows the DG to the door.

'At least the weather's changed,' the DG says. 'Raining cats and dogs. I suppose you could say we need it.'

Once the visitor has left, Lever tells Rosslyn she's overheard most of what the DG said.

'All this shit about you leaving flowers at King's Cross or something,' she says. 'What do they think this is, Remembrance Day?'

'I don't see any objection to doing what they want,' says Rosslyn. 'Look, Wendy, it's all over now.'

She shrugs.

'You're not jealous, are you?' he asks. 'Jealous of Caroline or something?'

'Jealous of her – me? No. I don't get this sudden display of generosity on the DG's part. Or Queron's. This flower-leaving stuff. Don't you worry, Alan. Go ahead and do it, Alan. Let me give you a bit of professional advice. Take that hand gun with you.'

He feels the stiffness of the muscles in his neck and shoulders. Where last night the gun holster had felt so tight. 'Forget it,' he says. 'My only problem is where to get the flowers.'

'Try the stall on Victoria station. There's a Greek-Cypriot woman there who never closes. Leg it to Victoria. Get the flowers. Do what Caroline wants. Wind it up. Then get back here. I've booked a dinner for two. For us. It'd be a pity to miss the celebration. Get it over and done with. Go and buy the red roses.'

The streets to Victoria are deserted. Rosslyn feels the emptiness of the first afternoon of the new century. Combined with the national hangover, the driving rain is keeping most people indoors. By the time he reaches Victoria station it's almost dark.

Lever turns out to be right about the flower stall being open on the station concourse. Come to think of it, how would she know? Maybe her people have used it in the past as cover for some surveillance operation. MI5 officers only fill their heads with odd facts for reasons that have nothing to do with the romance of buying flowers at stations.

He buys a bouquet of roses and heads for the underground. He could be forgiven for being impatient to have done with the business on this empty afternoon.

His impatience explains why he fails to spot the

legmen. Had he seen them he'd have recognized their faces.

They board the train to King's Cross St Pancras separately. One of them finds a seat in a carriage ahead of Rosslyn. The other, a discreet distance behind Rosslyn on the platform, boards the train just as the doors close.

Rosslyn relaxes in the warmth. Closes his eyes. And for most of the journey he keeps them closed. Glad it's over.

Wasteland. King's Cross St Pancras and the territory is bleak.

The usual sort of down-and-outs are in the darkened doorways. A few hunched saddos brave the chill rain to pick at the litter in the waste bins. A pair of shivering druggies and their panting dog watch a mother and child examining a discarded Macdonald's carton in a bus shelter. A wino drains the contents of a cider bottle by the cab rank. And none of the regular King's Cross tarts of either sex is braving the freezing rain to seek out punters this Millennial New Year's Day evening.

Heading into the rain with the bouquet of roses, Rosslyn takes much the same route he took when he had first followed Caroline and Lever to the wasteland beyond Battle Bridge Road. He passes the derelict building that once housed the British Rail Staff Association's recreation club. No lights shine from the American Car Wash Company but, even in the rain, the tang of spray paint and fibreglass lingers. At the crossing of St Pancras Road and Goodsway, he sees the smeared white letters of the painted legend:

There's a smell of gas from the barely visible Goodsway gasometers. His shoe strikes a squashed beercan, then crunches broken glass that glints in the beam of a passing car's headlights. The lights show the surrounding walls and the coils of razor wire just visible in the pouring rain.

Is there a figure there ahead of me?

Or could his stinging eyes be playing tricks?

He can feel the presence of someone near.

Before walking up Cheney Road, he pauses. He's outside the Cabot Centre for Body Mind Training, listening for footsteps, staring into the darkness. *Is there a legman ahead of me?* He turns and is certain there's the vague shadow of a figure on the cobblestones of Battle Bridge Road. Or is this a phantom? Is his mind playing games?

On his left, at the end of the cul-de-sac, he sees the open gates to the scrapyard. The wasteland where Jane Moorfield's body had been found is beyond the dilapidated gates. His pulse quickens. The security lights on in the stairwells of the Culross Buildings reveal a green weatherproof jacket.

The coat is identical to Wendy's. Have you taken it upon yourself to get here first? For what?

He curses the rain streaming down his face. When he looks back to the Culross Buildings entrance, the figure in the green weatherproof jacket is no more to be seen.

Nerves on edge, he walks on through the gates to the scrapyard. There's the stench of rotten animal flesh, vegetable débris and sewage, and the sound of water sluicing from a broken gutter into an overflowing oil drum.

The DG will have put two legmen on my tail. In his shoes I'd have done the same. He needs me more than I need him, to testify at the inquests.

From beyond what seems to be the wall of rain he hears the echo of an InterCity train's klaxon. It blares out at the mouth of one of the two King's Cross tunnel entrances, then the noise is sucked into the tunnel and goes dead. Quickening his pace, the mud sticking to his shoes, he reaches the stretch of open wasteland beside the great stacks of salvaged car wrecks.

Come to think of it, I don't know exactly where Jane Moorfield was found, anyway. Through the rain a light shows in the construction workers' huts bordering the railtrack. Beyond the single-storey huts and to his right is the single yellow and reddish blur of the station's lights. They seem somehow reassuring in this miserable place.

A single floodlight shows the nearest twisted stacks of smashed car bodies.

He gently sets down the roses beside the upside-down wreck of a Mercedes. Bows his head. Takes two steps backwards in the mud. Then turns to leave.

It's one of those rare moments when fear allows you to recognize what you don't want to see. He sees the figure in the rain. This isn't a legman. Quite the contrary. *Who is this? Take your time. Who knows I'm here? Wendy. Caroline. Queron. The DG. Who the hell is this?* The figure standing with its legs apart and the rush of fear allows him to catch the glimpse of what's pointing at him. The Barrett M82A1 Light Fifty A.

His mind begins to scream. *Dive for it. Make the bastard run. Get out of vision. Use the rain.*

As the figure approaches nearer, Rosslyn moves suddenly for the nearest of the vehicle wrecks. He's failed to notice the small sunken trench and the water fills his shoes and comes up to his knees. He's heaving himself forward behind the stack of twisted steel when the gunman opens fire. Several rounds strike the steel panels above him with metallic thuds. Others ricochet against another pile of car wrecks. Ahead of him he thinks he can see a gap between the stacks. It curves downwards and away in what he remembers is the direction of those lights in the construction workers' huts. They should be no more than fifty yards away.

I'm well in range. But he can't see me. That's what he wants to believe.

Stumbling forward in a crouch, he struggles to keep his feet on the slime. Glancing back twice, he sees no sign of the gunman.

Some twenty yards from the first of the huts, he slips behind a pile of scaffolder's planks. The lights he'd seen before are security lights. There's no one in the huts, at any rate no one that he can see. And if he tries to smash the windows or force the door, say to find an emergency telephone, he'll present a sitting target. So he moves further into the darkness towards the main embankment of the Goodsway Bridge that leads into York Way.

Ahead and below him he can make out the rail-tracks, the brick sides of the bridges and what seems to be the two great mouths of the railway tunnels. Beyond the tracks he can make out the lights in the main signal box on the opposite and eastern side. It's the safety of the manned signal box he's aiming to get to before the gunman takes another shot.

Where the earth has crumbled and subsided, he squeezes through the metal fence and then, steadying himself against the brick wall, he slides slowly down the steep embankment. To his left now is the vast entrance to the first of the tunnels. Rainwater pours like a waterfall from the parapet above. Ahead there's a stretch of gravel, the rails, and the second tunnel entrance. Beyond that there is the third and disused tunnel affording year-round foul sanctuary to vagrants.

He's on the rails, beneath the arch of the second

tunnel, when he sees the lights of the InterCity train come on. It's about to leave from King's Cross Platform One. At the same moment, somewhere far above, he hears a rumble that then becomes the roar of a helicopter.

It's when he's crossing the tracks at the entrance to this second tunnel that the rain is penetrated by both the Nitesun beam and the SkyShout voice. He's momentarily dazzled by the beam. The echoing voice is deafening: '**Move into the next tunnel, Mr Rosslyn. We have you covered from the bridge above you.**'

He can't tell whose voice is coming at him from the darkness. Less than a hundred yards away, the InterCity train prepares to pull out of the station. Heading towards him, its twin lights are raised. He can vaguely hear the voice on the tannoy system announcing its imminent departure.

Why in the name of God don't they stop the thing?

The Nitesun from the Bell helicopter swivels and focuses on the figure sliding down the embankment.

Don't scare the bastard into action.

Then Rosslyn slips inside the tunnel entrance as the first shots from the Barrett M82A1 Light Fifty A strike the brickwork around him. Then suddenly it stops.

He stares down the line at the lights of the train. With the gunman nearing the rails, and even though the train is about to leave, he stays put and peers ahead.

Now he can see the second figure. No friendly legman. Also armed, the figure in the gloom is aiming what seems to be a hand gun directly at him.

'**We have you covered from the bridge above you.**'

But whoever's covering him offers no shielding fire.

'**Stay in the tunnel, Mr Rosslyn.**'

Like hell.

He stays out of the Nitesun light, steps into the dark, out of the beam of the locomotive, and then he sees the Nitesun swivel and pick out the gunman with the Barrett who's sliding out of control down the slope.

If the gun has jammed . . .

He can see the figure's reloading.

Rosslyn breaks into a run. His lungs are raw. Risking a sudden fall, he takes long strides, looks up at the circling helicopter. At the figure struggling with the gun. At the train moving slowly along the tracks now illuminated by the Nitesun.

He sees the second pursuer is running towards him across the tracks.

Keeping his balance, with only a few feet left as the gun is being raised, he hurls himself at the first figure in the gloom.

The Barrett M82A1 Light Fifty A falls away. A nylon balaclava masks the face.

Rosslyn has his hands at the figure's throat. Through the nylon he can feel the warmth of the neck inside the collar, and he jams his thumbs down and keeps on jamming. His knees pinning the figure's chest, he releases his right thumb and tears away the mask. Marcus Luke. Squirming in the dirt, Luke brings a knee up hard into Rosslyn's groin.

Pain between his legs forces Rosslyn to release his grip. He rolls sideways towards the Barrett M82A1 Light Fifty A. Grabbing for it, he can hear the prostrate, wheezing Luke fight for breath. He seems to be getting to his feet. In his right hand he's carrying something like a blade.

Out of the darkness the woman's voice is saying: 'Don't move, Rosslyn.'

The Nitesun beam illuminates her. 'Kill him,' she yells at Luke. 'Kill him.'

Rosslyn points the gun at her. 'Drop it.'

She's masked but Queron's voice is unmistakable, and she has the hand gun levelled at his head.

Glancing sideways a fraction, he sees Luke is up on his feet, running fast towards the rail tracks.

'Don't move, Rosslyn.'

Without hesitating, he squeezes the trigger of the Barrett M82A1 Light Fifty A and the shot rips into the target. First into the chest. Then twice into the head. He watches the figure slump quickly to the ground. The left foot jerks sideways. Then the body settles, masked face up, askew in the mud and lies still, the steam rising from the mask's mouth slit.

The InterCity train gathers speed. Slowly at first.

Heading for the entrance to the centre tunnel, gathering speed from ten to fifteen to twenty miles per hour. There's no sign of Luke. He must by now have made it to the nearest tunnel's entrance. Rosslyn heads after him towards the tracks.

He can hear the rails creak as if stretched and compressed by the weight of the heaving locomotive. There's no stopping its progress to the entrance now. The spreading brightness of the advancing lights illuminates the entrance to the nearest tunnel. *He has to be in there.* The light seems to focus on the centre tunnel. There's no sign of him.

Until Luke moves up silently behind him.

Rosslyn feels the vicious pressure grip. The warm breath against his neck. The sudden twist of his arm as it's driven up behind him and the blade cutting through the fabric of his coat.

'Drop it,' Luke says.

Rosslyn feels the terrible pressure of the blade near his kidneys as the Barrett M82A1 Light Fifty A falls to the ground. Steadying himself, Luke gradually forces Rosslyn inch by inch towards the train. Then he steps quickly sideways and reaches for the weapon.

Ignoring the blade, Rosslyn throws all his weight against Luke's side. The blade slashes diagonally in front of Rosslyn's eyes. As it reaches the end of its arc, Rosslyn puts a leg behind Luke's and leans against him with all his weight. He lunges for the throat but Luke won't let go of his grip of the knife or of Rosslyn's coat. The voice overhead yells: **'Get clear of the train!'**

Rosslyn sees the blade slash the air. The sleeve of his coat is almost ripped clean away. And the light from the train shows the blade's point like a gleaming needle. It's as if Luke is mesmerized. Three times the blade carves the sign as he jerks Rosslyn towards the rails, pulling him down with him to the rails and the oncoming snout and wheels of the locomotive shining in the dazzling Nitesun.

The fourth and final lunge cuts a line in Rosslyn's skin. From the tip of his thumb to the palm of his hand. He heaves his arm away. The fabric of his sleeve is ripped apart and the final cord that might have saved Luke splits.

He topples backwards clean away. The left front wheel severs the arm, splits the shoulder and then amputates the head.

Once inside the King's Cross signal box Rosslyn calls Lever. 'You'd better tell the DG that the total's now up to thirty-eight. Luke and Queron. They're dead. The bodies are here at King's Cross.'

There's a pause on the line. The audible gasp. 'You found them there?' she whispers.

'Yes,' Rosslyn says slowly. 'You could say so. Or that they found me.'

He can hear the wailing of the sirens on York Way. Ambulances. Police and Fire Service vehicles. One of the signalmen is bandaging Rosslyn's hand.

'They found you, Alan,' she says. 'Queron was the person who made the so-called identification of Luke's corpse. Stay where you are and I'll come and pick you up.'

Shortly before nine on the night of 1 January 2000 they leave by cab for Chez Moi in Addison Avenue.

Rosslyn asks the driver if he wouldn't mind making a detour. 'Make sure to avoid Trafalgar Square.'

'It's off the route.'

'Just don't go there.'

'You weren't there last night, were you?' the driver asks.

'No,' says Rosslyn.

'You were lucky, then.'

'Yes,' says Rosslyn.

'So was I,' the driver says. 'Those people shouldn't have died the way they did '

'No,' says Rosslyn.

'I know what I believe,' says the cab driver with considerable conviction. 'What do you believe?'

'That we're late for dinner.'

'You're wrong,' says the cab driver. 'I'm a conviction man myself. I don't doubt. That's what the world needs now. Conviction. Certainty in the uncertain world.'

'Maybe,' says Rosslyn, not quite sure what the driver's saying.

Outside Chez Moi in the snow.

When Rosslyn pays the fare he understands the man's source of certainty. The conviction man follows Rosslyn's eye to the preferred reading matter clipped to the dashboard:

TRINITY
THE DIVINE TESTAMENT
| | | |

'Let me tell you about this,' the driver says. He leans down to retrieve a second copy from a plastic bag. 'You look the sort of couple who might be interested –'

The Calendar of Trinity the Divine
Anniversaries for Holy Month

1999   December

||||

1	Wednesday	Friedrich Engels d. 1895
2	Thursday	BIRTH OF ||| MOTHER THE DIVINE 1958
		ST LUCIUS OF BRITAIN
3	Friday	CHANUCAH BEGINS. Joseph Conrad b. 1857
4	Saturday	Mary Baker Eddy d. 1910
5	Sunday	**Advent Sunday.** W. A. Mozart d. 1791
6	Monday	BIRTH OF ||| SON THE DIVINE. 1970
7	Tuesday	G. L. Bernini b. 1598
8	Wednesday	Paul Gauguin b. 1848
9	Thursday	Karl Barth d. 1968
10	Friday	Alfred Nobel d. 1896
11	Saturday	Hector Berlioz b. 1803
12	Sunday	**2nd S. in Advent.** Gustave Flaubert b. 1821
13	Monday	Laurens van der Post b. 1906. Paul Gauguin d. 1903
14	Tuesday	BIRTH OF ||| TRINITY THE DIVINE 1945
		George Washington d. 1799
15	Wednesday	Izaak Walton d. 1683
16	Thursday	Jane Austen b. 1775
17	Friday	**St Begga.** L. van Beethoven b. 1770
		Vincent van Gogh b. 1853
18	Saturday	Carl Maria von Weber b. 1786
19	Sunday	**3rd S. in Advent.** Emily Bronte d. 1848
20	Monday	Sir Robert Menzies b. 1894
21	Tuesday	Lockerbie Air Disaster, 1988. Joseph Stalin b. 1870
22	Wednesday	**Winter Solstice**
23	Thursday	Thomas Malthus d. 1834
24	Friday	**Christmas Eve.** King John b. 1167.
		Ivan Turgenev b. 1818
25	Saturday	**Christmas Day. The Birth of Christ**
26	Sunday	**1st after Christmas. St Stephen**
27	Monday	**St John the Evangelist.** Johann Kepler b. 1571
28	Tuesday	**Holy Innocents.** Theodore Dreiser d. 1945
29	Wednesday	Christina Rossetti d. 1894
30	Thursday	Michael Bakunin d. 1876
31	Friday	Henri Matisse b. 1896. Leon Trotsky b. 1877

Leap Year   MILLENNIUM

2000   January

| 1 | Saturday | THE RESURRECTION OF ||| TRINITY THE DIVINE |